Money Magic

by

Hamlin Garland

MONEY MAGIC

CHAPTER I

THE CLERK OF THE GOLDEN EAGLE

Sibley Junction is in the sub-tropic zone of Colorado. It lies in a hot, dry, but immensely productive valley at an altitude of some four thousand feet above the sea, a village laced with irrigating ditches, shaded by big cotton-wood-trees, and beat upon by a genial, generous-minded sun. The boarders at the Golden Eagle Hotel can sit on the front stoop and see the snow-filled ravines of the mountains to the south, and almost hear the thunder crashing round old Uncompahgre, even when the broad leaves above their heads are pulseless and the heat of the mid-day light is a cataract of molten metal.

It is, as I have said, a productive land, for upon this ashen, cactus-spotted, repellent flat men have directed the cool, sweet water of the upper world, and wherever this life-giving fluid touches the soil grass and grain spring up like magic.

For all its wild and beautiful setting, Sibley is now a town of farmers and traders rather than of miners. The wagons entering the gates are laden with wheat and melons and peaches rather than with ore and giant-powder, and the hotels are frequented by ranchers of prosaic aspect, by passing drummers for shoes and sugars, and by the barbers and clerks of near-by shops. It is, in fact, a bit of slow-going village life dropped between the diabolism of Cripple Creek and the decay of Creede.

Nevertheless, now and then a genuine trailer from the heights, or cow-man from the mesas, does drop into town on some transient business and, with his peculiar speech and stride, remind the lazy town-loafers of the vigorous life going on far above them. Such types nearly always put up at the Eagle Hotel, which was a boarding-house advanced to the sidewalk of the main street and possessing a register.

At the time of this story trade was good at the Eagle for two reasons. Mrs. Gilman was both landlady and cook, and an excellent cook, and, what was still more alluring, Bertha, her pretty daughter, was day-clerk and general manager. Customers of the drummer type are very loyal to their hotels, and amazingly sensitive to female charm—therefore Bertha, who would have been called an attractive girl anywhere, was widely known and tenderly recalled by every brakeman on the line. She was tall and straight, with brown hair and big, candid, serious eyes—wistful when in repose, boyishly frank and direct as she stood behind her desk attending to business, or smiling as she sped her parting guests at the door.

"I know Bertie ought to be in school," Mrs. Gilman said one day to a sympathetic guest. "But what can I do? We got to live. I didn't come out here for my health, but goodness knows I never expected to slave away in a hot kitchen in this way. If Mr. Gilman had lived—"

It was her habit to leave her demonstrations—even her sentences—unfinished, a peculiarity arising partly from her need of hastening to prevent some pot from boiling over and partly from her failing powers. She had been handsome once—but the heat of the stove, the steam of the washtub, and the vexation and prolonged effort of her daily life had warped and faded and battered her into a pathetic wreck of womanhood.

"I'm going to quit this thing as soon as I get my son's ranch paid for. You see—"

She did not finish this, but her friend understood. Bertha's time for schooling was past. She had already entered upon the maiden's land of dreams—of romance. The men who had hitherto courted her, half-laughingly, half-guiltily, knowing that she was a child, had at last dropped all subterfuge. To them she was a "girl," with all that this word means to males not too scrupulous of the rights of women.

"I oughtn't to quit now when business is so good," Mrs. Gilman returned to the dining-room to add. "I'm full all the time and crowded on Saturday. More and more of the boys come down the line on purpose to stay over Sunday. If I can stick it out a little while—"

The reason why "the boys came down the line to stay over Sunday," was put into words one day by Winchell, the barber, who took his meals at the Eagle.

He was a cleanly shaven young man of twenty-four or five, with a carefully tended brown mustache which drooped below the corners of his mouth.

He began by saying to Bertha:

"I wish I could get out of my business. Judas, but I get tired of it! When I left the farm I never s'posed I'd find myself nailed down to the floor of a barber-shop, but here I am and making good money. How'd you like to go on a ranch?" he asked, meaningly.

"I don't believe I'd like it. Too lonesome," she replied, without any attempt to coquette with the hidden meaning of his question. "I kind o' like this hotel business. I enjoy having new people sifting along every day. Seems like I couldn't bear to step out into private life again, I've got so used to this public thing. I only wish mother didn't have to work so hard—that's all that troubles me at the present time."

Her speech was quite unlike the birdlike chatter with which girls of her age entertain a lover. She spoke rather slowly and with the gravity of a man of business, and her blunt phrases made her smile the more bewitching and her big, brown eyes the more girlish. She did not giggle or flush—she only looked past his smirking face out into the street where the sun's rays lay like flame. And yet she was profoundly moved by the man, for he was a handsome fellow in a sleek way.

"Just the same, you oughtn't to be clerk," said the barber. "It's no place for a girl, anyway. Housekeeping is all right, but this clerking is too public."

"Oh, I don't know! We have a mighty nice run of custom, and I don't see anything bad about it. I've met a lot of good fellows by being here."

The barber was silent for a moment, then pulled out his watch. "Well, I've got to get back." He dropped his voice. "Don't let 'em get gay with you. Remember, I've got a mortgage on you. If any of 'em gets fresh you let me know—they won't repeat it."

"Don't you worry," she replied, with a confident smile. "I can take care of myself. I grew up in Colorado. I'm no tenderfoot."

This boast, so childish, so full of pathetic self-assertion, was still on her lips when a couple of men came out of the dining-room and paused to buy some cigars at the counter. One of them was at first sight a very handsome man of pronounced Western sort. He wore a long, gray frock-coat without vest, and a dark-blue, stiffly starched shirt, over which a red necktie fluttered. His carriage was erect, his hands large of motion, and his profile very fine in its bold lines. His eyes were gray and in expression cold and penetrating, his nose was broad, and the corners of his mouth bitter. He could not be called young, and yet he was not even middle-aged. His voice was deep, and harsh in accent, but as he spoke to the girl a certain sweetness came into it.

"Well, Babe, here I am again. Couldn't get along without coming down to spend Sunday— seems like Williams must go to church on Sunday or lose his chance o' grace."

His companion, a short man with a black mustache that almost made a circle about his mouth, grinned in silence.

Bertha replied, "I think I'll take a forenoon off to-morrow, Captain Haney, and see that you both go to mass for once in your life."

The big man looked at her with sudden intensity. "If you'll take me—I'll go." There was something in his voice and eyes that startled the girl. She drew back a little, but smiled bravely, carrying out the jest.

"I'll call you on that. Unless you take water, you go to church to-morrow."

The big man shoved his companion away and, leaning across the counter, said, in a low and deeply significant tone:

"There ain't a thing in this world that you can't do with Mart Haney—not a thing. That's what I came down here to tell you—you can boss my ranch any day."

The girl was visibly alarmed, but as she still stood fascinated by his eyes and voice, struggling to recover her serenity, another group of diners came noisily past, and the big man, with a parting look, went out and took a seat on one of the chairs which stood in a row upon the walk. The hand which held the cigar visibly trembled, and his companion said:

"Be careful, Mart—"

Haney silenced him with a look. "You're on the outside here, partner."

"I didn't mean to butt in—"

"I understand, but this is a matter between that little girl and me," replied the big man in a tone that, while friendly, ended all further remark on the part of his companion, who rose, after a little pause, and walked away.

Haney remained seated, buried in thought, amazed at the fever which his encounter with the girl had put into his blood.

It was true that he had been coming down every Saturday for weeks—leaving his big saloon on the best evening in the week for a chance to see this child—this boyish school-girl. In a savage, selfish, and unrestrained way he loved her, and had determined to possess her—to buy her if necessary. He knew something of the toil through which the weary mother plodded, and he watched her bend and fade with a certainty that she would one day be on his side.

When at home and afar from her, he felt capable of seizing the girl—of carrying her back with him as the old-time savage won his bride; but when he looked into her clear, calm eyes his villiany, his resolution fell away from him. He found himself not merely a man of the nearer time, but a Catholic—in training at least—and the words he had planned to utter fell dead on his lips. Libertine though he was, there were lines over which even his lawlessness could not break.

He was a desperate character—a man of violence—and none too delicate in his life among women; but away back in his boyhood his good Irish mother had taught him to fight fair and to protect the younger and weaker children, and this training led to the most curious and unexpected acts in his business as a gambler.

"I will not have boys at my lay-out," he once angrily said, to Williams, his partner, "and I will not have women there. I've sins enough to answer for without these. Cut 'em out!" He was oddly generous now and then, and often returned to a greenhorn money enough to get home on. "Stay on the farm, me lad—'tis better to milk a cow with a mosquito on the back of your neck than to fill a cell at Cañon City."

In other ways he was inexorable, taking the hazards of the game with his visitors and raking in their money with cold eyes and a steady hand. He collected all notes remorselessly—and it was in this way that he had acquired his interests in "The Bottom Dollar" and "The Flora" mines—"prospects" at the time, but immensely valuable at the present. It was, indeed, this new and measurably respectable wealth which had determined him upon pressing his suit with Bertha. As he sat there he came to a most momentous conclusion. "Why not marry the girl and live honest?" he asked himself; and being moved by the memory of her sweetness and humor, he said, "I will," and the resolution filled his heart with a strange delight.

He presented the matter first to the mother, not with any intention of doing the right thing, but merely because she happened into the room before the girl returned, and because he was overflowing with his new-found grace.

Mrs. Gilman came in wiping her face on her apron—as his mother used to do—and this touched him almost like a caress. He rose and offered her a chair, which she accepted, highly flattered.

"It must seem warm to you down here, Captain?" she remarked, as she took a seat beside him.

"It does. I wouldn't need to suffer it if you were doing business in Cripple. I can't leave go your Johnny-cake and pie; 'tis the kind that mother didn't make—for she was Irish."

"I've thought of going up there," she replied, matter-of-factly, "but I can't stand the altitude, I'm afraid—and then down here we have my son's little ranch to furnish us eggs and vegetables."

"That's an advantage," he admitted; "but on the peak no one expects vegetables—it's still a matter of ham and eggs."

"Is that so?" she asked, concernedly.

"'Tis indeed. I live at the Palace Hotel, and I know. However, 'tis not of that I intended to speak, Mrs. Gilman. I'm distressed to see you working so hard this warm weather. You need a rest—a vacation, I'm thinkin'."

"You're mighty neighborly, Captain, to say so, but I don't see any way of taking it."

"Furthermore, your daughter is too fine to be clerkin' here day by day. She should be in a home of her own."

"She ought to be in school," sighed the mother, "but I don't see my way to hiring anybody to fill her place—it would take a man to do her work."

"It would so. She's a rare little business woman. Let me see, how old is she?"

"Eighteen next November."

"She seems like a woman of twenty."

"I couldn't run for a week without her," answered the mother, rolling down her sleeves in acknowledgment that they had entered upon a real conversation.

"She's a little queen," declared Haney.

It was very hot and the flies were buzzing about, but the big gambler had no mind to these discomforts, so intent was he upon bringing his proposal before the mother. Straightened in his chair and fixing a keen glance upon her face, he began his attack. "'Tis folly to allow anything to trouble you, my dear woman—if anny debt presses, let me know, and I'll lift it for ye."

The weary mother felt the sincerity of his offer, and replied, with much feeling: "You're mighty good, Captain Haney, but we're more than holding our own, and another year will see the ranch clear. I'm just as much obliged to you, though; you're a true friend."

"But I don't like to think of you here for another year—and Bertie should not stand here another day with every Tom, Dick, and Harry passin' their blarney with her. She's fitter to be mistress of a big house of her own, an' 'tis that I've the mind to give her; and I can, for I'm no longer on the ragged edge. I own two of the best mines on the hill, and I want her to share me good-fortune with me."

Mrs. Gilman, worn out as she was, was still quick where her daughter's welfare was concerned, and she looked at the big man with wonder and inquiry, and a certain accusation in her glance.

"What do you mean, Captain?"

The big gambler was at last face to face with his decision, and with but a moment's hesitation replied, "As my wife, I mean, of course."

She sank back in her chair and looked at him with eyes of consternation. "Why, Captain Haney! Do you really mean that?"

"I do!" He had a feeling at the moment that he had always been honorable in his intentions.

"But—but—you're so old—I mean so much older—"

"I know I am, and I'm rough. I don't deny that. I'm forty, but then I'm what they call well preserved," he smiled, winningly, "and I'll soon have an income of wan hundred thousand dollars a year."

This turned the current of her emotion—she gasped. "One hundred thousand dollars!"

He held up a warning hand. "Sh! now that's between us. There are those younger than I, 'tis true, but there is a kind of saving grace in money. I can take you all out of this daily tile like winkin'—all you need to do is to say the wan word and we'll have a house in Colorado Springs or Denver—or even in New York. For what did you think I left me business on the busiest day of every week? It was to see your sweet daughter, and I came this time to ask her to go back with me."

"What did she say?"

"She has not said. We had no time to talk. What I propose now is that we take a drive out to the ranch and talk it over. Williams will fill her place here. In fact, the house is mine. I bought it this morning."

The poor woman sat like one in a stupor, comprehending little of what he said. The room seemed to be revolving. The earth had given way beneath her feet and the heavens were opening. Her first sensation was one of terror. She feared a man of such power—a man who could in a single moment, by a wave of his hand, upset her entire world. His enormous wealth dazzled her even while she doubted it. How could it be true while he sat there talking to her—and she in her apron and her hair in disorder? She rose hurriedly with instinct to make herself presentable enough to carry on this conversation. As she stood weakly, she apologized incoherently.

"Captain, I appreciate your kindness—you've always been a good customer—one I liked to do for—but I'm all upset—I can't get my wits—"

"No hurry, madam," he said, with a generous intent. "To-morrow is coming. Don't hurry at all—at all."

She hurried out, leaving him alone—with the clock, the cat, and the hostler, who was spraying the sidewalk under the cotton-wood-trees. Quivering with fear of the girl's refusal, the gambler rose and went out into the sunsmit streets to commune with this new-found self.

Life was no longer simple for Mrs. Gilman. It was, indeed, filled with a wind of terror. Haney's promise of relief from want was very sweet, yet disturbingly empty, like the joy of dreams, and yet his words took her breath—clouded her judgment, befogged her insight.

She went back to the dining-room, where her daughter sat eating dinner, with a numbness in her limbs and a sense of dizziness in her brain, and dropping into a chair at the table gasped out:

"Do you know—what Captain Haney just said to me?"

"Not being a mind-reader, I don't," replied the girl, calmly, though she was moved by her mother's white, awed face.

"He wants you!"

Bertha flushed and braced both hands against the table as she replied, "Well, he can't have me!"

With the opposition in her daughter's tone, Mrs. Gilman was suddenly moved to argue.

"Think what it means, Bertie! He's rich. Did you know that? He owns two mines."

"I know he is a gambler and runs two saloons. You see, the boys keep me posted, and I'm not marrying a gambler—not this summer," she ended, decisively.

"But he's going to give that up, he says." He hadn't said this, but she was sure he would. "His income is a hundred thousand dollars a year. Think of that!"

"I don't want to think of it," the girl answered, frowning slightly. "It makes my head ache. Nobody has a right to so much money. How did he get it?"

"Out of his mine—and oh, Bertie, he says if you'll speak the word we needn't do another day's work in this hot, greasy old place! The house is his, anyway. Did you know that?"

Bertha eyed her mother closely—with cool, bright, accusing eyes—for a moment, then she softened. "Poor old mammy, it's pretty tough lines on you—no two ways about that. You've got the heavy end of the job. I'd marry most anybody to give you a rest—but, mother, Captain Haney is forty, if he's a day, and he's a hard citizen. He has been a gambler all his life. You can't expect me to marry a sport like him. And then there's Ed."

The mother's face changed. "A barber!" she exclaimed, scornfully.

"Yes, he's a barber now, but he's going to make a break soon and get into something else."

"Don't bank on Ed, Bertie; he'll never be anything more than he is now. No man ever got anywhere who started in as a barber."

"Would you rather I married a gambler and a sure-shot? They tell me Haney has killed his man."

"That may be all talk. Well, anyhow, he wants to see you and talk it over; and oh, Bertie, it does seem a wonderful chance—and my heart's so bad to-day it seems as though I couldn't see to another meal! I don't want you to marry him if you don't want to—I'm not asking you to. You know I'm not. But he is a noble-looking man—and I get awfully discouraged sometimes. It scares me to think of dying and leaving you without any security."

One of the waiters, half-dead with curiosity, was edging near, under pretense of brushing the table, and so the mistress rose and took up the burdens of her stewardship.

"But we'll talk it over to-night. Don't be hasty."

"I won't," replied the girl.

She was by no means as unmoved as she gave out. She had always admired and liked Captain Haney, though he never moved her in the same way that the young barber did for Ed Winchell had youth as well as comeliness, and there is a divine suppleness in youth, yet he had been a welcome guest. "A hundred thousand dollars a year! And yet he's been coming to our little hotel for a year—to see me!"

This consideration was the one that moved her most. All the bland words, the jocular phrases of his singular wooing came back to her now, weighted with deep significance. She had called it "joshing," and had put it all aside, just as she had parried the rude jests of the brakemen of her acquaintance. Now she saw that he had been in earnest.

She was wise beyond her years, this calm-faced, keen-eyed girl, trained by adversity to take care of herself. She knew instinctively that she lived surrounded by wolves, and, much as she admired the big frame and bold profile of Captain Haney, she had placed him among her enemies. His coming always pleased her but at the same time put her upon the defensive.

Strange to say, she enjoyed her position there in her battered little hotel. "If it weren't for poor old mother—" She arrested herself and went back to the counter with a certain timidity, a self-consciousness new to her, fearing to face the gambler now that she knew his intent was honorable.

The room was empty, all the men having gone out upon the walk to escape the heat, and she took her seat behind her desk and gave herself up to a consideration of the life to which the possession of so much wealth would introduce her. She could have unlimited new gowns, she could travel, and she could rescue her mother from drudgery and worry. These things she could discern—but of the larger life which money could open to her she could only vaguely dream.

The first effect of marrying Marshall Haney would be to cut short her life in Sibley; the second, the establishment of a home in the great camps about them.

As she looked around the dingy room buzzing with flies, she experienced a premonitory pang of the pain she would suffer in going out of its doors forever.

When Haney came back an hour later, he read in the cold, serious look she gave him a warning, therefore he spoke but a few words on commonplace subjects, and returned to his seat on the walk to await a change in her mood.

This meekness on the part of a powerful man moved the girl, and a little later she went to the doorway and said to the crowd generally, "It's a wonder some fellow wouldn't open a cantaloupe or something."

Haney put his finger to his mouth and whistled to the grocer opposite. He came on the run, alert for trade.

"Roll up a couple of big melons," called Haney, largely. "We're all drying to cinders over here."

The loafers cheered, but the girl said, in a lower voice, "I was only joking."

"What you say goes," he replied, with significance.

She did not stay to see the melons cut, but went back to her desk, and he brought a choice slice in to her.

She took it, but she said, "You mustn't think you own me—not yet." Her tone was resentful. "I don't want you to say things like that—before people."

"Like what?" he asked.

She did not answer.

He went on: "I don't mean to assume anything, God knows. I'm only waitin' and hopin'. I'll go away if you want me to and let you think it over alone."

"I wish you would," she said, realizing that this committed her to at least a consideration of his proposal.

He held out his hand. "Good-bye—till next Saturday."

She put her small, brown hand in his. He crushed it hard and his bold face softened. "I need you, my girl. Sure I do!" And in his eyes was something very winning.

CHAPTER II

MARSHALL HANEY CHANGES HEART

It was well for Haney that Bertie did not see him as he sat above his gambling boards, watchful, keen-eyed, grim of visage, for she would have trembled in fear of him. "Haney's" was both saloon and gambling hall. In the front, on the right, ran the long bar with its shining brass and polished mahogany he prided himself on having the best bar west of Denver, and in the rear, occupying both sides of the room, stood two long rows of faro and roulette outfits, together with card-tables and dice-boards. It was the largest and most prosperous gambling hall in the camps, and always of an evening was crowded with gamesters and those who came as lookers-on.

On the right side, in a raised seat about midway of the hall, Haney usually sat, a handsome figure, in broad white hat, immaculate linen, and well-cut frock-coat, his face as pale as that of a priest in the glare of the big electric light. On the other side, and directly opposite, Williams kept corresponding "lookout" over the dealers and the crowd. He was a bold man who attempted any shenanigan with Mart Haney, and the games of his halls were reported honest.

To think of a young and innocent girl married to this remorseless gambler, scarred with the gun and the knife, was a profanation of maidenhood—and yet, as he fell now and then into a dream, he took on a kind of savage beauty which might allure and destroy a woman. Whatever else he was, he was neither commonplace nor mean. The visitors to whom he was pointed out as "a type of our modern Western desperado" invariably acknowledged that he looked the part. His smile was of singular sweetness—all the more alluring because of its rarity—and the warm clasp of his big, soft hand had made him sheriff in San Juan County, and his bravery and his love of fair play were well known and admired among the miners.

The sombre look in his face, which resembled that of a dreaming leopard, was due to the new and secret plans with which his mind was now engaged. "If she takes me, I quit this business," he had promised himself. "She despises me in it, and so does the mother, and so I reckon 'tis up to me to clean house."

Then he thought of his own mother, who had the same prejudice, and who would not have taken a cent of his earnings. "I see no harm in the business," he said. "Men will drink and they will gamble, and I might as well serve their wish as any other—better, indeed, for no man can accuse me of dark ways nor complain of the order of me house. I am a business man the same as him that runs a grocery store; but 'tis no matter, she dislikes it, and that ends it. She's a clear-headed wan," he thought, with a glow of admiration for her. "She's the captain."

He no longer thought of her as his victim—as something to be ruthlessly enjoyed—he trembled before her, big and brave and relentless as he was in the world of men. "What has come over me?" he asked himself. "Sure she has me on me knees—the witch. Me mind is filled with her."

All through the week his agents were at work attempting to sell his saloons. "I'm ready to close out at a moment's notice," he declared.

At times, as he sat in his place, he lost consciousness of the crowding, rough-hatted, intent men and the monotonous calls of the dealers. The click of balls, the buzz of low-toned comment died out of his ears—he was back in Troy, looking for his father, whom he had not seen or written to in twenty years. He saw himself, with a dainty little woman on his arm, taking the boat to New York. "I will go to the biggest hotel in the city; the girl shall have the best the old town has. Nothing will be too good for her—"

He roused himself to a touch on his elbow. One of his agents had a new offer for the two saloons. It was still less than he considered the business worth, but in his softened mood he said, "It goes!"

"Make out your papers," replied the other man, with almost equal brevity.

During the rest of the evening the gambler sat above his lay-out with mingled feelings of relief and regret. After all, he was in command here. He knew this business, and he loved the companionship and the admiration of the men who dropped round by his side to discuss the camp or the weather, or to invite him to join a hunting trip. He felt himself to be one of the chief men of the town, and that he could at any time become their Representative if he chose. For some years he couldn't have told why he had taken on a thrift unknown to him before, and had been attending strictly to business. He now saw that it must have been from a foreknowledge of Bertha. In him the superstitions of both miner and gambler mingled. The cards had run against him for three years, now they were falling in his favor. "I will take advantage of them," he declared.

Slowly the crowd thinned out, and at one o'clock only a few inveterate poker-players and one or two young fellows who were still "bucking" the roulette wheel remained and, calling one of his men to take charge, Haney nodded to Williams and they went out on the street.

As he reached the cold, crisp, deliciously rarefied air outside, he took off his hat and involuntarily looked up at the stars blazing thick in the deep-blue midnight sky. With solemn voice he said to his partner: "Well, 'Spot,' right here Mart Haney's saloon business ends. We're all in."

Williams felt that his partner was acting rashly. "Oh, I wouldn't say that! You may get into it again."

"No—the little girl and her mother won't stand for it, and, besides, what's the use? I don't need to do it, and if I'm ever going to see the world now is my chance. I'm goin' back East to discover how many brothers and sisters I have livin'. The old father is dodderin 'round somewheres back there. I'll surprise him, too. Now, have those papers all made out ready to sign by eleven o'clock to-morrow. I'm goin' down the valley on the noon train."

"All right, Mart, but you're makin' a mistake."

"Never you mind, me bucko. 'Tis me own game, and the mines will take all the gray matter you can spare."

As the big man was walking away towards his hotel a woman met him. "Hello, Mart!"

"Hello, Mag; what's doing?"

She was humped and bedraggled, and her face looked white in the moonlight. "Nothing. Stake a fellow to a hot soup, won't you?"

"Sure thing, Mag." He handed her a five-dollar gold piece. "Is it as bad as that? What's t' old man doin' these days?"

"Servin' time," she answered, bitterly.

"Oh, so he is!" replied Haney, hastily. "I'd forgotten. Well, take care o' yourself," he added, genially, walking on in instant forgetfulness of the woman's misery, for his mind was turned upon the talk which his younger brother Charley had given him not long before in Denver.

It was not a cheerful conversation, for Charley flippantly confessed that he didn't hold any family reunions, and that all he knew of his brothers he gained by chance. "They're all great boozers," he said, in summing them up. "Tim is a ward heeler in Buffalo—came to see me at the stage-door loaded to the gunnels. Tom is a greasy, three-fingered brakeman on the Central. Fannie married a carpenter and has about seventeen young ones. Mary died, you know?"

"No, I didn't know."

"Yes, died about four years ago. She was like mother—a nice girl. Dad sent me a paper with a notice of her death. He never writes, but now and then, when Tim has a fight or Tom gets drunk and slips into the criminal column, I hear of them."

Charles did not say so, but Mart knew that he was lumped among the other poverty-stricken, worthless members of the family. He did not at the time undeceive his brother, but now that he was no longer a gambler and saloon-keeper, now that he was rich, he resolved not only to let his father know of his good-fortune and his change of life, but also and this was due to Bertie's influence he earnestly desired to help his family out of their mire.

"We had good stuff in us," he said, "but we went wrong after the mother left us."

As he walked on down the street a strange radiance came into the world. The distant peaks of the Sangre de Cristo range rose in dim and shadowy majesty to the south, and, wondering, astonished at the emotion stirring in his heart, the regenerated desperado turned to see the moon lifting above the crown of the great peak to the east. For the first time in many years his heart was filled with a sense of the beauty of the world.

CHAPTER III

BERTHA YIELDS TO TEMPTATION

Bertie looked older and graver when Haney entered the Eagle Hotel, and his heart expanded with a tenderness that was partly paternal. She seemed so young and looked so pale and troubled.

She greeted him unsmilingly and calmly handed him the pen with which to register.

"How are you all?" he asked, with genuine concern.

"Pretty bum. Mother gave out this week. It's the heat, I guess. Hottest weather we've had since I came to town."

"Why didn't you let me know?"

She avoided his question. "We're too low here at Junction. Mother ought to go a couple of thousand feet higher. She needs rest and a change. I've sent her out to the ranch."

"You're not running the house alone?"

"Why, cert!—that is, except my brother's wife is taking mother's place in the kitchen. I'm runnin' the rest of it just as I've been doin' for three years."

He looked his admiration before he uttered it. "You're a wonder!"

"Don't you think it! How does it happen you're down to-day? You said Saturday."

"I've sold out—signed the deeds to-day. I'm out of the liquor trade forever."

She nodded gravely. "I'm glad of that. I don't like the business—not a little bit."

He took this as an encouragement. "I knew you didn't. Well, I'm neither saloon-keeper nor gambler from this day. I'm a miner and a capitalist—and all I have is yours," he added, in a lover's voice, bending a keen glance upon her.

The girl was standing very straight behind her desk, and her face did not change, but her eyes shifted before his gaze. "You'd better go in to supper while the biscuit are hot," she advised, coolly.

He had tact enough to take his dismissal without another word or glance, and after he had gone she still stood there in the same rigid pose, but her face was softer and clouded with serious meditation. It was wonderful to think of this rich and powerful man changing his whole life for her.

Winchell, the young barber, came in hurriedly, his face full of accusation and alarm. "Was that Haney who just came in?" he asked, truculently.

"Yes, he's at supper—want to see him?"

"See him? No! And I don't want *you* to see him! He's too free with you, Bert; I don't like it."

She smiled a little, curious smile. "Don't mix it up with *him*, Ed—I'd hate to see your remains afterwards."

"Bert, see here! You've been funny with me lately." By funny he meant unaccountable. "And your mother has been hinting things at me—and now here is Haney leaving his business to come down the middle of the week. What's the meaning of it?"

"It isn't the middle of the week. It's Friday," she corrected him.

He went on: "I know what he keeps coming to see you for, but for God's sake don't you think of marrying an old tout and gambler like him."

"He isn't old, and he isn't a gambler any more," she significantly retorted.

"What do you mean?"

"He's sold out—clean as a whistle."

"Don't you believe it! It's a trick to get you to think better of him. Bert, don't you dare to go back on me," he cried out, warningly—"don't you dare!"

The girl suddenly ceased smiling, and asserted herself. "See here, Ed, you'd better not try to boss me. I won't stand for it. What license have you got to pop in here every few minutes and tell me what's what? You 'tend to your business and you'll get ahead faster."

He stammered with rage and pain. "If you throw me down—fer that—old tout, I'll kill you both."

The girl looked at him in silence for a long time, and into her brain came a new, swift, and revealing concept of his essential littleness and weakness. His beauty lost its charm, and a kind of disgust rose in her throat as she slowly said, with cutting scorn:

"If you really meant that!—but you don't, you're only talking to hear yourself talk. Now you shut up and run away. This is no place for chewing the rag, anyway—this is my busy day."

For a moment the man's face expressed the rage of a wild-cat and his hands clinched. "Don't you do it—that's all!" he finally snarled. "You'll wish you hadn't."

"Run away, little boy," she said, irritably. "You make me tired. I don't feel like being badgered by anybody, and, besides, I'm not mortgaged to anybody just yet."

His mood changed. "Bertie, I'm sorry. I didn't mean to be fresh. But don't talk to me that way, it uses me all up."

"Well, then, stop puffing and blowing. I've troubles of my own, with mother sick and a new cook in the kitchen."

"Excuse me, Bert; I'll never do it again."

"That's all right."

"But it riled me like the devil to think—" he began again.

"Don't think," she curtly interrupted; "cut hair."

Perceiving that she was in evil mood for his plea, he turned away so sadly that the girl relented a little and called out:

"Say, Ed!" He turned and came back. "See here! I didn't intend to hurt your feelings, but this is one of my touchy days, and you got on the wrong side of me. I'm sorry. Here's my hand— now shake, and run."

His face lightened, and he smiled, displaying his fine, white teeth. "You're a world-beater, sure thing, and I'm going to get you yet!"

"Cut it out!" she slangily retorted, sharply, withdrawing her hand.

"You'll see!" he shouted, laughing back at her, full of hope again.

She was equally curt with two or three others who brazenly tried to buy a smile with their cigars. "Do business, boys; this is my day to sell goods," she said, and they took the hint.

When Haney came out from his supper, he stepped quietly in behind the counter and said: "I'll take your place. Get your grub. Then put on your hat and we'll drive out to see how the mother is." The girl acknowledged a sense of relief as she left him in charge and went to her seat in the far corner of the dining-room—a relief and a dangerous relaxation. It was, after all, a pleasure to feel that a strong, sure hand was out-stretched in sympathy—and she was tired. Even as she sat waiting for her tea the collapse came, and bowing her head to her hands she shook with silent sobs.

The waitresses stared, and young Mrs. Gilman came hurrying. "What's the matter, Bertie; are you sick?"

"Oh no—but I'm worried—about mother."

"You haven't heard anything—?"

"No, but she looked so old and so worn when she went away. She ought to have quit here a month ago."

"Well, I wouldn't worry. It's cooler out to the ranch, and the air is so pure she'll pick up right away—you'll see."

"I hope so, but she ought to take it easy the rest of her days. She's done work enough—and I'm kind o' discouraged myself."

Slowly she recovered her self-possession. She drank her tea in abstracted silence, and at last she said: "I'm going out there, Cassie; you'll have to look after things. I'll get some of the boys to 'tend the office."

"You're not going alone?"

"No, Mart Haney is going to drive me."

"Oh!" There was a look of surprise and consternation in the face of the young wife, but she only asked, "You'll be back to-night?"

"Yes, if mother is no worse."

Haney had the smartest "rig" in town waiting for her as she came out, but as he looked at her white dress and pretty hat of flowers and tulle he apologized for its shortcomings—"'Tis lined with cream-colored satin it *should* be."

She colored a little at this, but quickly replied: "Blarney. Anybody'd know you were an Irishman."

"I am, and proud of it."

"I want to take the doctor out to see mother."

"Not in this rig," he protested.

She smiled. "Why not? No, but I want to go round to his office and leave a call."

"I'll go round the world fer you," he replied.

The air was deliciously cool and fragrant now that the sun was sinking, and the town was astir with people. It was the social hour when the heat and toil of the day were over, and all had leisure to turn wondering eyes upon Haney and his companion. The girl felt her position keenly. She was aware that a single appearance of this kind was equivalent to an engagement in the minds of her acquaintances, but as she shyly glanced at her lover's handsome face, and watched his powerful and skilled hands upon the reins, her pride in him grew. She acknowledged his kindness, and was tired and ready to lean upon his strength.

"When did your mother quit?" he asked, after they had left the town behind.

"Sunday night. You see, we had a big rush all day, and on top of that, about twelve o'clock, an alarm of fire next door. So she got no sleep. Monday morning she didn't get up, Tuesday she dressed but was too miserable to work, so finally I just packed her off to the ranch."

"That was right—only you should have sent for me."

She was silent, and her heart began to beat with a knowledge of the demand he was about to make. She felt weak and unprotected here—in the office they were on more equal terms—but she enjoyed in a subconscious way the swift rush of the horses, the splendor of the sunset, and the quiet authority in his voice—even as she lifted eyes to the mesa towards which they were driving he began to speak.

"You know my mind, little girl. I don't mean to ask you till to-morrow—that's the day set—but I want to say that I've been cleaning house all the week, thinkin' of you. I'm to be a leading citizen from this day on. You won't need to apologize for me. I've never been a drinking man, but I have been a reckless devil. I don't deny that I've planted a wide field of wild oats. However, all that I put away from this hour. 'Tis true I'm forty, but that's not old— I'm no older than I was at twenty-one, sure—and, besides, you're young enough to make up." He smiled, and again she acknowledged the charm of his face when he smiled. "You'll see me grow younger whilst you grow older, and so wan day we'll be of an age."

Her customary readiness of reply had left her, and she still sat in silence, a sob in her throat, a curious numbness in her limbs.

He seemed to feel that she did not wish to talk. "If you come into partnership with me you need never worry about the question of bread or rent or clothes, and that's worth considerin'—Which road now?"

She silently pointed to the left, and they drew near the foot of the great mesa whose level top was cutting the sun in half.

The miner was filled with grateful homage. "'Tis a great world!" he exclaimed, softly. "Sure, 'tis only yesterday that I found it out, and lifting me head took a look at the hills and the stars for the first time in twenty years. 'Tis a new road I'm enterin'—whether you come to me or not."

All this was wonderful to the girl. Could it be that she was capable of changing the life of a powerful man like this? It filled her with a sense of duty as well as exaltation, an emotion that made a woman of her. She seemed suddenly to have put the hotel and all its worriments far, far behind her.

Seized by an impulse to acquaint her with his family, Haney began to tell about his father and his attempts to govern his five sons. "We were devils," he admitted—"broncos, if ever such walked on two legs. We wouldn't go to school—not wan of us except Charley; he did pretty well—and we fished and played ball and went to the circus—" He chuckled. "I left home the first time with a circus. I wanted to be a lion-tamer, but had to content meself with driving the cook wagon. Then I struck West, and I've never been back and I've never seen the old man since, but now I've made me pile, I think I'll go home and hunt him up and buy him new spectacles; it's ace to the three-spot he's using the same horn-rimmed ones he wore when I left."

Bertha was interested. "How long did you stay with the circus?"

"Not very long. I got homesick and went back, but the next time I left, I left for fair. I've been everywhere but East since. I've been in Colorado mostly. 'Tis a good State."

"I like it—but I'd like to see the rest of the country."

"You can. If you join hands with me we'll go round the ball together."

She did not follow this lead. "I've been to Denver once—went on one of these excursion tickets."

"How did you like it there?"

"Pretty good; but I got awful tired, and the grub at the hotel was the worst ever—it was a cheap place, of course. Didn't dare to look in the door of the big places."

"You can have a whole soot of rooms at the Royal Flush—if you will."

Again she turned away. "I can't imagine anybody rich enough to live at such hotels—There's our ranch."

"Shy as a coyote, ain't it?" he commented, as he looked where she pointed. "I'd prefer the Eagle House to that."

"I love it out here," she said. "I helped plant the trees."

"Did you? Then I want the place. I want everything your pretty hands planted."

"Oh, rats!" was her reproving comment, and it made him laugh at his own sentimental speech.

The ranch house stood at the foot of the mesa near a creek that came out of a narrow gorge and struck out upon the flat valley. It was a little house—a shack merely, surrounded by a few out-buildings, all looking as temporary as an Indian encampment, but there were trees—thriftily green—and some stacks of grain to testify to the energy and good husbandry of the owner.

Mrs. Gilman was lying in a corner room, close to the stream which rippled through the little orchard, and its gentle murmur had been a comfort to her—it carried her back to her home in Oxford County State of Maine, where her early girlhood had been spent. At times it seemed that she was in the little, old, gray house in the valley, and that her father's sharp voice might come at any moment to break her delicious drowse.

Her breakdown had been caused as much by her mental turmoil as by her overtaxing duties. She was confronted by a mighty temptation through her daughter at a time when she was too weak and too ill to carry forward her ordinary duties. To urge this marriage upon Bertha would be to bring it about. That she knew, for the girl had said, "I'll do it if you say so, mother."

"I don't want you to do it if you'd rather not," had been her weak answer.

Bertie entered quietly, in a singularly mature, almost manly way, and bending to her mother, asked cordially, "Well, how are you to-day?"

The sick woman took her daughter's hand and drew it to her tear-wet cheek. "Oh, my baby! I can't bear to leave you now."

"Don't talk that way, mother. You're not going to leave me. The doctor is coming out to see you, and everything is going all right at the house, so don't you worry. You set to work to get well. That's your little stunt. I'll look after the rest of it."

Bertie had never been one to bestow caresses, even on her parents, and her only sign of deep feeling now lay in the tremble of her voice. She drew her hand away, and putting her arm about her mother's neck patted her cheek. "Cassie's doing well," she said, abruptly, "and the girls are fine. They brace right up to the situation, and—and everybody's nice to us. I reckon a dozen of the church ladies called yesterday to ask how you were—and Captain Haney came down to-day on purpose to find out how things were going."

The sufferer's eyes opened wide. "Bert, he's with you!"

"Yes, he drove me out here," answered the girl, quietly. "He's come for an answer to his proposition. It's up to us to decide right now."

The mother broke into a whimper. "Oh, darling, I don't know what to think. I'm afraid to leave this to you—it's an awful temptation to a girl. I guess I've decided against it. He ain't the kind of man you ought to marry."

She hushed her mother's wail. "Sh! He'll hear you," she said, solemnly. "There are lots o' worse men than Mart Haney."

"But he's so old—for you."

"He's no boy, that's true, but we went all over that. The new fact in the case is this: he's sold out up there—cleared out his saloon business—and all for *me*. Think o' that—and I hadn't given him a word of encouragement, either! Now that speaks well for him, don't you think?"

The mother nodded. "Yes, it surely does, but then—"

The girl went on: "Well, now, it ain't as though I hated him, for I don't—I like him, I've always liked him. He's the handsomest man I know, and he's treated me right from the very start. He didn't come down to hurry me or crowd me at all, so he says. Well, I told him I wouldn't answer yet awhile—time isn't really up till to-morrow. I can take another week if I want to."

The mother lay in silence for a few moments, and then with closed eyes, streaming with hot tears, she again prayed silently to God to guide her girl in the right path. When she opened her eyes the tall form of Marshall Haney towered over her, so handsome, so full of quiet power that he seemed capable of anything. His face was strangely sweet as he said: "You must not fret about anything another minute. You've but to lie quiet and get strong." He put his broad, soft, warm, and muscular hand down upon her two folded ones, and added: "Let me do fer ye as I would fer me own mother. 'Twill not commit ye to a thing." He seemed to understand her mood—perhaps he had overheard her plea. "I'm not asking a decision till you are well, but I wish you would trust me now—I could do so much more fer you and the girl. Here's the doctor, so put the whole thing by for the present. I ask nothing till you are well."

If this was policy on his part it was successful; for the poor tortured mother's heart was touched and her nerves soothed by his voice, as well as by the touch of his hand, and when they left the house she was in peaceful sleep, and the doctor's report was reassuring. "But she must have rest," he said, positively, "and freedom from care."

"She shall have it," said Haney, with equal decision.

This bluff kindness, joined to the allurement of his powerful form, profoundly affected the girl. Her heart went out towards him in admiration and trust, and as they were on the way home she turned suddenly to him, and said:

"You're good to me—and you were good to mother; you needn't wait till to-morrow for my answer. I'll do as you want me to—some time—not now—next spring, maybe."

He put his arm about her and kissed her, his eyes dim with a new and softening emotion.

"You've made Mart Haney over new—so you have! As sure as God lets me live, I'll make you happy. You shall live like a queen."

CHAPTER IV

HANEY MEETS AN AVENGER

Haney took the train back to his mountain town in a mood which made him regard his action as that of a stranger. Whenever he recalled Bertha's trusting clasp of his hand he felt like removing his hat—the stir of his heart was close akin to religious reverence. "Faith, an' she's taking a big risk," he said. "But I'll not see her lose out," he added, with a return of the gambler's phrase. "She has stacked her chips on the right spot this time."

With all his brute force, his clouded sense of justice, this gambler, this saloon-man, was not without qualifying characteristics. He was a Celt, and in almost every Celt there is hidden a poet. Quick to wrath, quick to jest and fierce in his loves was he, as is the typical Irishman whom England has not yet succeeded in changing to her own type. Moreover, he was an American as well as a Celt and the American is the most sentimental of men—it is said; and now that he had been surprised into honorable matrimony he began to arrange his affairs for his wife's pleasure and glory. The words in which she had accepted him lingered in his ears like phrases of a little hesitating song. For her he had sold his gambling halls, for her he was willing at the moment to abandon the associates of a lifetime.

He was sitting in the car dreamily smoking, his hat drawn low over his brows, when an acquaintance passing through the car stopped with a word of greeting. Ordinarily Haney would have been glad of his company, but he made a place for him at this time with grudging slowness.

"How are ye, Slater? Set ye down."

"I hear you've sold your saloons," Slater began, as he settled into place.

Haney nodded, without smiling.

His neighbor grinned. "You don't seem very sociable to-day, Mart?"

"I'm not," Haney replied, bluntly.

"I just dropped down beside you to say that young Wilkinson went broke in your place last night and has it in for you. He's plum fuzzy with drink, and you better look sharp or he'll do you. He's been on the rampage for two days—crazy as a loon."

"Why does he go after me?" Haney asked, irritably. "I'm out of it. 'Tis like the fool tenderfoot. Don't he know I had nothing to do with his bust-up?"

"He don't seem to—or else he's so locoed he's forgot it. All I know is he's full of some pizen notion against you, and I thought I'd put you on your guard."

They talked on about this a few minutes, and then Slater rose, leaving Haney to himself. But his tender mood was gone. His brow was knit. He began to understand that a man could not run a bad business for twenty years, and then at a day's notice clear himself of all its trailing evil consequences. "I'll vamoose," he said to himself, with resolution. "I'll put me mines in order, and go down into the valley and take the girl with me—God bless her! We'll take a little turn as far as New York. I'll put long miles between the two of us and all this sporting record of mine. She don't like it, and I'll quit it. I'll begin a new life entirely." And a glow of new-found virtue filled his heart. Of Wilkinson he had no fear—only disgust. "Why should the fool pursue me?" he repeated. "He took his chances and lost out. If he weren't a 'farmer' he'd drop it."

He ate his supper at the hotel in the same abstraction, and then, still grave with plans for his new career, went out into the street to find Williams, his partner. It was inevitable that he should bring up at the bar of his former saloon; no other place in the town was so much like home, after all. Habit drew him to its familiar walls. He was glad to find a couple of old friends there, and they, having but just heard of the sale of his outfit, hastened to greet and congratulate him. Of his greatest good-fortune, of his highest conquest, they, of course, knew nothing, and he was not in a mood to tell them of it.

The bar-room was nearly empty, for the reason that the miners had not yet finished their evening meal, and Haney and his two cronies had just taken their second round of drinks when the side door was burst violently open, and a man, white and wild, with a double-barrelled shotgun in his hand, abruptly entered. Darting across the floor, he thrust the muzzle of his weapon almost against Haney's breast and fired, uttering a wild curse at the moment of recoil.

The tall gambler reeled under the shock, swinging half way about, his hands clutching at the railing, a look of anguish and surprise upon his face. The assassin, intent, alert, would have fired again had not a by-stander felled him to the floor. The room filled instantly with excited men eager to strike, vociferous with hate; but Haney, with one palm pressed to his breast, stood silent—curiously silent—his lips white with his effort at self-control.

At length two of his friends seized him, tenderly asking: "How is it, old man? Are you hurt bad?"

His lips moved—they listened—as he faintly whispered: "He's got me, boys. Here's where I quit."

"Don't say that, Mart. You'll pull through," said his friend, chokingly. Then with ferocious impatience he yelled: "Somebody get the doctor! Damn it all, get moving! Don't you see him bleed?"

Haney moved his head feebly. "Lay me down, Pete—I'm torn to pieces—I'm all in, I'm afraid. Get me little girl—that's all I ask."

Very gently they took him in their arms and laid him on one of the gambling-tables in the rear room, while the resolute barkeeper pushed the crowd out.

Again Haney called, impatiently, almost fiercely: "Send for Bertie—quick!"

The men looked at each other in wonder, and one of them tapped his brow significantly, for no one knew of his latest love-affair. While still they stared Williams came rushing wildly in. All gave way to him, and the young doctor who followed him was greeted with low words of satisfaction. To his partner, whom he recognized, Haney repeated his command: "Send for

Bertie." With a hurried scrawl Williams put down the girl's name and address on a piece of paper, and shouted: "Here! Somebody take this and rush it. Tell her to come quick as the Lord will let her." Then, with the tenderness of a brother, he bent to Haney. "How is it, Mart?"

Mart did not reply. His supreme desire attended to, he sank into a patient immobility that approached stupor, while the surgeon worked with intent haste to stop the flow of blood. The wound was most barbarous, and Williams' eyes filled with tears as he looked upon that magnificent torso mangled by buckshot. He loved his big partner—Haney was indeed his highest enthusiasm, his chief object of adoration, and to see him riddled in this way was devil's work. He lost hope. "It's all over with Mart Haney," he said, chokingly, a few minutes later to the men crowding the bar-room—and then his rage against the assassin broke forth. He became the tiger seeking the blood of him who had slain his mate. His curses rose to primitive ferocity. "Where is he?" he asked.

To him stepped a man—one whose voice was quiet but intense. "We've attended to his case, Williams. He's toeing the moonlight from a lamp-post. Want to see?"

For an instant his rage flared out against these officious friends who had cheated him of his share in the swift delight of the avenger. Then tears again misted his eyes, and with a dignity and pathos which had never graced his speech before he pronounced a slow eulogy upon his friend: "No man had a right to accuse Mart Haney of any trick. He took his chances, fair and square. He had no play with crooked cards or 'doctored' wheels. It was all 'above board' with him. He was dead game and a sport, you all know that, and now to be ripped to bits with buckshot—just when he was takin' a wife—is hellish."

His voice faltered, and in the dead silence which followed this revelation of Haney's secret he turned and re-entered the inner room, to watch beside his friend.

The hush which lay over the men at the bar lasted till the barkeeper softly muttered: "Boys, that's news to me. It does make it just too tough." Then those who had hitherto opposed the lynching of the murderer changed their minds and directed new malediction against him, and those who had handled the rope took keener comfort and greater honor to themselves.

"Who is the woman?" asked one of those who waited.

This question remained unanswered till the messenger to the telegraph office returned. Even then little beyond her name was revealed, but each of the watchers began to pray that she might reach the dying man before his eyes should close forever. "He can't live till sunrise," said one, "and there is no train from the Junction till morning. She can't get here without a special. Did you order a special for her?"

"No, I didn't think of it," the messenger replied, with a sense of shortcoming.

"It must be done!"

"I'll attend to that," said Slater. "I know the superintendent. I'll wire him to see her—and bring her."

"Well, be quick about it. Expense don't count now."

It was beautiful to see how these citizens, rough and sordid as many of them were, rose to the poetic value of the situation. As one of them, who had seen and loved the girl, told of her youth and beauty, they all stood in rigidly silent attention. "She's hardly more than a child," he explained, "but you never saw a more level-headed little business woman in your life. She runs the Golden Eagle Hotel at Junction, and does it alone. That's what caught Mart, you see. She's as straight as a Ute, and her eyes are clear as agates. She's a little captain—just the mate for Mart. She'll save him if anybody can."

"Will she come? Can she get away?"

"Of course she'll come. She'll ride an engine or jump a flat-car to get here. You can depend on a woman in such things. She don't stop to calculate, she ain't that kind. She comes—you can bet high on that. I'm only worrying for fear Mart won't hold out till she gets here."

Meanwhile, every man in the room where Haney lay, sat in silence, with an air of waiting— waiting for the inevitable end. The bleeding had been checked, but the sufferer's breathing was painful and labored, and the doctor, sitting close beside him, was studying means to prolong life—he had given up hope of saving it. With stiffened lips Haney repeated now and again: "Keep me alive till she comes, doctor. She must marry me—here. I want her to have all I've got—*everything*!"

At another time he said: "Get the judge—have everything ready!"

They understood. He wished to dower his love with his wealth, to place in her hands his will, beyond the reach of any contestant, and this resolution through the hours of his agony, through the daze of his weakness persisted heroically—till even the doctor's throat filled with sympathetic emotion, as he thought of the young maiden soon to be thrust into this tragic drama. He answered, soothingly: "I'll do all I can, Mart. There's a lot of vitality in you yet. We won't give up. You'll pull through, with her help."

To this Haney made no reply, and the hours passed with ghostly step. It was a most moving experience for the young doctor to look round that wide room littered with scattered cards, the wheels of chance motionless at the hazard where the last gambler's bet had ended. In the "lookout's chair," where Haney himself used to sit, an unseen arbiter now gloomed, watching a game where life was the forfeit. A spectral finger seemed to rest upon the blood-red spot of every board. No sound came from the drinking-saloon in front. The miners had all withdrawn. Only the barkeeper and a few personal friends kept willing vigil.

About nine o'clock an answering telegram came to Slater: "Girl just leaving on special. Will make all speed possible."

Haney faintly smiled when Williams read this message to him. "I knew it," he whispered, "she'll come." Then his lips set in a grim line. "And I'll be here when she comes." Thereafter he had the look of a man who hangs with hooked fingers in iron resolution above an abyss, husbanding every resource—forcing himself to think only of the blue sky above him.

A little later the priest knocked at the door and asked to see the dying man, but to this request Haney shook his head and whispered. "No, no; I've no strength to waste—'tis good of him. Wait! Tell him to be here—to marry us—" And with this request the priest was forced to be content. "May the Lord God be merciful to him!" he exclaimed fervently, as he turned away.

Once again, about midnight, the wounded man roused up to say: "The ceremony must be legal—I want no lawsuits after. The girl must be protected." He was thinking of his brothers, of his own kind, rapacious and selfish. Every safeguard must be thrown around his sweetheart's life.

"We'll attend to that," answered Williams, who seemed able to read his partner's thoughts. "We'll take every precaution. He wants the judge to be present as well as the priest," he explained to the doctor, "so that if the girl would rather she can be married by the Court as well as by the Church."

Every man in the secret realized fully that the girl was being endowed with an immense fortune, and that she would inevitably be the quarry of every self-seeking relative whose interest would be served by attacking her rights in the premises. "The lawsuits must be cut out," was Williams' order to the judge. "Mart's brothers are a wolfish lot. We don't want any loose ends for them to catch on to."

From time to time messages flashed between the oncoming train and the faithful watchers. "It's all up grade, but Johnson is breaking all records. At this rate she'll reach here by daylight," said Slater. "But that's a long time for Mart to wait on that rough bed," he added to Williams, with deep sympathy in his voice.

"I know that, but to move him would hasten his death. The doctor is afraid to even turn him. Besides, Mart himself won't have it. 'I'm better here,' he says. So we've propped him into the easiest position possible. There's nothing to do but wait for the girl."

CHAPTER V

BERTHA'S UPWARD FLIGHT

Bertha was eating her supper, after a hard day's work in her little hotel, when a little yellow envelope was handed to her. The words of the message were few, but they were meaningfull: "Come at once. Mart hurt, not expected to live." It was signed by Williams. While still she sat stunned and hesitant, under the weight of this demand, another and much more explicit telegram came: "Johnson, superintendent, is ordered to fetch you with special train. Don't delay. Mart needs you—is calling for you. Come at once!"

The phrase "is calling for you" reached her heart—decided her. She rose, and, with a word of explanation to her housekeeper, put on her hat, and threw a cloak over her arm. "I've got to go to Cripple. Captain Haney is sick, and I've got to go to him. I don't know when I'll be back," she said. "Get along the best you can." Her face was white but calm, and her manner deliberate. "Send word to mother that Mart is hurt, and I've gone up to see him. Tell her not to worry."

To her night clerk, who had come on duty, she quietly remarked: "I reckon you'll have to look after things to-morrow. I'll try to get back the day after. If I don't, Lem Markham will take my place." While still she stood arranging the details of her business a short, dark man stepped inside the door, and very kindly and gravely explained his errand. "I'm Johnson, the division superintendent. They've telegraphed me for a special, and I'm going to take you up myself. Mart is a friend of mine," he added, with some feeling.

She thanked him with a look and a quick clasp of his hand, and together they hurried into the street and down to the station, where a locomotive coupled to a single coach stood panting like a fierce animal, a cloud of spark-lit smoke rolling from its low stack. The coach was merely a short caboose; but the girl stepped into it without a moment's hesitation, and the engine took the track like a spirited horse. As the fireman got up speed the car began to rock and roll violently, and Johnson remarked to the girl: "I guess you'd better take my chair; it's bolted to the floor, and you can hang on when we go round the curves."

She obeyed instantly, and with her small hands gripping the arm-rests of the rude seat cowered in silence, while the clambering monster rushed and roared over the level lands and labored up the grades, shrieking now and again, as if in mingled pain and warning. Johnson and the brakeman, for the most part, kept to the lookout in the turret, and the girl rode alone—rode far, passing swiftly from girlhood to womanhood, so full of enforced meditation were the hours of that ride. It seemed that she was leaving something sweet and care-free behind her, and it was certain that she was about to face death. She had one perfectly clear conception, and that was that the man who had been most kind to her, and to whom she had given her promise of marriage, was dying and needed her—was calling for her through the night.

Burdened with responsibility from her childhood, accustomed to make her own decisions, she had responded to this prayer, knowing dimly that this journey denoted a new and portentous experience—a fundamental change in her life.

She had admired and liked Haney from the first, but her feeling even yet was very like that of a boy for a man of heroic statue—her regard had very little of woman's passion in it. She was appalled and benumbed by the thought that she was soon to look upon him lying prone. That she might soon be called upon to meet those bold eyes closing in death she had been warned, and yet she did not shrink from it. The nurse, latent in every woman, rose in her, and she ached with desire of haste, longing to lay her hand upon the suffering man in some healing way. His kindness, his gentleness, during the days of his final courtship had sunk deep—his generosity had been so full, so free, so unhesitating.

She thought of her mother, and as a fuller conception of the alarm and anxiety she would feel came to her, she decided to send her a telegram. "She will know it was my duty to go," she decided. "As for the hotel—what does it matter now?" Nothing seemed to matter, indeed, save the speed of her chariot.

The night was long, interminably long. Once and again Johnson came down out of his perch, and spoke a few clumsy words of well-meaning encouragement, but found her unresponsive. Her brain was too busy with taking leave of old conceptions and in mastering new duties to be otherwise than vaguely grateful to her companions. Her mind was clear on one other point—this journey committed her to Marshall Haney. There could be no further hesitation. "Some time, soon, if he lives, I must marry him," she thought, and the conception troubled her with a new revelation of what that relationship might mean. She felt suddenly very small, very weak, and very helpless. "He must be good to me," she murmured. And then, as the words of his prayer to her came back, she added: "And I'll be good to him."

Far and farther below her shone the lights in the little hotel, and the busy and jocund scenes of her girlish life receded swiftly. At this moment her desk and the little sitting-room where the men lounged seemed a haven of peace and plenty, and the car, rocking and plunging through the night, was like a ship rising and falling on wild seas under unknown stars.

* * *

The clear light of the mountain dawn was burnishing brass into gold as the locomotive with its tolling bell slid up the level track at the end of its run, and came to a stealthy halt beside the small station.

"Here we are!" called Johnson from his turret, and Bertha rose, stiff and sore with the long night's ride, her resolution cooled to a kind of passive endurance. "I'm ready!" she called back.

Williams met her at the step. "It's all right, sis. Mart's still here—and waiting for you."

Instantly, at sight of his ugly, familiar, friendly face, she became alert, clear-brained. "How is he?"

"Pretty bad."

"What's it all about? How did it happen?"

"I'll clear that up as we go," he replied, and led the way to a carriage.

Once inside, she turned her keen gaze upon him. "Now go ahead—straight."

He did so in the blunt terms of a man whose life had been always on the border, and who has no nice shading in act or word.

"Is he dying?" she asked at the first pause.

"I'm afraid he is, sister," he replied, gently. "That's what's made the night seem long to us; but you're here and it's all right now."

That she was to look on him dying had been persistently in her mind, but that she was to see him mangled by an assassin added horror to her dread. In spite of her intrepid manner, she was still girl enough to shudder at the sight of blood.

Williams went on. "He's weak, too weak to talk much, and so I'm going to tell you what he wants. He wants you to marry him before he dies."

The girl drew away. "Not this minute—to-night?"

"Yes; he wants to give you legal rights to all he has, and you've got to do it quick. No tellin' what may happen." His voice choked as he said this.

Bertha's blood chilled with dismay. Her throat filled and her bosom swelled with the effort she made at self-control, and Williams, watching her with bright eyes of admiration, hurried on to the end. "Everything is ready. There is a priest, if you want him, and Judge Brady with a civil ceremony, if that will please you better, or we'll get a Protestant minister; it's for you to say. Only the knot must be tied good and tight. I told the boys you'd take a priest for Mart's sake. He says: 'Make it water-proof.' He means so that no will-breaking brothers or cousins can stack the cards agin you. And now it's up to you, little sister. He has only a few hours anyway, and I don't see that you can refuse, specially as it makes his dying—" He stopped there.

The street was silent as they drew up to the saloon door, and only Slater and one or two of his friends were present when Bertha walked into the bar-room, erect as a boy, her calm, sweet face ashen white in the electric light. For an instant; she stood there in the middle of the floor alone, her big dark eyes searching every face. Then Judge Brady, a kindly, gray-haired man, advanced, and took her hand. "We're very glad to see you," he gravely said, introducing himself. Williams, who had entered the inner room, returned instantly to say: "Come, he's waiting."

Without a word the bride entered the presence of her groom, and the doctor, bending low to the gambler, said: "Be careful now, Mart. Don't try to rise. Be perfectly still. Bertie has come."

Haney turned with a smile—a tender, humorous smile—and whispered: "Bertie, acushla mavourneen, come to me!"

Then the watchers withdrew, leaving them alone, and the girl, bending above him, kissed him. "Oh, Captain, can't I do something? I *must* do something."

"Yes, darlin', ye can. You can marry me this minute, and ye shall. I'm dyin', girl—so the doctor says. I don't feel it that way; but, anyhow, we take no chances. All I have is for you, and so—"

She put her hand ever his lips. "You must be quiet. I understand, and I will do it—but only to make you well." She turned to the door, and her voice was clear as she said to those who waited: "I am ready."

"Will you have Father Kearney?" asked Williams.

She turned towards Haney. "Just as he says."

The stricken miner, ghastly with the pain brought on by movement, responded to the doctor's question, only by a whisper: "The priest—first."

The girl heard, and her fine, clear glance rested upon the face of the priest. Tears were on her cheeks, but a kind of exultation was in her tone as she said: "I am willing, father."

With a look which denoted his appreciation of the girl's courage, the priest stepped forward and led her to her place beside her bridegroom. She took Haney's big nerveless hand in her firm grasp, and together they listened to the solemn words which made them husband and wife. It seemed that the gambler was passing into the shadow during the opening prayer, but his whispered responses came at the proper pauses, and only when the final benediction was given, and the priest and the judge fell back before the rush of the young doctor, did the wounded man's eyes close in final collapse. He had indeed reached the end of his endurance.

The young wife spoke then, imperiously, almost fiercely, asking: "Why is he lying here? This is no place for him."

The doctor explained. "We were afraid to move him—till you came. In fact, he wouldn't let me move him. If you say so now, we will take him up." With these words the watchers shifted their responsibility to her shoulders, uttering sighs of deep relief. Whatever happened now, Mart's will had been secured. At her command they lifted the table on which her husband lay, and the wife walked beside it, unheeding the throngs of silent men walling her path. Every one made way for her, waited upon her, eager to serve her, partly because she was Marshall Haney's wife, but more because of her youth and the brave heart which looked from her clear and candid eyes.

She showed no hesitation now, gave out no word of weakness; on the contrary, she commanded with certainty and precision, calling to her aid all that the city afforded. Not till she had summoned the best surgeons and was sure that everything had been done that could be done did she permit herself to relax—or to think of rest or her mother.

When she had sunk to sleep upon a couch beside her husband's bed, Williams, with a note of deep admiration, demanded of the surgeon: "Ain't she a little Captain? Mart can't die now, can he? He's got too much to live for."

CHAPTER VI

THE HANEY PALACE

One day early in the following summer a tall, thin man, with one helpless side, entered the big luminous hall of the Antlers Hotel at the Springs, upheld by a stalwart attendant, and accompanied by a sweet-faced, calm-lipped young woman. This was Marshall Haney and his young wife Bertha, down from the mountain for the first time since his illness, and those who knew their story and recognized them, stood aside with a thrill of pity for the man and a look of admiration for the girl, whose bravery and devotion had done so much to bring her husband back to life and to a growing measure of his former strength.

Marshall Haney was, indeed, but a poor hulk of his stalwart self. One lung had been deeply torn, his left shoulder was almost wholly disabled, and he walked with a stoop and shuffle; but his physical weakening was not more marked than his mental mellowing. He was softened—"gentled," as the horsemen say. His eyes were larger, and his face, once so stern and masterful, gave out an appealing expression by reason of the deep horizontal wrinkles which had developed in his brow. He had grown a mustache, and this being gray gave him an older look—older and more military. It was plain, also, that he leaned upon his keen-eyed, impassive little wife, who never for one moment lost her hold upon herself or her surroundings. Her flashing glances took note of everything about her, and her lips were close-set and firm.

Williams, ugly and wordless as ever, followed them with a proud smile till they entered the handsome suite of rooms which had been reserved for them. "There's nothing too good for Marshall Haney and his side-partner," he exulted to the bell-boy.

Thereupon, Mart, with a look of reverence at his young bride, replied: "She's airned it—and more!"

A sigh was in his voice and a singular appeal in his big eyes as he sank into an easy-chair. "I believe I do feel better down here; my heart seems to work aisier. I'm going to get well now, darlin'."

"Of course you are," she answered, in the tone of a daughter; then added, with a smile: "I like it here. Why not settle?"

To her Colorado Springs was a dazzling social centre. The beauty of the homes along its wide streets, the splendor of its private carriages, affected her almost as deeply as the magnitude and glory of Denver itself; but she was not of those who display their weaknesses and diffidence. She ate her first dinner in the lofty Antlers dining-hall with quiet dignity, and would not have been particularly noticed but for Haney, who was well-known to the waiters of the hotel. Her association with him had made her a marked figure in their mountain towns, and she was accustomed to comment.

She met the men who addressed her with entire fearlessness and candor she was afraid only of women in good clothes, speaking with the easy slanginess of a herder, using naturally and unconsciously the most picturesque phrases of the West. Her speech was incisive and unhesitating, yet not swift. She never chattered, but "you bet" and "all right" were authorized English so far as she was concerned. "They say you can't beat this town anywhere for society, and I sure like the looks of what we've seen. Suppose we hang around this hotel for a while— not too long, for it's mighty expensive." Here she smiled—a quick, flashing smile. "You see, I can't get used to spending money—I'm afraid all the time I'll wake up. It's just like a dream I used to have of finding chink—I always came to before I had a chance to handle it and see if it was real."

Haney answered, indulgently: "'Tis all real, Bertie. I'll show you that when I'm meself again."

"Oh, I believe it—at least, part of the time," she retorted. "But I'll have to flash a roll to do it—checks are no good. I could sign a million checks and not have 'em seem like real money. I'm from Missouri when it comes to cash."

Mrs. Gilman, who had always stood in bewilderment and wonder of her daughter, was entirely subject now. She and Williams usually moved in silence, like adoring subjects in the presence of their sovereigns. They had no doubts whatsoever concerning the power and primacy of gold; and as for Haney himself, his unquestioning confidence in his little wife's judgment had come to be like an article of religious faith.

After breakfast on the second day of her stay Bertha ordered a carriage, and they drove about the town in the brilliant morning sunshine, looking for a place to build. She resembled a little home-seeking sparrow. Every cosey cottage was to her an almost irresistible allurement. "There's a dandy place, Captain," she called several times. "Wouldn't you like a house like that?"

He, with larger notions, shook his head each time. "Too small, Bertie. We've the right to a fine big place—like that, now." He nodded towards a stately gray-stone mansion, with the sign "For Sale" planted on its lawn.

She was aghast. "Gee! what would we do with a state-house like that?"

"Live in it, sure."

"It would need four chamber-maids and two hired men to take care of a place like that. And think of the money it would spoil to stock it with furniture!" Nevertheless, she gazed at it longingly. "I'd sure like that big garden and that porch. You could sit on that porch and see the mountains, couldn't you? But my ears and whiskers, the expense of keeping it!"

They passed on to other and less palatial possibilities, and returned to the hotel undecided. The two women, bewildered and weary, diverged and discussed the matter of dress till the mid-day meal.

"I like being rich," remarked the young wife, as they took their seats in the lovely dining-room, and looked about at the tables so shining, so dainty. "It would be fun to run a house like this, don't you think?" She addressed her mother.

"Good gracious, no! Think of the bill for help and the worry of looking after all this silver! No, it's too splendid for us."

Haney still retained enough of his ancient humor to smile at them. "I'd rather see you manage that big stone house with the porch which I'm going to buy."

"You don't mean it?" said Bertha, while Mrs. Gilman stared at him over her soup.

He went on quietly. "Sure! Me mind's made up. You want the garden and I like the porch; so 'phone the agent after dinner, and we'll go up and see to it this very afternoon."

Bertha's bosom heaved with excitement, and her eyes expanded. "I'd like just once to see the *inside* of a house like that. It must be half as big as this hotel—but to own it! You're crazy, Captain."

The remote possibility of walking through that wonderful mansion took away the young wife's appetite, and she became silent and reflective in the face of a delicious fried chicken. The magic of her husband's wealth began to make itself most potently felt.

Haney insisted on smoking a cigar in the lobby. Bertha took her mother away to talk over the tremendous decision which was about to be thrust upon them. "We want a house," said she, decisively, "but not a palace like that. What would we do with it? It scares me up a tree to think of it."

"I guess he was only joking," Mrs. Gilman agreed.

"I can see the porch would be fine for him," Bertha went on. "But, jiminy spelter, we'd all be lost in the place!"

Haney called Williams to his side, and told him of the house. "It's a big place, but I want it. Go you and see the agent. My little girl needs a roof, and why not the best?"

"Sure!" replied Williams, with conviction. "She's entitled to a castle. You round up the women, and I'll do the rest."

The house proved to be even more splendid and spacious than its exterior indicated, and Bertha walked its wide halls with breathless delight. After a hurried survey of the interior, they came out upon the broad veranda, and lingered long in awe and wonder of the outlook. To the west lay a glorious garden of fruits and flowers; a fountain was playing over the rich green grass; high above the tops of the pear and peach trees which made a little copse rose the purple peaks of the Rampart range.

"Oh, isn't it great!" exclaimed Bertha.

Haney turned to the agent with a tense look on his pale face—a look of exultant power.

"Make out your papers," said he, quietly. "We take the place—as it stands."

Bertha was overwhelmed by this flourish of the enchanter's wand—but only for a moment. No sooner was the contract signed than she roused herself as to a new business venture. "Well, now, the first thing is furniture. Let's see! There is some carpets and curtains in the place, isn't there? And a steel range. It's up to me to rustle the balance of the outfit together right lively."

And so she set to work quite as she would have done in outfitting a new hotel—so many beds, so many chairs in a room, so many dressers, and soon had a long list made out and the order placed.

She spent every available moment of her time for the next two days getting the kitchen and dining-room in running order, and when she had two beds ready insisted on moving in. "We can kind o' camp out in the place till we get stocked up. I'm crazy to be under our own roof."

Haney, almost as eager as she, consented, and on the third day they drove up to the door, dismissed their hired coachman, and stepped inside the gate—master and mistress of an American chateau.

Mart turned, and, with misty eyes and a voice choked with happiness, said: "Well, darlin', we have it now—the palace of the fairy stories."

"It's great," she repeated, musingly; "but I can't make it seem like a home—mebbe it'll change when I get it filled with furniture, but the garden is sure all right."

They took their first meal on the porch overlooking the mountains, listening to the breeze in the vines. It was heavenly sweet after the barren squalor of their Cripple Creek home, and they did little but gaze and dream.

"We need a team," Bertha said, at last.

"Buy one," replied Haney.

So Bertha bought a carriage and a fine black span. This expenditure involved a coachman, and to fill that position an old friend of Williams'—a talkative and officious old miner—was employed. She next secured a Chinese cook, the best to be had, and a girl to do the chamber-work. They were all busy as hornets, and Bertha lived in a glow of excitement every waking hour of the day—though she did not show it.

Haney's check-book was quite as wonderful in its way as Aladdin's lamp, and little by little the women permitted themselves to draw upon its magic. The shining span of blacks, with flowing manes and champing bits, became a feature of the avenue as the women drove up and down on their never-ending quest for household luxuries—they had gone beyond mere necessities. Mart usually went with them, sitting in the carriage while they "visited" with the grocery clerks and furniture dealers. They were very popular with these people, as was natural.

"Little Mrs. Haney" became at once the subject of endless comment—mostly unfavorable; for Mart's saloon-made reputation was well-known, and the current notion of a woman who would marry him was not high. She was reported, in the alien circles of the town, to be a vulgar little chamber-maid who had taken a gambler for his money at a time when he was supposed to be on his death-bed, and her elevation to the management of a palatial residence was pointed out as being "peculiarly Western-American."

The men, however, were much more tolerant of judgment than their women. They had become more or less hardened to seeing crude miners luxuriating in sudden, accidental wealth; therefore, they nodded good-humoredly at Haney and tipped their hats to his pretty wife with smiles. As bankers, tradesmen, and taxpayers generally they could not afford to neglect a citizen possessed of so much wealth and circumstance.

Mrs. Gilman presented a letter of introduction to the nearest church of her own persuasion, and went to service quite as unassumingly as in Sibley, and was greeted by a few of the ladies there cordially and without hint of her son-in-law's connections. Two or three, including the pastor's wife, made special effort to cultivate her acquaintance by calling immediately, but they were not of those who attracted Bertha; and though she showed them about the house and answered their questions, she did not promise to call. "We're too busy," she explained. "I haven't got more than half the rooms into shape, and, besides, we're to have my brother's folks down from the Junction—we're on the hustle all day long."

This was true. She had been quite besieged by her former neighbors in Sibley, who found it convenient to "put up with the Haneys" while visiting the town. They were, in fact, very curious to study her in her new and splendid setting; and though some of them peeked and peered amid the beds, and thumped the mattresses in vulgar curiosity, the young housewife merely laughed. All her life had been spent among folk of this directly inquisitive sort. She expected them to act as they did, and, being a hearty and generous soul, as well as a very democratic one, she sent them away happy.

Indeed, she won praise from all who came to know her. But that small part of the Springs— alien and exclusive—which considered itself higher if not better than the rest of the Western world, looked askance at "the gambler's wife and her freak friends," and Mrs. Crego, who was inclined to be very censorious, alluded to the Haneys as "beggars on horseback" as she met them on the boulevard.

Of all this critical comment Bertha remained, happily, unconscious, and it is probable that she would soon have won her way to a decent circle of friends had not Charles Haney descended upon them like a plague. Mart had been receiving letters from this brother, but had said nothing to Bertha of his demands. "Charles despised me when he met me in Denver," he explained to Williams. "I was busted at the time, ye mind." He winked. "And now when he reads in the papers that Mart Haney is rich, he comes down on me like a hawk on a June bug. 'Tis no matter. He may come—I'll not cast him out. But he does not play with me double-eagles—not he!"

Charles Haney was not fitted to raise his brother's wife in the social scale, for he belonged to that marked, insistent variety of actor to be distinguished on trains and in the lobbies of hotels—a fat, sleek, loud-voiced comedian, who enacted scenes from his unwritten plays while ladling his soup, and who staggered and fell across chairs in illustration of highly emotional lines and, what was worse, he was of those who regard every unescorted woman as fair game. Bold of glance and brassy of smile, he began to make eyes at his sister-in-law from their first meeting.

She amazed him. He had expected a woman of his own class—an adventuress, painted, designing; and to find this sweet little girl—"why, she's too good for Mart," he concluded, and shifted his hollow pretensions of sympathy from his brother to his sister-in-law. Before the first evening of his visit closed he sought opportunity to tell her, in hypocritic sadness, that Mart was a doomed man, and that she would soon be free of him. Bertha was disturbed by his gaze and repelled by his touch, but tried to like him on Mart's account. His mouthing disgusted her, and the good-will with which Haney greeted his brother turned into bitterness as the boaster and low wit began to display himself.

"We all grew up in the street or in the saloon," Haney sadly remarked, "and you finished your education in the variety theatre, I'm thinking."

The actor took this as a joke, and with a grin retorted: "That's better than running a faro-layout."

"I dunno; a good quiet game has its power to educate a man," replied the gambler.

That night, as she was preparing the Captain for bed, he remarked, with a sigh: "Life is a quare game! I mind Charley well as a cute little yellow-haired divil, always laughing, always in mischief, and me chasin' after him—a big slob of a boy. I used to carry him up an' down the tenement stairs. I learned him to skate—and now here he is drinkin' himself puffy, whilst I am an old broken-down hack at forty-five." He looked up at her with a sheen of tears in his eyes. "Darlin', 'tis a shame to be leanin' on you."

She put her arm around his big grizzled head and drew it to her.

"You can lean hard, Mart. I'm standin' by."

"No, I'll not lean too hard," he answered. "I don't want your fine, straight back to stoop. I make no demands. I'll not spoil your young life. I'm not worth it. You're free to go when you can't stand me any longer."

"Now, now, no more of that!" she warned. "When I have cause to knock, you won't need no ear-trumpet. Put up your hoof." He obeyed, and, stooping swiftly, she began to unlace the shoe which he could no longer reach. Her manner was that of a daughter who tyrannizes over an indulgent father. Her admiration and gratitude, so boyish once, were now replaced by an affection in which the element of sex had small place, and his love for her sprang also from a source far removed from the fierce instinct which first led him to seek her subduing.

CHAPTER VII

BERTHA REPULSES AN ENEMY

Charles Haney had no scruples. From the moment of his first meeting with his brother's young wife he determined to make himself "solid" with her. Convinced that Mart was not long for this world, he set to work to win Bertha's favor, for this was the only way to harvest the golden fortune she controlled.

"Mart is just fool enough and contrary enough to leave every cent of his money to her." Here he placed one finger against his brow. "Carlos, here is where you get busy. It's us to the haberdasher. We shine."

Notwithstanding all his boasting, he was not only an actor out of an engagement, but flat broke, badly dressed, and in sorry disrepute with managers. "I've been playing in a stock company in San Francisco," he had explained, "and I'm now on my way to New York to produce a play of my own. Hence these tears. I need an 'angel.'"

He distinctly said "the first of the month" in this announcement, but as the days went by he only settled deeper into the snug corners of the Haney home, making no further mention of his triumphal eastward progress. On the contrary, he had the air of a regular boarder, and turned up promptly for meals, rotund and glowing in the opulence of his brother's hospitality.

On the strength of his name he found favor with the tailors, and bourgeoned forth a few days later in the best cloth the shops afforded, and strutted and plumed himself like a turkey-cock before Bertha, keeping up meanwhile a pretension of sympathy and good-fellowship with Mart.

In this he miscalculated; for Bertha, youthful as she seemed, was accustomed, as she would say, to "standing off mashers," and her impassive face and keen, steady eyes fairly disconcerted the libertine. "For Mart's sake, we'll put up with him," she said to her mother. "He's a loafer; but I can see the Captain kind o' likes to have him around—for old times' sake, I reckon."

This was true. When alone with his brother, Charles dropped his egotistic brag and dramatic bluster, and touched craftily upon the dare-devil, boyish life they had led together. He was shrewd enough to see and understand that this was his most ingratiating rôle, and he played it "to the limit," as Bertha would have said.

And yet no one in the house realized how his presence reacted against Bertha.

"What are we to think of a girl so obtuse that she permits a man like this fat, disgusting actor to dangle about her?" asked Mrs. Crego of her husband, who was Haney's legal adviser.

"He's her husband's brother, you know," argued Crego.

"All the same, I can't understand her. She looks nice and sweet, and you say she is so; and yet here she is married to a notorious gambler, and associating with mountebanks and all sorts of malodorous people. Why, I've seen her riding down the street with the upholsterer, and Mrs. Congdon told me that she saw her stop her carriage in front of a cigar store and talk with a barber in a white jacket for at least ten minutes."

Crego laughed. "What infamy! However, I can't believe even the upholsterer will finally corrupt her. The fact is, my dear, we're all getting to be what some of my clients call 'too a-ristocratic.' Bertha Haney is sprung from good average American stock, and has associated with the kind of people you abhor all her life. She hasn't begun to draw any of your artificial distinctions. I hope she never will. Her barber friend is on the same level with the clerks and grocery-men of the town. They're all human, you know. She's the true democrat. I confess I like the girl. Her ability is astonishing. Williams and Haney both take her opinion quite as weightily as my own."

Mrs. Crego was impressed. "Well, I'll call on her if you really think I *ought* to do so."

"I don't. I withdraw my suggestion. I deprecate your calling—in that spirit. I doubt if she expects you to call. I hardly think she has awakened to any slights put upon her by your set. Indeed, she seems quite happy in the society of Thomas, Richard, and Harry."

"Don't be brutal, Allen."

"I'm not. The girl is now serene—that's the main thing; and you might raise up doubts and discontents in her mind."

"I certainly shall not go near her so long as that odious actor is hanging about. His smirk at me the other day made me ill."

This conversation was typical of many others in homes of equal culture, for Bertha's position as well as her face and manner piqued curiosity. After all, the town was a small place—just large enough to give gossip room to play in—and the sheen of Mrs. Haney's wealth made her conspicuous from afar, while her youth and boyish beauty had been the subject of admiring club talk from the very first. Haney was only an old and wounded animal, whose mate was free to choose anew.

"It makes me ache to see the girl go wrong," said Mrs. Frank Congdon, wife of a resident portrait-painter, also in delicate health she was speaking to Mrs. Crego. "Think of that great house—Frank says she runs it admirably—filled with tinkers and tailors and candlestick-makers, not to mention touts and gamblers—when she might be entertaining—well, us, for example!" She laughed at the unbending face of her friend; then went on: "Dr. Cronk says the mother is a sweet old lady and of good New England family—a constitutional Methodist, he calls her. I wish she kept better company."

"But what can you expect of a girl brought up in a pigsty. Her mother was mistress of a little miners' hotel in Junction City, Allen says, and the girl boasts of it."

Mrs. Congdon smiled. "I'm dying to talk with her. She's far and away the most interesting of our newly rich, and I like her face. Frank has called, you know?"

"Has he?"

"On business, of course. She has decided to have him paint her husband's picture. She's taken her first step upward, you see."

"I should think she'd be content to have her saloon-keeper husband's face fade out of her memory."

"Frank is enthusiastic. I'm not a bit sure that he didn't suggest the portrait. He is shameless when he takes a fancy to a face. He's wild to paint them both and call it 'The Lion Tamer and the Lion.' He considers Haney a great character. It seems he saw him in Cripple Creek once, and was vastly taken by his pose. His being old and sad now—his face is one of the saddest I ever saw—makes it all the more interesting to Frank. So I'm going to call—in fact, we're going to lunch there soon."

"Oh, well, yes. You artists can do anything, and it's all right. You must come over immediately afterwards and tell me all about it, won't you?"

At this Mrs. Congdon laughed, but, being of generous mind, consented.

Crego was right. Bertha had not yet begun to take on trouble about her social position. She had carried to her big house in the Springs all the ideas and usages of Sibley Junction—that was all. She acknowledged her obligations as a householder, carrying forward the New England democratic traditions. To be next door made any one a neighbor, with the right to run in to inspect your house and furniture and to give advice. The fact that near-at-hand residents did not avail themselves of this privilege troubled her very little at first, so busy was she with her own affairs; but it was inevitable that the talk of her mother's church associates should sooner or later open her eyes to the truth that the distinctions which she had read about as existing in New York and Chicago were present in her own little city. "Mrs. Crego and her set are too stuck up to associate with common folks," was the form in which the revelation came to her.

From one loose-tongued sister she learned, also, that she and the Captain were subjects of earnest prayer in the sewing-circle, and that her husband's Catholicism was a source of deep anxiety, not to say proselyting hostility, on the part of the pastor and his wife, while from another of these officious souls she learned that the Springs, beautiful as it was, so sunlit, so pure of air, was a centre of marital infelicity, wherein the devil reigned supreme.

Her mother's pastor called, and was very outspoken as to Mart and Charles—both of whom needed the Lord's grace badly. He expressed great concern for Bertha's spiritual welfare, and openly prayed for her husband, whose nominal submission to the Catholic Church seemed not merely blindness to his own sin, but a danger to the young wife.

Haney, however, though wounded and suffering, was still a lion in resolution, and his glance checked the exhortation which the minister one day nerved himself to utter. "I do not interfere with any man's faith," said he, "and I do not intend to be put to school by you nor any other livin'. I was raised a Catholic, and for the sake of me mother I call meself wan to this day, and as I am so I shall die." And the finality of his voice won him freedom from further molestation.

Bertha's concern for her creed was hardly more poignant than Haney's, and they never argued; but she did begin to give puzzled thought to the social complications which opened out day by day before her. Charles, embittered by his failures, enlightened her still more profoundly. He had a certain shrewdness of comment at times which bit. "Wouldn't it jar you," said he one day, "to see this little town sporting a 'Smart Set' and quoting *Town Topics* like a Bible? Why, some of these dinky little two-spot four-flushers draw the line on me because I'm an actor! What d'ye think o' that? I don't mind your Methodist sistern walking wide of me, but it's another punch when these dubs who are smoking my cigars at the club fail to invite me to their houses."

Bertha looked at him reflectively throughout this speech, putting a different interpretation on the neglect he complained of. She had gone beyond disliking him, she despised him for he was growing bolder each day in his addresses, and took every precaution that he should not be alone with her; and she rose one morning with the determination to tell Mart that she would not endure his brother's presence another day. But his pleasure in Charles' company was too genuine to be disturbed, and so she endured.

The actor's talk was largely concerned with the scandal-mongery of the town, and very soon the young wife knew that Mrs. May, whose husband was "in the last stages," was in love with young Mr. June, and that Mr. Frost, whose wife was "weakly," was going about shamelessly with Miss Bloom, and all this comment came to her ears freighted with its worst significance. Vile suggestion dripped from Charles Haney's reckless tongue.

This was deep-laid policy with him. His purpose was to undermine her loyalty as a wife. His approaches had no charm, no finesse. Presuming on his relationship, he caught at her hand as she passed, or took a seat beside her if he found her alone on a sofa. At such moments she was furious with him, and once she struck his hand away with such violence that she suffered acute pain for several hours afterwards.

His attentions—which were almost assaults—came at last to destroy a large part of her joy in her new home. Her drives, when he sat beside her, were a torture, and yet she could not bring herself to accuse him before the crippled man, who really suffered from loneliness whenever she was out of the house or busy in her household work. He had never been given to reading, and was therefore pathetically dependent upon conversation for news and amusement. He was much at home, too, for his maiming was still so fresh upon him that he shrank from exhibiting himself on the street or at the clubs there are no saloons in the Springs. Crego, whom he liked exceedingly, was very busy, and Williams was away at the mines for the most part, and so, in spite of Bertha's care, he often sat alone on the porch, a pitiful shadow of the man who paid court to the clerk of the Golden Eagle.

Sometimes he followed the women around the house like a dog, watching them at their dusting and polishing. "You'll strain yourself, Captain," Bertha warningly cried out whenever he laid hold of a chair or brush. And so each time he went back to his library to smoke, and wait until his wife's duties were ended. At such hours his brother was a comfort. He was not a fastidious man, even with the refinement which had come from his sickness and his marriage, and the actor so long as he cast no imputations on any friend could talk as freely as he pleased.

Slowly, day by day, Charles regained Mart's interest and a measure of his confidence. Having learned what to avoid and what to emphasize, he now deplored the drink habits of his brothers, and gently suggested that the old father needed help. They played cards occasionally during such times as household cares drew Bertha away, and held much discussion of mines and mining—though here Mart was singularly reticent, and afforded little information about his own affairs. His trust in Charles did not go so far as that. With Crego, however, he freely discussed his condition, for the lawyer had written his new will, and was in possession of it.

"I'm like a battered old tin can," he said once. "Did ye ever try to put a tin can back into shape? Ye cannot. If ye push it back here, it bulges there. The doctors are tryin' hard to take the kinks out o' me, but 'tis impossible—I see that—but I may live on for a long time. Already me mind misgives me about Bertie—she's too young to be tied up to a shoulder-shotten old plug like mesilf."

To this Crego soothingly responded. "I don't think you need to worry. She's as happy as a blackbird in spring."

Once he said to Bertha: "I niver intended to limp around like this. I niver thought to be the skate I am this day," and his despondency darkened his face as he spoke. "I could not blame you if you threw me out. I'm only a big nuisance."

"You will be if you talk like that," she briskly answered, and that is all she seemed to make of his protest. She had indeed been reared in an atmosphere of loyalty to marriage as well as of chastity, and she never for a moment considered her vows weakened by her husband's broken frame.

This fidelity Charles discovered to his own confusion one night as he came home inflamed by liquor and reckless of hand, to find her sitting alone in the library writing a letter. It was not late, but Mart, feeling tired, had gone to bed, and Mrs. Gilman was in Sibley.

Bertha looked up as he entered, and without observing that he was drunk, went on with her writing, which was ever a painful ceremony with her. Dropping his coat where he stood, and with his hat awry on the red globe of his head, the dastard staggered towards her, his eyes lit with a glare of reckless desire.

"Say," he began, "this is luck. I want 'o talk with you, Bertie. I want 'o find out why you run away from me? What's the matter with me, anyhow?"

She realized now the foul, satyr-like mood of the man, and sprang up tense and strong, silently confronting him.

He mumbled with a grin: "You're a peach! What's the matter? Why don't you like me? Ain't I all right? I'm a gentleman."

His words were babble, but the look in his eyes, the loose slaver of his lips, both scared and angered her, and as he pushed against her, clumsily trying to hook his arm about her waist, she struck him sharply with the full weight of her arm and shoulder, and he tottered and fell sprawling. With a curse in his teeth he caught at a chair, recovered his balance, and faced her with a look of fury that would have appalled one less experienced than she.

"You little fool," he snarled, "don't you do that again!"

"*Stop!*" She did not lift her voice, but the word arrested him. "Do you want to die?" The word *die* pierced the mist of his madness. "What do you think Mart will say to this?"

He shivered and grew pale under the force of his brother's name uttered in that tone. He began to melt, subsiding into a jelly-mass of fear.

"Don't tell Mart, for Christ's sake! I didn't mean nothing. Don't do it, I beg—I beg!"

She looked at him and seemed to grow in years as she searched his wretched body for its soul. "If you don't pull out of this house to-morrow I'll let him know just the kind of dead-head boarder you are. You haven't fooled me any—not for a minute. I've put up with you for his sake, but to-night settles it. You go! I've stood a lot from you, but your meal-ticket is no good after to-morrow morning—you *sabe*? It's you to the outside to-morrow. Now get out, or I call Mart."

He turned and shuffled from the room, leaving his battered hat at her feet.

She waited till she heard him close his door; then, with a look of disgust on her face, picked up his hat and coat, and hung them on the rack in the hall. "I'm sorry for Mart," she said to herself. "He *was* company for him, but I can't stand the loafer a day longer. I hope I never see him again."

He did not get down to breakfast, and for this she was glad; but he sought opportunity a little later to plead for clemency. "Give me another chance. I was drunk. I didn't mean it."

She remained inexorable. "Not for a second," she succinctly replied. "I don't care how you fix it with Mart. Smooth it up as best you can, but fly this coop." And her face expressed such contempt that he crept away, flabby and faltering, to his brother.

"I've been telegraphed for, and must go," he said. "And, by the way, I need a little ready mon to carry me to the little old town. As soon as I get to work I'll send you a check."

Mart handed him the money in silence, and waited till he had folded and put away the bills. Then he said: "Charles, you was always the smart one of the family, and ye'd be all right now if ye'd pass the booze and get down to hard work. It's *time* ye were off, for ye've done nothin' but loaf and drink here. I've enjoyed your talk—part of the time; but I can see ye'd grow onto me here like a wart, and that's bad for you and bad for me, and so I'm glad ye're going."

"Can't you—" He was going to ask for a position—something easy with big pay—when he saw that such a request would make his telegram a lie.

As he hesitated Mart continued: "No, I'll back no play for ye. I'm a gambler, but I take no chances of that kind. If you see the old father, write and tell me how he is."

Charles, though filled with rising fury, was sober enough to know in what danger he stood, and forcing a smile to his face, shook hands and went out to his carriage—alone.

As Mart met Bertha a few minutes later he remarked, with calm directness: "There goes a cheap rounder and a sponge. I've been a gambler and a saloon-keeper, but I never got the notion that I could live without doin' something. Charles was a smart lad, but the divil has him by the neck, and to give money is to give him drink."

Bertha remained silent, her own indictment was so much more severe.

CHAPTER VIII

BERTHA RECEIVES AN INVITATION

Colorado Springs lies in a shallow valley, under a genial sun, at almost the exact level of the summit of Mt. Washington. From the railway train, as it crawls over the hills to the east, it looks like a toy village, but is, in fact, a busy little city. To ride along its wide and leafy streets in summer, to breathe its crystalline airs in winter, is to lose belief in the necessity of disease. The grave seems afar off.

And yet it was built, and is now supported, by those who, fearing death, fled the lower, miasmatic levels of the world, and who, having abandoned all hope or desire of return, are loyally developing and adorning their adopted home. These fugitives are for the most part contented exiles—men as well as women—who have come to enjoy their enforced stay here beside the peaks; and their devotion to the town and its surroundings is unmistakably sincere, for they believe that the climate and the water have prolonged their lives.

Not all even of these seekers for health are ill, or even weakly, at present; on the contrary, many of them are stalwart hands at golf, and others are seasoned horsemen. In addition to those who are resident in their own behalf are many husbands attendant upon ailing wives, and blooming wives called to the care of weazened and querulous husbands, and parents who came bringing a son or daughter on whom the pale shadow of the White Death had fallen. But, after all, these Easterners color but they do not dominate the life of the town, which is a market-place for a wide region, and a place of comfort for well-to-do miners. It is, also, a Western town, with all a Western town's customary activities, and the traveller would hardly know it for a health resort, so cheerful and lively is the aspect of its streets, where everything denotes comfort and content.

In addition to the elements denoted above, it is also taken to be a desirable social centre and a charming place of residence for men like Marshall Haney, who, having made their pile in the mountain camps, have a reasonable desire to put their gold in evidence—"to get some good of their dust," as Williams might say. Here and there along the principal avenues are luxurious homes—absurdly pretentious in some instances—which are pointed out to visitors as the residences of the big miners. They are especially given to good horses also, and ride or drive industriously, mixing very little with the more cultured and sophisticated of their neighbors, for whom they furnish a never-ending comedy of manners. "A beautiful mixture for a novelist," Congdon often said.

Yes, the town has its restricted "Smart Set," in imitation of New York city, and its literary and artistic groups small, of course, and its staid circle of wealth and privilege, and within defined limits and at certain formal civic functions these various elements meet and interfuse genially if not sincerely. However, the bitter fact remains that the microcosm is already divided into classes and masses in a way which would be humorous if it were not so deeply significant of a deplorable change in American life. Squire Crego, in discussing this very matter with Frank Congdon, the portrait-painter, put it thus: "This division of interest is inevitable. What can you do? The wife of the man who cobbles my shoes or the daughter of the grocer who supplies my sugar is, in the eyes of God, undoubtedly of the same value as my own wife, but they don't *interest* me. As a social democrat, I may wish sincerely to do them good, but, confound it, to wish to do them good is an impertinence. And when I've tried to bring these elements together in my house I have always failed. Mrs. Crego, while being most gracious and cordial, has, nevertheless, managed to make the upholsterer chilly, and to freeze the grocer's wife entirely out of the picture."

"There's one comfort: it isn't a matter of money. If it were, where would the Congdons be?"

"No, it isn't really a matter of money, and in a certain sense it isn't a matter of brains. It's a question of—"

"*Savoir faire.*"

"Precisely. You haven't a cent, so you say frequently—" Congdon stopped him, gravely.

"I owe you fifty—I was just going down into my jeans to pay it, when I suddenly recalled—"

"Don't interrupt the court. You haven't a cent, we'll say, but you go everywhere and are welcome. Why?"

"That's just it. Why? If you really want to know, I'll tell you. It's all on account of Lee. Lee is a mighty smart girl. She has a cinch on the gray matter of this family."

"You do yourself an injustice."

"Thank you."

Crego pursued his argument. "There isn't any place that a man of your type can't go if you want to, because you take something with you. You mix. And Haney, for example—to return to the concrete again—Haney would make a most interesting guest at one's dinner-table, but the wife, clever as she is, is impossible—or, at least, Mrs. Crego thinks she is."

Congdon fixed a finger pistol-wise and impressively said: "That little Mrs. Haney is a wonder. Don't make any mistake about her. She'll climb."

"I'm not making the mistake, it's Mrs. Crego. I've asked her to call on the girl, but she evades the issue by asking: 'What's the use? Her interests are not ours, and I don't intend to cultivate her as a freak.' So there we stand."

Congdon looked thoughtful. "She may be right, but I don't think so. The girl interests me, because I think I see in her great possibilities."

"Her abilities certainly are remarkable. She needs but one statement of a point in law. She seems never to forget a word I say. Sometimes this realization is embarrassing. When she fixes those big wistful eyes on me I feel bound to give her my choicest diction and my soundest judgments. Haney, too, for all his wild career, attaches my sympathy. You're painting his portrait—why don't you and Lee give them a dinner?"

"Good thought! I told Lee this morning that it was a shame to draw the line on that little girl just because that rotten, bad brother-in-law of hers was base enough to slur her at the club. But, as you say, women can't be driv. However, I think Lee can manage a dinner if anybody can. As you say, we're only artists, and artists can do anything—except borrow money. However, if you want to know, Lee says that this barber lover of Mrs. Haney's has done more to queer her with our set than anything else. They think her tastes are low."

"That incident is easily explained. Winchell knew her in Sibley, and though he has undoubtedly followed her over here for love of her, he seems a decent fellow, and I don't believe intends any harm. I will admit her stopping outside his door to talk with him was unconventional, but I can't believe that she was aware of any impropriety in the act. Nevertheless, that did settle the matter with Helen. 'You can dine with them any day if you wish,' she says, 'but—' And there the argument rests."

"Of course, you and I can put the matter on a basis of trade courtesy," said Congdon; "but I confess they interest me enormously, and I would like to do them some little favor for their own sakes. Poor Haney will never be more of a man than he is to-day, and that little girl is going to earn all the money she gets before she is done with him."

And so they parted, and Congdon went home to renew the discussion with his wife. "You must call. It's only the decent thing to do, now that the portrait is nearly done," he said.

"I don't mind the calling, Frank," she briskly replied, "and I don't much mind giving a little dinner, but I don't want to get the girl on my mind. She has so much to learn, and I haven't the time nor energy to teach her."

Congdon waved his finger. "Don't you grow pale over that," said he. "That girl's no fool— she's capable of development. She will amaze you yet."

"Well, consider it settled. I'll call this afternoon and ask her to dinner; but don't expect me to advise her and follow her up. Now, who'll we ask to meet her—the Cregos?"

"Yes, I'd thought of them."

"Oh, I know all about it. You needn't stammer. You and Allen are getting a good deal out of the Haneys, and want to be decent in return. Well, I think well of you for it, and I'll do my mite. I'll have young Fordyce in, and Alice; being Quakers and 'plain people,' they won't mind. Ben is crazy to see the rough side of Western life, anyway. Now run away, little boy, and leave the whole business to me."

As Crego had said, the Congdons were privileged characters in the Springs. They were at once haughty with the pride of esthetic cleverness, and humble with the sense of their unworthiness in the wide old-world of art. Lee was contemptuous of wealth when they had a pot of beans in the house, and Frank was imperiously truculent when borrowing ten dollars from a friend or demanding an advance of cash from a prospective patron. They both came of long lines of native American ancestry, and not only felt themselves as good as anybody, but a little better than most. They gave wit for champagne, art instruction for automobile rides, and never-failing good humor for house-room and the blazing fires of roomy hearths.

Mrs. Congdon, of direct Virginian ancestry, was named Lee by a state's-rights mother, who sent her abroad to "study art." She ended by pretending to be a sculptor—and she still did occasionally model a figurine of her friends or her friends' babies; mainly, she was the aider and abettor of her husband, a really clever portrait-painter, whose ill health had driven him from New York to Colorado, and who was making a precarious living in the Springs—precarious for the reason that on bright days he would rather play golf than handle a brush, and on dark days he *couldn't* see to paint so he said. In truth, he was not well, and his slender store of strength did not permit him to do as he would. To cover the real seriousness of his case he loudly admitted his laziness and incompetency.

Lee was a devoted wife, and when she realized that his interest in the Haneys was deep and genuine her slight opposition gave way. It meant a couple of thousand dollars to Frank, but money was the least of their troubles—credit seemed to come along when they needed it most, and each of them had become "trustful to the point of idiocy," Mrs. Crego was accustomed to say. Mrs. Crego really took charge of their affairs, and when they needed food helped them to it.

Starting for the Haneys on the street-car that very afternoon, Lee reached the gate just as Bertie was helping Mart into his carriage. There was something so genuine and so touching in this picture of the slender young wife supporting her big and crippled husband that Mrs. Congdon's nerves thrilled and her face softened. Plainly this consideration on the part of Mrs. Haney was habitual and ungrudging.

Bertie, as she faced her caller, saw only a pale little woman with flashing eyes and smiling mouth, whose dress was as neat as a man's and almost as plain Lee prided herself on not being "artistic" in dress, and so waited for further information.

"How do you do, Mrs. Haney?" Lee began. "I'm Mrs. Congdon."

Bertha threw the rug over Mart's knees before turning to offer her hand. "I'm glad to meet you," she responded, with gravity. "I've seen you on the street."

Lee couldn't quite make out whether this remark was intended for reproach or not, but she went on, quickly: "I was just about to call. Indeed, I came to ask you and Mr. Haney to dine with us on Thursday." She nodded and smiled at Mart, who sat with impassive countenance listening with attention—his piercing eyes making her rather uncomfortable. "We dine at seven. I hope you can come."

Bertha looked up at her husband. "What do you say, Captain?"

"I don't see any objection," he answered, without warmth.

Bertha turned, with still passive countenance. "All right," she said, "we'll be there. Won't you jump in and take a ride with us?"

Lee, burning with mingled flames of resentment and humor, replied: "Thank you, I have another call to make—Thursday, then, at seven o'clock."

"We'll connect. Much obliged," replied Bertha, and sprang into the carriage. "Go ahead, Dan. Good-day, Mrs. Congdon."

Lee stood for an instant in amazement at this easy, not to say indifferent, acceptance of her tremendous offering. "Well, if that isn't cool!" she gasped, and walked on thoughtfully.

Humor dominated her at last, and when she entered Mrs. Crego's house she was flushed with laughter, and recounted the words of the interview with so many subtle interpretations of her own that Mrs. Crego was delighted.

Mrs. Congdon did not spare herself. "Helen, she made me feel like a bill-collector! 'All right,' said she, 'I'll be there,' and left me standing in the middle of the street. You've got to come now, Helen, to preserve my dignity."

"I'm wild to come, really. I want to see what she'll do to us 'professional people.' Maybe she will patronize us too."

When Lee told Frank about it at night he failed to laugh as heartily as she had expected. "That's all very funny, the way you tell it, but as a matter of fact the girl did all she knew. She accepted your invitation and civilly asked you to take a ride. What more could mortal woman proffer?"

"She might have invited me into the house."

"Not at the moment. It was Mart's hour for a drive, and you were interfering with one of her duties. I think she treated you very well."

"Anyhow, she's coming, and so is Helen. It tickled Helen nearly into fits, of course, and she's coming—just to see me 'put to it to manage these wet valley bronchos.'"

"The girl may look like a bronk, but she's got good blood in her. She'll hold her own anywhere," replied Congdon, with conviction.

CHAPTER IX

BERTHA MEETS BEN FORDYCE

For all her impassivity, Bertha was really elated by this invitation, for she liked Congdon, and had a very high opinion of his powers. She experienced no special dread of the dinner, for it appeared to her at the moment to be a simple sitting down to eat with some friendly people. She was not in awe of Mrs. Congdon, however much she might admire her husband's skill, and she knew their home. It was a small house on a side street, and did not compare for a moment with her own establishment, in which she had begun to take a settled pride.

As they rode away she was mentally casting up in her mind a choice of clothes, when Haney remarked: "Bertie, I don't believe I'll go to that dinner."

"Why not?"

"Well, I'm not as handy with a cold deck as I used to be, and I don't think I ought to put me lame foot into another man's lap."

"You're all right, Captain, and, besides, I'll be close by to help out in case you run up against a hard knock in the steak. Course you'll go—I want you to get out and see the people. Why, you haven't taken a meal out of the house since we moved, except that one at the Casino. You need more doin'."

Haney was in a dejected mood. "So do you. I'm a heavy handicap to you, Bertie, sure I am. As I see ye settin' there bloomin' as a rose and feel me own age a-creepin' on me, I know I should be takin' me *congé* out of self-respect—just to give you open road."

"Stop that!" she warningly cried. "Hello, there's Ed! He seems in a rush. Wonder what's eating him?"

Winchell, dressed in a new suit of clothes, darted from the sidewalk to the carriage, his face shining. "Say, folks, I'm called East. Old man died yesterday, and I've got to go home." He was breathing hard with excitement.

"Get in and tell us about it," commanded Bertha.

He climbed up beside the driver, and turned on his seat to continue. "Yes, I've got to go; and, say, the old man was well off. I don't do no more barberin', I tell you that. I'm goin' to study law. I'm comin' back here just as soon as things are settled up. I've been talking with a fellow here—Lawyer Hansall; he says he'll take me in and give me a chance. No more barberin' for me, you hear me!"

"'Tis a poor business, but a necessary," remarked Haney.

Bertha was sympathetic. "I'm glad you're goin' to get a raise. Of course, I'm sorry about your father."

"I understand—so am I. But he's gone, and it's up to me to think of myself. I know you always despised my trade."

"No, I didn't. Men have to be shaved and clipped. It's like dish-washin', somebody has to do it. We can't all sit in the parlor."

Winchell acknowledged the force of this. "Well, I always felt sneakin' about it, I'll admit, but that was because I was raised a farmer, and barbers were always cheap skates with us. We didn't use 'em much, in fact. Well, it's all up now, and when I come back I want you to forget I ever cut hair. A third of the old farm is mine, and that will pay my board while I study."

Neither Haney nor his young wife was surprised by this movement on his part any more than he was surprised at their rise to wealth and luxury; both were in accordance with the American tradition. But as they rode down the street certain scornful Easterners schooled in European conventions smiled to see the wife of an Irish millionaire gambler in earnest conversation with a barber.

Mrs. Crego, driving down-town with Mrs. Congdon, stared in astonishment, then turned to Lee. "And you ask me to meet such a woman at dinner!" she exclaimed, and her tone expressed a kind of bewilderment.

Lee laughed. "You can't fail me now. Don't be hasty. Trust in Frank."

"I'd hate to have my dinner partners selected by Frank Congdon. I draw the line at barbers."

"You're a snob, Helen. If you were really as narrow as you sound I'd cut you dead! Furthermore, the barber isn't invited."

"I can't understand such people."

"I can. She don't know any better. You impute a low motive where there is nothing worse than ignorance. As Frank says, the girl is a perfectly natural outgrowth of a little town. I hope our dinner won't spoil her."

Mrs. Congdon had put the dinner-hour early, and when the Haneys drove up in their glittering new carriage, drawn by two splendid black horses, she too had a moment of bewilderment, but her sense of humor prevailed. "Frank," she said, "you can't patronize a turnout like that— not in my presence."

"To-night art's name is mud," he replied, with conviction, and hastened down the steps to help Haney up.

The gambler waved his proffered arm aside. "I'm not so bad as all that," said he. "I let me little Corporal help me—sometimes for love of it, not because I nade it."

He was still gaunt and pale, but his eyes were of unconquerable fire, and the lift of his head from the shoulders was still leopard-like. He was dressed in a black frock-coat, with a cream-colored vest and gray trousers, and looked very well indeed—quite irreproachable.

Bertha was clad in black also—a close-fitting, high-necked gown which made her fair skin shine like fire-flushed ivory, and her big serious eyes and vivid lips completed the charm of her singular beauty. Her bosom had lost some of its girlish flatness, but the lines of her hips and thighs still resembled those of a boy, and the pose of her head was like that of an athlete.

"Won't you come in and take off your hat?" asked Mrs. Congdon. And she followed without reply, leaving the two men on the porch.

Without appearing to do so she saw everything in the house, which was hardly more than an artistic camp, so far as the first floor was concerned. Navajo rugs were on the floor, Moqui plaques starred the walls, and Acoma ollas perched upon book-shelves of thick plank. The chairs were rude, rough, and bolted at the joints. The room made a pleasant impression on Bertha, though she could not have told why. The ceiling was dark, the walls green, the woodwork stained pine, and yet it had charm.

Mrs. Congdon explained meanwhile that Frank had made the big centre-table of plank, and the book-shelves as well. "He likes to tinker at such things," she said. "Whenever he gets blue or cross I set him to shifting the dresser or making a book-shelf, and he cheers up like mad. He's a regular kid anyway—always doing the things he ought not to do."

In this way she tried to put her guest at her ease, while Bertha sat looking at her in an absent-minded way, apparently neither frightened nor embarrassed—on the contrary, she seemed to be thinking of something else. At last, to force a reply, Mrs. Congdon asked: "How do you like my husband's portrait of Mr. Haney?"

"I don't know," she slowly replied. "It looks like him, and then again it don't. I guess I'm not up to hand paintin's. Enlarged photographs are about my size."

"You're disappointed, then?"

"Well, yes, I don't know but I am. I didn't think it was going to look just that way. Mr. Congdon says blue shadows are under anybody's ears in the light, but I can't see 'em on the Captain, and I do see 'em in the picture; that's what gets me twisted. When I look at the picture I can't see nothin' else."

Her hostess laughed. "I know just how you feel, but that's the insolence of the painter—he puts on canvas what *he* sees, not what his patron sees. The more money you pay for a portrait the more insolent the artist."

At this moment Mrs. Crego came in, and as she said afterwards was presented to the gambler's wife "as though I were a nobody and she a visiting countess." Bertha rose, offered her hand, like a boy, in silence; she stood very straight, with very cold and unmistakably suspicious face. And Alice Heath, who entered with Mrs. Crego, shared this chill reception.

Bertha, in truth, instantly and cordially hated Mrs. Crego; but she pitied the younger woman, in whom she detected another fugitive fighting a losing battle with disease. Miss Heath was very fair and very frail, with burning deep-blue eyes and a lovely mouth. She greeted Bertha with such sincere pleasure that the girl inclined to her instantly, and they went out on the porch together. Alice put her hand on Bertha's arm, saying: "I've wanted to meet you, Mr. Congdon has told us so much of you. Your life seems very romantic to me."

The men all rose to meet Mrs. Congdon, and before Bertha had time to recover from the effect of the girl's words she found herself confronted by Ben Fordyce, who looked like a college boy, athletic and smiling. He was tall and broad-chested, with a round blond face and yellow hair. His manner was frank, and his voice deep. His hand, broad and strong, was hardened by the tennis-racket and calloused by the golf-stick, and somehow its leathery clasp pleased the girl. The roughness of his palm made him less alien than either Congdon or Crego.

They went out to dinner immediately, and as she walked beside Mart she felt the young athlete's eyes resting upon her face, and the knowledge of this troubled her unaccountably. Mrs. Congdon seated him opposite her at the table, and he continued to stare at her with the frankest curiosity. She returned his gaze at last with a certain defiance, but found no offence in his eyes, which were round as his face, and of a sincere, steady gray. He was smooth-shaven, and his blond hair was rather short. All these peculiarities appeared one by one in the intervals between her attentions to Mart and her study of the furnishings of the table, which was decorated with candles and flowers in a way quite new to her.

Fordyce was as fine as he looked. Nothing equivocal was in "that magnificent boy," as his friends called him, and his interest in little Mrs. Haney was that of the Easterner who, having been told that strange things take place in the West, is disappointed if they do not happen under his nose. He had heard much of the Haneys from Congdon, and had been especially impressed with the story of Bertha's midnight ride to the bedside of the dying gambler. The wedding in the saloon, her devotion to the wounded man, their descent upon the Springs, and their domestication in a stone palace—all appealed to his imagination. Such things could not happen in Chester; they were of the mountain West, and most satisfying to his taste.

Bertha, on her part, had to admit that the people at the table were most kindly, even considerate. They made her husband the centre of interest, and passed politely over all his disastrous attempts to use his left hand. There were no awkward pauses, for, excepting one or two slips of tongue, Haney rose to the occasion. He was big enough and self-contained enough not to apologize for what he had been or what he was, and under Congdon's skilful guidance told of his experiences as amateur miner and gambler, growing humorous as the wine mellowed and lightened his reminiscences. He felt the sympathy of his audience. All listened delightedly with no accusation in their eyes—except in the case of Mrs. Crego, who still breathed, so it seemed to Bertha, a certain contempt and inner repugnance.

Young Fordyce glowed with delight in these tales, reading beneath the terse lines of Haney's slang something epic, detecting a perfect willingness to take any chance. The fact that his bravery led to nothing conventionally noble or moral did not detract from the inherent interest of the tale; on the contrary, the young fellow, being of unusual imaginative reach and freedom, took pleasure in the thought that a man would risk his life again and again merely for the excitement of it. Occasionally he glanced at Judge Crego, to find him looking upon Haney with thoughtful glance. It was a little like listening to a prisoner's confession of guilt as he afterwards said, but to him, as to Congdon, it was a most interesting monologue.

It added enormously to the romance, so far as Ben Fordyce was concerned, to look across the table at the grave, watchful face of the girl who unfolded her husband's napkin or cut up his roast with deft hand—always careful not to interrupt his talk.

As he thought of the quiet Quaker neighborhood from which he came, and contrasted these singular and powerfully defined personalities with the "men of weight" and the demure maidens of his acquaintance, Ben's blood tingled with a sense of the bigness and strangeness of the greater America. The West was no longer a nation; it was a world. To be in it at last was a delight as well as an education.

Bertha, on her part, felt no strangeness in her position. Her marriage was a logical outcome of her life and surroundings. The incomprehensible lay in the shining women about her. Their ideas of life, their comment, puzzled her. Their clothes were of a kind which her own money could buy, but their manners, their grace of speech, their gestures, came of something besides money. Mrs. Crego was especially formidable, and made her feel the inadequacy of the black gown which she had thought very fine when she selected it, ready made, in a Denver store. She did not know that Mrs. Crego had dressed "very simply," at the suggestion of her hostess; but she did feel a certain condescension of manner, even in Alice, and was glad the Captain absorbed so much of the table-talk.

Her time of trial came when the ladies rose and, at Mrs. Congdon's suggestion, returned to the porch, leaving the men to finish their cigars. Not one of Ben's little courtesies towards the women escaped her. His acquiescence, Congdon's tone of exaggerated respect, Crego's compliments, were all new to her, and in a certain sense she resented them. She doubted their sincerity a little, notwithstanding their grateful charm.

Alice took her to herself and this was a great relief; for she feared Mrs. Crego's sharp tongue, and was not entirely sure of her hostess.

Laying a slim hand on her arm, the Eastern girl began: "I am fascinated by you, Mrs. Haney. You have had such an interesting life, and you have such an opportunity for doing good."

Bertha looked at her in blank surprise. "What do you mean?"

"With your great wealth you can accomplish so much. Had you thought of that?"

"No, I hadn't." The answer was blunt. "I've been so busy getting settled and looking after the Captain, I haven't had time to think of anything else."

"Oh, of course; but by and by you'll begin to look about you for things to help—I mean hospitals and charities, and all that. The only time when I envy great wealth is when I see some wrong which money can right. Mr. Fordyce is a lawyer, but not a very famous one— he's only twenty-eight; and while we are likely to have all we really need, we can't begin to do what we'd like to do for others. I suppose Mrs. Congdon has told you of us?"

"Where do you live?"

"We live in Chester, but Mr. Fordyce has an office in Philadelphia. We have been engaged a long time, but I couldn't think of marrying while I was so ill. I'm afraid I stayed so long that not even this climate can help me."

This was indeed Bertha's conviction, and her untactful silence said as much. Therefore, Alice hastened on to other more general topics. She was very sprightly, but Bertha maintained a determined silence through it all, quite unable to understand the girl's confidences.

When the men came out Alice took Haney to herself, and they seemed to enjoy each other's society very keenly; indeed, their mutual absorption became so complete that Ben remarked upon it to Bertha. "Miss Heath has been crazy to meet your husband, Mrs. Haney. His adventurous life appeals to her, as to me, very deeply. We don't mean to be offensive, but to us you seem typical of the West."

What he said at this time made less impression on her than the way in which he spoke. The light of an electric street-lamp fell upon his face, revealing its charming lines. On his fine hand a ring gleamed. Autumn insects were singing sleepily in the grass and from the trees. The laughter of girls came from the dusk of neighboring lawns, and over all descended the magical light of a harvest moon, flecking the surface of the little garden with shadows almost as definite as those cast by the flaming white globes of the street-lamps. It is on such nights that the heart of youth expands with longing and sadness.

Crego and Congdon fell into hot argument their usual method of conversation, leaving the young people to themselves, and, Ben with intent to provoke the grave little wife to laughter, told a funny story which reflected on Congdon's improvidence.

Bertha was really grateful, for she felt herself at a great disadvantage among these fluent and interesting folk, who talked like the characters in novels. Their jests, their comment, meant little to her; but their gestures, their graceful attitudes, their courtesies to each other, meant much. They were something more than polite; they were considerate in a way which showed their thoughtfulness to be deeply grounded in habitual action. They used slang, but they used it as a garnish, not as a habit of speech. Expressions which she had read in books, but had never before heard spoken, flowed from their lips. Their sentences were built up for effect; in Crego's case this was more or less expected, but the phrases of Fordyce and Congdon were still more disconcerting. The art of their stories was a revelation of the neatness and precision of cultivated speech.

When Mrs. Congdon led the way back into the house Ben stepped to Alice's side, saying, in a low tone: "I hope you haven't taken a chill. I beg your pardon, dearest; I should have watched you more closely."

Once within-doors Mrs. Congdon insisted on Ben's singing, which he did with smiling readiness, expressing, however, a profound ignorance of music. "I never take my songs as seriously as my friends seem to do," he explained to Bertha. "Music with me is a gift rather than an acquirement."

His voice was indeed fresh and sweet, and he sang—as Bertha had never heard any one sing—certain love ballads, whose despairing cadences were made the more profoundly piercing, someway, by his happy boyish face and handsomely clothed and powerful figure. "'But I and my True Love Will Never Meet Again!'" seemed to be a fatalistic cry rather than a wail of sadness as it came from his lips, but its melody sank deep into the girl's heart. She sat in rigid absorption, her eyes fixed upon the splendid young singer as a child looks upon some new and complicated toy. The grace with which he pronounced his words, the spread of his splendid chest, his easy pose, his self-depreciating shrugs enthralled her. Surely this was one of the young princes of the earth. His voice came to her freighted with the passion of ideal manhood.

He sang other songs—tunes not worthy of him—but ended with a ballad called "Fair Springtide," by MacDowell—a song so stern, so strange, so inexorably sad that the singer himself grew grave at last and rose to his best. Bertha was thrilled to the heart, saddened yet exalted by his voice. Her horizon—her emotional horizon—was of a sudden extended, and she caught glimpses of strange lands and dim peaks of fabled mountains; and when the singer declared himself at an end she sat benumbed while the others cheered—her hands folded on her lap. It seemed a profanation to applaud.

Haney gloomed in silence also, but not for the same reason. "I might have sung like that once," he thought, for he had been choir-boy in his ragamuffin youth, and had regained a fine tenor voice at eighteen. Age and neglect had ruined it, however. For ten years he had not attempted to sing a note. This youth made him dream of the past—as it caused Bertha to forecast the future.

While young Fordyce was putting away his music the Captain struggled to his feet, and Bertha, seeing a sudden paleness overspread his face, hastened to him.

"I reckon we'd better be going," she said to Mrs. Congdon, with blunt directness.

"It's early yet," replied her hostess.

Haney replied: "Not for cripples. Time was when I could sit all night in the 'lookout's chair,' but not now. Ten o'clock finds me wishful towards the bed." He said this with a faint smile. But the pathos of it, the truth of it, went to Bertha's heart, as it did to Mrs. Congdon's. Not merely was his body maimed, but his mind had correspondingly been weakened by that tearing charge of shot.

Something of his native Celtic gallantry came back to him as he said: "Sure, Mrs. Congdon, we've had a fine evening. You must come to see us soon."

Ben was addressing himself to Bertha. "Do you ever ride?"

"I used to—I don't now. You see, the Captain can't stand the jolt of a horse, so we mostly drive."

"I was about to say that Alice and I would be glad to have you join us. We ride every morning—a very gentle pace, I assure you, for I'm no rough-rider, and, besides, she sets the pace."

Bertha's face was pale and her eyes darkly luminous as she falteringly answered. "I'd like to—but—Perhaps I can some time. I'm much obliged," and then she gave him her hand in parting.

Mrs. Congdon was subtly moved by something in the girl's face as she said good-night, and to her invitation to come and see her cordially responded: "I certainly shall do so."

Little Mrs. Haney rode away from her first dinner party in the silence of one whose thoughts are too swift and too new to find speech. Her brain, sensitive as that of a babe, had caught and ineffaceably retained a million impressions which were to influence all her after life. The most vivid and most powerful of these impressions rose from the glowing beauty of young Fordyce, whose like she had never seen; but as background to him was the lovely room, the shining table, the grace and charm of the conversation, and, dominating all, the music—quite the best she had ever heard. The evening—so simple, almost commonplace, to her hostess— was of unspeakable significance to the uncultured girl.

She did not wish to talk, and when Haney spoke she made no reply to his comment. "A fine bunch of people," he repeated. "They sure treated us right. Crego's the fine man—we do well to make him our lawyer." As Bertha again failed to respond he resumed, with a little chuckle: "But Mrs. Crego is saying, 'I dunno—them Haneys is queer cattle.' And the little sick lady, sure she was as interested in me talk as Patsy McGonnigle. She drug out o' me some of me wildest scrapes. Poor little girl, 'twill soon be all up with her.... It's a fine young fellow she has. A Quaker by training, she says. My! my! What a prizefighter he'd make if his mind ran that way! Think of a Quaker with a chest like that—'tis something ferocious! He can sing, too, can't he? A fine lad—as fine as iver I see. Think of shoulders like his all wasted on a man of peace. I'm afraid the little lady will never put on the ring if she waits till she gets well."

To this Bertha listened intently, but gave out no sign of interest. She was eager to be alone, eager to review all that had happened—all that had been said.

For the first time since her marriage she felt Haney's presence to be just the least bit of a burden; and when they entered the house she urged his immediate retirement, though he was disposed to sit in the library and talk. "They were high-class," he said, again. "I never supposed I could make easy camp with such people. They sure treated us noble. They made us feel at home.... We must have some liquor like that. I've always despised wine and those that took it; but, bedad! I see there are two sides to that question. 'Tis not so thin as I thought it."

Bertha at last got him safely bestowed, and was free to seek her own apartment, which she did at once. Her chamber, which adjoined her husband's to the west he liked the morning sun, was a big room, and the young wife looked like a doll as she dropped into a broad tufted chair which stood in a square bay-window, and with folded hands looked out upon the ghostly shapes of the great peaks, snow-covered and moonlit.

A thousand revelations of character as well as of manners lay in that short evening's contact with cultivated and thoughtful people. It argued much for her ancestry, for her own latent powers, that she responded with such bewildering readiness to the suggestions which rose like sparks of fire from that radiant hour.

She had been made to feel dimly, vaguely, but multitudinously, the fibres and reaches of another world—the world of art, and that indefinable thing which the books call culture; and finally, in that splendid young Quaker, she was brought to know a man who could be jocular without being coarse, and whose glance was as sincere as it was flattering and alluring.

She did not think of him as husband to Alice Heath, who seemed so much older in spirit as in body more like an elder sister than a bride elect, and his consideration of her was that of brother rather than the devotion of a lover. How far he stood removed from Ed Winchell and the young fellows of Sibley! "And yet I can understand him," she thought. "He ain't funny, like Mr. Congdon. He don't say queer things, and he don't make game of people. And he don't orate like Judge Crego. He isn't laughing at us now, the way the others are. I bet they're havin' a good time over our blunders."

She saw Marshall Haney in a new light also. For the first time he seemed like an old man, sitting there, supine, garrulous, in the midst of those self-contained people. "Gosh! how he did talk! He took too much wine, I reckon, but that didn't make all the difference." In truth, his imperiousness, his contempt, had been melted and charmed away by the genial smiles of his auditors. Even Mrs. Crego had listened with a show of interest. It was as if a lonely old man had at last found companionship.

What did all this mean? "Are they interested in him only because he's what they call a desperado? Did they ask us there to hear him tell stories of his wild life?" Questions of this kind also troubled her.

The moon slid behind the mountain range while still the girl sat with pale face and wide dark eyes thinking, thinking, the wings of her expanding soul fluttering with vague unrest. Only once in a lifetime can such an experience come to a human being. Her swift ride to Marshall Haney's side that summer night—now so far away—was momentous, but its import was simple compared with the experiences through which she had just passed.

She rose at last, chilled and stiffened, and went to her bed with a sense of foreboding rather than of new-found happiness.

Mart rose late next morning. "I had a bad night," he explained. "The mixed liquors I tuck got into me wound, I guess. It woke me twice, achin' and burnin'. You're lookin' tired yersilf, little girl. This high life seems to be wearin' on the both of us."

CHAPTER X

BEN FORDYCE CALLS ON HORSEBACK

Ben Fordyce and his affianced bride rode home talking of the Haneys. "Aren't they deliciously Western!" she said.

"Mrs. Haney certainly is a quaint little thing," he replied, quite soberly; "she's like a quail—so bright-eyed, and so still. I think her devotion to her old husband very beautiful. She's more like a daughter than a wife, don't you think so?"

"They're great fun if you don't feel sorry for him as I do," Alice thoughtfully responded. "They say he was magnificent as a gambler. He admitted to me to-night that he longed to go back to the camp, but that he had promised his wife and mother-in-law not to do so. I never ran a gambling-saloon, but I can imagine it would be exciting as a play all the time, can't you? Here, as he said to me, he can only sit in the sun like a lizard on a log. It must seem wonderful to her—having all this money and that big castle of a house. Don't you think so? Wasn't she reticent! She hardly uttered a word the whole evening. Some way I feel sorry for them both. They can't be happy. Don't you see that? It is plain she doesn't love him as a wife should, while he worships her. When she's away he is helpless. 'I'm no gairdner,' he said, pathetically; 'I was raised on the cobble-stones. I wouldn't know a growin' cabbage from a squash.' So you see he can't pass his time in gardening."

Ben's reply was a question. "I wonder if she would ride with us?"

"Perhaps we would do better not to follow up the acquaintance, Ben. It's all very interesting to meet them as we did to-night, but they are impossible socially—that you must admit. If there is any possibility of our settling down here I suppose we must be careful to do the right thing from the start."

Ben was a little irritated by this. "If I'm to settle here as a lawyer I can't draw social distinctions of that sort."

"Certainly not—as a lawyer. Of course, you ought to know Haney; but for me to ride or drive with Mrs. Haney is quite a different matter. However, I don't really care. She attracts me, and, so far as I know, is just a nice little uncultivated woman. We might call on her in the morning, and see if she can go with us. It will commit us; but really, Ben, I am not going to drag Eastern conventions into this fresh big country. I'm willing to risk the Haneys."

"I'm glad you take that view of it," said Ben.

Bertha was in the yard when they rode up to the gate next morning. Dressed in a white sweater and a short skirt, and holding biscuits for a handsome collie to snatch from her hand, she made a charming picture of young and vigorous life. Her slim body was as strong and supple as the dog's, and her face glowed like a child's. Haney, sitting on the porch, was watching her with a proud smile.

Alice glanced at her lover with admiration in her eyes. "What a glorious creature she really is!"

Seeing visitors at her gate, Bertha came down without confusion to say good-morning, and to ask them to dismount.

Ben, with doffed cap, replied by saying: "We've come to ask you to ride with us."

Bertha looked up at him composedly. "Haven't a saddle, and I don't know that any of our horses are broken. But come again to-morrow, and I'll have an outfit."

"There's no time like the present. Let me ride down to the barn and bring one up," volunteered Ben.

"Don't need to do that, I'll 'phone. I didn't really expect you," she explained. "Get off and come in a few minutes, and I'll see what I can hustle together for an outfit. I haven't rode a lick since I left Sibley."

Ben helped Alice to dismount, and Bertha led her to the house while he tethered the horses.

"What a superb place you have here!" exclaimed Alice. "It is one of the best in the city."

"We bought it for the porch," calmly replied the girl. "The Captain likes to sit where he can see the mountains. I'm not entirely done with the outfitting yet, but it beats a barn."

Haney rose as they drew near, and smilingly greeted his visitors. "I should be out gatherin' the peanuts and harvestin' the egg-plants, but the dinner last night, not mentionin' Congdon's pink liquor, kept me awake till two."

"Moral: Stick to Irish whiskey—or Scotch," laughed Ben.

"I will. These strange liquors are not for strong men like ourselves."

Ben took a seat at his invitation, while Bertha went in to 'phone for a horse and to "dig up" a riding-skirt. Alice was eager to see the interior of the house, but held her curiosity in check by walking about the beautiful garden, which ran to the very edge of a deep ravine. The trees hid the base of the mountain peaks, whose immitigable crags took on added majesty from the play of the delicate near-by branches against their distant rugged slopes.

"You have a magnificent outlook here, Captain Haney."

"'Tis so, and I try to be content with it; but it's hard for one who has roamed the air like a hawk all his life to be content with ridin' a wooden horse. I couldn't endure it if it weren't for me wife."

His big form rested in his chair with a ponderous inertness which was a telltale witness to his essential helplessness. His left hand still failed to participate in the movements of his right, and yet, as he showed, he could, by special effort of will, use it. "I'm gaining all the time— but slowly," he went on. "I want to make a trip back up to the mines, and I think I'll be able to do it soon." He put aside his own troubles. "And you, miss, I hope the climate is doing you good?"

"Oh, indeed, yes," she brightly responded. "I feel stronger every day."

Ben at the moment experienced a sharp pang of uneasiness and pain, for Alice was looking particularly worn and thin and yellow; and when Bertha returned, flushed with her haste, the contrast between them was quite as distressing as that between the withered, dying rose and the opening, fragrant bud. The young man's heart rose to his throat. "We have waited too long," he thought, and resolved to again urge upon her a new treatment which they had discussed.

"Come in and see the house," said Bertha, in brusque invitation. "It isn't ship-shape yet. I wanted to do it all myself, but I find it's a big proposition to go up against. It sure is. But I like it. I'd like nothing better than running a big hotel—not too big, but just big enough. I tell the Captain that when our mines 'pinch out' I'll go to Denver and start a hotel."

She was quite communicative, but not at ease as she led them from room to room. Her manner was rather that of one seeking to conceal trepidation, and her fluency seemed a little out of character.

In fact, she was trying to make the best possible impression on these people, whose sincere interest she felt; but with Ben's eyes fixed upon her so constantly, and a knowledge of Alice's delicate wit to trouble, she was more deeply embarrassed than ever before in her life. It was not her habit to blush or stammer, and she did not do so now, but she was carried out of her wonted reticence.

"As I say, we bought the place for the porch. I didn't realize what I was being let into—if I had I might have shied. We're practically lost in the place. Except when some of the people come down from camp, we're alone. My mother helps out some, but she's up at the ranch a good deal." She opened the library door, and led the way before an easel, on which stood a huge canvas. "Here's the picture Mr. Congdon is paintin' of the Captain. I wanted him taken with his hat on, but Mr. Congdon said no, and his word went. I don't know whether I like this or not. It's got me twisted."

Congdon had been after psychology rather than costume, that was evident at a glance, for the clothing counted for little in the portrait. Out of the shadow the face peered sadly, yet with a kind of ferocity, too—a look which made Alice Heath recoil from the man. In a certain way the artist had taken advantage of Mart's helplessness and loneliness. He had caught the sadness, sullenness, and remorselessness of his sitter rather than his gay, good-tempered smile. The face of this man was concerned with the past, not with the future; and yet on its surface it was a good likeness, as Ben said, and had both power and distinction. "I think it a cracker-jack piece of work," he ended.

Bertha replied: "I suppose it is, and yet I can't see it. I'd rather it looked the way the Captain used to when he came down to the Junction. I'm sorry to have his sickness painted in that way."

"That can't be helped. These artists are queer cattle; you can't drive 'em," Ben remarked.

Bertha smiled. "He wants to paint me now. 'Not on your life' says I. 'You'd be doing double stunts with my freckles, and I won't stand for it.'" She laughed. "No sir-ree, I don't let any artist tip my freckles edgewise just to see how flip he is at it. I like Mr. Congdon, but I don't trust him—he's too much of a joker."

Thereupon she led the way to the second floor, and showed them the furniture, which was mostly very costly and very bad, and at last said: "The third story is pretty empty yet. I don't know just what I'm going to do with it." She was looking at Alice. "I wish you'd come over and help me decide some day."

"What fun!" cried Alice, speaking on the impulse. "I'd like to very much."

"You see," Bertha went on, "my folks have always been purty poor, and I've lived in jay towns all my life; and when I came here I didn't know any more about life in a city than a duck does of mining. I had it all to learn, and they's a whole lot yet that I don't know." She smiled quaintly, then grew sober. "And what's worse, I haven't any one to tell me—except Mr. Congdon, and he's such a josher I don't trust him. He did give me a few points on the library, which ain't so bad, we think; but all the rest of it I had to dig out myself, and it's slow work. But I guess we better go down; my horse will be here in a few minutes." Then, with lowered voice, she added: "I can't stay out but a little while. The Captain dreads to have me leave him even to go down-town. I hadn't ought to go at all."

Ben began to perceive a real slavery in her life, and reassured her. "I'm glad you're coming. It will do you good, and it will be a pleasure to us too. We'll only be away an hour."

As they returned to the porch, Bertha put her hand on Haney's shoulder, in the manner of one man to another, saying: "I'm going for a little ride with these people, Captain, if you don't mind."

"Not a whiff," he answered. "I'll be here when you come back." Again a subtle cadence in his voice so belied his smile that Alice's heart responded to it.

Bertha's horse proved to be a spirited animal, but she mounted him with the ease and celerity of a boy—riding astride, in the mountain fashion. "I haven't a long skirt," she carelessly remarked to Alice. That was all the explanation she offered, and Ben thought he had never seen anything more alert, more graceful, than her slim figure poised alertly in the saddle, her face glowing, her hair blown across her face.

Alice, a timid rider, admired them both from her position, which was always behind, though they tried to accommodate their pace to hers. A pang of envy that was almost jealousy pierced her heart as she looked at them—so young, so vigorous, and so blithe.

"I should be sitting with Captain Haney on the porch," she thought, with bitterness. "I am out of place here."

The words which passed between Bertha and her cavalier meant little, but their glances meant much. It was, indeed, a fateful ride. The liking, the deep interest, born of their first meeting, swept irresistibly into admiration. Their faces turned towards each other, youth to youth, as naturally as flowers swing towards the light.

They fell into argument over saddles, over the difference between his manner of riding and her own. Her speech, so direct, so full of quaint slang, enchanted him, and Alice soon found herself the third party. And when they were for pushing into a gallop she acknowledged herself a clog. Concealing her disgust of herself under a bright smile, she called out: "Why don't you people gallop ahead, and let me jog along at my own gait?"

"Oh no," replied Ben, "we don't want to do that. Are you tired?" He became anxious at once.

"No, no! Please go! Mrs. Haney wants to race—I can see that; and I'd really like to see her ride—she sits her horse so beautifully."

"Very well," Ben acquiesced, "we'll take a run ahead, and come back to you."

Thereupon they set off, Bertha leading in a rushing gallop up a fine road which wound along a ravine, towards the top of a broad mesa. Alice, with slack rein in her small hand, rode slowly on in the vivid sunlight, a chill shadow rolling in upon her soul. As young as her lover in years, she nevertheless seemed at the moment twice his age. Everything interested him. Nothing interested her. He was never tired mentally or physically, and his smooth, unwrinkled face still reflected the morning sunlight of the world. "He is still the boy, while I am old and wrinkled and nerveless," she bitterly confessed.

When they returned to her at the top of the mesa, flushed and laughing, her pain had deepened into despair. Up to that moment she had checked disease with a belief that some day she was to recover her health, that some day her wrinkles would be smoothed out and her cheeks resume their youthful charm; but now she knew herself as she was—a broken thing.

The divine glow and grace of youth would never again come to her, while this vigorous and joyous girl would grow in womanly charm from month to month. "She is going to be very beautiful," she admitted; and even in the midst of her own discouragement she could not but admire Bertha's skill with the horse. She rode in the manner of a cowboy, holding her hands high and guiding her horse by pulling the reins across his neck. Ben was receiving lessons from her—absorbed and jocular.

At the top of the mesa they all halted to look away over the landscape—a gray-green, tumbled land, out of which fantastic red rocks rose, and over which, to the west, the snowy peaks loomed. Ben drew a deep breath of joy. It seemed that the world had never been so beautiful. "Isn't it magnificent!" he cried. "I like this country! Alice, let's make our home here."

She smiled a little constrainedly. "Just as you say, dear."

"Why shouldn't we, when the climate is doing you so much good?"

The horse that Bertha rode was prancing and foaming, eager for a renewal of the race, and Ben, seeing it, cried out: "Shall we go round by the hanging rock?"

"I'm willing!" answered Bertha, her eyes shining with excitement.

Alice shook her head. "I think I'll let you young things go your own gait, and I'll poke along back towards home."

Ben rode near her, searching her face anxiously. "You're not tired—are you, sweetness?"

"No, but I would be if I took that big circuit. But never mind me, I like to poke."

"Very well," he answered, quite relieved, "we'll meet you at the bridge." And off they dashed with furious clatter, leaving her to slowly retrace her lonely way, feeling very tired, very old, and very sad.

Bertha was perfectly, perilously happy. It was almost her first escape from the brooding care and weight of Haney's presence. She felt as she used to feel when speeding away on swift gallop to the ranch with some companion as care-free as herself. Since that fateful day when her mother fell ill and Marshall Haney asked her to marry him, she had not been permitted an hour's holiday. Even when absent from her husband her mind carried an inescapable picture of his loneliness and helplessness, and no complete relaxation had come with her temporary freedom. This day, this hour, she was suddenly free from care, from pain, from all uneasiness.

She considered this feeling due to the saddle and to the clear air of the morning. "I will ride every day," she declared to Ben, with shining face, as they drew their horses to a walk. "I don't know when I've enjoyed a ride so much. I can't see why I haven't been out before. I used to ride a good lot; lately I've dropped it."

"We'll call for you every morning," he replied. "As Alice gets stronger, we can go up into the cañons and take long rides."

"I'll tell you what we'll do," she said; "we'll let her ride in the cart with the Captain, and take our dinner, and we'll all go up the North Cañon some day, and eat picnic dinner there."

"Good idea," he said, accepting her disposition of Alice without even mental dissent. "That will be jolly fun."

They planned this and other excursions, with no sense of leaving any one behind or of cutting across conventional boundaries. Their native honesty and innocence of any ill intention prevented even a suspicion of danger, and by the time they joined Alice at the bridge they were on terms of intimacy and good-fellowship which seemed to rise from years of long acquaintance. Ben had promised to help her select a horse, and she had agreed to bring the Captain to call on Alice, who was staying with some friends not far away.

This change in Bertha's manner extended to Alice, who returned it in kind. The guilelessness which shone from the young wife's clear eyes was unmistakable. She was growing handsome, too. The flush of blood in her cheeks had submerged her freckles, and Alice began to realize how the poor child's devotion to Marshall Haney had reacted against her native good health. "She is but a child even now," she thought.

Haney was sitting on the porch where they had left him, the collie at his feet, but at sight of them returning he rose and hobbled slowly down the walk, his heart filled with tenderness and admiration for his wife. He had never ridden with her, but he had once seen her mounted, and one of his expressed wishes had been that he might be able to sit a saddle once more and ride by her side.

"Come in and stay to dinner!" he called, hospitably, and Bertha eagerly seconded the invitation.

But Alice replied: "I'm pretty tired; I think I'll go home. You can stay if you like, Ben."

Ben, smitten with sudden contrition, quickly said: "Oh no; I will go with you. I'm afraid you've ridden too far."

She protested against this, for Bertha's relief. "Not at all. It's a good tiredness. It's been great fun."

And with promises of another expedition of the same sort they rode away, while Bertha and Haney remained at the gate to examine the new horse.

As little Mrs. Haney re-entered the house with her husband the day seemed to lose its magical brightness, and to decline to a humdrum, shadowless flare. The house became cold and gloomy and the day empty. For the first time since its purchase she mentally asked herself: "What will I do now?" It was as if some ruling motive had suddenly been withdrawn from her life.

This empty, aching spot remained with her all through the day, even when she took Haney for his drive down-town, and only disappeared for a few moments as they met young Fordyce on the street. It troubled her as she returned to the house, and she was glad that Williams came in to take supper with them, for his talk of the mine diverted her and deeply interested her husband.

Williams eyed his boss critically. "You're gainin', Captain. You'll soon be able to make camp again."

"I hope so, but the doctor says my heart's affected and it wouldn't be safe for me to go any higher—for a while."

Williams smiled at Bertha. "Better send the missus, then. The men all have a great idea of her. They say she's a kind of mascot. McGonnigle asks me every time what she thinks of our new shaft. I've a kind of reverence for her judgment myself. They say women kind o' feel their way to a conclusion. Now, I'd like her to pass judgment on our work in *The Diamond Ace*."

"I'd like to go up," said Bertha. But, in truth, she was no longer thinking of the mine: she was considering how she might make her table look as pretty as Mrs. Congdon's. Her first dissatisfaction with her own way of life filled her mind. "I must have some of those candles," she said to herself, while the men were still intent upon the mine. Her first step towards social conformity was at this moment taken.

She felt herself akin to these people, and this assertion, subconscious and unuttered, brought something between Marshall Haney and herself. It was not merely that she was younger and clearer of record, but she was perfectly certain that with education she could hold her own with the Congdons or any one else. "If my father had lived, I wouldn't be the ignoramus I am to-day." But she had no plan for acquiring the knowledge she needed other than by reading books. She resolved to read every day, though each hour so spent must be taken from her husband, now piteously dependent upon her.

He managed his morning paper very well, but when she read aloud to him he almost always went to sleep.

CHAPTER XI

BEN BECOMES ADVISER TO MRS. HANEY

Bertha was astir early the next morning, and quite ready to join the Fordyces as soon as breakfast was over; but they did not come. She waited and watched the whole forenoon, and when at twelve o'clock they had neither called nor sent word, her day suddenly sank into nothingness, like a collapsed balloon, and she faced her tasks with a weakness of will not native to her.

Haney and Williams were both down street discussing some business matter with Crego, and this left her hours the more empty and unsatisfactory. As the dinner-hour drew near she drove to fetch her husband, hoping for a glimpse of the Fordyces on the way, but even this comfort was denied her, and she ached with dull pain which she could not analyze.

As Haney settled himself in the carriage, he said: "Well, little woman, did ye have a good ride?"

"I didn't go," she responded, with curt emphasis.

"Ye did not—Why not?"

"I had too much to do." This was a prevarication which she instantly repented. "Besides, they didn't turn up."

"I'm sorry. I was hoping you'd had a good try at the new horse. Ye must mount him for me to see this afternoon." Later he said: "I'm feeling better each day now; soon I'll be able to take that trip East. Do you get ready at your ease."

The thought of this trip, hitherto so wonderful in its possibilities, afforded her no pleasure; it scarcely interested her. And when another day went by with no further call or word from Ben Fordyce, she began to lose faith in her new-found friends and in herself.

"They had enough of me," she said, bitterly. "I'm not their style." And in this lay her first acknowledgment of money's inefficiency: it cannot buy the friends you really care for.

On the third day Fordyce called her up on the 'phone to say that Alice had been ill. "Our ride that day was a little too much for her," he explained, "but she will be all right again soon. I think we can go again to-morrow."

This explanation brought sunshine back into the Haney castle, and its mistress went about the halls singing softly. In the afternoon, as she and Mart were starting on their "constitutional" she proposed that they call to see how Alice was. This Haney was glad to do. "I liked the little woman," said he; "she's sharp as a tack. And, besides, she listened to me gabble," he added.

Miss Heath was stopping in the home of a friend—a rather handsome house, in the midst of thick shrubbery; and they found her wrapped in a blanket and sitting on the porch in a steamer-chair, with Ben reading to her. They were both instant and cordial in their demands that the Captain alight and come in, and Ben went down the walk to get him, while Alice, with envious, wistful eyes answered the glowing girl: "Oh no, I don't think the ride did me any harm. I have these little back-sets now and then. I'm glad you came."

"How thin her hands are," thought Bertha. And she saw, too, that the delicate face was wrinkled and withered.

Reading compassion in the girl's glance, Alice continued, brightly: "I'll be up to-morrow. I'm like a cork—nothing permanently depresses me. I'm suffering just now from an error of thought!"

Bertha only smiled, and the gleam of her teeth, white and even as rows of corn, produced in her face the effect of innocent humor like that of a child. Then she said: "I've bought a new horse."

"Have you, indeed?"

"Yes, and I've been expecting you to ride up to the line fence and call me out—I wanted to show him to you. He's a cracker-jack, all right."

"We'll come over in a day or two. I never stay *down* more than three days."

Haney, lumbering round the corner of the house, called out, mellowly: "Here you are! Now don't move a hair." He bent and offered a broad white hand. "How are ye the day?"

"Better, thank you. Ben, put a chair beside me; I want to talk to Captain Haney. He was interrupted the other night in the very middle of one of his best stories, and I'm going to insist on his finishing it."

Haney faced Bertha with a look of humorous amazement on his face. "Think o' that, now! She remembers one of my best."

"Indeed I do, Captain, and I can tell you just where you left off. You had just sighted the camp of the robbers."

Haney clicked with his tongue, as if listening to a child. "There now! I must have been taking more grape-juice than was good for me to start on that story, for it's all about meself and the great man I thought I was in those days."

"I love to hear about people who can ride a hundred miles in a night, and live on roots and berries, and capture men who bristle with revolvers. Please go on. Ben, you needn't listen if you don't want to. You can show Mrs. Haney the automobile or the garden."

Ben laughed. "I like to hear Captain Haney talk quite as well as anybody, but I'll be glad to show Mrs. Haney any of your neighbors' things she cares to see."

Alice turned to Bertha. "I suppose the Captain's tales are all old songs in your ears?"

"No, they're mostly all new to me. The Captain never tells stories to me."

Haney winked. "She knows me too well. She wouldn't believe them."

"Go on, please," said Alice. And so Haney took up the thread, though he protested. "'Tis a tale for candle-light," he explained.

Ben was studying Bertha with renewed admiration. "Where did she get that exquisite profile?" he thought.

The story was again interrupted by a group of callers, among them Mrs. Crego, and though Alice loyally stood by the Haneys and introduced them boldly, Mrs. Crego's cold nod and something that went out from the eyes of her companions made Bertha suffer, and she went away with a feeling of antagonism in her heart. Did these people consider her beneath their respect?

Haney remarked as they rode away: "If black eyes could freeze, sure we'd be shiverin' this minute. Did ye see Mrs. Crego pucker up when she sighted us?"

"I did, and it settled her for me," replied Bertha.

The intimacy thus established between the Haneys and the Congdon circle furnished the gossip of the "upper ten" with vital material for discussion. Mrs. Crego most decidedly disapproved of their calling, and advised Alice Heath against any further connection with the gambler's wife.

"What good can it possibly lead to? It's only curiosity on your part, and it isn't right to disturb the girl's ideals—if she has any."

To this Alice made no reply, but Ben stoutly defended the young wife. "She would have been as good as any of us with the same education. The poor little thing has had to work since her childhood, and that has cut off all training. As for Haney, he isn't a bad man. I suppose he argues that as some one must keep a gambling-house, it is best to have a good man do it."

The sense of being to a degree freed from the ordinary restraints of social life made Alice very tolerant. But, as it chanced, they did not go out the next day; indeed, it was several days before they again rode up to the Haney gate. They found Bertha dressed and ready for them as she had been each morning, and when she came out to them her heart was glowing and her face alight.

"We've come to see the new horse!" called Ben.

Haney was at the gate with a smile of satisfaction on his face when the horse was brought round. "There is a steed worth the riding!" he boasted. "I told Bertie to get the best. I would not have her riding a 'skate' like that one the other morning. She'll keep ye company this day."

Ben exclaimed, with admiration: "I see you know horse-kind, Captain!"

"I do," responded Haney. "And now be off, and remember you take dinner with us to-day."

As they moved away he took his customary seat on the porch to wait for their return—patient in outward seeming, but lonely and a little resentful within.

Bertha suggested a ride up the Bear Cañon, but Ben was quick to say: "That is too far, I fear, for Alice."

Bertha's glance at Alice revealed again, but in clearer lines, the sickness and weariness and the hopelessness of the elder woman's face, and Ben's consideration and watchful care of her took something out of the ride. The rapture, the careless gayety, of their first gallop was gone.

An impatience rose in the girl's soul. With the cruelty of youth she unconsciously accused the other, resenting the interference with her own plans and pleasures. She felt cheated because Ben permitted himself no racing, no circuits with her—and yet outwardly and in reality she was deeply sympathetic. She pitied while she accused and resented.

Their ride was short and unsatisfying. But as her guests remained for luncheon—Bertha was learning to call it that—the outing ended in a rare delight; for while "the two invalids" sat on the piazza, Bertha showed Ben her garden and stables, and the greenhouses she was building, and this hour was one of almost perfect peace.

Ben, once outside Alice's depressing presence, grew gay and single-minded in his enjoyment of his hostess and her surroundings.

"It must seem like Aladdin and his wonderful lamp to you," he said, as they stood watching the workmen putting in the glass to the greenhouses. "All you have to do is rub it, and miracles happen."

"That's just what it does," she answered, with gravity. "I give myself a knock in the head every time I write out a check, just to see if I am awake; but I can see I'll get used to it in time. That's the funny thing: a feller can get used to anything. The trouble with me is I don't know what to do nor how to do it. I ought to be learning things: I ought to go to school, but I can't. You see, I had to buckle down to work before I finished the high-school, and I don't know a thing except running a hotel. I wish you'd give me a few pointers."

"I'll do what I can, but I am afraid my advice wouldn't be very pertinent. What can I help you on?"

"Well, I don't know. Alice"—she spoke the word with a little hesitation—"said something to me the other day about charity, and all that. Well, now, I'm helping mother's church—a little—and I'm helping up at Sibley, but I don't know what else to do. I suppose I ought to do some good with the money that's rolling in on us. I've got my house pretty well stocked and fitted up, and I'm about stumped. I can't sit down, and just eat and sleep, ride and drive, can I?"

"There are women who do that and nothing else."

"Well, I can't. I've always had something to do. I like to play as well as the next one, but I don't believe I could spend my time here just sitting around."

"It's no small matter to run such a house as this."

"Well, there's something in that; but the point is, what's it all for? We're alone in it most of the time, and it don't seem right. Another thing, most of our old friends fight shy of us now. I invite 'em in, and they come, but they don't stay—they don't seem comfortable. They are all wall-eyed to see the place once, but they don't say 'hello' as they used to. And the people next door here—well, they don't neighbor at all. You and the Congdons are the only people, except a few of mother's church folks, who even call. Now, what's the matter?"

He was now quite as serious as she. "I suppose your own folks feel that your wealth is a barrier."

"Why should they? I treat 'em just the same as ever. I'm not the kind to go back on my friends because I'm Marshall Haney's wife. If I'd earned this money I might put on airs; but I haven't—I've just married into it."

"How did you come to do it?" he asked, quickly—almost accusingly.

Her tone again faltered, and her eyes fell. "Well, it was like this: Mother was sick and getting old, and I was kind o' tired and discouraged, and the Captain was mighty nice and kind to us;

and then I—And so when the word came that he was hurt—and wanted me—I went." Here she looked up at him. "And I did right, don't you think so?"

He was twisting a twig in his fingers. "Oh yes, certainly. You've been a great comfort to him. You saved his life probably, and he really is a fine man in spite of—" He broke off.

She took up his phrase. "In spite of his business. I know, that was mother's main objection to him. But, you see, he cleaned all out of that before I married him. He hasn't touched a card since."

He was almost apologetic. "I've been brought up to despise gamblers—I'm a Quaker, you know, by family. But I like Captain Haney, and I can see that from his point of view a 'straight game,' as he calls it, is not a crime."

"Yes, that's one good thing in his favor—he never let a crooked deal pass in his place. But, after all, I can't forget that he was a gambler, and other people can't, and his record is dead against us here." Her face was dark as she resumed. "I'm a gambler's wife. Ain't that so? Didn't you hear of me in that way? Weren't you warned against us?"

His honest eyes quailed a little. "It is true your husband is called a gambler rather than a miner."

"Well, he was. That's right, but he isn't now. I'm not complaining about the part that can't be helped, but I want to do something to show we are in line to-day, and so does the Captain. We want to make our money count, and if you can tell us what to do we'll be mightily obliged."

The young Quaker was more profoundly enthralled by this unexpected confession of the girl than by any other word she could have uttered. His own knowledge of life was neither wide nor deep, and his sense of responsibility not especially keen; and yet he experienced a thrill of pleasure and a certain lift of spirit as he stood looking down at her—the attitude of confidential spiritual adviser began at the moment to yield a sweet satisfaction as well as an agreeable realization of power. How much Haney's mines were pouring forth he did not know, but their wealth was said to be enormous. Every day added to the potentiality of this gray-eyed girl who stood so trustfully, so like a pupil, before him.

He spoke with emotion. "I'll do what I can to advise you and help you, and so will Alice. Allen Crego is a good man—he has your legal business, I believe?"

"Yes, I think he's square, and I like him. But I can't go to Mrs. Crego; she despises us—that's one good reason." She smiled faintly. "But it ain't legal advice I want—it's something else. I don't know what it is. Our minister isn't the man, either. I guess I want somebody that knows life, and that ain't either a lawyer or a minister. I want some one to take our affairs in hand. I need all kinds of advice. Won't you give it to me?"

He smiled. "I'd like to help, but I am only a lawyer—and a very young one at that."

"I don't think of you as a lawyer; you're more than that to us."

"What am I, then?"

The color danced along her cheek as she uttered a phrase so current in the West that it has a certain humorous sound: "You're a gentleman and a scholar."

"Thank you. But I fear you mean by that that I take life very easily."

She grew serious again. "No, I don't. Anybody can see you're honest. I trust you more than I do Judge Crego, and so does the Captain. You can tell us things we want to know. We both know a little about business, but we don't know much about other things. That's where we both fall down."

This frank expression of regard brought about a moment of emotional tension, and Ben hesitated before replying. At last he said: "I hope I shall always deserve your confidence. I wish I had the wisdom you credit me with. I wonder what I can tell you?"

"Tell me what you would do if you were in my place."

Quick as a sunbeam his smile flashed out. "Be your own good, joyous self. Whatever you do, don't lose what you are now—the quality which attracted Alice and me to you. Don't try to be like other rich people."

The sight of the Captain and Alice walking slowly towards them cut short the further admission of his own careless inexperience, and they all took seats beneath a big pear-tree which shaded a semicircular wire settee.

Haney had been confessing a little of his loneliness. "I will not believe that me work in the world is done. 'Tis true, I took very little care of me good days; but I was happy in me business, such as it was. Me little wife there saves me from the blue divils when she's about, but when I'm alone, sure it's deep in the dumps I go. Sometimes me mind misgives me, to think of her tied to an old stump of a tree like me! But maybe she's right—maybe I'm to recover me powers and be of use."

To this Alice could only reply, as comfortingly as she could: "You've given her a good deal, Captain."

"So I have, but I mean to give more. As soon as I'm able to travel we're going down the hill to see the world. Sometimes when we sit on our porch and talk of it, it seems as if I could see the whole of the States spread out before us—Chicago, Washington, New York, and all to choose from. I can't get over the surprise of having the stream of money keep comin'. I used to work hard—you may not believe that, but 'twas so. I used to have long days and nights of watching. 'Twas work of a kind, though you may not admire the kind. And now I have nothing to do but sit and twist me two thumbs—and one of them bog-spavined, at that."

To this Alice had made no reply, for they were within earshot of Ben and Bertha. Haney called out: "Sure, it must be near dinner-time, Bertie!—I mean luncheon, ma'am—I'm lately instructed."

They all laughed in tune to his humor, and Bertha replied: "No more twelve-o'clock dinners for us, Captain."

Haney groaned. "This fashionable life will be the death of me. Sure, I eat and talk by rule a'ready. Where it will end I dunno."

Happily the bell soon relieved the strain, but the talk at the table continued to be very personal—it could not be prevented, for each of these four people was at a turning-point in his or her life. Haney, feeling the slow tide of returning vigor in his limbs, was in trouble thinking of what he was to do. Bertha, just beginning to tremble beneath the mysterious stir of an all-demanding love, was uneasy, feverish, and self-conscious. Alice, sensing the approach of weakness and decay, yet struggling against it, was inwardly in despair. While Ben, hitherto careless, facing life with unwrinkled brow, was appreciating, for the first time, the positive responsibilities of manhood. Bertha's expressed wish to employ his best judgment exalted him while it troubled him.

For a time the burden of the conversation was his. Haney was in a reflective mood, and Bertha busied with the table service, which she was trying to raise to the level of her honored guests, was distracted. Alice, tired and a little dispirited, added nothing to the youthful spirit of the meal.

At last, just when the conversation seemed about to flag out, Haney, lifting his head, began in a new tone: "Mr. Fordyce, my little girl and I have decided we want you to take Crego's place as our lawyer. I hope you'll be able to do it."

Alice looked up in surprise. "But you don't mean to take it from Mr. Crego?"

Haney's face grew hard. "I am under no obligation to Crego, and I prefer to have as me lawyer a man who can neighbor with me, and whose wife is not above nodding when me own wife passes by."

Alice hastened to defend the Cregos. "You mustn't be unjust to Mrs. Crego."

"I'm not," said Haney, "nor to Crego either. I've paid for his time, and paid well—as I'm willing to pay for yours." He turned to Ben. "I need advice, and I want to feel free to go for it."

Ben replied: "I'd like to accept your business, Captain, but you see it would not be professional for me to profit at the expense of my friend, and, besides, I haven't really settled here yet."

Haney looked disappointed. "I thought ye had. Well, I am going to cut loose from Crego anyhow, and I shall tell him why."

Bertha cried out: "No, don't do that."

He acquiesced. "Very well, then I won't tell him why; but I'm going to quit him! So if you don't care to take on me business, I'll give it to Jim Beringer. It pays a good bit of money, and will pay more. I'll make it profitable to ye."

Alice looked at Ben. "Of course, if he is going to leave Mr. Crego anyway—"

"But that would mean making our permanent home here, and setting up an office."

"Well, why not? I can't live in the East any more; that we have tested. I am willing to decide now. It would give you a start here, and, besides, I think you can be of use to the Captain."

Ben still hesitated. "It seems rather treacherous to Crego some way. But if you have definitely decided against him—"

"We have," said Bertha. "We talked it all over yesterday. We want you."

Haney's face was very grave now. "There is one thing more, Mr. Fordyce. Mart Haney's reputation must be taken into account. It won't do you anny good to be associated with him. I don't know that it will do you anny harm, but I'm dom sure it will do you no good to be associated with me."

Alice interposed, quickly. "A lawyer can't choose his clients—at least, a *young* lawyer can't."

Haney ignored the implications of her speech. "I'm not tryin' to cover up me tracks," said he. "I was a gambler for thirty years. Me whole life has been a game of chance. There are many who think gambling one of the high crimes an' misdemeanors, but I think a square game between men is defensible. I am a gambler by nature. Why shouldn't I be? I grew up a fat squab of a boy rollin' about on the pavin'-stones of Troy. 'Twas all luck, bedad, whether I lived or died. I lived, it fell out, and when I had learned to read I read wild-West stories. Of course, that led me to go West and jine the Indians, and by stealin' rides and beggin' me bread I reached Dodge City. 'Twas all chance that I didn't die on the way. Me mother, poor soul, was worried and I knew it, and finally I put me fist to it and wrote her a letter to say I was all right. She wrote beggin' me to return, which I did a couple of years later; but Troy was too slow for me then, and again I pulled out. I was always takin' risks. Danger was me delight. I had no trade, but I had faith in me luck. I won—I almost always won. And so I came to be a gambler along with bein' sheriff and city marshal, and the like o' that, in one mountain town or another, but I always played fair. A man who plays a square game is a gambler. The man who deals underhand is a crook. I'm no crook. I love the game. To know that the cards are stacked against the other player takes all the fun out of the deck for me. I want the other felly to have an equal chance with me—else 'tis no game, but a hold-up. No man ever rightfully accused me of dealing against him. Yes, 'tis true, me world is a world of risk." He looked at Alice. "Sure, the Look-Out up above—if there is such—is there to see that we all have a show for our ace. If anything interferes with that the game is a crooked one."

Alice began to perceive something big and admirable in this man's spirit. She was not of his faith—quite the contrary. She was a fatalist. Nothing happened in her world. But she was imaginative enough to understand his point of view.

Haney went on. "I know all the tricks. I lairned them, not to use in the game, but to keep them *out* of the game. I had too much faith in me luck to ever weaken."

"Did you never lose?" asked Ben.

"Many the time, indeed, but only for a short streak. Take this mine, for instance. A man comes into me house full of confidence in himself, plays, and goes broke. The fury of the game bein' in him, he says: 'I'll put me prospect hole against five hundred dollars.' 'Roll the wheel,' says I, and I won his hole in the ground. 'Twas me luck. That prospect turned out a mine. 'Twas his luck to lose. He was a full-grown man; he knew the game and went into it with his eyes open. Truth was, he considered the mine a 'dead horse,' and was hopin' to take a fall out o' me. Me little girl here is disturbed about the way the mine came to us, but she needn't be. 'Twas all in the game. I'm sayin' 'twas in the game that another crazy fool should blow me to pieces—I don't complain. I take me chances. Now"—here he faced Ben, and his grave tone lightened—"as I understand it, you're not a rich man?"

Ben flushed a little. "No, I haven't earned much so far; but it's up to me to get busy."

"And ye expect to marry soon?"

This question sent a thrill to the heart of each of the three young people listening—a thrill of fear, of doubt. And Ben said, slowly, perceiving Haney's fatherly good-will: "Yes, we expect to set up housekeeping, as the old-fashioned people say, as soon as Alice is a little stronger."

"Very well, then," Haney went on like one who has made his point, "here's *your* chance. Your fee with me will pay your coal bills anyway. We're likely to take a good dale of your time, but you'll lose nothing by that."

Bertha, with big yearning eyes fixed upon Ben's face, waited in a quiver of hope as he replied: "Of course, Captain Haney, I can't subscribe to your defense of gambling, and if you were still a gambler, in the strict sense of the word, I couldn't accept this position, for it is something more than legal. But as you have given up all connection with cards and liquor selling, I see no reason why I should not accept your offer—provided I can be of service in the manner you expect." He looked across the table at Bertha, and reading there the same entreaty which she had expressed in the garden, he added, firmly and definitely: "Yes, I will accept, and be very much obliged to you."

Haney extended his hand, and they silently clasped palms in the compact.

They parted in a glow of mutual confidence and liking, and Alice's voice quivered as she thanked their host. "I think it very fine of you, Captain Haney. This may be the means of establishing Mr. Fordyce in business here."

His eyes twinkled in reply. "I will do all I can to help him, for he takes me eye."

Ben's last glance and the pressure of his hand left in Bertha's brain a glow which remained with her all the rest of the day, and she carolled like a robin as she trod her swift way about the house.

The next morning, as they sat at breakfast, Mart briskly said: "Well, little woman, I've decided, now that I have a man I can trust with me business, to make the trip East. As soon as he has the mines in hand we'll start. Can you be ready to go Monday week?"

"Sure thing," she answered, quickly. But even as she spoke a nameless pang that was neither joy nor exultation shot through her heart. For the first time she realized that she had lost her keen desire to explore the glittering plain which lay below her feet. A fairer world, a perfectly satisfying world, was opening before her in the high country which was her home.

CHAPTER XII

ALICE HEATH HAS A VISION

This change of legal adviser, while very important to Ben Fordyce and the Haneys, did not seem to trouble Allen Crego very much. As a matter of fact, he was about to run for Congress, and had all the business he could attend to anyway. He liked the young Quaker, and responded "All right" in the frank Western fashion, sending the Haneys away quite as solidly friendly as before. To Ben he was most cordial. "I'm glad you're going to settle here, and I'm specially glad you've got a retainer; for the field is overcrowded, and it may take a long time for you to get a place. We old fellows who came down along with the pioneers have an immense advantage. I wish you every success." And he meant it.

Only when he got home to Mrs. Crego did he come to realize what a horrible injury he had permitted "a young and inexperienced Eastern boy" to do himself. "This connection will ostracize them both," his wife said.

He answered a little wearily. "Oh, now, my dear, I think you take your social Medes and Persians too seriously. We lawyers can't afford to inquire into the private affairs of our clients too closely—especially if they are derived from the pioneer West. Ben Fordyce doesn't become responsible for Haney's past; it is a business and not a social arrangement."

"That's like a man," she responded; "they never see anything till it bumps their noses. They've both called on the Haneys and gone riding with them—or with the girl. They've even eaten luncheon there!"

"How dreadful! Mrs. Crego, you shock me!"

"If any evil comes of this—and there will be sorrow in it—you'll be morally responsible. In the old days it didn't matter, but now nobody who is anybody in this town can associate with people like the Haneys and not be hurt by it."

The judge ceased to smile. "Now, let this end the discussion. Fordyce has sense enough to take care of himself. He's just the man for Haney—he has time, good nature, and splendid connections. I am glad to be rid of the business, and I am delighted to think this young fellow has pleased Haney—"

"It isn't Haney. Don't you see? It's that girl. She has urged it—I'm perfectly sure."

"Stop right there!" he commanded, sharply. "I don't want to hear a word of your insinuations. I'm tired of them. I'm ashamed of you." And he took up his paper and walked away from her.

She was defeated at the moment, but hurried to the Congdons with her news. Lee looked quite serious enough. "I don't believe I like that either. What do you think, Frank?"

"All depends on Ben. If he makes it a business deal and keeps it so all right; if he don't, it may go against him in the town, as Helen says."

"Don't you think you'd better go see him and have a talk?"

"Nixie!" he answered, in swift negation. "Little Willie don't want to tackle that delicate job. I'm subtle, but not so subtle as that. Alice Heath knows all we know and more, and you can bet they've talked the whole thing over."

"But they may not realize the position of the Haneys."

"They may not; but I suspect they think they can carry any connection they choose to make, and I mostly think they can—ten generations of Quaker ancestry—"

"But the people there don't know their ancestry."

"Well, go talk to them. I abdicate. Besides, I like the Haneys."

Mrs. Crego now laid her joker on the table. "Here's the point. That girl is *taken* with Ben—it's all her plan."

Congdon started. "Sh! Don't say that out loud, Nell. That little wife is true as steel."

"I don't care. My prophetic soul—"

Lee put in. "Prophetic pollywogs! Why, Helen, the girl is as simple and straightforward as a boy of twelve."

"She seems that way, but I could see she was wonderfully attracted by Ben and his singing that night here."

"That may be; so was I. Anyhow, I agree with Frank: it would be cruel to say such a thing—even if it were so, which I don't for an instant believe. At the same time, I admit the connection will make talk and may create a prejudice. Maybe we'd better see Ben." She looked at her husband.

He waved a protesting finger before his face. "Not on your life! Ben and I are friends. I like him immensely—too much to think of running such a frightful risk of offending him. If you interfere you do so at your own peril."

Lee finally acquiesced in his judgment, and Mrs. Crego went home more deeply troubled than her acquaintance with Alice Heath would seem to warrant. "Helen's an estimable person," said Frank Congdon, "and on the whole I like her; but I wish she didn't take quite so much evil for granted."

So as no one warned Ben Fordyce, he went gayly forward and hired a couple of nice rooms in a sightly block, and hung out a gilded sign. "I am a citizen of Colorado now," he said to the Captain and Bertha the first time they called at his office.

Alice was there, and they were deep in discussion of the merits of a pile of new rugs which were to match the wall-paper. Ben stoutly stood for the "ox-blood" and she for the "old gold." Ben explained. "The entire extravagance of this office is due to her." He pointed an accusing finger at Alice, who nodded shamelessly. "I was all for second-hand stuff, both for economy's sake and to show I'd been in practice a long time."

"You'd need a battered second-hand set of whiskers to match," she replied, and they all laughed at the notion. "No, Captain, being sure Ben couldn't deceive anybody as to his age and experience, I argued for signs of prosperity. New-born success has its weight, you know."

"Sure it has."

"People like silken rugs and mahogany furniture, even in the West."

"They do," Haney agreed.

Bertha, standing silently by, was vaguely resenting Alice's presence. This feeling was not defined, but it was strong enough to darken her face and take the sparkle out of her eyes. She would have liked to do this work of fitting up his rooms; and he, on his part, saw that she was in sombre mood, and sought opportunity to come to where she stood. "I'm being congratulated on all sides for becoming a citizen of Colorado. It's quite like being initiated into some new club. In an Eastern town they'd let me jolly well alone. I'm going to like it immensely, I know, and it's really due to you."

She found words difficult at the moment. His face and voice dazzled her like an open door towards sunshine, and after a moment's pause she looked round the room, saying: "It's going to be fine."

"I want it comfy, so that you and the Captain will feel like coming down often. We have a great deal to talk over before I shall really have a full understanding of your affairs. I'm going to bone into my books hard," he added, boyishly. "To tell the truth, I've taken life pretty easy. You see, my father left me a regular income, big enough to support me while I was studying law, but not enough to marry on." She couldn't have told why, but this subject troubled her and confused her. She turned away again as he continued: "Alice has a little, not much, in her own right, and so it is really up to me to settle down and get to work. Please don't think you are taking the time of a rich and busy man like Crego. I am very grateful to you. It will enable us to plan a home here in the West."

Again that keen pang went through her heart, and he, looking towards Alice, so worn and drooping, was touched with dismay, almost fear.

She was talking to the Captain, but was furtively watching Bertie and Ben. "How erect and radiant and happy they are," she thought, and a doubt of the girl came into her mind. "She is so untrained and so young!" And in this mental exclamation she put her first fear that Ben might find his position as legal adviser complicated by the admiration of the Captain's wife.

Something weirdly intuitive had come to Alice Heath in these later years. As her health declined and her flesh purified, she had come to possess uncanny powers of vision, and at times seemed to read the very innermost thoughts of those about her. The loss of her beauty, which had been exquisite as that of a rose, had made her morbid—which she knew and struggled against. She forecast the future, and this is disquieting to any one. "Here at this moment," she often said to herself, "my world is flooded with sunshine—a static world in appearance. But how will it be ten years from now? The clock ticks, the sun passes, the universal sway of death extends." With the same acuteness with which she read other minds she read her own; but knowing that such imaginings were unnatural and distressing, she fought against them; yet they came in spite of herself. And the picture of Bertha standing there beside Ben filled her with a prophetic vision of what the girl-wife was to become: "She will grow in grace and in dignity, in understanding. She's of good stock. She's like a man in her power to raise herself above lowly conditions. Why are there not female Lincolns? There are, and she is one of them. Nearly all our great men were born and reared under conditions ruder than those which surrounded this girl. Why can't she rise? She will rise—and then—"

She did not pursue the clew further, for the Captain was speaking. "And you, miss, can be of just as great service to me wife. She's alone with me here in this town, and I'm a heavy load for her to carry. I am so. Now that her house is in order the days are long. The people she'd like to know don't drop in, and I suspect it's because she's Mart Haney's wife."

She resumed her sprightly manner. "Oh no; I'm afraid if she were a poor girl she'd find these same people still more indifferent."

"True, miss. But would they act the same if she were Mart Haney's widow?"

She flashed a deep-piercing, wondering glance at him. "Ah, that would be different. And yet," she hastened to say, "that would not make her acceptable to the really best people."

"What would, miss?" he asked, simply. "I'm a rough man, and I've led a rough life. I begin to see things now that I never saw before. What would give Bertha standing among the people you speak of?"

"Education, character. By character I mean she must be a personality."

"That she is!" He was emphatic in this.

"She certainly is a fascinating girl, and she promises to be a still more interesting woman."

"I'm not a wooden-head, miss. As a gambler, it was me business to read men's faces. I see more than my little girl gives me credit for. I think I know why Mrs. Crego can't see us as we pass by, and I was wise to them friends of yours the other day when they curled their tails and showed their teeth at sight of us. It's because Bertie is the wife of a gambler. Isn't that so, now?"

She rose with a start, for Bertha was coming towards them. "Hush! don't talk about it any more—at present." And at this moment there passed before her eyes a vision of this big man, crushed and writhing on a mountain-side, among deep green ferns. It lasted but an instant, like the memory of an event in childhood; a spot transient as a shadow—disconnected, without precursor or sequence; like a cloud over the wheat it gloomed a moment and was gone, and she gave herself up to the influence of the sunny room and Ben's joyous plans.

This vision came back to her when she was alone in her own room an hour later, and stayed with her persistently. What did it mean? Did it presage an accident to him, or had it arisen from a vague knowledge of the cause of his wounding?

This singular and distressing rule governed her dreams of the future. They were all of sorrow, death, physical calamities; never, or very rarely, of health and happiness; therefore, she seldom spoke of them. "Sufficient unto the day is the evil thereof," her father was wont to say, and she had come to the same conclusion. Besides her faith in her predictive dreams was by no means fixed. She had reached but one comforting conclusion, and that was negative. If no vision came to reveal the future of any friend, she rested secure in the belief that he or she at least was to be free of disaster. It was a sweet and comforting fact to remember that no vision of Ben's future had ever entered her consciousness. She did not even dream of him. And this was still more wonderful, for she had always understood that those we love are ever in our thoughts in slumber.

For some reason the day had been most wearing, and to dress for dinner was an effort. But she made herself as lovely as she could for Ben's sake—and for the sake of the Congdons with whom they were to dine. "We are to be alone," Lee had 'phoned, "for I want to talk with you like a Dutch aunt."

Alice knew as well as if Lee had spoken it what was coming. They were going to protest against Ben's intimacy with the Haneys. And as soon as they were in their carriage she warned Ben. "You want to be on your guard to-night. The Congdons are going to advise you against accepting this retainer from Captain Haney."

He was too happy to do more than jokingly reply: "Too late! Bribe is in hand, and money mostly spent. What I want to ask you is more important. When are we to start our 'love in a cottage' idyl? It really looks possible now. Isn't it beautiful to think we can really keep house out here and pay our way?"

"Oh, Ben!"—there was a wail in her voice—"I don't seem to gain as I should! I'm completely tired out to-night."

He was all concern instantly, and putting his arm about her, tenderly exclaimed: "Dear heart, it was my fault. You shouldn't have gone down at all."

"But don't you see how revealing it is? If I can't go down to your office to superintend the arrangement of a few rugs and chairs, how can I keep a house—your house—in order? No, dear boy, we mustn't think of it—not now; perhaps by spring, but certainly not now."

He was both saddened and perplexed, and yet his disappointment was not so keen as it had been when she had put off their wedding-day the first time, and when she turned a white, despairing face up to him, saying wildly: "Oh, Benny, why don't you give me up and marry some nice young girl?" He only took her in his arms and shut her lips with a kiss.

"No more such talk," he said; "you're tired and a little morbid. Lee's lecture will do you good. I hope she gets after you for letting yourself down into these detestable moods."

Signs of their troubled ride were on their faces as they entered the Congdon sitting-room which also served as hall, and Lee put her arm about her guest with compassion uppermost in her heart. "You don't look a bit well to-night. What have you been doing?"

"Nothing. That's the worst of it. If I'd been scrubbing floors or cleaning silver I'd feel that I had a right to be tired, but I've only been down to Ben's new office overseeing the laying of three rugs. I didn't lift a hand, and now look at me!"

When they were in the privacy of Lee's dressing-room the hostess studied her guest critically. "You've something on your mind," she announced.

"I always have something on my mind."

"I know you do, and if you're ever going to get well you must get it off your mind. Do I know what it is?"

"If you don't, you ought to. Since this retainer from Captain Haney, Ben is urging an immediate marriage."

Lee Congdon was an unconquerable realist and truth-teller, and she could not at the moment utter any other than a divergent word. "We got you here to-night to talk over that Haney business. We don't entirely like it; at least, I don't. Frank has no responsibility, never had. Haney is not a bad man, and she isn't a bit low or common; but folks think she is. And it's going to hurt you both, I'm afraid, to have anything to do socially with them."

"Oh, socially!" Alice cried, in disgust. "I thought we were coming to the big and boundless West, where such things don't count."

"You have, and you haven't. The Springs is a little of the West, a little of England, and a good deal of the East. It's a foolish town in some ways, and I warn you lots of nice people will find it inconvenient to call on you for fear of meeting Mrs. Haney."

"Oh, rats!"

"Absurd, isn't it? I'm glad you put on that dress. You don't look tired now; your cheeks are blazing."

"With wrath—not health."

"At me?"

"Oh no. At these people who assume to dictate whom we shall know."

"They don't do that, dear; they only think you're paying too much for Ben's new office. But come down to dinner; we'll fight this out later."

Congdon was outspoken in his admiration. "By the Lord, the climate is getting in its work! Why, Alice, you're radiant. You're ten years younger to-night!"

"That's because I'm angry."

"What about?"

"Your townspeople. Lee has made me feel as if I were the club-bar topic to-night."

Congdon became solemn—grim as a brazen image. "Mrs. Congdon, you've been making some of your tactful remarks."

"I have not. I've been talking straight from the shoulder, as I advise you to do."

He capitulated. "After the turkey. Come on, Ben, we're in for a lecture by the Professor-Doctor Lee Congdon."

Under the influence of his humor they took seats about the pretty, candle-lit table as gay a group as the city held—apparently; for Alice was of that temperament which responds quickly and buoyantly to humor, and Frank Congdon never took anything quite seriously—except his portrait-painting. He could do a cake-walk with any one, but he would not discuss art with the unsympathetic. He always had a new story to tell of his amazing experience. Something was always happening to him. Other men come and go up and down the whole earth without an adventure, but no sooner does Frank Congdon slip out of the door than the fates—generally the humorous ones—pounce upon him. Drunken women claim him for a son. Sheriffs arrest him in the mountains and transport him long distances, only to find him the wrong man. Confused Swedish mothers give him babies to hold in the cars, and rush out just in time to get left. And these tales lose nothing in his recount of them.

In the present instance he took up half the dinner-hour with a description of his latest mishap. A neighbor's cook had suddenly gone mad, and had charged him with putting a spell over her. "Somebody calls me up on the 'phone this morning: 'Is this Frank Congdon?'... 'Yes.' ... 'Hello, Frank, this is Henry. What you been doing to my cook?' ... 'What does she say I have?' ... 'Says you've hypnotized her—put a spell over her.' ... 'I pass.' ... 'Fact; she's crazy as a bed-bug, and we can't do a thing with her—and she was *such* a good girl. How could you, Frank?' ... 'I never saw the creature in my life.' ... 'Well, you'll see her now. You're to come right over and remove this spell, or we won't have any breakfast.'" Here Congdon looked solemnly round at his guests. "Now wouldn't that convulse a body? I didn't know her name; on my word, I couldn't remember how she looked. But my curiosity was roused, and over I toddled. It was all true. Karen was in the kitchen, armed with the jig-saw bread-knife and calling for me. Henry was all for my appearing suddenly at the door à la Svengali, and with a majestic wave of the hand lift the cloud from her brain. 'Not on your tintype,' says I; 'I guess this is a case for the police. If I put this spell on that hell-cat it must have been by "absent treatment" during sleep, and it's me to my studio again.' ... 'No you don't,' said Henry. 'You stay till this incubus is cleared away. It ain't reasonable to suppose that an ignorant maid like this is going to charge a complete stranger with a crime of this kind unless—'

"'That's what I say. It isn't reasonable, I refuse to believe it.' Just then something seemed to break loose in the back part of the house. Wash-boilers seemed to be falling on the kitchen range, and wild yells made Mrs. Henry turn pale.

"'That's your work, monster!' shrieked Henry.

"'Is it?' I said. 'My opinion is she's broke into your wine-cellar. It's you to the police.'

"'Go calm her. Come, it's a fine chance to experiment.'

"'So it is—with a cannon. Do you mean to tell me seriously that she thinks I've hypnotized her?'

"Then he got down to business, and assured me that he was telling the truth. This interested me, and I thought I'd chance opening the door—particularly as everything was quiet inside."

His company was very tense now, so vividly had he set the whole scene before them. "I opened the door, and found her standing at the far side of the room, her hair in ropes and her eyes wild. She was 'bug-house' all right. 'Karen,' I said, in my most hypnotic voice, 'I lift the spell. You are free. Go back to work.'"

"What happened?" asked Alice, breathless with excitement.

His face was grave and his voice sad. "Not a thing! My Svengali pass didn't work. I was as the idle wind to her. Therefore, I withdrew and 'phoned the police."

"What an extraordinary thing," said Ben.

Mrs. Congdon brightly answered: "It would be for any one else, but I'm so used to that now I don't mind. Whenever the telephone bell rings I expect to hear that Frank is sued for breach of promise, or arrested for burglary, or some little thing like that. If he were only a novelist he'd make our everlasting fortune. But I know why he started this story—he wants to head off my talk with you about the Haneys, and I don't intend to let him do it. Have you taken on Haney's legal business?"

"Yes."

"For good and all?"

"Yes. He's advanced me part of my fee, and I've spent it for desks, rugs, and office rent. I think I may say the offer is accepted."

"I'm sorry," she said, simply.

Her husband objected. "I don't see why. Haney is a man of large means, his mines are paying hugely, and he needs some one to look after the investment side of his income, and to keep tab on the output of the mines, and to be ready to settle any legal points that may come up. Ben's just the boy to do this."

Lee was firm. "That's one side of it. But these young people should not start in wrong. Haney's past is said to be criminal, and Mrs. Haney is called low—"

Congdon hotly interrupted. "Who says so? It's a lie!"

"That's the talk over town. It was all right for Crego to transact their business, for he is an old and well-known lawyer here; but it's different with Ben, who is just starting."

Ben laughed. "Yes, it is different. Crego didn't need the job, and I do."

"How bad do you need it?" she asked.

"Well, it makes it possible for us to marry at once and settle here." He looked at Alice with a renewal of the admiration he had felt for her in the days of their dancing feet. She shrank from his gaze, and Mrs. Congdon perceived it.

"You're not so poor as all that," she stated rather than asked.

"I don't suppose we're likely to need bread of a sort, but I don't feel able to buy or rent and keep house—or I didn't till Haney made this offer."

"How did he come to make it?"

His fair skin flushed at her question, for he couldn't quite bring himself to tell the whole truth. He knew the decision came from Bertha, and at the moment, and for the first time, he saw how it might be misconstrued. He evaded her. "Modesty forbids, but I suppose it must come out. It is all due to my open-faced Waterbury countenance. He thinks I am at once able and honest."

"There you have it, Lee. Haney knows a good thing when he sees it."

Mrs. Congdon, putting the rest of her lecture aside for future use, said: "Well, if it's all settled, then I've no more to say. Probably I'm too fussy about what the town thinks, anyway."

"Precisely my contention, Mrs. Congdon," replied her husband.

She was audaciously frank and truth-seeking, but she could not say to any one but her husband that Little Mrs. Haney, expanding into a dangerously attractive woman, was already in love with Ben Fordyce. "There are limits to advice, after all," she said to Frank, when they were alone.

"I'm glad you recognize the limit in this case," he replied, "but I don't intend to worry. Ben is all right, and the girl has got to have her tragedy sooner or later. If it isn't Ben, it will be somebody else. A wonder it wasn't with me."

"Oh, I don't know." She laughed. "I feel very secure about you."

"Am I such a bad shape?" he asked, with comical inflection.

CHAPTER XIII

BERTHA'S YELLOW CART

Ben found his office a most cheerful and pleasant resort—just what he needed. And each morning as soon as his breakfast was eaten, he went to his desk to write, to read his morning paper, and to glance at the law journals. He called this "studying." About eleven o'clock the Haneys regularly drove down, and they went over some paper, or some proposal for investment, or Williams came in with a report of the mines. This filled in the time till lunch. Not infrequently he got into the carriage, and they rode up to get Alice to fill out the table. In the afternoon they sometimes went out to the mesas, and it was this almost daily habit of driving and lunching with the Haneys which infuriated Mrs. Crego who really loved Alice and troubled Lee Congdon who was, as she said, frankly in love with Ben. Gossips were already discussing the outcome of it all.

"Just such a situation as that has produced a murderess," said Mrs. Crego to the judge one night. But he only shook his paper and scowled under its cover, refusing to say one word further concerning the Haneys.

Alice, studying Ben with those uncanny eyes of hers, saw him slowly yielding to the charm of Bertha's personality, which was maturing rapidly under the influence of her love. She was as silent as ever, but her manner was less boyish. The swell of her bosom, the glow that came into her face, had their counterparts in the unconsciously acquired feminine grace of her bearing. She was giving up many of the phrases which jarred on polite ears, and she did this, naturally, by reason of her association with Alice. She saw and took on many of the little niceties of the older woman's way of eating and drinking.

At Lee Congdon's suggestion, she abandoned the cross-saddle. It required a great deal of character to give up the free and natural way of riding the way in which all women rode until these latter days, and to assume the helpless, cramped, and twisted position the side-saddle demands; but she did it in the feeling that Ben liked her better for the change. And he did. She could see approval in his eyes when she rode out for the first time in conventional riding-skirt, looking very slim and strong and graceful. "I can't stand for the 'hard hat,'" she confessed. "I'll wear a cap or a sombrero, but no skillet for me."

These were perfect days for the girl-wife. Under these genial suns, with such companionship, such daily food, she rushed towards maturity like some half-wild colt brought suddenly from the sere range into abundant and peaceful pasture, the physical side of her being rounded out, glowing with the fires of youth, at the same time that the poor old Captain sank slowly but surely into inactivity and feebleness. She did not perceive his decline, for he talked bravely of his future, and called her attention to his increasing weight, which was indeed a sign of his growing inertness.

And so the months passed with no one of the little group but Alice suffering, for Mart had attained a kind of resignation to his condition. He still talked of going up to the camp, but the doctor and Bertha persuaded him to wait, and so he endured as patiently as he could, and if he suffered, gave little direct sign of it.

Alice, fully alive now to the gossip of the town thanks to Mrs. Crego, found herself helpless in the matter. She believed the young people to be—as they were—innocent of all disloyalty, and she could not assume the rôle of the jealous woman. She was frightened at thought of the suffering before them all, and it was in this fear that she said to Ben one day: "Boy, you're giving up a deal of time to the Haneys."

He answered, promptly. "They pay me for it."

"I know they do. But, dearest, you ought to take more time to study—to prepare yourself for other clients—when they come."

He laughed. "They're not likely to come right away, and, besides, I do get in an hour or two every day."

"But you ought to study *six* hours every day. Aren't the traditions of Lincoln and Daniel Webster all to that effect: work all day with the ax, and study in the light of pine knots all night?"

He took her words as lightly as they were spoken. "Something like that. But I'm no Daniel Webster; I'm not sure I want to go in for criminal law at all."

She spoke, sharply. "You mustn't think of getting your fees too easy, Ben. I don't think any good lawyer wins without work. Do you?"

"I didn't mean that," he hastened to say. "You do me an injustice. I really read more than you think, and my memory is tenacious, you know. Besides, I can't refuse to give the Haneys the most of my time; for they are my only clients, and the Captain is most generous."

"The mornings ought to be enough," she hazarded.

"I know what you mean. I do go out with them afternoons a good deal, but I consider that a part of my duty. They are so helpless socially. You've always felt that yourself."

"I feel it now, Bennie boy, but we mustn't neglect all friends for them. Other people don't know that you do this as a matter of business, and of course you can't tell any one; for if the Haneys heard of it they would be cut to the heart. Do they put it on a business basis?"

"They never mention it. Bertha isn't given to talking subtleties, as you know, and the Captain takes it all as it comes these days."

It hurt her to hear him speak of Mrs. Haney in that off-hand, habitual way, and she foretold further misconception on the part of Mrs. Crego in case he should forget—as he was likely to do—and allude to "Bertha" in her presence. But how could she tell him not to do that? She merely said: "I like Mrs. Haney, and I feel sorry for her—I mean I'm sorry she can't have a place in the town to which she is really entitled. She is improving very rapidly."

"Isn't she!" he cried out. "That little thing is reading right through the town library—a book every other day, she tells me."

"Novels, I fear."

"No; that's the remarkable thing. She's reading history and biography. Isn't it too bad she couldn't have had Bryn Mawr or Vassar? I've advised her to have in some one of the university people to coach her. I've suggested Miss Franklin. I wish you'd uphold me in it."

He had never told Alice of the talk in the garden that day, nor of the look in Bertha's eyes which decided him to assume the position of mentor as well as legal adviser, and he did not now intimate more than a casual supervision of her reading. As a matter of fact, he was directing her daily life as absolutely as a husband—more absolutely, in fact; for she obeyed his slightest wish or most minute suggestion. He withheld these facts from Alice, not from any perceived disloyalty to her, but from his feeling that his advice to Bertha was paid for and professional, and therefore not to be spread wide before any one. He did not conceal anything; he merely outlined without filling in the bare suggestion.

He not merely gave his fair client lists of books, he talked with her upon them, and so far as he was able spoke seriously and conscientiously about them. She seized upon his suggestion, and got Miss Franklin, one of the teachers of the schools, to come in now and again of an evening to help her, and, being fond of music, she bought a piano and began to take lessons.

All of which Lee Congdon would have said threatened to render her commonplace and uninteresting; but Alice Heath felt quite differently about that.

"No; the more that girl gets, the more she'll have, Lee. As Ben says, she's the kind that if she were a boy would turn out a big self-made man. That's a little twisted as to grammar, but you see what I mean. Sex is one of the ultimate mysteries, isn't it? Now, why didn't I inherit my father's ability?"

"You did, only you never use it. But this girl hasn't your father to draw from."

"No; but her father was an educated man—a civil engineer, she tells me, who came out here for one of the big railroads. He was something of an inventor, too. That's the reason he died poor—they nearly all do."

"But the mother?"

"Well, she's weak and tiresome now, but she's by no means common. She's broken by hard work, but she's naturally refined. No, the girl isn't so bad; it's the frightful girlhood she endured in that little hotel. I think it's wonderful that she could associate with the people she did—barbers and railway hands, and all that—and be what she is to-day. If she had married a man like young Bennett, for example, she would have gone far."

"She can't go far with Haney chained to her wrist," said the blunt Mrs. Congdon.

"But think what will happen when she is his widow!"

"And his legatee!"

"Precisely."

"She'll cut a wide swath. She's going to be handsome."

They had reached a danger-point, for Lee was on the verge of saying something about Ben's infatuation; but she didn't, and Alice knew why she didn't, for she asked, rather abruptly: "Won't you come over Thursday night? I'm going to take the Haneys to dinner at the hotel." She flushed under Lee's gaze. "It's really Bennie's party, and I'm going to make it as pretty as I can."

"Alice, I don't understand you. Why do you do this?"

"Because I must. She and the Captain are going East on a visit, and Ben wants to give them a 'jolly send-off,' as he calls it. Besides, I like the girl."

Lee mused in silence for a few moments. "I guess you're right. Of course I'll come. Who else will?"

"Several of Ben's new friends and the Cregos—"

"Not the missus?"

"Yes; she comes because she's consumed with curiosity. Oh, it really promises to be smart!"

Congdon came in just in time to hear these words, "Who promises to be smart—Mrs. Haney?"

The women laughed. "Another person going about with a mind full of Mrs. Haney."

"Well, why not? I just passed her on the street in her new dog-cart, and she was ripping good to look at. Say, that girl is too swift for this town. You people better keep close to her if you want to know what's doing in gowns and cloaks. Did you ever see such development in your life? Say, girls, I always believed in clothes. But, my eyes! I didn't think cotton and wool and leather could make such a change. Who is putting her on?"

"The cart is a new development," said Alice. "I hope it wasn't yellow?"

"Well, it was."

"The Captain was in it?"

"Not on your life. The Captain was at home in the easy-chair by the fire."

The women looked at each other. Then Lee said: "The beginning of the end. Poor old Captain."

Congdon was loyalty itself. "Now don't you jump at conclusions. Yes, she pulled up, and I went out to see her. She gave me her hand in the old way, and said; 'Isn't this a joke. The Captain ordered it from Chicago. He saw a picture in one of my magazines of a girl driving one of these things, and here I am. You don't think they'll charge me a special license, do you?' Oh, she's all right. Don't you worry about her. Then she said: 'What I don't like about it is the Captain can't ride in it. I'm not going to keep it,' she said."

"That was for effect," remarked Lee.

"Don't be nasty, Mrs. Congdon. You can't look into her big serious eyes and say such things."

Lee looked at Alice. "Oh, well, if it comes down to 'big serious eyes,' then all criticism is valueless. Aren't men curious? Character is nothing, intellect is nothing—it's all a question of whether we're good-lookin' or not. Sometimes I'm discouraged. An artist husband is so hard to please."

"I didn't use to be, dovey," he replied, with a mischievous gleam.

"He means when he took me. I'm used to his slurs. Just think, Alice, I accepted this man fresh from Paris, with all his sins of omission and commission upon him, and now he reviles me to my teeth." She patted the hand he slipped round her neck. "Tell us more about Mrs. Haney. How was she dressed?"

"In perfect good taste—almost too good. She looked like one of Joe Meyer's early posters. Gee! but she was snappy in drawing. She carries that sort of thing well—she's so clean and nifty in line. If she could have a year in Paris—wow!—well, us to Fifth Avenue, sure thing!"

"All depends on what is at the bottom of that girl's soul," retorted Lee, sententiously. "A light woman with money is a flighty combination. I don't pretend to say what your little Mrs. Haney is at bottom. Thus far I like her. I talk about her freely, but I defend her in public. But, at the same time, fifty thousand dollars a year is a corrupting power."

Congdon gravely assented to this. "You're perfectly right; that's the reason I keep our income down to fifteen hundred. I'd hate to see you look like a ready-made cloak advertisement."

Alice rose rather wearily. "Thursday night, you said?"

"Yes; and I guess, following the latest bulletin concerning Mr. Haney, we better put on our swellest ginghams."

Alice, on her way home, continued to think of Mrs. Haney; indeed, she was seldom out of her mind. And she had a feeling of having known her for a long time—since girlhood; and yet less than a year had passed since that dinner at Lee Congdon's. Spring was coming; the hint of it was in the sweet air, and in the clear piping of a prairie lark in a vacant lot. Spring! And how long it had been since Ben had referred to their marriage! Perhaps he took it for granted. "Perhaps he sees in me only failing health, and dares not speak."

She was not gaining; that she knew, and so did Lee. She had stayed too long in the raw climate of her native city. "He must not marry me!" she despairingly cried. "I must not let him ruin his life in that way!" And she sank back in the corner of her carriage with wrinkled, pallid face, and quivering lips; for Bertha was passing up the avenue, driving a smart-stepping cob, in her cart, and in the seat beside her, as radiant as herself, sat Ben Fordyce.

CHAPTER XIV

THE JOLLY SEND-OFF

The Mrs. Haney who came to Alice Heath's dinner at the Antlers was in outward seeming an entirely different person from the constrained young wife who stepped into Lee Congdon's home that night of her first dinner. She was gowned now in that severe good taste which betokens a high-priced "ladies' tailor" combined with very judicious criticism. Her critic she had found in Miss Franklin, a young lady from the university who had passed easily and naturally from teaching history and etiquette up to the higher function of advising as to the cut and color of gowns. Bertha's black velvet was this time a close-clasping sheath which revealed her slender figure, and delicately and modestly disclosed the growing grace of her bosom. She wore, too, some jewels of diamond and turquoise—not showy her mentor had taken great pains to warn her of all that. And she was not merely irreproachable, she was radiant, as she slowly entered with the Captain, who, having submitted like a martyr to evening dress, was uneasy as a colt in harness, and more than usually uncertain of step.

Ben's eyes expanded with surprise and his heart warmed with pride as he greeted her. "You are beautiful!" he exclaimed to her, and the tone of his exclamation as well as the words exalted her. Her brain filled with a mist of gold. She hardly felt the floor beneath her feet. To be called beautiful—and by him—had been outside the circle of her most daring hope, and the repetition of this word in her mind was like the clash of musical bells—entrancing her. Mechanically she took her place at his right hand, silently, and with a far-away look, listening to the merry clamor of the table. She hardly knew what she ate or what any one said—except when Ben spoke to her. But she was aware of the Captain down at Alice's right, and wondered vaguely how he was getting on with his napkin and his fork.

The first words that really roused her and stopped the musing smile on her lips were spoken by Ben in a lower voice—half-laughing, but tender also. "You mustn't stay away too long. I'll feel as if I weren't earning my salary while you're gone."

"I wish you were going too," she said. She had thought this many times, but had not permitted herself to utter it. "Why can't you—and Alice—come with us?"

"I can't afford it, for one thing. The Captain spoke of it, but it's out of the question."

"He'll pay you wages just the same."

"I wouldn't want pay. No, it isn't that; but Alice isn't able to go, and I can't think of going without her."

This was a good reason, and Bertha, looking towards Alice, saw in her face the pain which masks itself in color and movement. The dinner-table was exquisite and the company gay, and Bertha felt herself a part of the great world of dignity and beauty, where eating is made to seem a graceful art, and wine is only a bit of color and not a lure. She vaguely comprehended that this little party was of a tone and quality of the best the world over—that it was of a part and interfused with the dining customs of London and Paris and New York. "It will be *au fait*," Miss Franklin had said, sententiously, "for Alice Heath *knows*."

Mrs. Crego, who sat nearly opposite, stared at the girl in stupefaction. "She makes me feel dowdy," she had confessed to Lee in the dressing-room. "Why didn't you warn me to come in my best? Who has been coaching her? Alice Heath, I suppose." She now wondered as sharply over the girl's manner; for Bertha, carried out of herself by Ben's word of praise, felt no desire to drink or to eat, and her reticence and the delicacy of her appetite conferred a distinction which concealed her lack of small talk, and protected her from the criticism to which exuberance of manner ordinarily exposed her.

She was deeply impressed, too, with Ben's management of the waiters, and with the ease and skill with which he supported Alice in carrying forward the courses. It was a revelation of training which instructed her absurdly, for her mind was quick to link and compare. It leaped so swiftly and so subtilely along connecting lines of thought that a hint alone sufficed to set in motion a hundred latent memories and inherited aptitudes. Her father had been a man of native refinement, and she possessed unstirred deeps of character, as Alice now well understood. And from her end of the table she glanced often at the sweetly smiling girl-wife whose beauty abashed Haney. At last she said to him: "Your wife is very lovely to-night, Captain."

He hesitated a moment; then replied, slowly: "She is. She's as fine as anny queen!" Then after another pause, added: "And the more shame to me, being what I am! She's a good girl, miss, true as steel. Never a word of complaint or a frown. She bears with me like an angel."

"You're doing a great deal for her."

His face lightened. "So she says. I mean to do more. I mean to show her the world. That's the only comfort I have; my money is giving her nice clothes and a home as good as anny, and to-night I feel 'tis giving her friends."

"But she is worth while, even without the money."

"True," he quickly said. "But I take comfort in the consideration that had I not carried her away she'd be in Sibley Junction this night."

"Sibley Junction! Can this radiant young creature sitting there at the head of my table be the clerk of the Golden Eagle Hotel?" thought Alice. "Money is magical! No wonder we all work for it—and worship it!"

The dinner was both early and short, in order that Bertha and the Captain might take the train at ten o'clock. And as they were to have the drawing-room in the sleeping-car Ben's suggestion, they went directly to the coach in their party clothes. And so it happened that this little woman, who had never occupied a berth in a Pullman, entered her compartment in the robes of a princess.

Alice had suggested a maid, but Bertha would not hear to that; but she was willing that their coachman should go along to help the Captain. Ben had interposed here, and said: "You need some one used to travelling. I know a colored fellow who is out of service just now, and would like to come to you. He's a good, reliable man, and a fine nurse." So she had engaged him. He was on the platform as they drove up—a slight, quiet man, of gentle speech and indeterminable age, who took charge of the Captain at once, as if he had been his servant for years.

Alice said good-bye at the carriage door, but Ben went with them into the coach. And in the excitement of getting to the train and into the car Bertha had been able to forget the sick feeling about her heart. But now, as he turned and said, "It's nearly time to start," and held out his hand in parting, a desolation, a loneliness, a helpless hunger swept over her, the like of which had never anguished her before.

"I wish you were going too!" she faltered, her speech broken and full of sad cadences.

He, too, was tense with emotion as he answered: "I wish I were, but I can't—I must not!" Then, with the gesture of a brother, he bent and kissed her and turned away, blind to everything else but his pain, and, so stumbling and shaken, vanished from her sight.

For a moment she remained standing in the aisle, the touch of his lips still clinging to her cheek, surprised, full of bewildered defence; then, as reckless of on-lookers as he had been, she rushed to the window in swift attempt to catch a final glimpse of him. But in vain; he had hurried away without looking back, her look of wonder and surprise still dazzling him with its significance. A kiss with him, as with her, had never been a thing lightly given or received, and this caress, so simple to others, sprang from an impulse that was elemental. That he had both shocked and angered her he fully believed; but the arch of her brows, the wistful curve of her lips, and the pretty, almost childish, push of her hands against his breast were still so appealingly vivid that he entered the carriage and took his seat beside Alice with a kind of rebellious joy hot in his blood.

However, as his passion ebbed his uneasiness deepened, and he went to his room that night with a feeling that his connection with the Haneys, so profitable and so pleasant, was in danger of being irremediably broken off. "She will be justified in refusing ever to see me again," he groaned. And in this spirit of self-condemnation and loneliness he took up his work next day.

Bertha's self-revelation was slower. She was so young and so innately honest and good that no sense of guilt attached to the pleasure she felt in the sudden revelation that this splendid young man loved her—a pleasure which grew as the first shock of the parting, the pain, and the surprise wore away. "He likes me! He said I was beautiful! He kissed me!" These were the rounds in the ladder of her ascent, and she was carried high, only to fall into despair. For was she not leaving him and all the pleasant people she had come so recently to know— hurrying away into darkness with a crippled man, old before his time, out into a world of which she knew little—for which, at this moment, she cared nothing?

She went back, a few moments later, with this sorrow written on her face, to find Lucius, the colored man, deftly preparing the Captain for bed. The old borderer looked up with a smile, in which shame and sadness mingled. "Well, Bertie, I didn't think I'd come to this—me, that could once sit in me saddle and pick a dollar out o' the dust. But so it is."

"I'll take care of you!" she cried, in swift contrition. Turning almost fiercely to the valet, she said: "You can go, I'll 'tend to him!"

The Captain stopped her gently. "No, darlin', Ben's right; I'm too clumsy and heavy for you. I need just such a handy man. Now, now! Let be!... Go ahead, Lucius, strip off these monkey-fixens, and dom the man that gets me into them again."

Efficient as she was, the girl could not but admit that Lucius was better able to serve her husband than herself. He was both deft and strong; and though the swaying of the car troubled his master, he steadied him and guided him and stowed him away as featly as if it were the fiftieth instead of the first time; then, with a few words of explanation to the wife, he quietly withdrew, and shut the door with a final touch of considerate care which was new to her.

She would have been less troubled by him had he been a black man, but he was not. He seemed more like a Spaniard, and his grizzled mustache, yellowish skin, and big dreamy black eyes lent him a curious distinction, and the thought that he was to take her place as crutch and cane to the Captain gave her a sense of uselessness which she had not, up to this moment, confessed.

His suggestions, combined to the minute instructions of Miss Franklin, enabled her to get to her bunk in fair order, but no sleep came to her for hours. She longed for her mother more childishly than at any time since her marriage. She reproached herself for not bringing Miss Franklin. "Why did I come at all?" she wailed, in final accusation.

There had been a time when the thought of this trip—of Chicago, New York, and Washington—was big in her mind, but it was so no longer. These great cities were but names—empty sounds compared to the realities she was leaving: her splendid house, her horses and dogs—and her daily joy in Ben Fordyce. She did not put these visits in their highest place, not even when remembering his parting kiss, but she dwelt upon the inspiriting morning drives, the talks in the mellow-tinted, sunshine-lighted office. She recalled the lunches they took together and the occasional wild gallops up the cañon—these she treasured as the golden realities, for the loss of which she was even now heart-sick.

One thought alone steadied her—gave her a kind of resignation: the Captain wanted to find his sisters, to revisit the scenes of his youth, and it was her duty to go with him. And in this somewhat dreary comfort she fell asleep at last.

She was awakened next morning by a pleasant voice saying: "The first call for breakfast has been made, Mrs. Haney." And she looked up to find Lucius peering in at the door with serious, kindly eyes. He added, formally: "If I can assist you in any way call me, and please let me know when you are ready to have me come in."

His speech was so precise and his manner so perfect that Bertha was puzzled and a little embarrassed by them. It seemed abnormal to have a hired servant so polished, so thoughtful. She dressed hurriedly, while the Captain yawned and talked between his yawning. "That yellow chap is sure handy. I wish I'd had him before; 'twould have saved you a power o' work and worry. Did ye sleep last night?"

"Not very well. I hope you did. You can't complain of the bunk."

"'Tis luxurious—'tis so! But there's nothing like the west side of Colorado Avenue, after all, or a bed of pine boughs beside a roaring mountain stream. 'Twas a fine little supper Ben gave us last night."

The level lands awed and depressed the mountain girl. They seemed to type the flat and desolate spiritual world into which she was entering, and the ride seemed interminable, carrying her every hour farther from the scenes and sounds to which her love clung. She was bitterly homesick, and nothing seemed to promise comfort. She gazed with lack-lustre eyes on the towns and rivers along the way, and she entered the great inland metropolis by the lake with dread and a deepening sense of her inexperience and youth.

On the neighboring track stood the return sleepers headed for the hills, and she acknowledged a wild desire to take her place among the jocund folk who stood on the observation-platform exchanging good-byes with friends. Thunderous, smothering, and vast the city seemed as they drove through it on their way to the hotel, and upon reaching her room she flung herself down on her bed and sobbed in a frenzy of homesickness.

Haney, who had never before perceived a tear on her face, was startled, and stood in puzzled pain looking down at her, while the tactful Lucius went about the unpacking of the trunks, confident that the shower would soon be over.

"What's the ail of it?" asked the Captain. "Tell me, darlin'. Are ye sick?"

She shook her head from side to side, like a suffering and weary child, and made no further answer.

CHAPTER XV

MART'S VISIT TO HIS SISTER

Bertha woke next morning with a sense of weariness and desolation still at her heart, but she dressed and went to breakfast with Haney at an hour so early that the dining-room was nearly empty. Lucius, with quiet insistence upon the importance of his employers, had secured a place at a window overlooking the lake, and was glad to see his mistress brighten as her eyes swept the burnished shoreless expanse.

Haney, still troubled by her languid air and gloomy face, took heart, and talked of what Chicago was in the days when he saw it and what it was now. "People say it don't improve. But listen: when I was here the Palmer House was the newly built wonder of the West, the streets were tinkling with bobtail horse-cars. And now look at it!"

Bertha went back to her room, still in nerveless and despondent mood, not knowing what to do. The Captain proposed the usual round. "We'll take an auto-car, and go to the parks, and inspect the Lake Shore Drive and the Potter Palmer castle. Then we'll go down and see where the World's Fair was. Then we'll visit the Wheat Pit. 'Tis all there is, bedad."

Lucius, who had been answering the 'phone in the hall, came in at the moment to say; "A lady wishes to speak with Mrs. Haney."

"A lady! Who?"

"A certain Mrs. Brent—a friend of Miss Franklin's."

Bertha's face darkened. "Oh I'd forgot all about her. Miss Franklin gave me a letter to her," she explained, as she went out.

She had no wish to see Mrs. Brent. On the contrary, she had an aversion to seeing or doing anything. But there was something compelling in the cool, sweet, quiet voice which came over the line, and before realizing it she had promised to meet her at eleven o'clock.

Mrs. Brent then added: "I am consumed with desire to see you, for Dor—I mean Miss Franklin—has been writing to me about you. You're just in time to come to a little dinner of mine—don't make any engagement for to-morrow night. I'm coming down immediately."

Bertha quite gravely answered, "All right, I'll be here," and hung up the receiver, committed to an interview that became formidable, now that the sweetness of the voice had died out of her ears.

"Who was it?" asked the Captain.

"A friend of Miss Franklin's—sounds just like her voice, but I think she's only a cousin. She wants to see me, and I've promised to be here at eleven."

The Captain looked a little disappointed. "Well, we can take a spin up the lake. Lucius, go hire a buckboard and we're off."

"There's an auto-car waiting, sir. I ordered it half an hour ago."

The gambler looked at him humorously. "Ye must be a mind-reader."

A tap on the door called the man out, and when he returned he bore a telegram. "For you, Captain," he said, presenting it on the salver.

The gambler took it with sudden apprehension in his face. "I hope there's no trouble at the mine," he muttered.

Bertha, leaning over his shoulder, read it first. "It's from Ben!" she called, joyously. "Ain't it just like him?"

This message seemed a little bit foolish to Haney.

"Just to say hello! All well here. Have a good time.

"Fordyce."

To Bertha it made all the difference between sunshine and shadow. She thrilled to it as if it had been a voice. "He knew I'd be homesick, and so he sent this to cheer me up," she said. And in this she was right. Her shoulders lifted and her face cleared. "Come on, Captain, if we're going."

As they came down the elevator, men in buttons met them, and attended them to the door, and turned them over to still other uniformed attendants, who were fain to help them into the auto-car; for Lucius had managed to convey to the hotel a proper sense of his employer's money value. He himself was always close to his master's side, for lately Haney had taken to stumbling at unexpected moments, and his increasing bulk made a fall a real danger.

A thrill of delight, of elation, ran through the young wife as she glanced up and down Chicago's proudest avenue. It conformed to her notion of a city. The level park, flooded with spring sunshine, was walled on the west by massive buildings, while to the east stretched the shining lake. From here the city seemed truly cosmopolitan. It had dignity and wealth of color, and to the girl from Sibley Junction was completely satisfying—almost inspiring.

It was uplifting also to be attended to a splendid auto-car by willing, alert servants, and to feel that the passers-by were all envious of her careless ease. Bertha forgot her homesickness, and took her seat in the spirit of one who is determined to have the worth of her money for once anyhow, and the pedestrians, if they had any definite notion of her at all, probably said: "There goes a rich old cattle king and his pretty daughter. It's money that makes the 'mobile go."

She held to this pose for half an hour, while they threaded the tumult of Wabash Avenue, and, crossing the river, swept up the Lake Shore Drive. But the lake filled her with other thoughts. "I wish we had this at the Springs," she said. "This is fine!"

"We have our share," answered he. "If we had this at our door, there wouldn't be anything left to go to."

They whizzed through the park, and down another avenue into the thick tangle of traffic, which scared them both, and so back to the hotel, the Captain saying: "My! my! but she has grown. 'Tis twenty years since I took this turn."

In some strange way Bertha had drawn courage, resolution, pride, and ambition from what she saw on this short ride. That she was in a car and mistress of it was in itself a marvellous distinction, and the thought of what she would have been—as a "round-tripper" from Sibley Junction—added to her pleasure and pride. She was always doing sums in her head now. Thus: "Suppose our excursion does cost twenty dollars per day; that's only one hundred and fifty per week, six hundred per month, and our income is ten times that, and more." She had not risen above the habit of calculation, but she was fast rising to higher levels of expenditure.

She met Mrs. Brent with something of this mood in her manner, but was instantly softened and won by her visitor, who did not in the least resemble Miss Franklin in appearance, though her voice was wonderfully the same. Her eyes were wide, her brow serene, and her lips smiling.

"Why, you're a child," she said—"a mere babe! Dorothy didn't tell me that."

Bertha stiffened a little, and Mrs. Brent laughingly added: "Please don't be offended—I am really surprised." And then her manner became so winning that before the Western girl realized it she had given her consent to join a dinner-party the following night. "Come early, for we are to go to the theatre afterwards. I'll have some of the university people in to see you. Miss Franklin has made us all eager to meet you."

Bertha had a dim perception that this eagerness to meet her was curiosity, but her loyalty to her teacher and the charm of her visitor kept her from openly rebelling.

The Captain was not so easily persuaded. "'Tis poor business for me," he said. "Time was when I went to bed like a wolf—when the time served; but now I'm as regular to me couch as a one-legged duck. However, to keep me wife in tune, I'll go or come, as the case may be."

Mrs. Brent did not attempt to be funny with this wounded bear, and they parted very good friends.

As her visitor was going, Bertha suddenly said, "Wait a minute," and, going to her hand-bag, brought out an envelope addressed in Congdon's big scrawling hand. "Do you know these people?"

Mrs. Brent glanced at it. "Why, yes, Joe Moss is an artist. He's well-known here, and you'll like him. His wife is a very talented woman, and will be of great advantage to you. They know all the 'artistic gang,' as they call themselves, and they live a delightfully Bohemian life. They're right near here, and if I were you I'd go in to see them. I'd thought of having the Mosses to-morrow night, and this settles it. They must come. Good-bye till to-morrow at 7 p.m." And she went out, leaving the girl in a glow of increasing good-will.

Haney was looking over a list of names and addresses which Lucius had brought to him, and as Bertha returned he put his finger on one, and said: "I believe, on me soul, that this Patrick McArdle is me second sister's husband. 'Patrick McArdle, pattern-maker.' Sure, Charles said he was in a stove foundry. 'Tis over on the West Side, Lucius says. How would it do to slide over and see?"

"I'm agreeable," she carelessly answered, her mind full of Mrs. Brent and the dinner.

Lucius interposed a word. "It's a very poor neighborhood, Captain. We can hardly get to it with a machine."

"Well, then we'll drive. I want to make a stab at finding my sister anyhow."

Lucius submitted, but plainly disapproved of the whole connection. On the way Haney talked of his sister Fanny. "She was a bouncing, jolly-tempered girl, always down at the heels, but good to me. She was two years older, and was mother's main guy, as the sailors say. She was fairly industrious, though none of us ever worked just for the fun of it. Fan married all the other girls off to saloon-keepers or aldermen, which is all the same in pay, and then ended up by takin' a man far older than herself, who was not very strong and not very smart. He makes patterns in sand for the leaves and acorns you see on stove doors. For all we know, he may have made them that's on your new range at home."

The mention of that range brought to Bertha's mind a picture of her lovely kitchen, so light and bright and shining, and another spasm of homesickness and doubt seized her. "Mart, we had no business to come away and leave that house and all our nice things in it."

"Miss Franklin will see after it."

"But how can she? She's gone nearly all day. And, besides, she's not up to housekeeping—it ain't her line. I feel like going right back this minute!"

This feeling of dismay was increased by the glimpses of the grimy West Side, into which they were plunging every moment deeper. After leaving the asphalt pavement the noise increased till they were unable to make each other hear without shouting, and so they sat in silence while the driver turned corners and dodged carts and cars till at last he turned abruptly into a side-street, and, driving slowly along over a rotting block pavement, drew up before a small, two-story frame house—a relic of the old-time city.

The yards were full of children, who all stopped their play to stare at this carriage, especially impressed by Lucius, who sat very erect on the seat beside the driver, resolutely doing a very disagreeable duty. At the door he got down and said: "Now, Captain, you give me a pointer or two, and I'll find out whether this is your McArdle or not."

"Just ask if Mrs. McArdle was Fan Haney, of Troy. That'll cover the specification," he answered.

By this time a large, fair-haired, slovenly woman had opened the door, and, with truculent voice, called out: "Who do you want to find?"

"Fan Haney, of Troy," answered the Captain.

"That's me," the woman retorted.

"Ye are so! Very well, thin, consider yourself under arrest this minute," said Haney, beginning to clamber out of the carriage.

The woman stared a moment; then a slow grin developed on her face so like to Haney's own that Bertha laughed. The lost sister was found.

As Haney neared her, he called out: "Well, Fan, ye're the same old sloven ye were when I used to kick your shins in Troy for soapin' me mouth."

"Mart Haney, by the piper!" she exclaimed, wiping her lips and hands in anticipation of a caress. "Where did ye borry the funeral wagon?"

He shook her hand—the kiss was out of his inclination—and responded in the same vein of mockery: "A friend of mine died the day, and I broke out of the procession to pay a call. Divil a bit the dead man cares."

"Who's with you in the carriage?"

"Mrs. Haney, bedad."

"Naw, it is not!"

"Sure thing!"

"She's too young and pretty—and Mart, ye're lame! And, howly saints, man, ye look old! I wouldn't have known ye but fer the mouth and the eyes of ye. Ye have the same old grin."

"The same to you."

"I get little chance to practise it these days."

"'Tis the same here."

"But how came ye hurt?"

"A felly with a grievance poured a load of buckshot into me side, and one of them lodged in me spine, so they say."

She clicked her tongue in ready sympathy. "Dear, dear! But come in and sit ye down. Ask yer girl to come in—I'm not perticular."

"She's me lawful wife," he said, and his tone changed her manner into something like sweetness and dignity.

"Go ye in, Mart. I'll fetch her."

As the young wife sat in her carriage before this wretched little home and watched that slatternly sister of her husband approach, she rose on a wave of self-appreciation. Haney lost in dignity and power by this association. For the first time in her life the girl acknowledged a fixed difference between her blood and that of Mart Haney. She was disgusted and ashamed as Mrs. McArdle, coming to the carriage side, said bluffly: "'Tis a poor parlor I have, Mrs. Haney, but if ye'll light out and come in I'll send for Pat. He'll be wantin' to see ye both."

Bertha would have given a good deal to avoid this visit, but seeing no way to escape she stepped from the carriage under the keen scrutiny of her hostess and walked up the rickety steps with something of the same squeamish care she would have shown on entering a cow-barn.

"Here, Benny!" called Mrs. McArdle. "Run you to Dad and tell him me brother Mart has come, and to hurry home. Off wid ye now!"

The poverty of this city working-man's home was plain to see. It struck in upon Bertha with the greater power by reason of her six months of luxury. It was not a dirty home, but it was cluttered and hap-hazard. The old wooden chairs were worn with scouring, but littered with children's rags of clothing. The smell of boiling cabbage was in the air, for dinner-time was nigh. There were three rooms on the ground-floor and one of these was living-room and dining-room, the other the kitchen, and a small bedroom showed through an open door. For all its disorder it gave out a familiar odor of homeliness which profoundly moved Haney.

"Ye've grown like the mother, Fan. And I do believe some of these chairs are her's."

"They are. When Dad broke up the house and went to live with Kate I put in a bid for the stuff and I brought some of it out here with me."

"I'm glad ye did. That old rocker now—sure it's the very one we used to fight for. I'll give ye twenty-five dollars for it, Fan."

"Ye can have it for the askin', Mart," she generously replied—tears of pleasure in her eyes. "Sure, after all the tales I heard of ye—it's to see you takin' fine to the mother's chair. She was a good mother to us, Mart."

"She was!" he answered.

"And if the old Dad had been as much of a man as she was, we'd all stand in better light to-day I'm thinkin'—though the father did the best he knew."

"The worst he did was to let us all run wild. A club about our shoulders now and then would have kept our tempers sweeter."

Bertha, in rich new garments, seemed as alien to the scene as any fine lady visiting among the slums. She was struggling, too, between disgust of her sister-in-law's slovenly house and untidy dress, and the good humor, tender sentiment and innate motherliness of her nature. There was charm in her voice and in her big gray eyes. Irish to the core, she could storm at one child and coo with another an instant later. She was like Mart, or rather Mart became every moment more of her kind and less of the bold and remorseless desperado he had once seemed to be. The deeper they dug into the past the more of his essential kinship to this woman he discovered. He greeted her children with kindly interest, leaving a dollar in each chubby, dirty fist, and when McArdle came into the room Fan had quite conquered her awe of Bertha's finery.

McArdle was a small bent man, with a black beard, a pale serious face and speculative eyes. He looked like a wondering, rather cautious animal as he came in. He wore a cheap gray suit and a celluloid collar, and was as careless in his way as his wife. It was plain that he was gentle, absent-minded, and industrious.

He listened to his wife's voluble explanations in silence, inwardly digesting all that was said, then shook hands—still without a word. And when all these preliminaries were over he laid his hat aside and ran his fingers through his thin hair with a perplexed and troubled gesture, asking, irrelevantly: "How's the weather out there?"

Nobody saw the humor of this but his wife, who explained: "Pat is a fiend on the weather. He was raised on a farm, ye see, and he can't get over it. I say to him: 'What difference does the state o' the weather make to you, that's under a roof all day?' But divil a change does it make in him. The first thing in the morning he turns to the weather report."

McArdle's eyes showed traces of a smile. "If it weren't for the papers and the weather reports, me days would be alike. But sit by," he added, hospitably, waving his hand towards the table, on which the dinner was steaming.

They were drawing up to the board when a puffing and blowing, and the furious clatter of feet announced the inrushing of the children.

Not the mother's shrill whooping, but the sight of the strange guests, transformed them into mutes. The carriage outside had filled them with wild alarms, but the sight of their parents alive, and entertaining guests of shining quality, was almost as satisfyingly unusual as death and a funeral.

They were a noisy, hearty throng, and Bertha's heart went out to poor Patrick McArdle, who sat amid the uproar, silent, patient, the heroic breadwinner for them all. No wonder he was old before his time. Slowly her antipathy died out. She began to find excuses even for the mother. To feed such a herd of little pigs and calves, even out of wooden troughs, would require much labor; to keep them buttoned, combed, and fit for school was an appalling task. "Mart must help these folks," she said to herself.

McArdle had nothing to say during the meal, and Bertha could see that his family did not expect him to do more than answer a plain question. Indeed, the children created a hubbub that quite cut off any connected intercourse, and Fan, with a grin of despair, at last said: "They'll be gorged in a few minutes, and then we'll have peace."

"This is what lack of money means," Bertha was thinking. And her house, her automobile, her horses, became at the moment as priceless, as remote, as crown jewels and papal palaces. Then, conversely, she grew to a larger conception of the possibilities which lay in sixty thousand dollars a year. Not only did it lift her and all hers above the heat and mire and distress of the world of toil, it enabled them to help others.

Swiftly the children filled their stomachs, and, seizing each a piece of cake or pie, withdrew, leaving the old folks and their guests in peace.

Thereupon, McArdle, taking a pipe from his pocket and knocking it absent-mindedly on the seat of the chair, dryly remarked: "Now that we can hear ourselves think, let's have it all over again. Who air ye, and why air ye here?"

Being told a second time that this was his brother-in-law, a miner from Colorado, he shook hands all over again, and accepted Mart's cigar with careful fingers, as if fearing to drop and break the precious thing.

Bertha said: "I think we'd better be going, Captain. Our carriage is outside."

"Gracious Peter," cried Mrs. McArdle, "I forgot all about it! Is he by the day or by the hour?"

Mart answered, with an amused smile. "Well, now, I don't know. I think by the hour."

"Ye're makin' a big bluff, Mart. We're properly impressed," said his sister. "Go pay him off, and save the money."

McArdle put in a query. "You must have a good thing out there?"

"'Tis enough to pay me carriage hire," answered Mart. And his tone satisfied McArdle, who, with reflective eye on Bertha, puffed away at his cigar, while Mart gave his promise to call again. "I'll come over and get you all, and take you to the theatre in me auto-car," he said, as he rose. "But we must be going now."

Fan was beginning to perceive in him more and more of the man of power and substance, and her manner changed. "Ye were always the smartest of the lot of us, Mart."

"No, I was not. Charles was the bright boy."

"So he was, but he was lazy. That was why he took up with play-acting—'tis an easy job."

"Even that is too much work for him," remarked McArdle.

"I reckon that's right," laughed Mart, as he turned towards the door.

"Come again, if ye find time," called Fan, as they went down the steps.

McArdle, with his cigar in his hand, waved it in a sign of parting. And so their visit to the McArdles closed.

Mart turned to his silent and thoughtful wife, and said, with a great deal of meaning in his voice: "Well, now, what do you think of that for a fine litter of pups?"

"They seem hearty."

"They do. 'Tis on such that the future of the ray-public rests." And then he added: "Sure, Bertie, it gripped me heart to see the mother's old chair!"

CHAPTER XVI

A DINNER AND A PLAY

Lucius seemed to know the city very well, and to have a list of its principal citizens in his memory. He knew the best places to shop and the selectest places to eat, and Bertha soon came to ask his advice about other and more intimate affairs. She showed him Mrs. Brent's card, and explained that they were going out there to dinner.

"I know the locality," he said, much impressed, "and I think I know the house. It's likely to be quietly swell, and you'd better wear your best gown."

"The black dress," said Haney, who was a deeply concerned witness. "I like that."

Lucius was respectful, but firm. "You are very well in that, Mrs. Haney. But if I were you I'd have a new gown; you'll need it. I know just the saleslady to fit you out."

"But I've only worn the black dress once!" she exclaimed, in dismay.

Lucius explained that people who went out much in the city made a point of not wearing the same gown in the same circle a second time. "And as you only have two presentable evening gowns, you certainly need another."

Haney joined in, emphatically. "Sure thing! What's the good of money if you don't use it to buy things?"

Tremulous with the excitement of it, she went with the Captain to several of the largest and most sumptuous establishments on State Street. And Lucius, who accompanied them, ostensibly to be of service to his master, was of the greatest service to his mistress, he was so quiet, so unobtrusive, so thoroughly the footman in appearance, so helpful, and so masterful, in fact; a faint shake of his head, a nod, a gesture decided momentous questions.

The girl, sitting there surrounded by scurrying clerks and saleswomen, had a return of her bewilderment and doubt. "Can it be true that I can buy any of these cloaks and hats?" she asked herself. What was the magic that had made her lightest wish realizable? When a splendid cloak fell round her shoulders, and she looked in the glass at the tall figure there, she glowed with pride.

"Madam carries a cloak beautifully," the saleswoman said, with sincerity. "This is our smartest model—perfectly exclusive and new. Only such a figure as the madam's properly sets it off."

While the women were making measurements for some slight alterations, Lucius said: "It would be nice if you decided on that automobile, and took Mrs. Haney to the dinner in it."

Haney's face lighted up. "I will! Sh! not a word. We'll surprise her."

"If you don't mind I'll hustle up a footman's livery."

"So do. Anything goes—for her, Lucius."

Bertha thought she had already rubbed the side of her wonderful lamp to a polish. But under the almost hypnotic spell of her West-Indian attendant she bought shoes, hats, hosiery, and toilet articles till her room looked "like Christmas morning," as Haney said, and yet there was little that could be called foolish or tawdry. She wore little jewelry, having resisted Haney's attempt to load her with rings and necklaces. Miss Franklin had impressed upon her the need of being "simple." When she put on her dinner-dress and faced him, Mart Haney was humbled to earth. "Sure, ye're beautiful as an angel!" he exulted, as if addressing a saint. And as she swept before the tall glass and saw her radiant self therein, she thought of Ben, and her face flamed with lovely color. "I wish he could see me now!" she inwardly exclaimed.

Miss Franklin, in writing to her friend, Mrs. Brent, had said: "In a sense, the Haneys are 'impossible'—he is an ex-gambler, and she is the daughter of a woman who kept a miner's boarding-house in the mountains. But this sounds worse than it really is. I like the Captain. Whatever he was in the days before his accident I don't know—they say he was a terror. But when I entered the family he was as he is now—a pathetic figure. He isn't really old; but he's horribly crippled, and takes it very hard. He is kindness itself to his wife and to every one round him, and will be grateful for anything you do for him. Bertha is young but maturing very rapidly, and there's no telling where she will stop. She's been studying with me, and I've told her you will advise her while she's in Chicago. You needn't go far with her if you don't want to. The Hallidays and Voughts won't mind the back pages of the Haney history, and you needn't say anything about the Captain's career if you don't want to. He's a big mine-owner now, and is out of the gambling and saloon business altogether. Bertha is perfectly eligible in herself. And as many of us started on farms or poor little villages, we can't afford to take on any airs over her. She's of good parentage, and as true as steel. She likes the Captain, and is devoted to him."

Dr. Brent was not connected with the university, but his wife's brother had been a student there, and was now an instructor in one of the scientific departments. And Mrs. Brent's charm of manner and the Doctor's easy-going hospitality made their fine little Kenwood home the centre of a certain intellectual Bohemia on the borders of the institution, and the "artistic gang" occasionally met and genially interfused with the professors round the big Brent fireplace. Being rich in his own right, Brent took his practice in such moderation as to be of the highest effectiveness when he consented to operate, and was in demand for difficult surgical cases. He was slender, blond, and languid of movement—not in the least suggestive of the Western hustle of Chicago, and yet he was born within twenty miles of the court-house. Indeed, it was the spread of the city which had enriched his father's estate, and which now permitted him to work when he felt like it, and to assemble round his hearthstone—an actual stone, by the way—the people he liked best. The amount of hickory wood he burned was stupendous.

Mrs. Brent was known as "the audacious hostess," because she was not afraid to invite anybody who interested her. "You take your reputation in your hand," her friends often said to those about to make their first call. "You may meet an actor from New York or a stone-mason from the West Side—one never knows." Their house was an adaptation of the "mission style" of California and possessed one big room on the first floor which their friends called Congress Hall.

Miss Franklin was certain that this circle would enjoy the Captain once he became at ease, and she really hoped Mrs. Brent would "advise the girl," and, as she put it, "Help her to get at the pleasant side of Chicago. She's very rich and she's intelligent, but she is very raw! She's very like a boy, but she's worth while. She wanted me to come with her, but I could have done so only by giving up here and going as her companion, and that I'm not ready to do—at present."

After carefully considering all these points, Mrs. Brent 'phoned her friends, being careful to explain that Dorothy Franklin had sent her "some fleecy specimens of Colorado society," and that she was asking a few of "the bold and fearless" among her set to meet them.

"Who are the guests of honor?" she was asked by each favored one.

Each received the same reply: "Marshall Haney, the gambler prince of Cripple Creek, and his bride, Dead-shot Nell, biscuit-shooter, from Honey Gulch."

"Honest?"

"Hope to die!"

"It's too good to be true! Of course I'll come. Do we have a quiet game after dinner?"

"Ah, no, that would be too cruel—to Captain Haney. No; we go to the theatre. So be on hand at 7 p.m., sharp."

In this way she had prepared her friends to be surprised by Bertha's good looks and the Captain's tame and courteous manner, but was herself soundly jarred when her "wild-West people" came up to the door in an auto-car that must have cost five or six thousand dollars, and when a colored footman, in bottle-green uniform, leaped out to open the door for them it was Lucius in his new suit—he was playing all the parts. Brent, with a comical look at his wife, remarked: "I suppose this is in lieu of broncos?"

"They *are* branching out!" she gasped. "And see her clothes!"

She might well exclaim, for Bertha, in her long cloak, her head bare, and her pretty dress showing, did not in the least resemble the picture Miss Franklin had drawn; neither did she resemble the demure, almost sullen girl Mrs. Brent had met in the hotel. The Captain, too, for the second time in his life, wore evening dress, but citing to his sombrero; so that he resembled a Tennessee congressman at the Inaugural Ball as he came slowly up the short walk, and Mrs. Brent deeply regretted that no one was present to take the shock with herself and the doctor.

The maid at the door, who knew nothing of the wild reputation of the Haneys, guided them up-stairs to their respective dressing-rooms, and helped to remove their wraps so expeditiously that they were on their way back to the first floor before any other guests arrived. Bertha was delighted but not awed by the fine room into which they were ushered, for was not her own house larger and more splendid? She had grown accustomed to big things—it was the tasteful beauty of the room that moved her.

In the side of the room a big plain brick fireplace was filled with a crackling fire, and in the light of it stood her host and hostess. Bertha was glad to find them alone—she had expected to face a room full of people. She was not specially attracted to Dr. Brent, and remained so coldly restrained that he was quite baffled and turned away to the Captain, who sought the fire, saying: "This looks good. I feel the cold now—I don't know why I should."

This opened the way to a very confidential talk on wounds and diet.

Bertha's new gown of pale blue made her look very young and very sweet, and the eager guests were sadly disappointed in her—that is to say, the ladies were; the men seemed quite content with her as she was. They took the "biscuit-shooter" description to be a piece of fooling on Mrs. Brent's part, and as they had no time after dinner to get the Captain started they remained quite convinced that he, too, had been maligned in their hostess's description.

As a result, Mrs. Brent and her other guests were forced to do the talking, for Bertha had not only warned Mart against reminiscence, but had determined to keep a tight hold on her own tongue; and though she listened with the alertness of a bird, she answered only in curt phrase, making "yes" and "no" do their full duty. She perceived that the people round her were of intellectual companionship to the Crego and Congdon circles, and these young men, so easy and graceful of manner, reminded her of Ben. None of them were entirely strange to her now, and yet she dimly apprehended something uncomplimentary veiled beneath their polite regard. She did not entirely trust any of them—not even her host. Indeed, she liked Mrs. Brent less than at their first meeting in the hotel.

The dinner was rather hurried, and they would have been late had it not been for Haney's new auto-car, which carried six, and made two trips to the station unnecessary. It was fine to see the Captain put his machine at the disposal of his hostess. "I told Lucius to wait," he boasted, "I thought we might need him."

Dr. Brent succeeded at last in drawing his pretty guest into conversation by remarking on the Captain's color. "He's feeding improperly, if you don't mind my saying so. He's putting on weight, he tells me, but feels cold and nerveless. Cut him down on starchy foods. How long is it since he was hurt?"

"About eight months."

"Must have been a tearing beast of an accident to wing a man of his frame."

"It was. Tore his whole side to pieces."

"Who put him together—Steele, of Denver?"

"No, a man in Cripple."

"Sure he was the right man?"

"He was the best I could get."

"You arouse my professional egotism. I'd like to examine the Captain if you don't object—not for any fee, you understand. But a fellow of his build and years—he tells me he's only forty-five—"

"Only forty-five," thought the girl. "What strange ideas these older people have! And Ben was twenty-six." Just what the doctor said afterwards she didn't hear, for she was thinking of the swift, wide arc of change through which her mind had swung from the time when Marshall Haney first came to Sibley—so grand of stride, so erect, so powerful. He, too, seemed young then; now he was old—old and feeble—a man to be advised, protected, humored. She dimly understood, too, that corresponding change had come to her; that she was far away from the girl who had stood behind the counter defending herself against the love-making of the bummers and drummers among her patrons—and yet she was the same, after all. "I've not changed as much as he has," was her conclusion. And she enjoyed the gayety and beauty of her companions, but she said little to express it.

The play that night appalled her by its fury of passion, its mockery of woman, its cynical disbelief in man. With startling abruptness and in most colloquial method it delineated the beginning of a young wife's wrong-doing, and when the lover caught the innocent, ensnared woman to his bosom a flaming sword seemed to have been plunged into Bertha's own breast. She quivered and flushed. And when the actress displayed the awakened conscience of the erring one, putting into words as well as into facial expression her feeling of guilt and remorse, the girl-wife in the box shrank and whitened, her big eyes fixed upon the sobbing, suffering character before her, defending herself against the dramatist as against an enemy. He was a liar! There was no wrong in Ben's kiss and no remorse in her own heart as she remembered the caress. "Even if he loves me, that doesn't make him horrible!"

The dramatist went remorselessly on. He showed the husband—old, coarse, brutal. He put him in sharpest relief in order that the woman should be tempted to her ruin, and in the end the lover—virile, handsome and unscrupulous—wins the tortured woman's soul—and they flee, leaving the usual note behind.

"What can you expect?" remarked the cynical friend of the injured husband. "Given a young and lovely wife like Rose and an old limping warrior like you, and an elopement follows as a matter of course, Q. E. D." And so the curtain fell.

Relentless realist in the first act, the dramatist in the second act began to hedge. He made the life of the erring woman conventionally miserable. Her lover beat her, neglected her, and finally deserted her. And in the last act she crawled back into her husband's home like a starved cat to die, while he, scarred old beast, cried out: "The wages of sin is death!" Whether the writer intended this scene to be ironical or not, the effect was to awaken a murmur of laughter among the ill-restrained of the auditors. But Bertha, hot with anger towards both author and players, could not join in Mrs. Brent's smiling comment: "Isn't that comical!"

The doctor coolly said: "A good conventional British ending. Why didn't he clap a pair of wings on the old reprobate and run him up on a wire, the way they used to do in translating little Eva in 'Uncle Tom's Cabin'?"

Afterwards Mrs. Brent proposed that they go to a German restaurant and have some beer and skittles; but this struck harshly on Bertha, who still palpitated with the passion of the play. "I reckon we'd better not. The Captain is pretty tired, and, if you don't mind, we'll quit now."

Without saying "I've had a lovely time," she shook hands all round, and, taking her husband's arm, moved off into the street, leaving her hostess a little uneasy and wholly perplexed. Mrs. Brent's joke about the Captain and his wife had, as the doctor expressed it, "queered the whole affair."

"But how did she know?"

"She's a good deal sharper than you gave her credit for being," he replied. "You Easterners never can learn to take diamonds in the rough."

Bertha's mind was in tumult, and she wished to be alone. Mart irritated her. She refused to talk to him about the play or the dinner, and, turning him over to Lucius, went at once to her own bed. Thus far she had not attempted to closely analyze her relationship to Marshall Haney. He had been to her a good friend rather than a husband, a companion who needed her, and who had given her everything she asked for. Keenly forward, almost precocious on the calculative side, she had remained singularly untroubled on the emotional side. She knew that certain problems of sex existed in the world, and she was only mentally aware of temptations—she had never really felt them. Now all at once her whole nature awoke. Her mind engaged a legion of vaguely defined enemies. Out of the shadow stepped words of no weight, of no significance hitherto, encircling her, panoplied with meaning. The half-heard comment of the camp, the dimly perceived gossip of the Springs, the flattering looks of the artists—all helped her to see herself as she was: a handsome young girl, like that on the stage, married to a crippled middle-aged man of evil history.

"But he is good to me," she argued against her new self. "I was poor, and he has made me rich; and all I've done is to nurse him and keep house for him." With this thought came a realization that she had never been a full and complete wife to him. And with a flush of shame and repulsion she added: "And now I never can be. No matter if he were to become as straight, as strong, and as handsome as he was in those days, I cannot love him as a wife should."

Once having admitted this feeling of repulsion, once having clearly perceived the vast distance between herself and her husband, the repulsion deepened, the separating space widened. He seemed ten years older as they met next morning, and his face was heavy and his frame lax. Her pity had not lessened, but it was mixed now with a qualifying emotion which she had not yet acknowledged to be disgust. His skin was waxy white and his jowls drooping. "I'm not at all up to the work," he said, with a return of his humor. "'Tis a killing pace we've struck, Bertie, and the old man must take the flag if you keep it up."

"I don't intend to keep it up," she answered, shortly. "I think we'd better go home." At the word "home" a little thrill went through her. It was so bright and big and desirable, that mansion under the purple peaks.

"No; I must go trail up me old dad, and leave him provided for. Fan doesn't even know his address the more shame to her, but I'll find him. If ye're tired and would rather go home, I'll go on alone."

"Oh no, you mustn't do that!" she exclaimed instantly, feeling the sincerity of his desire to please her. "I'll go, but we mustn't stay long." And she took up the direction of his life again.

The mood of the night had passed away, leaving only a clearer perception of his growing age and helplessness.

"You must let Dr. Brent examine you," she said, a little later. "He don't think your lameness is caused by your wound. He says you're out of condition."

He looked at her with shadowed face and sorrowful eyes. "I'm only a poor old skate, wind-broken and lazy. Ye have the right to cut me loose any time."

"You mustn't talk like that," she said, sharply. "When I want to cut loose I'll let you know."

"I hold ye to that," he answered, with intent look.

CHAPTER XVII

BERTHA BECOMES A PATRON OF ART

Bertha, deeply engrossed in the conceptions called up by this visit, did not feel like calling upon the Mosses, even though they were almost next door. She was troubled, too, with a feeling of helplessness in the use of a pen. She wanted to write to Fordyce, but was afraid to do so, knowing that a letter would disclose her ignorance of polite forms; but this, instead of discouraging her, roused her to a determination to learn. This was the saving clause in her character. She acknowledged shortcomings, but not defeats. Here again she was of the spirit that lifts the self-made man.

The Congdons had been most generous of letters of introduction, and in addition to those to Mrs. Brent and the Mosses, Bertha was in possession of two or three envelopes addressed to people in New York City, presumably artists also, as they bore the names of certain studios. The note to Moss was unaffected and simple in itself, quite innocent of any qualification, but the letter which had privately preceded it was in the true Congdon vein, and Moss, like Mrs. Brent, did not delay his call. His card was in the Haney box when they returned. "Sorry to miss you. Come into my studio at five if you can," he had pencilled on the back.

"Your artistic bunch," Congdon had written, "won't mind meeting one of the most successful and picturesque of our gamblers, Marshall Haney, especially as the walls of his big house are bare and his wife is pretty. They are ripping types, old man; not in the 'best society,' you understand, but I know you'll like 'em. Be as good to 'em as you can without involving anybody. Little Mrs. Haney is a corker. Good start on a self-made career. They're both unsophisticated in a way, and a little real sympathy will drag their secret history to the light. Do a sketch of her for me. She's likely to be famous. Haney is rolling in dough these days— miner—and she's bound for some whooping big thing, I don't know what, but she's like a country boy with a stirring ambition. It wouldn't surprise me to see her on Fifth Avenue one of these days. With these few burning words I commend them into your plastic hands. Don't let Sammy paint her, for God's sake. Oh yes, I worked 'em for a couple of canvases. What do you think. In this buoyant climate we all move. Yours in the velvet."

With such a letter before him Joe Moss awaited his amazing guests with impatience, cautioning the few who were in the secret not to dodge when the Captain reached for his pocket-handkerchief. "And, above all, you are to praise Colorado and condemn the East as a place of residence." Joe prided himself on his *savoir faire* and on his apparel, which had nothing about it to distinguish the sculptor. "In fact," he often said, "there *are* people who say I'm not a sculptor. Be that as it may, I manage by daily care to look like a clerk in a hardware store."

And he did. He customarily wore a suit of pepper and salt, neat and trig, a "bowler hat" as they say in London, a ready-made four-in-hand tie, and a small pearl scarf-pin. "No more fuzzy hair for me, no red tie, no dandruff," he had said on his return from Paris. "Right here we melt into the undistinguishable ocean of the millions, unless we can be distinguished by reason of our sculpture." He always included Julia, his wife, in this way although she never "modelled a lick", for she wrote all his letters, made out all his checks, and took charge of him generally. Some said his success was due to her management. She was a dark-eyed, smiling little woman, exquisite in her dress and brisk in her manner.

Their studio occupied the whole north side of the attic of a big office building in the heart of the city's traffic. "We want to be in the midst of trade, but above it," Moss explained to those who wondered at his choice of location. "Sculpture, as I see it, is a part of architecture. I'm not above modelling a door-knocker if they'll only let me do it my way. Sculpture was a part of life in the old days, and we don't want to make it a thing too 'precious' now. I want to get close to the business men, not to avoid them. I like the roar of trade."

The Haneys, therefore, led by the sagacious Lucius, soon found themselves in the Wisconsin Block, and shooting aloft in a bronze elevator that seemed fired from a cannon "express to the 10th floor", with nothing to suggest art in the men or in the signs about them. On the thirteenth story they alighted, and, walking up one flight of stairs, found themselves at the end of a bright hall, before a door which bore, in simple gold letters, "Jos. Moss, Sculptor." Bertha heard laughter within, and her heart misgave her. It was not easy for her to meet these artist folk. Of business men, miners, railway managers she was unafraid, but these people who joke and bully-rag each other and talk high philosophy one minute and gossip the next, like the Congdons, were "pretty swift" for her. After a moment's pause she said to the Captain, "They can't kill us; here goes!" and knocked gently.

Moss himself opened the door, and his cordial, "How de do, Mrs. Haney," established him in her mind at once as a good fellow. He was quite as direct as Congdon. "I'm glad to see you," he said to the Captain. "Come in." He looked keenly at Lucius, who composedly explained himself. "The Captain is a little lame, and I just came along to see that he got here all right. I'll be back at 5.30."

The door opened into a big room, which was darkened at the windows and lighted by shaded electric globes. It was cool and bare in effect. Around a small table in a far corner a half-dozen people were sitting. Mrs. Moss, who was pouring tea, rose in her place at the tea-urn as her husband approached, and cordially shook hands with her guests. "I'm very glad you came. Please tell me how you'll have your tea," she said.

Bertha was accustomed to take her tea "any old way," and said so, being influenced by Mrs. Moss' candid eyes and merry smile. Haney, with a queer feeling of being on the stage as a character in a play, sank heavily into the chair at his hostess' right hand and said: "I never took tea in my life, but I'm not dodgin' anything you mix."

Joe earnestly protested. "Don't do it, Captain, there's some Scotch down cellar."

Mrs. Moss indicated one or two other dimly seen faces about her and introduced their owners in a most casual manner while she compounded a hot drink for her Western guest.

"How long have you been in our horrible town, Mr. Haney?" she asked, heedful of Joe's warning.

"One day, ma'am."

"You're just 'passing through,' I presume—that's the way all Colorado people do."

Haney smiled. He was getting the drift of her remarks. "'Tis natural, ma'am; for, you see, 'tis a long run and a heavy grade, and hard to side-track on the way."

Bertha, to whom Moss addressed himself, was candidly looking about her—profoundly interested in what she saw. Dim forms in bronze and plaster stood on shelves, brackets, and pedestals, and at the end of the long room a big group of figures writhed as if in mortal combat. It was a work-shop—that was evident even to her—with one small nook devoted to tea and talk.

"Would you like to poke about?" he asked, anticipating her request.

"Yes, I would," she bluntly replied.

"There isn't much to see," he said. "I'm the kind of sculptor who works on order. I believe in the 'art for service' idea, and when I get an order I fill it as well as I can, make it as beautiful as I can, and send it out on its mission. I'd like to model mantel-pieces and andirons, because they are seen and actually influence people's lives. What I started to say was this: my stuff all goes out—my real stuff; my fool failures stay by me—this thing, for instance." He indicated the big clump of nude forms. "I had an 'idea' when I started, but it was too ambitious and too literary. Moreover, it isn't democratic. It don't gibe with the present. I'd be a wild-animal sculptor if I knew enough about them."

It was a profoundly moving experience for this raw mountain-bred girl to stand there beside that colossal group while the man who had modelled it took her into his confidence. There was no affectation in Moss's candor. He had come to a swift conclusion that Congdon had attempted to let him into a trap, for Bertha's reticence and dignity quite reassured him. If she had uttered a single one of the banal compliments with which visitors "kill" artists he would have stopped short; but she didn't, she only looked, and something in her face profoundly interested him. Suddenly she turned and said:

"Tell me what it means."

"It don't mean anything—now. Originally I intended it to mean 'The Conquest of Art by the Spirit of Business,' or something like that. I started it when I was fresh from Paris, and wore a red tie and a pointed beard. I keep it as a record of the folly into which exotic instruction will lead a man. If I were to go at it now I'd turn the whole thing around—I'd make it 'Art Inspiring Business.'"

Bertha did not follow his thought entirely, but she felt herself in the presence of a serious problem and listening to something deep down in the heart of a strong man. Here was another world—not an altogether strange world, for Congdon had also talked to her of his work—but a world so far removed from her own life that it seemed some other planet. "How well he talks," she thought. "Like a book."

"How charming she is," he was thinking. And the alert, aspiring pose of her head made his thumb nervously munch at the bit of clay he had picked up.

They wandered up and down the long room while he showed her tiles for mantel decoration, bronze cats' heads for door-knobs, and curious and lovely figures for lamps and ash-trays. "I take a shy at 'most everything," he explained.

"Do you sell these?" she asked, indicating some designs for electric desk-lamps.

He smiled. "Sometimes—not as often as I'd like to."

"How much are they?"

"Fifty dollars each."

"I'll take them both," she said, and her pulse leaped with the pride of being a patron of art.

"Now see here, Mrs. Haney, I'm not displaying these to you as a salesman—not that I'm so very delicate about offering my things, but I try to wait till a second visit." He really did feel mean about it. "Don't take 'em—wait till to-morrow. They're pretty middling bad anyway. They're supposed to be mountain lions, but as a matter of fact I never saw a mountain lion outside the Zoo."

"They're lions, all right. I want 'em, and I know the Captain will like 'em." She stepped back to call Haney. But finding him surrounded by all of the other callers they had "got him going" telling stories of his wild life in the West, she turned to the sculptor with a smile, saying: "Never mind, *I* know they're what he needs—if he don't." And Moss, recalling Congdon's description of the Haneys' material condition, answered: "Very well, if you insist; but I really feel as though I had played a confidence game on you."

"Can you fix 'em up with lights?" she asked, eager as a child. "I mean right now."

"Certainly." He unscrewed a couple of small bulbs from a near-by bracket, and, putting them into place on the lamps, turned on the current. She laughed out in delight. One of the lions was playing with the stem which supported the light. As if rising from a sleep, he lay upholding the globe on one high-raised paw. The other—a counterpart, or nearly so in pose— had a different expression. The cub was snarling and clutching at the light, as if it were a bird about to escape.

"I had an idea of putting them on the corners of a mantel to light a piece of low relief," he explained, "but I never got at the relief. It ought to be characteristic Western scenery, and I've never seen the West. Shameful, isn't it?"

"I want you to do that mantel for me," she said. "I don't know what you mean by 'low relief,' but I know it would be up to these, and they are *right*!"

"Your trust in me is beautiful, Mrs. Haney, and maybe I'll come out this summer and try to meet it."

"I wish you would," she said, and she meant it. "I'll show you Colorado."

"If you're starting to be a patron of art, Mrs. Haney, don't overlook Congdon; he's a first-class man." He became humorous again. "We're moving swiftly, but I'm going to tell you that he wanted me to make a sketch of you. If you'll be so good as to give me two or three sittings, I'll do something we can send out to him—if you wish."

"What do you mean by a sketch?"

"Something like this." And, leading her before a curious, half-human, veiled object, he began to unwind damp yellow cloths till at last the head of a young woman appeared on a small revolving stand. It was very dainty, very sweet, and smiling.

Bertha was puzzled. "It ain't your wife, and yet it looks like her."

"It is my wife's sister—a quick study from life—just the kind of thing Frank wants. Will you sit for me A couple of mornings will answer." He was eager to do her now. Her profile, so clear, so firm, so strangely boyish, pleased him. He could feel the "snap" that the sketch would have when it was done.

Bertha considered. She owed a great deal to the Congdons, and she liked this man. Her homesickness at the moment was abated, and to stay two, or even three, days in Chicago promised at the moment to be not so dreadful, after all.

"Yes, I'll do it," she decided. "I don't know what Mr. Congdon will do with a picture of me, but that's his funeral." And her laughing lip made her seem again the untaught girl she really was.

As they went back to the group around the Captain, Julia Moss treated her husband to a glance of commiseration, thinking him a bored and defeated man. "You've missed the Captain's racy talk," she whispered.

Haney was enjoying himself very well in the "centre of the stage," and doing himself credit. Never in his life had he known a keener audience than these artists, who studied him from every point of view.

"Yes," Haney was saying, "'tis possible to bust a bank if the game is straight—that is, at faro; but most machine games are built so that 'the house'—that is, the bank—is protected. My machines was always straight. I'd as soon turn a sausage-grinder as run a wheel that was 'fixed' in me favor."

Bertha did not like this talk of his abandoned trade, and her cheeks burned as she put her hand on his shoulder. "I reckon we'd better be going."

He recovered himself. "Of course I quit all that when I married," he explained, and dutifully rose.

"Oh, Mrs. Haney," pleaded Mrs. Moss, "don't take him away! We were just getting light on the game of faro. Please sit down again."

Bertha resented this tone. "No, we've got to go. Glad to have met you." She nodded towards the men who had risen. "Much obliged," she said again to Moss. "I'll send for them things to-morrow."

Mrs. Moss cordially insisted on their coming again.

"She's going to pose for me," reported Moss. "To-morrow morning at ten?" he inquired.

"Ten suits me as well as any time," Bertha replied.

Mrs. Moss beamed at Haney. "You come, too, Captain. I want to know more about those delightful games of chance."

Bertha went back to her hotel with throbbing brain. The day had been so full of experience! She was tired out and fairly bewildered by it all.

As her excitement ebbed and she had time to recover her own point of view, Colorado, her home, the Springs, and the memory of her own people came rushing back upon her, making the city and all it contained but a handful of east wind. Ben's kiss burned vividly again upon her lips. "Was it wrong of him to say what he did?" she began to ask herself. A good-bye kiss would not have so deeply stirred her; it was his face, his voice, his intensely uttered words which deeply thrilled her, even now, as she recalled them one by one. "You are beautiful and I love you." These were the most important words to a woman, and they had come at last to her.

Then her cheek flushed with shame of her husband as she remembered his gambling talk at the studio. "Why *must* he always go back to that?" she asked, hotly.

They ate their dinner in the big dining-room surrounded by waiters, while the Captain discussed his sister and her family. "I'll do something for Fan," he said. "She's a different sort from Charles. McArdle seems a hard-workin' chap, the kind that a little help wouldn't spile. What do you think of buyin' them a bit of a house somewhere?"

Bertha listened with a languor of interest new to her, and when he repeated his question and asked her if she were tired, she answered: "Yes; and I think I'll go to bed early to-night. It's been a hard day."

CHAPTER XVIII

BERTHA'S PORTRAIT IS DISCUSSED

Joe Moss was delighted with the Haneys, for they talked of their native West as people should talk. They were as absolute in their convictions as a Kentuckian. For them there was no other "God's country," and as it was his latest dream to go West and "do a big thing on a cliff or something" he put off every other engagement to enjoy their racy speech. He said at the first sitting: "I've had an idea of working the Thorwaldsen trick: find some fine site out there, some wall of rock close to the railway, and hew out a monster grizzly or mountain lion. The railway could then advertise it, you see; trains could stop there 'five minutes to permit a view of Moss's Lion'; they could use a cut of it on all their folders. If there was a spring near by they could advertise the water and bottle it, a picture of my lion on the label. Ah, it is a fine scheme!"

"'Tis so," said Haney. "I wonder nobody thought of it before."

"It takes a Yankee, after all, to plan new suspender buttons," the sculptor replied. And all the time he talked his hands were dabbling, his thumbs gouging, his dibble cutting and smoothing.

Haney watched him with amused glance. "Sure, I didn't know ye went at it so. I thought ye chipped each picture out o' stone." And when the process of molding in plaster was explained to him, he said: "'Tis like McArdle's trade entirely. He takes a rise in the world since I know he's an artist like yourself."

"What is his 'line'?"

"Pattern-maker for a stove foundry."

Moss beamed. "Just what I'd like to be if they'd only pay a little more wages and furnish a better place to work."

Bertha never knew when he was in earnest, so habitually mocking was his tone. But she grew towards a perception of his ideal, and dimly apprehended in him a mind far beyond any she had ever known. Mrs. Moss, almost as reticent as Mrs. Haney herself, came and went about the studio brightly, briskly, keeping vigilant eye on her husband's mail, moistening his "mud ladies," and defending him from inopportune callers, insistent beggars, and wandering models. Bertha, though sitting with the stolid patience of a Mississippi clam-fisher, was thinking at express speed. Her mind was of that highly developed type where a hint sets in motion a score of related cognitions, and a word here and there in Moss's rambling remarks instructed her like a flash of light. She was at school, in a high sense, and improving her time. The sketch was expanding into a carefully studied portrait bust and Moss was happy.

One day a fellow-artist came in casually, and they both squinted, measured, and compared the portrait and herself with the calm absorption of a couple of prize-pig committeemen at a cattle-show. "You see, this line is shorter," the stranger said, almost laying his finger on Bertha's neck. "Not so straight, as you've got it. That's a fine line—"

"I know it is!"

"And you don't want to spoil it. I don't like your fad for cutting down the bust. The neck is nothing but a connecting link between the head and the bust. Now here you have a charming and youthful head and face—let the neck at least suggest the woman below."

"Oh yes, that's good logic, provided you're after that. But what I want here is spring-time—just a fresh, alert, lovely fragment. This pure line must be kept free from any earthiness."

"I suppose you know what you want; I won't say you don't. But if I were painting her, I'd get that sweeping line there that ends by suggesting the summer."

They talked disjointedly, elliptically, and of course mainly of the clay; and yet Bertha grew each moment more clearly aware that they considered her not merely interesting but beautiful, and this was a most momentous and developing assurance. She had hoped to be called "good-looking," but no one thus far excepting Ben Fordyce had ever called her beautiful; and these judgments on the part of Joe Moss and his brother artist were made the more moving by reason of their precision of knowledge and their professional candor. They spoke as freely in discussion of her charm as if she were deaf and dumb.

The painter, who had been introduced in a careless way as "Mr. Humiston, of New York," turned to Bertha at last, and, assuming the ordinary politeness of a human being, said: "I'd like to make a study of you, too, Mrs. Haney, if you'll permit. I can bring my canvas in here and work with Joe, so that it needn't be any trouble to you."

Bertha, her wealth still new upon her, had no suspicion of the motives of those who addressed her, was deeply flattered by this request, and as Moss made no objection, she consented.

The only thing that troubled Moss was her growing tendency to lapse into troubled thought. "Remember, now, you're the crocus, the first violet, or something like that—not the last rose of summer. Don't think, don't droop! There, that's right! What have you to think or droop about? When you're as old and blasé as Humiston there, you'll have a right to ponder the mysteries, but not now. You and I are young, thank God!"

Humiston was dabbling at his small canvas swiftly, lightly, as unmoved by his fellow-artist as if his voice were the wind in the casement. He was a tall, sickly looking man with grizzled hair, and pale, deeply lined face. He was fresh from Paris with a small exhibition of his pictures, which were very advanced, as Mrs. Moss privately explained to Bertha. "And he's rather bitter against Americans because they don't appreciate his work. But Joe asks: 'Why should they?' They're undemocratic—little high-keyed 'precious' bits; pictures for other artists, not real paintings, or they are unacceptable otherwise. He's a wonderful technician, though, and he'll make an exquisite sketch of you."

The Western girl-wife was completely fascinated by this small, dusky, dim, and richly colored heart of the fierce and terrible city whose material bulk alone is known to the world. To go from the crash and roar of the savage streets into this studio was like climbing from the level of the water in the Black Cañon to the sunlit, grassy peaks where the Indian pink blossoms in silence. She was of the aspiring nature. She had commonly played with children older than herself. She had read books she could not understand. She had always reached upward, and here she found herself surrounded by men and women who excited her imagination as Congdon had done. They helped her forget the doubt of herself and her future, which was gnawing almost ceaselessly in her brain, and she was sorry when Moss said to her:

"Come in once more, to-morrow, and see me do the real sculptor's act. No, don't look at it" he flung a cloth over his work; "you may look at it to-morrow."

"May I see my picture?" she asked of Humiston.

He turned the easel towards her without a word.

"Good work!" cried Moss.

Mrs. Moss came from her dark corner. "I knew you'd do something exquisite."

Bertha looked at it in silence. It was as lovely in color as a flower, a dream-girl, not Bertha Haney. And at last she said: "It's fine, but it isn't me."

Humiston broke forth almost violently. "Of course it isn't you; it's the way you look to me. I never paint people as they look to themselves nor to their friends. I am painting my impression of you."

"Do you really see me like that?" she both asked and exclaimed. And at the moment she was more moving than she had ever been before, and Humiston, in a voice of anguish, cried:

"My God, why didn't I do her like that?" And he fell to coughing so violently that Bertha shuddered.

Moss defended himself. "I couldn't do her in *all* her fine poses," he complained. "I had to select. Why didn't you do her that way yourself?"

The painter put his short-hand sketch away with a sigh. "If you venture as far as New York, I hope you and the Captain will visit my studio," he said.

With no suspicion of being passed from hand to hand, she promised to send him her address, and said: "I'd like to see the pictures you have here."

Moss became abusive. "Now see here, Jerry, I can't let you take Mrs. Haney to that show of yours. I'll go myself to point out their weak points."

"I know their weak points a bloody sight better than you do," answered Humiston, readily.

"If you do you don't speak of 'em."

"Why should I? You don't call out the defects of your 'hardware,' do you?"

Mrs. Moss interposed. "That's just what he does do, and it hurts trade. I think I'll take Mrs. Haney over to see the pictures myself."

Humiston brightened. "Very well; but you must all lunch with me. You're about the only civilized people I know in this crazy town, and I need you."

"No," said Bertha. "It's our treat. You all come over and eat with us."

Haney, who had been keeping in the background, now came forward. "I second that motion," he heartily said. "We don't get a chance every day to feed a bunch of artists."

"You can have that pleasure any day here," said Moss. "Our noses are always over the bars, waiting."

When she emerged from the gallery an hour later Bertha enjoyed an exalted sense of having been carried through some upper, serener world, where business, politics, and fashion had little place. It was "only a dip," as Mrs. Moss said—just to show the way; but it set the girl's brain astir with half-formed, disconnected aspirations. Only as she re-entered the hotel the centre of obsequious servants did she become again the wife of Marshall Haney, and Mrs. Moss, noting the eager attention of the waiters, was amazed and delighted at the look of calm command which came over the girl's face.

"Art is fine and sweet as a side issue," said Julia to her husband, as they were going in, "but money makes the porters jump."

Bertha, composed and serious, seated her guests at a table which had been reserved for her near a window and charmingly decorated with flowers. She put Moss at her left hand and Humiston at her right, and as the Eastern man settled into place, he said: "Really, now, this isn't so bad." His experienced eye had noted the swift flocking of the waiters, and with cynical amusement he commented upon it. "These people must *smell* of money!" and in his heart acknowledged that he and Moss were not so very different from the servitors, after all. "They're out for tens, we're after thousands; that's the main point of difference."

Bertha, once the cutlets were served, was able to give attention to the talk—Humiston's talk he was celebrated as a monologist, for he had resumed the discussion into which he and Moss had fallen. "I don't believe in helping people to study art. I don't believe in charity. This interfering with the laws of the universe that kill off the crippled and the weakly is pure sentimentalism that will fill the world with deformed, diseased, and incapable persons."

"You're a vile reactionary!" cried Moss.

"I am not—I'm for the future. I want to see the world full of beauty."

"Physical beauty?"

"Yes, physical beauty. I want to see vice and crime and crooked limbs and low brows die out—not perpetuated. I believe in educating the people to the lovely in line and color."

As he pursued this line of inexorable argument Bertha looked at him in wonder. Did he mean what he said? His burning eyes seemed sincere—and yet he did not fail to accept a second helping of the mushrooms. There was power in the man. He pushed the walls of her intellectual world very wide apart. He came from a strange, chaotic region—from a land where ordinary modes and motives seemed lost or perverted. He took a delight in shocking them all. Morality was a convention—a hypocritic agreement on the part of the few to reserve freedom to themselves at the expense of the many. "Art is impossible to little people, to those who starve the big side of their nature, for fear of Mrs. Grundy. Look at the real people— Rachel, Wagner, Turner, Bernhardt, and a thousand others. Were they bound by the marriage laws? What will these crowds of tiny men and petty women do who come from the country parlors and corn-shocks of the West? They will puddle around a little while, paint and muddle a few petty things, then marry and go back to the ironing-board and the furrow where they belong. What's the matter with American art? It's too cursed normal, that's what. It's too neat and sweet and restrained—no license, no "go" to it. What's the matter with you, to be personal?"

"Too well balanced."

"Precisely. You *talk* like a man of power, but model like a cursed niggling prude. You're bitten with the new madness. You're the Bryan of art. 'The dear people' is your cry. Damn the people! They don't know a good thing when they see it. Why consider the millions? Consider the few, those who have the taste and the dollars. That's the way all the big men of the past had to do. Look at Rubens and Michael Angelo and Titian—all the big bunch; they were all frank, gross feeders, lovers of beauty, defiant of conventions."

He had forgotten where he sat, but he was not neglecting his hostess. He took a satanic satisfaction in seeing her lovely eyes widen and glow as he went on. Subtly flattering her by including her among the very few who could understand his ideals, he seemed to draw her apart to his side—appealing to her for support against the coarse and foolish hosts represented by the Mosses, while Marshall Haney sat in a kind of stupor, his eyes alone speaking, as if to ask: "What the divil is the little man with the cough so hot about?"

Moss, accustomed to Humiston's savage diatribes, roared out objections or laughed him to scorn, while Mrs. Moss tried her best to turn the mad artist's mind upon more suitable subjects. He had been deeply hurt and financially distressed by the failure of his exhibits in Pittsburg and Chicago, and was now taking it out on his friends. His passion, his bitter, vengeful cry against the ignorant masses of the world was something Bertha had read about, but never felt; but she quivered now with the half-disclosed fury of the disappointed austere soul.

Could it be possible that this savage man, so worn and ill, had painted those dim, vague pictures of flower-like girls whose limbs were involved in blossoming vines?

He concluded at last: "The only place in the world to-day for an artist is Paris. In no other city can he live his own life in frank fulness, and find patrons who see the subtlest meaning of a line."

Bertha was tired of all this—mentally weary and confused; and she felt very grateful to Mrs. Moss, who came to the rescue the moment Humiston paused.

"There, Mrs. Haney, that is the end of Professor Jerry Spoopendyke's lecture on the undesirability of America as a place of residence—*for him*. Of course, he don't mind selling his pictures just to enlighten our night of ignorance, but as for going to Sunday-school or keeping the decalogue, that's our job."

Humiston had the grace to smile. "I beg your pardon, Mrs. Haney, I have been a fool. But that monkey over there—Joe Moss—provoked me with his accursed heresies about the democracy of art. Art has no democracy, and democracy will never have an art—"

"There, there!" warned Moss, "you said all that before."

The painter wrenched himself away and turned to Bertha. "You *are* coming to New York, Mrs. Haney?"

"I don't know," she said. "We may."

"If you do, don't fail to let me know. I would like to see you."

"All right," said Bertha, "I'll send you a line." And her frank smile made him sorry to say good-bye even for the day.

As Mart was going up the elevator he sighed and said: "It takes all kinds of people to make up a world—Mr. Hummockstone is wan of the t'others. He has a grouch agin the universe. Sure but he's been housin' a gnawin' serpent. How 'twill all end I dunno."

When alone in her room, Bertha's mind again reverted to Ben Fordyce. As she compared him with Humiston, he seemed handsomer and more boyishly frank than ever. What did Joe Moss mean by calling Mr. Humiston "blasé." She had seen that word in novels and it always meant something wicked. How could this weary, sick man be wicked? She pitied him and wished to help him. "Why should he take so much interest in me? He don't have to. Of course the Mosses are nice to me on Congdon's account, but why does this great artist want me to come to his studio in New York? He talks poor, so maybe he wants me to buy some of his pictures." That her money was a lure for wasps she did not yet realize. That the waiters and clerks buzzed round her because she was rich, she knew; but that these men, who talked of beauty and the higher life, could flatter her with attentions with a base motive was incredible.

She was shrewd as her Yankee forbears, but she was also an idealist, and these artist folk now seemed to her the highest types she had ever known or was likely to know. She felt the mystery and the power in Humiston's personality, and his bitter and rebellious, almost blasphemous, words were counterpoised by his paintings, which she acknowledged to be beautiful—too beautiful for her to comprehend. He looked like a man of sorrow and weary of battle, and she longed to know more about him. When he was not fierce he was melancholy; evidently his life had been a failure. "Why shouldn't I buy some of his pictures?" she asked herself.

Hitherto the answer to any such question had been, "Can we afford it?" but now another and deeper query came in answer, like an echo: "Is it right to spend Mart Haney's money? I am only his trained nurse, not his wife," and she now knew that she could not be his wife. She shrank from the weight of his hand, and each day made clearer the wide spaces of years, of family, of ideals, which lay between them. The kiss Ben Fordyce had pressed upon her lips had brought this revelation. But of this she was not yet aware; she was only conscious of a growing dread of the future. Her duties as his nurse were lightening. Lucius, indeed, now took many of her tasks upon himself, and she no longer helped him with his shoes or coat, and, what was still more significant, she could not calmly think of going back to these wifely services.

She dwelt treacherously on Haney's own admission: that she had been in a sense entrapped. He had believed himself a dying man at the time, and she had been too excited, too exalted by the lurid romance of the scene to be clear about anything save the wish and the will to save him; and now she knew that at bottom of all her willingness to serve him lay the consciousness that he was on his death-bed. Afterwards he had been to her only a big-hearted, generous friend, in need of love and companionship. This understanding had made it easy for her to prepare his meals, to help him, as a nurse would help him, to dress and undress. She had lost all of the fear and much of the admiration in which she used to greet him as he swung into the office of her little hotel. He had become to her an invalid, a child to be jollied and humored, and yet respected; for no one could have been kinder or more scrupulously just than he. And it was the recollection of all his acts of self-sacrifice and loving patience which gave her assurance that he would never require obedience, though he might sue for it.

Her danger lay in herself. "If he *does* ask me to be his real wife—then I must either agree or leave. It won't be right for me to take all these benefits unless—"

And with this thought, the big house in the Springs, the sleek horses, their shining carriages, the auto-car, her dresses, the service of the big hotel, and the consideration her husband's money gave to her, all assumed a new and corrupting lustre. She was growing accustomed to luxury and the thought of giving it up made her shiver like one who faces a plunge into a dark night and an icy river. Besides, her sacrifice would involve others. Her mother, her brother, were already roundly ensnared in Mart's bounty.

Her head was aching with it all, when a comforting thought came to her. It was not necessary to decide it at that moment, and with a sigh of relief she threw it aside and sat down to write a letter to her mother.

"I ought to have written before, but I've been jumped right into the middle of things here. The letters Frank Congdon gave me took me into an artistic bunch about as gay and queer as Frank is, but they've been mighty nice to me. I've been setting for my bust to Mr. Moss, who is a sculptor. He has a big studio clear on the top of one of the tallest blocks here and has some dandy lamps and things. I've bought some to bring back. I met a Mr. Humiston there from New York, and he made a sketch of me—wants me to see his studio in New York. I don't know whether I'll go on or let Mart go with Lucius. Lucius is all right—I don't see how I got on without him. He knows everything. I wish I had half the education he's got. He's up on all the society ways and puts me on. For instance, he told me the nice thing would be to give a dinner to this artist push and to the people that Dorothy give me a letter to, and I'm going to do it. Lucius will look out for the whole thing. You should see the way the waiters tend. I reckon Lucius has told 'em we're made of money. I'm afraid we're getting spoilt, Muzz. It would be pretty tough to go back to the hotel now, wouldn't it?

"We went to see Mart's sister, Fanny. Her house was a sight. It was clean enough, but littered—well, litter is no name for it—but she's a good old thing and so is McArdle. He sat and looked at us the whole time like a turkey blind in one eye—never said a word the whole time but 'pass the p-taties.' I liked him though. He's a kind of sculptor, too—makes patterns for all these little acorns and leaves and do-funnies on stoves. They've got forty-'leven children and need help and I'm perfectly willing Mart should help 'em. We're looking up houses now. He's going to buy a place for 'em on the west side. Wednesday night I went to see the Doctor Brents, Dorothy's friends. They had a dinner—very nice, but they all kind o' sat 'round and waited for us to perform. I guess they thought we were mountain lions. But they didn't make much out o' me. They was one chap there with goggles who looked at Mart like an undertaker. He's a scientific doctor—one of these fellers that invent new ways of doing things. His name is Halliday. I liked Dr. Brent pretty well—but Mrs. Brent only so-so. The doctor wants to 'dagnose' Mart's case—says it won't cost a cent. We all went to a show at night and the Captain was just about petered to a point. He's better though. The lower altitude helps his circulation. I guess his heart *is* affected. He's afraid now he won't ever be able to go back to the mines. He wants to slide on to New York and see his father and wants me to go—but I'd rather come home—I'm homesick for the hills. They're nice to me here—but I want to see the old Peak once more. Tell" here she wrote "Ben" and blotted it "tell Mr. Fordyce that we're all right and to keep us posted every day. We see by the papers that the mine-owners are going to throw the unions out of business. If they try that they'll be war again. We'll be home soon—or at least I will. I'm getting home-sicker every minute as I write."

She added a postscript. "Don't show my letters to *any one*. I wish I'd 'a' had a little more schooling."

CHAPTER XIX

THE FARTHER EAST

Haney visibly brightened as the days went by, and took long rides in his auto, sometimes with Bertha, sometimes alone with Lucius, and now and then with some old acquaintance, who, having seen his name in the paper, ventured to call. They were not very savory characters, to tell the truth, and he did not always introduce them to Bertha, but as his health improved he called upon a few of the more reputable of them, billiard-table agents, and the like of that, and to these proudly exhibited his wife.

Bertha had hitherto accepted this with boyish tolerance, but now it irritated her. Some of these visitors presumed on her husband's past and treated her with a certain freedom of tone and looseness of tongue which made plain even to her unsuspecting nature that they put no high value on her virtue—in fact, one fellow went so far as to facetiously ask, "Where did Mart find you? Are there any more out there?" And she felt the insult, though she did not know how to resent it.

Haney, so astute in many things, saw nothing out of the way in this off-hand treatment of his wife. He would have killed the man who dared to touch her, and yet he stood smilingly by while some chance acquaintance treated her as if she had been picked out of a Denver gutter. This threw Bertha upon her own defence, and at last she made even impudence humble itself. She carried herself like a young warrior, sure of her power and quick of defence.

She refused to invite her husband's friends to lunch, and the first real argument she had thus far held with him came about in this way. She said, "Yes, you can ask Mr. Black or Mr. Brown to dinner, but I won't set at the same table with them."

"Why not?" he asked.

"Because they're not the kind of men I want to eat with," she bluntly replied. "They're just a little too coarse for me."

"They're good business men and have fine homes—"

"Do they invite you to their homes?"

"They do not," he admitted, "but they may—after our dinner."

"Lucius says it's their business to lead out—and he knows. I don't mind your lunching these dubs every day if you want to, but I keep clear of 'em. I tell you those!"

And so it fell out that while she was going about with the Mosses and their kind, Mart was explaining to Black and Brown that his wife "was a little shy." "You see she grew up in the hills like a doe antelope, and it's hard for her to get wonted to the noise of a great city," he laboriously set forth, but at heart he did not blame her. He was coming to find them a little "coarse" himself.

Humiston was deeply enthralled by Bertha's odd speech, her beauty, her calm use of money, and lingered on day by day, spending nearly all his time at Moss's studio or at the hotel, seeking Mrs. Haney's company. He had never met her like, and confessed as much to Moss, who jocularly retorted: "That's saying a good deal—for you've seen quite a few."

Humiston ignored this thrust. "She has beauty, imagination, and immense possibilities. She don't know herself. When she wakes up to her power, then look out! She can't go on long with this old, worn-out gambler."

"Oh, Haney isn't such a beast as you make him out. Bertha told me he had never crossed her will. He's really very kind and generous."

"That may be true, and yet he's a mill-stone about her neck. It's a shame—a waste of beauty—for the girl is a beauty."

It was with a sense of relief that Moss heard Bertha say to his wife: "I guess I've had enough of this. It's me to the high ground to-morrow."

"Aren't you going on to the metropolis?"

"I don't think it. I'm hungry for the peaks—and, besides, our horses need exercise. I think I'll pull out for the West to-morrow and leave the Captain and Lucius to go East together. I don't believe I need New York."

To this arrangement Haney reluctantly consented. "You're missin' a whole lot, Bertie. I don't feel right in goin' on to Babylon without ye. I reckon you'd better reconsider the motion. However, I'll not be gone long, and if I find the old Dad hearty I may bring him home with me. He's liable to be livin' with John Donahue. Charles said he was a shiffless whelp, and there's no telling how he's treating the old man. Anyhow, I'll let you know."

She relented a little. "Ma'be I ought to go. I hate to see you starting off alone."

"Sure now! don't ye worry, darling. Lucius is handy as a bootjack, and we'll get along fine. Besides, I may come back immegitly, for them mine-owners are cooking a hell-broth for us all. Havin' a governor on their side now, they must set out to show their power."

Ben kept them supplied with home papers, and as Bertha took up one of these journals she found herself played upon by familiar forms and faces. The very names of the streets were an appeal. She saw herself sporting with her hounds, riding with Fordyce over the flowery Mesa, or facing him in his sun-bright office discussing the world's events and deciding upon their own policies and expenditures. She grew very homesick as these pleasant, familiar pictures freshened in her vision, and her faith in Ben's honesty and essential goodness came back to her. Moreover her mind was not at rest regarding Haney; much as she longed to go home, she felt it her duty to remain with him, and as she lay in her bed she thought of him with much the same pity a daughter feels for a disabled father. "He's given me a whole lot—I ought to stay by him."

She admitted also a flutter of fear at thought of meeting Ben Fordyce alone, and this unformulated distrust of herself decided her at last to go on with Mart and to have him for shield and armor when she returned to the Springs.

There are certain ways in which books instruct women—and men, too, for that matter—but there are other and more vital processes in which only experience individual or inherited teaches. In her desultory reading, little Mrs. Haney, like every other citizen, had taken imaginative part in many murders, seductions, and marital infidelities; and yet the motives for such deeds had never before seemed human. Now the dark places in the divorce trials, the obscure charges in the testimony of deserted wives, were suddenly illumined. She realized how easy it would be to make trouble between Mart and herself. She understood the stain those strangers in the car could put upon her, and she trembled at the mere thought of Mart's inquiring eyes when he should know of it. Why should he know of it? It was all over and done with. There was only one thing to do—forget it.

Surely life was growing complex. With bewildering swiftness the experiences of a woman of the world were advancing upon her, and she, with no brother or father to be her guard, or friend to give her character, with a husband whose very name and face were injuries, was finding men in the centres of culture quite as predatory as among the hills, where Mart Haney's fame still made his glance a warning. These few weeks in Chicago had added a year to her development, but she dared not face Ben Fordyce alone—not just yet—not till her mind had cleared.

In the midst of her doubt of herself and of him a message came which made all other news of no account. He was on his way to Chicago to consult Mart so the words ran, but in her soul she knew he was coming to see her. Was it to test her? Had he taken silence for consent? Was he about to try her faith in him and her loyalty to her husband?

His telegram read: "Coming on important business." That might mean concerning the mine— on the surface; but beneath ran something more vital to them both than any mine or labor war, something which developed in the girl both fear and wonder—fear of the power that came from his eyes, wonder of the world his love had already opened to her. What was the meaning of this mad, sweet riot of the blood—this forgetfulness of all the rest of the world— this longing which was both pleasure and pain, doubt and delight, which turned her face to the West as though through a long, shining vista she saw love's messenger speeding towards her?

Sleep kept afar, and she lay restlessly turning till long after midnight, and when she slept she dreamed, not of him, but of Sibley and her mother and the toil-filled, untroubled days of her girlhood. She rose early next morning and awaited his coming with more of physical weakness as well as of uncertainty of mind than she had ever known before.

Haney was also up and about, an hour ahead of his schedule, sure that Ben's business concerned the mine. "It's the labor war breaking out again," he repeated. "I feel it in my bones. If it is, back I go, for the boys will be nading me."

They went to the station in their auto-car, but, at Bertha's suggestion, Mart sent Lucius in to meet their attorney and to direct him where to find them. The young wife had a feeling that to await him at the gate might give him a false notion of her purpose. She grew faint and her throat contracted as if a strong hand clutched it as she saw his tall form advancing, but almost instantly his frank and eager face, his clear glance, his simple and cordial greeting disarmed her, transmuted her half-shaped doubts into golden faith. He was true and good—of that she was completely reassured. Her spirits soared, and the glow came back to her cheek.

Fordyce, looking up at her, was filled with astonishment at the picture of grace and ease which she presented, as she leaned to take his hand. She shone, unmistakable mistress of the car, while Haney filled the rôle of trusted Irish coachman.

As he climbed in, the young lawyer remarked merrily, "I don't know whether I approve of this extravagance or not." He tapped the car door.

"It's mighty handy for the Captain," she replied. "You see he can't get round in the street-cars very well, and he says this is cheaper than cabs in the long run."

"It has never proved economical to me; but it *is* handy," he answered, with admiration of her growing mastery of wealth.

And so with something fiercely beating in their hearts these youthful warriors struggled to be true to others—fighting against themselves as against domestic traitors, while they talked of the mine, the state judiciary, the operators, and the unions. Their words were impersonal, prosaic of association, but their eyes spoke of love as the diamond speaks of light. Ben's voice, carefully controlled, was vibrant with the poetry that comes but once in the life of a man, and she listened in that perfect content which makes gold and glory but the decorations of the palace where adoration dwells.

The great, smoky, thunderous city somehow added to the sweetness of the meeting—made it the more precious, like a song in a tempest. It seemed to Ben Fordyce as if he had never really lived before. The very need of concealment gave his unspoken passion a singular quality—a tang of the wilding, the danger-some, which his intimacy with Alice had never possessed.

The Haneys' suite of rooms at the hotel called for comment. "Surely Haney is feeling the power of money—but why not; who has a better right to lovely things than Bertha?" Then aloud he repeated: "How well you're looking—both of you! City life agrees with you. I never saw you look so well."

This remark, innocent on its surface, brought self-consciousness to Bertha, for the light of his glance expressed more than admiration; and even as they stood facing each other, alive to the same disturbing flush, Lucius called Haney from the room, leaving them alone together. The moment of Ben's trial had come.

For a few seconds the young wife waited in breathless silence for him to speak, a sense of her own wordlessness lying like a weight upon her. Into the cloud of her confusion his voice came bringing confidence and calm. "I feel that you have forgiven me—your eyes seem to say so. I couldn't blame you if you despised me. I won't say my feeling has changed, for it hasn't. It may be wrong to say so—it is wrong, but I can't help it. Please tell me that you forgive me. I will be happier if you do, and I will never offend again." His accent was at once softly pleading and manly, and, as she raised her eyes to his in restored self-confidence, she murmured a quaint, short, reassuring phrase: "Oh, that's all right!" Her glance, so shy, so appealing, united to the half-humorous words of her reply, were so surely of the Mountain-West that Ben was quite swept from the high ground of his resolution, and his hands leaped towards her with an almost irresistible embracing impulse. "You sweet girl!" he exclaimed.

"Don't!" she said, starting back in alarm—"don't!"

His face changed instantly, the clear candor of his voice reassured her. "Don't be afraid. I mean what I said. You need have no fear that I—that my offence will be repeated;" then, with intent to demonstrate his self-command, he abruptly changed the subject. "The Congdons sent their love to you, and Miss Franklin commissioned me to tell you that she will give you all her time next summer—if you wish her to do so."

She was glad of this message and added: "I need her, sure thing. Every day I spend here makes me seem like Mary Ann—I don't see how people can talk as smooth as they do. I'm crazy to get to school again and make up for lost time. Joe Moss makes me feel like a lead quarter. Being here with all these nice people and not able to talk with them is no fun. Couldn't I whirl in and go to school somewhere back here?"

"Oh no, that isn't necessary. You are getting your education by association—you are improving very fast."

Her face lighted up. "Am I? Do you mean it?"

"I do mean it. No one would know—to see you here—that you had not enjoyed all the advantages."

"Oh yes, but I'm such a bluff. When I open my mouth they all begin to grin. They're onto my game all right."

He smiled. "That's because of your picturesque phrases—they like to hear you speak. I assure you no one would think of calling you awkward or—or lacking in—in charm."

Haney's return cut short this defensive dialogue, and with a sense of relief Bertha retreated—almost fled to her room—leaving the two men to discuss their business.

At the moment she had no wish to participate in a labor controversy. She was entirely the woman at last, roused to the overpowering value of her own inheritance. Her desire to manage, to calculate, to plan her husband's affairs was gone, and in its place was a willingness to submit, a wish for protection which she had not hitherto acknowledged. She brooded for a time on Ben's words, then hurriedly began to dress—with illogical desire to make herself beautiful in his eyes. As she re-entered the room she caught Haney's repeated declaration—"I will be loyal to the men"—and Ben's reply.

"Very well, I'll go back and do the best I can to keep them in line, but Williams says the governor is entirely on the side of the mine-operators."

"Does he?" retorted Haney. "Well, you say to the governor that Mart Haney was a gambler and saloon-keeper during the other 'war,' and now that he's a mine-owner, with money to hire a regiment of deppyties, his heart is with the red-neckers—just where it was. Owning a paying mine has not changed me heart to a stone."

Ben, as well as Bertha, understood the pride he took in not whiffling with the shift of wind, but at the same time he considered it a foolish kind of loyalty. "Very well, I'll take the six-o'clock train to-night in order to be on hand."

"What's the rush?" said Haney; "stay on a day or two and see the town with us—'tis a great show."

Bertha, re-entering at this moment in her shining gown, put the young attorney's Spartan resolution to rout. He stammered: "I ought to be on the ground before the mine-owners begin to open fire, and, besides—Alice is not very well."

At the mention of Alice's name Bertha's glance wavered and her eyelids fell. She did not urge him to stay, and Haney spoke up, heartily: "I'm sorry to hear she's not well. She was pretty as a rose the night of the dinner."

"She lives on her nerves," Ben replied, falling into sadness. "One day she's up in the clouds and dancing, the next she's flat in her bed in a darkened room unwilling to see anybody."

"'Tis the way of the White Death," thought Haney, but he spoke hopefully: "Well, spring is here and a long summer before her—she'll be herself against October."

"I trust so," said Ben, but Bertha could see that he was losing hope and that his life was being darkened by the presence of the death angel.

Haney changed the current of all their thinking by saying to Bertha: "If you are minded to go home, now is your chance, acushla. You can return with Mr. Fordyce, while Lucius and I go on to New York the morning."

"No, no!" she cried out in a panic. "No, I am going with you—I want to see New York myself," she added, in justification. The thought of the long journey with Ben Fordyce filled her with a kind of terror, a feeling she had never known before. She needed protection against herself.

"Very well," said Haney, "that's settled. Now let's show Mr. Fordyce the town."

Ben put aside his doubt and went forth with them, resolute to make a merry day of it. He seemed to regain all his care-free temper, but Bertha remained uneasy and at times abnormally distraught. She spoke with effort and listened badly, so busily was she wrought upon by unbidden thoughts. The question of her lover's disloyalty to Alice Heath, strange to say, had not hitherto troubled her—so selfishly, so childishly had her own relationship to him filled her mind. She now saw that Alice Heath was as deeply concerned in Ben's relationship to her as Haney, and the picture of the poor, pale, despairing lady, worn with weeping, persistently came between her and the scenes Mart pointed out on their trips about the city. Did Alice know—did she suspect? Was that why she was sinking lower and lower into the shadow?

With these questions to be answered, as well as those she had already put to herself concerning Mart, she could not enjoy the day's outing. She rode through the parks with cold hands and white lips, and sat amid the color and bustle and light of the dining-room with only spasmodic return of her humorous, girlish self. The love which shone from Ben's admiring eyes only added to her uneasiness.

She was very lovely in a new gown that disclosed her firm, rounded young bosom, like a rosebud within its calyx—the distraction upon her brow somehow adding to the charm of her face—and Ben thought her the most wonderful girl he had ever known, so outwardly at ease and in command was she. "Could any one," he thought, "be more swiftly adaptable?"

They went to the theatre, and her beauty and her curiously unsmiling face aroused the admiration and curiosity of many others of those who saw her. At last, under the influence of the music, her eyes lost their shadow and grew tender and wistful. She ceased to question herself and gave herself up to the joy of the moment. The play and the melody—hackneyed to many of those present—appealed to her imagination, liberating her from the earth and all its concerns. She turned to Ben with eyes of rapture, saying, "Isn't it lovely!"

And he, to whom the music was outworn and a little shoddy, instantly agreed. "Yes, it is very beautiful," and he meant it, for her pleasure in it brought back a knowledge of the charm it had once possessed.

They dined together at the hotel, but the thought of Ben's departure brought a pang into Bertha's heart, and she fell back into her uneasy, distracted musing. She was being tempted, through her husband, who repeated with the half-forgetfulness of age and weakness, "You'd better go back with Mr. Fordyce, Bertie," but there was something stronger than her individual will in her reply—some racial resolution which came down the line of her good ancestry, and with almost angry outcry she answered:

"There's no use talking that! I'm going with you," and with this she ended the outward siege, but the inward battle was not closed till she had taken and dropped the hand her lover held out in parting next morning, and even then she turned away, with his eyes and the tender cadences of his voice imprinted so vividly on her memory that she could not banish them, and she set face towards the farther East with the contest of duty and desire still going forward in her blood.

CHAPTER XX

BERTHA MEETS MANHATTAN

It was a green land in which she woke. The leaves were just putting forth their feathery fronds of foliage, and the shorn lawns, the waving floods of growing wheat, and the smooth slopes of pastures presented pleasant pictures to the mountain-born girl. These thickly peopled farm-lands, the almost contiguous villages, the constant passing of trains roused in her a surprise and wonder which left her silent. Such weight of human life, such swarming populations, appalled her. How did they all live?

At breakfast Haney was in unusual flow of spirits. "'Twas here I rode the trucks of a freight-car," he said once and again. "In this town I slept all night on a bench in the depot.... I know every tie from here to Syracuse. I wonder is the station agent living yet. 'Twould warm me heart to toss him out ten dollars for that night's lodging. Them was the great days! In Syracuse I worked for a livery-stableman as hostler, and I would have gone hungry but for the scullion Maggie. Cross-eyed was Maggie, but her heart beat warm for the lad in the loft, and many's the plates of beef and bowls of hot soup she handed to me—poor girl! I'd like to know where she is; had I the power of locomotion I'd look her up, too."

Again Bertha was brought face to face with the great sacrifice she was obscurely contemplating. The magic potency of money was brought before her eyes as she contrasted the ragged, homeless boy with the man who sat beside her. The fact that he had not earned the money only made its magic the more clearly inherent in the gold itself. It panoplied the thief's carriage. It made dwarfs admirable, and gave dignity and honor to the lowly. It made it possible for Marshall Haney to retrace in royal splendor the perilous and painful journey he had made into the West some thirty years ago—rewarding with regal generosity those who threw him a broken steak or a half-eaten roll—and she could imaginatively enter into the exquisite pleasure this largess gave the man.

"And there was Father McBreen," he resumed, with a chuckle—"'sure the mark of Satan is on the b'y,' he used to say every time my mother told him of one of my divilments. And he was right. All the same, I'd like to drop in on him and surprise him with a check"—at the moment he forgot that he was old and a cripple—"just to let him know the divil hadn't claimed me yet. I'd like to show him me wife." He put his hand on her arm and smiled. "Sure the old man would revise his prediction could he see you; he might say the divil had got *you*—but he couldn't pity me."

She turned him aside from this by saying: "I reckon New York is a great deal bigger than Chicago. Mr. Moss says it makes any other town seem like a county seat. I'm dead leery of it. I want to see it, but it just naturally locoes me to think of it."

"'Tis the only place to spend money—so the boys tell me. I've never been there but once, and then only for three days. I went on to get a man when I was sheriff in San Juan. I saw it then mostly as a wonderful fine swamp to lose a thief in."

"Did you get your man?" she asked, with formal interest.

"I did so—and nearly died for want of sleep on the way home; he was a desprit character, was black Hosay; but I linked him to me arm and tuck chances."

Once she had listened to these stories with eager interest; now they were but empty boasting—so deeply inwrought was her soul with matters that more nearly concerned her woman's need and woman's nature. The potency of gold!—could any magic be greater? They lived like folk in a flying palace with books and papers, easy-chairs and card-tables, eating carefully cooked meals, served by attendants as considerate and as constant as those at their own fireside. The broad windows gave streaming panorama of town and country, hill and river, and the young wife accepted it all with the haughty air of one who is wearied with splendor, but inwardly the knowledge that it all came to Haney as to her unearned troubled her. Luck was his God, but she, while accepting from him these marvellous, shining gifts, had another God—one derived from her Saxon ancestors, one to whom luxury was akin to harlotry.

They left the train at Albany and went to the best hotel in the city to spend the night. "To-morrow I'll see if I can find anybody who knows where the old dad is," said Haney. "'Tis too late, and I'm too weary to do it to-night."

Bertha was tired, too—mentally wearied, and glad of a chance to be alone. She went at once to her room, leaving the Captain and Lucius busy with the Troy directory.

Haney set about his search next day with the eager zeal of a lad. He took an almost childish pleasure in displaying his good-fortune. Through Lucius he hired an auto-car as good as the one he had left in Chicago, and together he and Bertha rode into his native town, up into the bleak, brick-paved ward through which he had roamed when a cub. It had changed, of course, as all things American must, but it was so much the same, after all, that he could point out the alleys where he used to toss pennies and play cards and fight. Every corner was historic to him. "Phil O'Brien used to keep saloon here—and I've earned many a dime sweepin' out for his barkeeper. I was never a drunken lad," he gravely said; "I don't know why—I had all the chance there was. I've been moderate of drink all me life. No, I won't say that—I'll say I tuck it as it came, with no fear and no favor. When playin', I always let it alone—it spiled me nerve—I let the other felly do the drinkin'."

Some of the signs were unchanged, and he sent Lucius in to ask the proprietor of the "Hoosac Market" to step out; and when he appeared, a plump man with close-clipped gray hair and smoothly shaven face, he shouted, "'Tis old Otto—just the man I nade. Howdy, Otto Siegel?"

Siegel shaded his eyes and looked up at Haney. "You haff the edventege off me alretty."

"I'm Mart Haney—you remember Mart Haney."

Siegel grasped the situation. "Sure! Vy, how you vass dis dime, eh! Vell, vell—you gome pack in style, ain't it? Your daughter—yes?"

"My wife," said Haney.

Siegel raised a fat arm, which a dirty blue undershirt imperfectly draped, and Bertha shook hands with curt politeness. "Vell, vell, Mart, you must haff struck a cold-mine by now, hah?"

"That's what."

"Vell, vell! and I licked you fer hookin' apples off me vonce—aind dot right?"

Mart grinned. "I reckon that's so. I said I'd cut you in two when I grew up; all boys say such things, but I reckon your whalin' did me good. But what I want to know is this, can you tell me where to find the old man?"

"Your fader? He's in Brooklyn—so I heart. I don't know. My, my! he'll be clad to see you—"

"You don't know his address?"

"No, I heart he was livin' mit your sister Kate."

"Donahue's in a saloon, I reckon."

"Always. He tondt know nodding else. You can fint him in the directory—Chon Donahue, barkeep."

"All right. Much obleeged." Haney looked around. "I don't suppose any of the boys are livin' here now?"

"Von or two. Chake Schmidt iss a boliceman, Harry Sullivan iss in te vater-vorks department, ant a few oders. Mostly dey are scattered; some are teadt—many are teadt," he added, on second thought.

"Well, good-luck," and Haney reached down to shake hands again, and the machine began to whiz. "Tell all the boys 'How.'"

For half an hour they ran about the streets at his direction, while he talked on about his youthful joys and sorrows. "You wouldn't suppose a lad could have any fun in such a place as this," he said, musingly, "but I did. I was a careless, go-divil pup, and had a power of friends, and these alleys and bare brick walls were the only play-ground we had. You can't cheat a boy—he's goin' to have a good time if he has three grains of corn in his belly and a place to sleep when he's tired. I was all right till me old dad started to put me into the factory to work; then I broke loose. I could work for an hour or two as hard as anny one; but a whole long day—not for Mart! Right there I decided to emigrate and grow up with the Injuns."

Bertha listened to his musing comment with a new light upon his life. She had little cause for the feeling of disgust which came to her while studying the scenes of his boyhood—her own childhood had been almost as humble, almost as cheerless—and yet she could not prevent a sinking at the heart. The gambler, so picturesque in his wickedness, was becoming commonplace. He rose from such petty conditions, after all.

Thus far the question of his family relations had not troubled her very much, for, aside from the chance coming of Charles, she had had little opportunity of knowing anything about the Haneys, and they had seemed a very long way off; but now, as she was rushing down upon New York City, with the promise of not only finding the father, but of taking him back with them to live, she began to doubt. His character was of the greatest importance, in view of his taking a seat beside their fire.

It was singular, it was bewildering, this change in her estimate of Marshall Haney. The deeper he sank in reminiscent meditation the farther he withdrew from the bold and splendid freebooter he had once seemed to her. She was now unjust to him for he was still capable of what his kind call "standing pat." The rough-and-ready borderman was still housed under the same thatch of hair with the sentimental old Irishman, and yet it would have sorely puzzled the keenest observer to discover the relationship of that handsome, rather serious-browed, richly clothed young woman and her big, elderly, garrulous companion. Bertha was not easy to classify, in herself, for she gave out an air of reserve not readily accounted for. She looked to be the well-clothed, carefully reared American girl, but her gestures, the silent, unsmiling way in which she received what was said to her—something indefinably alert and self-masterful without being self-conscious—gave her a mysterious charm.

She was profoundly absorbed in the great, historic river on her right, and yet she did not cry out as other girls of her age would have done. She read her folder and kept vigilant eyes upon all the passing points of interest—even as Haney rumbled on about Charles and his father and Kate—more than half distraught by the vague recollections she had of her school histories and geographies. How little she knew! "I must buckle down to some kind of study," she repeatedly said to herself, as if it helped her to a more inflexible resolution.

Soon the mighty city and its fabled sea-shore began to scare her soul with vague alarms and exultations. Manhattan was as remote to her as London, and as splendidly alien as Paris. It was, indeed, both London and Paris to her. Its millions of people appalled her. How could so many folk live in one place?

Again the magic power of money bucklered her. It was good to think that they were to go to the best hotels, and that she had no need to trouble herself about anything, for Lucius settled everything. He telegraphed for rooms, he assembled all their baggage and tipped their porters: and when they rushed into the long tunnel in Harlem he was free to take the Captain by the arm and help him to the forward end of the car ready to alight, leaving Bertha to follow without so much as a satchel to burden her arm. Haney had accepted Lucius' assurance that the Park Palace was the smart hostelry, and to this they drove as to some unknown inn in a foreign capital.

It was gorgeous enough to belong in the tale of Aladdin's lamp—a palace, in very truth, with entrance-hall in keeping with the glittering, roaring Avenue through which they drove, and which was to Bertha quite as strange as a boulevard in Berlin would have been. Lucius conducted them into the reception-room with an air of proprietorship, and soon had waiters, maids and bell-boys "jumping." His management was masterful. He knew just what time to give each man, and just how much to say concerning his master and mistress. He conveyed to the clerk that while Captain Haney didn't want any foolish display, he liked things comfortable round him, and the colored man's tone, as he spoke that word "comfortable," was far-reaching in effect. The best available places were put at his command.

Bertha accepted it all with cold impassivity; it was only a little higher gloss, a little more glitter than they had suffered in Chicago; and she was getting used to seeing men in braid and buttons "hustle" when she came near. The suite of rooms to which they were conducted looked out on Fifth Avenue, as Lucius proudly explained; and from their windows he designated some of the houses of the millionaires who receive the homage of the less rich and of the very poor which only nobility can command in Europe. Bertha betrayed no eager interest in these notables, but she was very deeply impressed by the far-famed Avenue, which was already thickening with the daily five-o'clock parade of carriages, auto-cars, and pedestrians.

Lucius explained this custom, and said: "If you'd like to go out I'll get a car."

"Let's do it!" she exclaimed to Haney.

"Sure! get one. These smell-wagons must have been invented for cripples like me."

Bertha took that ride in the spirit of one who never expects to do it again, and so deeply did the city print itself upon her memory that she was able to recall years afterwards a hundred of its glittering points, angles, and facets. She felt herself up-borne by money. Without Haney's bank-book she would have been merely one of those minute insects who timidly sought to cross the street, and yet philosophers marvel at the race men make for gold! So long as silken parasols and automobiles mad with pride are keenly enjoyed, so long will Americans—and all others who have them not—struggle for them; for they are not only the signs of distinction and luxury, they are delights. A private car is not merely display; it is comfort. To have a suite of rooms at the Park Palace is not all show; it makes for homely ease, cleanliness, repose. And these people riding imperiously to and fro in Fifth Avenue buy not merely diamonds, but well-cooked food, warm and shining raiment, and freedom from the scramble on the pave.

Some understanding of all this was beating home to Bertha's head and heart. She had as yet no keen desire for the glitter of wealth, but its grateful shelter, its power to defend and nurture, were qualities which had begun to make its lure almost irresistible. Haney liked the auto-car, not for its red and gold which delighted Lucius, but for its handiness in taking him about the city. It saved him from climbing in and out of a high car door; it was swifter and safer than a carriage; therefore, he was ready to purchase its speed and convenience. He cared little for the sensation he would create in riding up to his sister's door in Brooklyn, though he chuckled mightily at the thought of what his old dad would say; and as they claimed a place among the millionaires he broke into a sly smile. "If ever a bog-trotter landed at Castle Garden, me father was wan o' them. I can remember the hat he wore. 'Twas a 'stovepipe,' sure enough. It had no rim at all at all! It was fuzzy as a cat. If he didn't have a green vest it was a wonder. He took me to see a play once just to show me how he did look. He was onto his own curves, was old dad. I hope he's livin' yet. I'd like to take him up the Avenue in this car and hear the speel he'd put up."

Bertha was in growing uneasiness, and when alone at the close of her wonderful ride through this marvellous city, so clean, so vast, so packed with stores of all things rich and beautiful, she went to her room in a blur of doubt. Now that an unspoken, half-formed resolution to free herself was in her mind, she realized that every extravagance like this ride, these gorgeous rooms, sank her deeper into helpless indebtedness to Marshall Haney. And this knowledge now took away the keen edge of her delight, making her food bitter and her pillow hot.

In the midst of her troubled thinking, Lucius knocked at the door to ask: "Will you go down to dinner or shall I have it sent up?"

"Oh no, I'll go down."

"They dress for dinner, ma'am."

"Do they? What'll I wear?"

He considered a moment. "Any light silk—semi-dress will do. I'll send a maid in to help you."

"No, I don't need a maid. They're a nuisance," she quickly answered.

Lucius' attitude towards her was more than respectful—it was paternal; for she made no more secret of her early condition than Haney, and the colored man enjoyed serving them. He seemed perfectly happy in advising, cautioning, directing them, and was deeply impressed with their powers of adaptability—was, in truth, developing a genuine affection for them both. He was a lonely little man, Bertha had learned, with no near kin in the States, and the fact that he came from an Island in the sea made him less of a "nigger" to the Captain, who had the usual amount of prejudice against both black and red men.

The high-keyed, sumptuous dining-hall was filled with small tables exquisitely furnished, and the carpets underfoot, thick-piled and deep-toned, gave a singular solemnity to the function of eating. It was a temple raised to the glory of terrapin and "alligator pears"; and as the Captain moved slowly across the aisles, closely attended by a zealous waiter he smiled and said to his wife: "This is a long ways from Sibley and the Golden Eagle, Bertie, don't you think?"

"It sure is," she replied, and her laughing lips and big pansy-purple eyes made her seem very young and very gay again.

Around her men and women in evening dress were feeding subduedly, while bevies of hawklike waiters swooped and circled, bearing platters, tureens, and baskets of iced wine-bottles. It made the hotel at Chicago appear like a plain, old-fashioned tavern, so remote, so European, so lavish, and yet so exaggeratedly quiet, was this service. Some of the women at the tables were spangled like the queens of the stage; mainly they were not only gloriously gowned, but in harmony with the sumptuous beauty around them. Their adornments made Bertha feel very rural and very shy.

"I wish I was younger," the Captain said, "I'd take ye to the theatre to-night, but I'm too tired. I could go for a couple of hours, but—to miss me sleep—"

"Don't think of it," she hastened to command. "I don't want to go. I'm just about all in, myself."

"'Tis a shame, darlin', surely it is, to keep you from havin' a good time just because I am an old helpless side o' beef. 'Tis not in me heart to play dog in the manger, Bertie. If ye'd like to go, do so. Lucius will take ye."

"Nit," she curtly replied; "you rest up, and we'll go to-morrow night. We might take another turn and see the town by electric light; you could kind o' lean back in the car and take it easy."

This they did; and it was more moving, more appalling, to the girl than by day. The fury of traffic on Broadway, the crowds of people, the endless strings of brilliantly lighted street-cars, the floods of 'busses, auto-cars, cabs, and carriages poured in upon the girl's receptive brain a tide of perceptions of the city's wealth, power, and complexity of social life which amazed while it exalted her. The idea that she might share in all this dazzled her. "We could live here," she thought; "the Captain's income would keep us just anyway we wanted to live."

But a vision of her own beautiful house under the shadow of the great peak came back to reproach her. Her horses and dogs awaited her. This tumultuous island was only a place to visit, after all.

"Do you suppose this goes on every night?" she said to Haney, as they turned off Broadway.

"I reckon it does," he said. "How is that, Lucius?" he asked. "Is this a special performance, or does the old town do this every night?"

"In the season, yes, sir. It's the last week of the Opera, and it'll be quieter now till November."

They returned to their hotel with a sense of having touched the ultimate in civic splendor, human pride, and social complexity. New York had met most of their ideals. They were glad it was on American soil and in the nation's metropolis; but, after all, it remained alien and mysterious, of a rank with Paris and London—the gateway city of the nation, where the Old World meets and mingles with the New.

CHAPTER XXI

BERTHA MAKES A PROMISE

As for Marshall Haney, as he went about New York and Brooklyn in search of his relations, he was astounded at the translation of the Irish laborer into something else. "In my time, when I left Troy, all the work in the streets was done by 'micks,' as they called 'em. Now they're gone—whisked away as ye'd sweep away a swarm of red ants, and here's these black Dagos in their places. Where's the Irishman gone—up or down? That's what's eatin' me. Is he dead or translated to a higher speer? 'Tis a mysterious dispensation, and troubles me much."

He found a good many Donahues in Brooklyn, and plenty of them barkeepers; and after he'd pulled up half a dozen times at these "joints" Bertha began to pout. She didn't like such places; and as they were riding in a showy auto-car the grandest Lucius could secure, they were pretty middling noticeable. At last she said, more sharply than she had ever spoken to him before: "Mart, I don't want any more of this. If you want to visit all the saloons in Brooklyn, I don't. Here's where I get out."

He was instantly remorseful. "I was thinkin' of that myself, Bertie. Lucius and I will go on alone. We'll send you back to the hotel in the 'mobile whilst we take a hack."

Half doubting, half glad, she consented to this arrangement, and was soon whirling back towards the ferry, her guilty feeling giving place to a sense of relief, as if a huge weight had been lifted from her shoulders—for a moment. She began to understand that half the pleasure she had taken in her hours with Moss and Humiston lay in the freedom from her husband's over-shadowing presence. He was not a man to be ignored, as she had seen wives ignore and put aside their meek partners. Marshall Haney even yet was a dominating personality, even though his family affairs were so insistent and so difficult to manage or explain. If the father came her joy in her home would be gone, and yet she had no right to refuse him shelter.

At the same time she was less sure of her place in the world, now that she was alone. She had the feeling that if anything were to happen—if the motorman should demand his pay at the door, or the hotel-keeper refuse to go her bond, she would be helpless. The Captain, for all his shortcomings and physical disability, was master of every situation. He had been schooled by stern powers, and his capabilities of defence were still equal to almost any need.

On the ferry-boat she found herself surrounded by the swarms of people who are forever calculating expenditures, who never desert a garment, and who finger a nickel lovingly; and she caught them looking at her as upon one of those who enjoy without earning it the product of their toil. They made way for her, as she got down and walked to the railing, as they would have done for a millionaire's daughter, a little surlily, and she divined without understanding this enmity, but was too exalted by the glittering bay, with its romance of ship and sea and shore and town, to very much mind what her threadbare fellow-passengers thought of her. These dark-hulled, ocean-going vessels, these alien flags, widened her horizon—deepened her sense of the earth's wonder and the wide-flung nerves of national interest. From this sea-level she looked up in fancy to her brother's ranch near Sibley as at a cabin on a mountain-side. How still and faint and far it seemed at the moment!

At the word of the chauffeur she climbed back into her car, returning to the isolation which money now provided for her. And so, girt about with velvet and costly wood and gilding, she rode up through the tearing throngs of the wharf, whirling past cars and trucks, outspeeding cabs and carriages, protected by a gambler's name, royally isolated and defensible by his money. As she spun through Fifth Avenue, so smooth of pave, so crowded, so sparkling, so far-reaching in its suggestions of security and power, the girl's soul entered upon a new and fierce phase of its struggle.

It was a larger and more absorbing fairy story than any in the *Arabian Nights*. Without Marshall Haney, without the gold he brought, she could never have even looked upon this scene. She would at this moment have been standing inside her little counter at the Golden Eagle, selling cigars to some brakeman or cowboy. Ed Winchell would be coming to ask her, as usual, to marry him, and her mother would still be toiling in the hot kitchen or be at rest in her grave. Did ever Aladdin's lamp translate its owner farther or lift him higher? Was not her refusal to be Marshall Haney's wife the basest ingratitude?

Not merely so, but the girl felt in herself potentialities not yet drawn upon, unlimited capabilities leading towards the accomplishment of good. Money had not merely the magic of exalting, educating, refining, and ennobling the individual herself; it had radiating, transforming power for others. It could diffuse warmth like a flame, and send forth joy like a bell. "With it I am safe, strong: I can help the poor. Without it I am only a struggling girl, like millions of others, with no chance and no power to aid those who suffer." But at this point her love re-entered and her sense of right was confused. After all the heart ruled.

At the hotel entrance the head porter was waiting to help her out, and the chauffeur, without a word or look of reminder, puffed away, secure in the reputation Lucius had given to Haney. As she went to her room the maid met her with gentle solicitude, and, after attending to her needs, considerately withdrew, leaving her deep-sunk in troubled musing.

Up to the coming of Ben Fordyce she had accepted all that Haney gave her as from one good friend to another. Once having satisfied herself that the money was clean of any taint from gambling-hall and saloon, she had not hesitated to use it. But now something was rising within her which changed the current of her purpose. Haney was no longer before the bar of her conscience; the soul under question was her own. Dimly, yet with ever-growing definiteness, she saw the moment of decision approach. She must soon decide whether to continue on the smooth, broad highway with Haney, or to return to the mountain-trail from which he had taken her.

While still she sat sombrely looking out over the city's roofs, Humiston's card was brought to her, and at the moment, in her loneliness and doubt, he seemed like an old friend. "Tell him to come up," she said, with instant cordiality, and her face shone with innocent pleasure when she met him. "I'm mighty glad to see you," she frankly said, in greeting.

He misconceived her feeling, and took advantage of it to retain her hand. "I assure you I am delighted to find *you* again."

"I thought you'd forgot us."

His eyes expressed a bold admiration as he answered: "I have done nothing but remember you. I've been in Pittsburg only got back to town yesterday, and here I am." He looked about. "Where is the Captain?"

She withdrew her hand. "He's out looking for his father. He'll return soon. He's liable to look in any minute now."

"You are lovelier than ever. How is the Captain?"

"Pretty well. He gets tired fairly easy, but he feels better than he did."

His look of eager intensity embarrassed her. After a little pause, he remarked: "I am holding you to your promise. Can't you come over to my studio this afternoon?"

"No, not to-day. I must be here when the Captain comes. He may bring the old father along, and he'd feel lost if I should be gone. Maybe I could come to-morrow."

"Don't bring the Captain unless you have to—he'll be bored," he said, in the hope that she would get his full meaning. "I want to introduce you to some friends of mine."

"Oh, don't do that!" she protested. "I'm afraid of your friends—they're all so way-wised while I am hardly bridle-broke."

"You need not fear," he replied; "you are most to be envied. No one can have more than health, wealth, and youth and beauty. I would not hesitate to introduce you anywhere." His admiration was so outspoken, so choicely worded, that she could not distrust him, though Mrs. Moss had more than once hinted to her that he was not to be entirely honored. "He isn't a man to be careless with," she had once said, and yet he seemed so high-minded, so profoundly concerned with the beautiful world of art. How could a single-hearted Western girl believe ill of him? He could not be evil in the ways in which men were wicked in Sibley. His sensitive face was too weary and his eyes too sad.

He was adroit enough to make his call short, and withdrew, leaving a very pleasant impression in her mind. She felt distinctly less lonely, now that she knew he was in the city, and she was still at the window musing about him when Haney returned, bringing his father with him.

The elder Haney interested and amused her in spite of her perplexities—he was so quaintly of the old type of Irishman and so absurdly small to be the father of a giant. He carried a shrewd and kindly face, withered and toothless, yet not without a certain charm of line. Mart's fine profile was like his sire's, only larger, bolder, and calmer.

With a chuckle he introduced him. "Bertie, this is me worthless old dad." And Patrick, though he was sidling and side-stepping with the awkwardness of a cat on wet ice, still retained his Celtic self-possession.

"Lave Mart to slander the soorce av aal his good qualities," he retorted. "He was iver an uncivil divil to me—after the day he first thrun me down, the big gawk."

Mart took the little man by the collar and twirled him about. "Luk at 'im! Did he ever feel the like of such cloes in his life?"

Patrick grinned a wide, silent, mirthful grimace. "Sure me heart is warmed wid 'em. I feel as well trussed as me lady's footman."

It was plain that every thread on the old man was new. Mart explained. "I stripped him to the buff and built him up plumb to his necktie, which is green—the wan thing he would have to his own taste. To-morrow we go to the tooth-factory."

"'Tis a waste of good money," interjected Patrick. "I ate soup."

"Soup be damned! Ye've many a steak to eat with me, ye contrary little baboon. 'Tis a pity if I can't do as I like with me own. Do as I say, and be gay."

Patrick cackled again, and his little twinkling eyes were half hid. "Ye may load me with jewels and goold, me lad, but divil a once do I allow a man wid a feet-lathe boring-machine to enter me head."

"Ye have nothing to bore, ye old jackass! Divil a rock is left to prospect in—so don't fuss."

Bertha interjected a question. "Where did you find him?"

"Marking up in a pool-room. Nice place for the father of Captain Haney! 'Come out o' that,' I says, 'or fight me.' And the old fox showed gooms at me, and says he: 'I notice ye're crippled, Mart. I think I'll jest take what ye owe me out of yer hide.'" They both chuckled at the recollection of it. Then Mart went on: "I'll not disgrace me wife by telling what the old tramp had on. I tuck him by the shoulder and I said: 'Have ye anny Sunday clothes?' I said. 'Narry a thread,' says he. 'Come along with me,' I says. 'You can't visit my wife in the hotel till every thread on yer corpus is changed,' for Donahue keeps a dirty place. So here he is—scrubbed, fumigated, barbered, and tailored; and when he gets his cellulide teeth he'll make as slick a little Irishman as ever left the old sod." Here his face became sadly tender. "I wish the mother was alive, too; I'd make her rustle in silks, so I would. Heaven rest her!"

The father's face grew suddenly accusing in line. "Ye waited too long, ye vagabond. Yer change of heart comes too late."

"I know it—I know it! But I could never find time till a man with a shotgun pointed the way to it. Now I have all the time there is, and she's gone."

In this moment of passing shadow Bertha caught a glimpse of the significance of the scene—of the wonder, almost alarm, which filled the old man's heart as he stood there scared of the flaming splendor of the room into which the sunlight fell, exaggerating its gold and pink and green, but bringing out the excellence of the furnishing, the richness of the silk tapestry.

The old man touched a gilded chair tenderly, and Mart cried out: "Lay hold, man, 'twill not rub off! Sit down and look about ye! Out with your new pipe and smoke up!"

He took a seat with forced confidence, and looked about him. "I wish Donahue and Kate could see this."

Mart turned a quietly humorous eye on Bertha. "Not this trip. I couldn't manage Kate," he explained. "She looks like Fan—only more so; and she has a litter o' young Donahues would make ye wonder could the world have room for them all."

Haney the elder had something more than the bog-trotter in him, for as he grew towards a little more assurance that Mart would not be thrown out of his hotel for non-payment of bills, he settled down to enjoy his glass of rare whiskey and a costly cigar with an assumption of ease that almost deceived the maid, though Lucius, being in the secret, watched him anxiously for fear he might expectorate on the rug.

Mart had some "p'otographs" of his house in the Springs, and showed them to Patrick. "Do ye see yerself smokin' a pipe on that porch?"

"I do not," the father energetically replied. "I see meself goin' the rounds of that garden with a waterin'-pot and a pair of shears."

"I thought ye was a bricklayer, or is it a billiard-marker?" asked Mart, with quizzical look.

"I can turn me hand to anny honest work," he replied, with dignity. "An' can ye say as much?"

"I cannot," confessed Mart. "Had ye put a club to me back and foorced me to a trade, sure I'd be layin' brick in Troy this day."

This retort fairly blinded the sturdy little father. The charge was false, and yet here sat Mart—a gentleman. While still he puzzled over the dangerous acknowledgment involved in his son's accusation, Mart turned to Bertha. "Do ye mind the old man's spendin' the rest of his days with us, darlin'?"

"You're the doctor, Mart. It's your house, not mine."

He felt the change in her. "Oh no, it isn't; it's *our* house. I never would have had it only for you." He paused a moment. "The dad is a well-meaning old rascal, and I'll go bail he don't do mischief."

Patrick took this up. "He is so, and he means to kape to his own way of life. If I go West, me b'y, 'tis on wages as a gardener—and, bedad, I'll draw 'em reg'ler, too. I'd like well to go West 'twould rejice me to see Fan and McArdle, and I don't object to spendin' a year with you in Coloraydo, but don't think Patrick Haney is to be pinsioner on anny one, not even his son."

Bertha's heart vibrated in sympathy with this note of independence, and she heartily said: "I hope you will come, Mr. Haney. The Captain is alone a good deal, and you'd be a comfort to him."

"I'll consider," the old man said. "I must have time to rea-lize it," he quaintly added. "I must smoke me pipe in me own garret once more, and talk it all over with Kate and the Donahues." He refused to stay to dinner with them which was a relief to Lucius, and went away jaunty as a bucko from County Clare.

He was no sooner gone from the room than Bertha turned to her husband, and said: "Mart, I want to talk things over with you."

Something in her voice, as well as in the words, made him turn quickly and regard her anxiously.

"What about? What is it, darlin'?"

"I have something on my mind, and I've got to spit it out before I can rest to-night. I've just about decided to leave you. I don't feel right livin' with you."

He looked at her steadily, but a gray pallor began to show on his face. He asked, quietly: "Do ye mean to go fer good?"

Her heart was beating fast, but she bravely faced him. "Yes, Mart, I don't feel right living with you, and spending your money the way I've been doing."

"Why not? It isn't mine—it's yours. Ye airn every cent ye spend."

"No, I don't!" she cried, passionately. "Now that you're getting better and Lucius has come, I'm not even a nurse."

"I'll send him away."

"No, no; he's worth more than I am."

"I'll not listen to such talk, Bertie. Ye well know you're the thing most precious to me. I can't live without ye." His voice thickened. "For God A'mighty's sake, don't say such things; they make me heart shake! Me teeth are chatterin' this minute! Ye're jokin'; say you don't mean it."

"But I do. Don't you see that I can't stay and let you do things for me like this"—she indicated their apartment—"when I do so little to earn it all? Mart, I've got to be honest about it. I can't let you spend any more money on me. Help your own people, and let me go. I do nothing to pay for what you do for me. It's better for me to go."

She could not bring herself to be as explicit as she should have been, but he was not far from understanding her real meaning, as he brokenly replied: "I've been afraid of this, my girl. I've thought of it all. The money I spend fer ye is but a small part of my debt. You say you do nothing for me. Why, darlin', every time you come into the room or smile at me you do much for me! I'm a selfish old wolf, but I'm not so bad as you think I am. If anny nice young felly comes along—a good square man—I'll get off the track; but I want you to let me stay near you as long as I live." His voice was hoarse with pleading. "Ye're all I have in the world; all I live for now is to make you happy. Don't pull away now, when me old heart has grown all round ye. I can't live and I daren't die without ye—now that's the eternal truth. Darlin', promise ye won't go—yet awhile."

Wordless, as full of pain as he, she sat silently weeping, unable to carry out her resolution—unable to express the change which had come into her life.

He went on. "I mark the difference between us. I see ye goin' up while I am goin' down. My heart is big with pride in ye. You belong with people like the Congdons and the Mosses—whilst I am only an old broken-down skate. I'm worse than you know. I went down to Sibley first with hell in me heart towards you, but that soon passed away—I loved ye as a man should love the girl he marries—and I love ye now as I love the saints. I wouldn't mar your young life fer anything in this world—'tis me wish to lave you as beautiful and fresh as I found you, and to give you all I have besides—so stay with me, if you can, till the other man comes." Here a new thought intruded. "Has he come now? Tell me if he has. Did ye find him in Chicago? Be honest, darlin'."

"No, no!" she answered. "It isn't that. It's just because—because it don't seem right."

"Then ye must stay with me," he said, "and don't worry about not doing things for me. You do things for me every minute—just by being in the world. If I can see ye or hear ye I'm satisfied. An' don't cut me off from spending money for ye, for that's half me fun. How else can I pay ye for your help to me? I've been troubled by your face ever since we left home. You don't smile as ye used to do. Don't ye like it here? If ye don't we'll go back. Shall we do that?"

She, overwhelmed by his generosity, could only nod.

His face cleared. "Very well, the procession will head west whenever you say the word. I hope you don't object to the old father. If ye do—"

"Oh no; I like him."

"Then we'll take him; but, remember, I'll let no one come into our home that will trouble you. I'd as soon have a cinder in me eye as a man I don't like sitting beside me fire; and if the old man is a burden to ye, out he goes." He rose, and came painfully to where she sat, and in a voice of humble sorrow, slowly said: "I don't ask ye to love me—now—I'm not worth it; and once I thought I'd like a son to bear my name, but 'tis better not. I'll never lay that burden upon ye. All I ask is the touch of yer hand now and then, and your presence when I come to die—I'm scared to die alone. 'Twill be a dark, long journey for old Mart, and he wants your face to remember when he sets forth."

CHAPTER XXII

THE SERPENT'S COIL

Lofty as Jerome Humiston talked, and poetic as his face seemed to Bertha Haney, he was at heart infinitely more destructive than any man she had ever known; for he took a satanic delight in proving that all women were alike in their frailty. He had reached also that period of decay wherein the libertine demands novelty—where struggle is essential, and to conquer easily is to fail of the joy of victory.

He, too, had rushed to the conclusion that this girl had married an old and broken gambler for his money, and that she was of those to be easily won. Her air of demure reserve piqued him—pleased him. "She is no silly kitten," he mentally remarked, after their second meeting. "She's in for a big career. With beauty and youth and barrels of money she will go far, and I will be her guide—unless I have lost my cunning. She will share her fortune with me some day, and I will teach her to live."

He met her at the door of his studio next day with a grave and tender smile. "I'm glad you've come," he said, "but I'll have to confess that I have very little to show you here. My pictures are all down at the gallery, and some of them not yet hung. Next week they will all be in place. But sit down while I boil some tea. My friends who own this work-shop are out; they'll be in soon."

"I don't believe I can stay to-day. The Captain is below."

"Please do sit down for a moment. I'll be hurt if you don't."

The studio was a big bare barn of a place with a few broad canvases upon the walls—not a bit like Humiston; and he explained that his stay in America being short, he could not afford to have a studio of his own. "I'm glad you came. You must let me take you to see my 'show' next week. Your fresh, young, Western eyes are just what I need." This was false, for he was impatient of all criticism. "I need comfort," he added, wearily smiling. "I didn't sell enough in the West to pay my railway fare."

He seemed ill as well as sad, and Bertha felt sorry for him. "Won't you come with us for a ride?"

"I'd rather have you stay and talk with me."

"Oh, I can't do that! The Captain is waiting for me. He said to bring you."

"But I don't want to go. I hate automobiles. I hate seeing sights. I despise this town. I've a grouch against everything in America—except you. Let me go down and tell the Captain to take his spin alone."

"No, no," she sharply said. "I keep my word. I said I'd be back in a few minutes, and I'm going."

He sighed resignedly. "Very well; but you'll let me come to see you?"

"Why, cert! Come to dinner any day. We don't browse around much outside the hotel. We're mostly always feeding at six."

"I'll come, and you must not fail to let me show you my pictures."

"Sure thing! I want to buy one to take home with me."

He assumed great candor. "I won't say that your ability to buy one of my pictures is not of interest to me, for it is; but quite aside from that, there is something in you that appeals to me. You make me think better of the West—of America. I feel that you will find something in my pictures which the critics miss." Then, with mournful abruptness, he added: "No doubt Joe told you of my unhappy marriage—"

"No, he didn't."

"My wife cares nothing for my work. She takes no interest in anything but the frippery side of life. That's what appeals to me in you—you are so aspiring. I feel that you have such wonderful possibilities. You would spur a man to big things."

They were both standing as if he had forgotten where he was, and she, embarrassed but fascinated by his words, and especially held by his voice, dared not make a motion till he released her. He looked round him. "I don't wonder you dislike this room; it's horribly cold and depressing to me. I can't work here. I wish you could see my den in Paris. Perhaps you will let me show it to you some day. All my happiest days have been spent in France. I am more French than American now."

He took her hand again, and with a return to his studiedly cheerful manner called her to witness that she had promised to come to see his paintings. "And please remember that I am going to take you at your word and dine with you—perhaps this very night."

"All right, come along," she replied, and went away filled with wonder at the familiar, almost humble attitude he had assumed towards her.

He did indeed dine with them that night, and quite won the Captain to a belief in him. "Come again," he heartily said. And the great artist feelingly answered: "I mean to, for, strange to say, I am almost as lonesome in this big town as anybody could be." This was a lie, but Haney's sympathy was roused. "There'll always be an empty chair for you," he repeated, with a feeling that he, too, was encouraging art.

Humiston pursued this game with singular and joyous skill. He talked of the West and of politics with the Captain, and of love and art and his essentially lonely life to Bertha. He returned often to the wish that they might meet in Paris. "A trip abroad would do you infinite good," he insisted. "What you need is three years of life in Paris. With your beauty and money, and, above all, with your personal magnetism, you could reign like a queen. I wonder that you don't go. It would be worth more to you than any other possible schooling. I don't know of anything in this world that would give me greater pleasure than to show you Paris."

Bertha's silence in face of these approaches deceived him. The throbbing of her bosom, the fall of her eyelashes, were due to instinctive distrust of him. That he was more dangerous than the rough miners and cowboys of the West she could not believe, and yet she drew back in growing fear of one who openly claimed the right to plow athwart all the barriers of law and custom. His mind's flight was like that of the eagle—now rising to the sun in exultation, now falling to the gray sea to slay. At times she felt a kind of gratitude that he should be willing to sit beside her and talk—he, so skilled, so learned, so famous.

The Chicago papers were still filled with criticism of his work and his theories, and this discussion, as well as the appearance of his portrait in the magazines, had made of him a very exalted person in little Mrs. Haney's eyes, and the interest he took in her was too subtly flattering not to affect her. He seemed fond of the Captain, too, and often joined them in their trips about the city, and the fellows who had known Humiston in Paris and who did not know Bertha nodded knowingly. "Jerry's amusing himself, as usual. I wonder who she is?"

He explained his poverty one day as he sat with her in the little gallery where his paintings were hung. "The fact is, while other men have been painting to order and doing 'stunts' for the Salon, I've gone on refining, seeking new shades, new allurements, subordinating line to color, story to harmony, till my work is sublimated beyond my public. The people that bought my things once can't follow me; it is only now and then that a man, or a woman *feels* what I'm after—and so I live. I hold all things beautiful to paint, America does not."

He liked her all the better because she did not try to say what she thought of his pictures, and when she insisted on taking one of them home he quickly stopped her. "I'm not asking you to take pity on me," he sharply said. And in this lay the subtlest touch of flattery he had yet used: the idea that she, an ignorant mountain girl, could be accused of patronizing a man so distinguished, so gifted as he, moved her in spite of all warnings. Why should she not use her money to help this wonderful artist?

She insisted on a picture, and asked him to select one for her. "I've got a big house out in the Springs, and I'd like something of yours."

"Not out of this collection," he declared. "These are not the ones on which my fame rests. The ones that represent me are in the cellar."

Her eyes were wide in question. "What do you mean by that?"

"American dealers won't include my best things in the exhibit—they are too 'direct.' They are stored over here in a warehouse. I'd like to show them to you. Will you come?" he asked, with eager eyes.

And she, with a sense of being distinguished above the great public, consented. Humiston rose animatedly. "Let's go over and see them now."

His gentle *camaraderie*, his eagerness, touched Bertha, and when he took her arm to help her into the elevator or to make sure she did not stumble at the crossing she was stirred—not as Ben's hand had moved her, but her blood nevertheless palpably quickened. Was it not wonderful that she, so lately from the mountains, should be walking here in the midst of the thronging multitudes of a great city street in the company of one of the chief artists of the world?

Humiston, crafty, cruel, unscrupulous, returned to his abuse of the city, and explained to her that American dealers had no real appreciation of art. "They sell anything that will sell, any cheap daub, and yet they dared to refuse to exhibit my best things! It was the same in Pittsburg and Buffalo; they're all alike. But what can you expect of these densely material towns? Beauty means only prettiness to them."

The salesman of the shop, accustomed to seeing Humiston pass in and out with friends, paid no special heed to the painter as he led Bertha into the farther room, where a few of his pictures hung among a dozen others. No one was in the gallery, and just as she was wondering where the other paintings could be, he opened a door which was cut out of the wall and partly concealed by paintings, and smilingly said: "Here is the inner temple. Enter."

She obeyed with a little hesitation, for the storeroom was not well lighted, and she had a wild bird's distrust of dark, enclosing walls.

Humiston shut the door behind him and followed her, plaintively saying: "Isn't it hard lines to have to bring my friends into this hole to show my masterpieces?" And by this she inferred that there was nothing unusual in the experience.

It was a long, bare hall, filled with boxes and littered with bits of excelsior, and Bertha looked about her uneasily while Humiston bent over some canvases stacked on the floor. He seemed to be selecting one with care. An electric lamp was swinging from the ceiling, and under it stood a large easel, and on this he placed a canvas, and, stepping back with eyes fixed on her, said with spirit: "This is one of my best. It was in the new Salon—here is the number. And yet it may not be exhibited in this rotten town."

Bertha inwardly recoiled from the canvas, for it was a painting of a nude figure of a girl at the bath. The critics had said, "It is naked, rather than nude," and the dealers objected to it on this ground, and to the Western girl it was both shocking and ugly. Before she had caught her breath he continued, in a tone that was at once a seduction and a defence: "There is nothing more beautiful in the world than the female form; it is the flower of flowers. Why should it not be painted?" And then, while still he argued for the return of the Greek's love of beauty, covering his moral depravity with the mantle of the philosopher, he placed another canvas before her—something so unrefined, so animal, so destructive of womanly modesty and of all reserve, that any one looking upon it would instantly know that the man who had painted it was a degenerate demon—an associate of dissolute models, an anarchist in the world of women. It was fit only for the banquet-halls of the damned.

Bertha stared at it—fascinated by the sense of the tempter's nearness. It was as if a satyr had suddenly revealed his lawless soul to her. Her thinking for an instant chained her feet, and her silence emboldened him.

Even as she turned to flee she felt his arm about her waist, his breath upon her cheek. "Don't go!" he pleaded, and in his eyes was the same look she had seen in the face of Charles Haney. At last he stood revealed. His artist soul could stoop as low in purpose as a drunken tramp. Beating him off with her strong hands, she ran down the hall and burst into the brilliantly lighted exhibition room such a picture of affrighted, outraged girlhood that the salesman stared upon her in wonder. His look of surprise warned Bertha of her danger. Composing herself by tremendous effort of the will, she closed the door and walked slowly out into the street, her brain in a tumult of anger and shame.

It seemed at the moment as if every man she had ever known was a brute-demon seeking to destroy her. She understood now the reason for the great painter's flattering deference to her opinion. From the first he had sought to blind her. His ways were subtler than those of Charles Haney and his like, but his soul was no higher; it was indeed more ignoble, for he was of those who claim to dispense learning and light. Pretending to add beauty to the world, he was ready to feed himself at the cost of a woman's soul. She recalled Mrs. Moss' hints about his life in Paris, and understood at last that he had wilfully misread her homage and trust. A realization of this perfidy filled her with a fury of hate and disgust. Was Ben Fordyce like all the rest? Did his candor, his sweetness of smile, but veil another mode of approach? Was his kiss as vile in its disloyalty, his embrace as remorseless in its design?

She walked back along the shining avenue to her hotel with drooping head. She knew the worst of Humiston now. She burned with helpless wrath as she dwelt upon his assumptions of superiority. She hated the whole glittering, unresting, lavish city at the moment, and her soul longed for the silence of the peaks to the west. She turned to her husband as one who seeks a tower of refuge in time of war.

CHAPTER XXIII

BERTHA'S FLIGHT

Before she had fairly recovered her poise next day Lucius brought to her a letter from Humiston—a suave, impudent note wherein he expressed the hope that she was well, and went on to plead in veiled phrase: "I'm sorry you did not stay to see the rest of my pictures. I meant it all as a compliment to your innate good taste and purity of thought. I expected you to see them as I painted them—in pure artistic delight. You misunderstood me. I hope you will let me see you again. You must remember you promised to let me make a portrait sketch of you."

Although not skilled in polite duplicity, Bertha was able to read beneath the serene insolence of these lines something so diabolically relentless that she turned cold with fear and repulsion. She had no experience which fitted her to deal with such a pursuer, and she shuddered at the rustling of the paper in her hand as she had once quivered in breathless terror of a rattlesnake stirring in the leaves near the door of her tent. Her first impulse was to lay the whole affair before the Captain, but the knowledge of his deadly temper when roused decided her to slip out at the other side of this fearsome thicket and leave the serpent in possession. She longed to return to the West. The little group of people in the Springs allured her; they were to be trusted. Congdon and Crego and Ben—these men she knew and respected. Her joy of the big outside Eastern world had begun to pass, and she dreaded to encounter again the bold eyes and coarse compliments of the men who loaf about the hotels and clubs.

She turned to Haney as he came into her room, and said: "Mart, I want to go home—to-day."

"All right, Bertie, I'm ready—or will be, as soon as I pick up the old father. But don't you want to see that show we've got tickets for?"

"No, I've had enough of this old town. I'm crazy to go home."

"Home it is, then." He called sharply; "Lucius!" The man appeared, impassive, noiseless, unhurried. The Captain issued his orders: "Thrun me garbage into a thrunk, and call some one to help the missus; we're goin' to hit the sunset trail to-night. 'Phone me old dad besides, and have him come over at wanst. Here we emigrate westward by the next express."

The man quietly took control of the situation, and in a few moments the Captain's commands were being carried out with the precision of a military camp.

Bertha, alarmed by Humiston's letter, refused to go down to the public dining-room. A fear that she might encounter the painter possessed her, and the thought of him was at once a shame and torment; therefore, she had her luncheon sent up, and Lucius himself found time to wait upon them.

As they were in the midst of their meal, Haney remarked rather than asked: "Of course, you're going back with us, Lucius."

"I have thought of it, sir, but it isn't in our contract."

"We can put it in," said Bertha.

"We can't do without you now," added Mart.

Lucius seemed pleased. "Thank you for that, Captain. I don't particularly care for the West, but I find service with you agreeable."

Haney chuckled. "Service, do ye call it? Sure, man, 'tis you are in command. I'm but a high private in the rear rank."

Lucius's yellow face flushed and his eyes wavered. "I hope I haven't assumed—"

"Assumed! No, 'tis we who are obligated. We need you as bad as a plainsman needs a guide in the green timber; and if you don't mind a steady job of looking after us social tenderfeet, I'm willing to make it right with you—and Mrs. Haney feels just the way I do."

"Sure, Mart—only trouble with Lucius is, he leaves so little for me to do. He's *too* handy—if anything."

"That'll wear off," replied Haney. "Well, then, it's all settled but the price, and I reckon we can fix that. If I can't pay cash, I'll let you in on the mine."

Lucius smiled. "Thank you, Captain; it's not entirely a question of pay with me; my wants are few."

Bertha seized the moment to put a question she had been minded many times to ask. "Lucius, what's your plan? You can't intend to do this all your life? Tell us your ambition—maybe we can help you."

He looked away, and a deeper shadow fell over his face. "I had ambitions once, Mrs. Haney, but my color was against me. Yes, I think I'll stay as I am. There is a certain security in being valet. You white people know exactly where to find me, and I know just how to meet you. In my profession it was different—I was always being cursed for presumption."

"What was your profession?" asked Haney.

"I studied law—and practised for a year or two in Washington; but I didn't like my position; I was neither white nor colored, so when I got a good chance I went out to service with a senator as body-servant." He stopped abruptly as though that were all of his tale.

Haney said: "Well, if you can put up with an ignorant old hill-climber like meself, I'll be grateful, and I'll try not rub your fur the wrong way."

Lucius became very earnest for the first time. "There, sir, is one point upon which I must insist. If I go with you, you are to treat me just as you have been doing—as a trusted servant. I'm sorry I told you anything about myself. My service thus far has been very pleasant, very satisfactory, and unless we can go on in the same way, I must leave."

"Very well," replied Haney. "It's all settled—you're adjutant-general of the Haneys' forces."

After Lucius went away Bertha said, thoughtfully: "I wish he hadn't told us that; I can't order him around the way I've been doing."

Haney smiled. "Did ye order him around? I niver chanced to hear ye do anything but ask him questions. 'Lucius, will ye do this?' 'Lucius, won't ye do that?'"

Bertha was troubled, and found herself embarrassed by the mulatto's services. She now perceived sadness beneath the quiet lines of his face and hard-won culture in the tones of his voice. The essential tragedy of his defeat grew more poignant to her as she watched him getting the trunks strapped, surrounded by maids and porters. How could she have misread his manner? He was performing his duties, not with quiet gusto, but in the spirit of the trained nurse.

This mountain girl had always regarded Illinois as "the East," but after a few weeks in New York City she now looked away to Chicago as a Western town. She was glad to face the sunset sky again, and yet as she wheeled away to the train she acknowledged a regret. Under the skilful guidance of Lucius she had seen a great deal of the splendid and furious Manhattan. She had gazed with unenvious admiration on the palaces of upper Fifth Avenue and the Park. Together with Haney she had spun up Riverside Drive, past Grant's Tomb, and on through Washington Heights, with joy of the far-spreading panorama. She had visited the Battery and sailed the shining way to Staten Island in silent awe of the ship-filled bay. She had heard the sunset-guns thunder at Fort Hamilton, and had threaded the mazes of the Brooklyn Navy-Yard, and each day the mast-hemmed island widened in grandeur and thickened with threads of human purpose, making the America she knew very simple, very quiet, and very remote.

Night by night she had gone to the music-halls and theatres, and her mind had been powerfully wrought upon by what she had seen and heard. In all these trips Haney had heroically accompanied his wife, though he frequently dropped asleep in his seat; and he, too, left the city with regret, though he said, "Thank God, I'm out of it," as they settled into their seats in the ferry. "'Tis not the night traffic that wears me down—I'm used to being on the night shift; 'tis the wild pace Lucius sets by day. Faith, 'twas the aquarium in the morning and the circus in the afternoon. Me dreams have been wan long procession of misbegotten fish, ballet-dancers, dirty monkeys, and big elephants the nights. 'Tis a great city, but I am ready to return to me peaceful perch above the faro-board; I think 'twould rest me soul to see a game of craps."

"Why didn't you order Lucius to let up on the sight-seeing business?" Bertha said.

"And expose me weak knees to me nigger? No, no, Mike."

"I wanted you to let me rummage about alone."

"You did. But I could not allow that, neyther. So long as I can sit the road-cart or run me arms into a biled shirt I'll stay by, darlin'. 'Tis not safe for you to go about alone in the hell-broth of these Eastern streets. Besides, while I'm losin' weight I'm lighter on me feet than when I came. I've enjoyed me trip, but it does seem sinful to think of our big house standing empty and the horses 'stockin'' in their stalls, and I'm glad we're edgin' along homeward."

"So am I," Bertha heartily agreed, even as she looked lovingly back upon the mighty walls and towers which filled the sky behind her. It was a gloriously exciting place to live in, after all. "Some day I may come back," she promised herself, but the thought of Humiston lurking like a wolf in the shadow came to make her going more and more like an escape.

The elder Haney amused her by his frank comment on everything that was strange to him. His new teeth, which did not fit him very securely, troubled him greatly, and he spoke with one hand held alertly, ready to catch them if they fell, but his smile was a radiant grin, and his shrewd old face was good to look at as he faced the splendors of the limited express.

"'Tis foine as a bar-room," said he. "To be whisked about over the world like this is no hairdship. Bedad, if I'd known how aisy it was I'd a visited McArdle befoore." He pretended to believe that everybody travelled this way, and that Mart was merely doing the ordinary in the matter of meals and state-room; and as he wandered from end to end of the train and found only luxurious coaches, and people taking their ease, he had all the best of the argument. Lucius he regarded as a man of his own level, and they held long confabulations together—the colored man accepting this comradeship in the spirit of democracy in which it was given. Mart, for his part, sat looking out of the window, dreaming of the past.

As she neared Chicago next day Bertha thought with pleasure of seeing the Mosses again. Now that Humiston was eliminated, she had only the pleasantest memories of the people she had met in the smoky city. It was as if in a dark forest of lofty trees she had found a pleasant mead on which the warm sunlight fell. The mellow charm of the studios was made all the more appealing by reason of the drab and desolate waste through which she was forced to pass to attain the light and laughter of those high places.

Chicago had grown more gloomily impressive, and at the same time—by reason of her knowledge of the larger plans and mightier enterprises of New York—it seemed simpler, and Bertha re-entered the hotel which had once dazzled her in confidence, finding it cheerful and familiar. She liked it all the better because it was less pretentious. It gave her a pleasant sense of getting back home to have the men in buttons smile and say, "Glad to see you, Mrs. Haney." The head clerk was very cordial; he even found time to come out and shake hands. "I can't give you precisely your old quarters," he said, "but I can fix you out on the next floor. I'm sure you'll be very comfortable." Thereupon she took up her quietly luxurious life at the point where she had dropped it some weeks before.

There lay in this Western girl a strongly marked tendency towards the culture and refinement of the East; and, though she had grown up far from anything æsthetic in home-life, she instinctively knew and loved the beautiful in nature, the right thing in art; and now that she was about to leave the East for the West—perhaps to abandon the town for the village—she found herself aching with a hunger which had hitherto been unconscious. She was torn with desire to go and a longing to stay. New York, Paris, the world, was open before her if only she were content to take Marshall Haney's money and use it to these ends.

That night as she lay in her bed hearing the rumble and jar of the city's traffic, her mind recalled and dwelt upon the wonderful scenes, especially the beautiful pictures which her eyes had gleaned from the East. The magical, glittering spread of Manhattan harbor, the silver sweep of the Hudson at West Point, the mighty panorama from Grant's Tomb, the silken sheen of Fifth Avenue on a rainy night, the crash and glitter of upper Broadway, the splendid halls of art, literature, and especially of music and the drama—all these came back one by one to claim a place beside her peaks and cañons, sharing the glory of the purple deeps and the snowy heights of the mountains she had hitherto loved so single-heartedly and so well.

She saw Sibley now for what it was—a village almost barren of beauty—a good, kindly, homey place, but so little and so dull! To go back there to live was quite impossible. "If I quit Mart I must find something to do here—in the East. I can't stand Sibley."

She longed for the Springs because of her home there and because of Ben—but she realized that it possessed, after all, but very limited opportunities for the purchase of culture. The great centres had begun to exercise dominion over her. She had ever been a lonely little soul, with no confidante of her own sex. Speech had never been fluent with her, and she was still elliptical, curt, and in a sense inexpressive. She had no chatter, and the ways of women were in many directions alien to her. Miss Franklin had been her teacher, and yet, while respecting her, she had never learned to love her. Next to Ben Fordyce she leaned upon the judgment and sympathy of the sculptor, whose fine eyes were aglow with a high purpose. She was certain that he was both good and wise.

Mart was much amused at his father, who refused to sleep a second night at the hotel. "It's too far from the street," said he. "I think I'll go stay with Fan if ye'll lay out the course that leads to her dure." So Lucius went with him, bearing a message from Haney: "Tell Fan I'll be over to see her to-morrow. I'm too tired to go to-day," and the father hurried away in joyous relief.

"'Tis unnatural to see a son of mine in such Babylonish splendor," he confided to Lucius. "Faith, it gives me a turn every time I see him unwind a bill from that big wad he carries in his pocket. 'Tis like palin' a red onion to him—nothing more."

The Captain was up early next day, and eager to see how his sister was getting along in her new house, and to please him Bertha went with him. The transposition of the McArdles, like most charitable enterprises, had not been entirely a success. The children had blubbered at being torn away from their playmates and the alleys and runways which they infested. They were like lusty rats suddenly let loose in a fine new barn with no dark corners, no burrows, no rotten planks, chips, or coal-heaps to dig into or hide beneath. The alleys in Glenwood were leafy lanes, the streets parked and concreted, and the school-yard unnaturally clean and shaded by fine young trees—which no one was allowed to climb.

Furthermore, there was work to do in the garden—and this was onerous to the boys. Then, too, they had to fight their battles all over again. However, they did this with pleasure, establishing dreadful reputations among the neat, knickerbocker "sissies" who were foolish enough to cross them. Dress, Mrs. McArdle declared, was now a real trial. The girls had to be "in trim all the time," and the boys were as violently in contrast to their fellows as a litter of brindle barn-kits beside a well-groomed tabby-cat's family. "I'm clean worn out with it, Mart," she confessed. "We've been here two weeks the day, and the children howlin' the whole time to go back and McArdle workin' himself to the figger of a spoon with a mind to polish the lawn and get the garden into seed."

But Mart only smiled. "'Tis good discipline, Fan."

Haney senior was delighted with his daughter's household. "Faith, the roar and tumble of the whelps brings back to me me own wife and childer. Them was good days. 'Twas hard skirmishin' some weeks for bacon and p'taties, but I got 'em someway, and you ate ivery flick of it—snappin' and snarlin', but happy as a box of pups."

His son and daughter looked at each other and laughed; then Mart said: "'Tis a sad memory the father has, a most inconvenient and embarrassing mind."

They all stayed to dinner, and Bertha rolled up her sleeves and helped in the kitchen while the Captain went to market with Lucius. McArdle having got a half-day off, came home highly wrought up again at thought of meeting Captain Haney and his handsome wife. He looked distinctly less care-worn, though he confessed that it was hard to rise at the hour necessary to reach his work at seven. Bertha's heart warmed to him. In a certain dreamy, speculative turn of eye he was like her father—a man inventing new forms as naturally as other minds copy worn models. He was gaining in conversational powers, as he came to know Mart better, and took occasion to lay before him the plans for several inventions, small in themselves, but of possible value, so Lucius said.

There was something hearty, wholesome, and satisfying in this visit, and Bertha went away with increased liking for the McArdles. "I'm glad you gave them a boost, Mart," she said, as they left the house, "and you fixed it fine. Mac talked to me a half-hour explaining that you hadn't put it on a charity basis—just sold the house on long time."

"That was Lucius's idea. Wasn't it, Lucius?"

Lucius did not appear to hear.

They were whirring down an avenue bordered by elms in expanding leaf, the sky was filled with big white clouds like those which come and go over the great domes of the Rockies, and the air was warm and sweet, not yet dusked by the city's chimneys. Bertha's heart rose on joyous wing. "Let's call and take the Mosses for a ride," she suggested.

"With all the pleasure in the world," he replied; and when they drew up before the side door of the huge block, Bertha sprang out and hurried in without waiting for Lucius to accompany her.

Mrs. Moss came to the studio door, and Bertha's shining face so wrought upon her that she seized her and kissed her with sincere pleasure. "Joe, here's Mrs. Haney."

Moss was modelling a small figure on a stand near one of the windows, but left his work and came towards her with beaming smile. "What a coincidence! We were just discussing you. How do you do? Shake my arm—my hands are muddy." She took his outbent wrist and shook it with frank heartiness. He explained: "I said you'd come back; Julia declared, 'No. Once she tastes the glories of New York, good-bye to Chicago and the West.'"

Bertha interrupted: "I want you to lay off and go out for a whirl in our machine."

"How gay!" cried Moss. "I ought to be working, for my rent is coming due; but what's the diff? Here goes! Come on, Julia, we'll shut up shop and let art wag."

Julia was doubtful. "You know you promised—"

"Of course I did—that's the prerogative of the artist. Come on, now; I'll work to-night."

"To-night is the Hall's circus party."

"So it is! Well, no matter. I'm hungry for some whizzing, lashing, cool, clear air."

Dodging behind a screen in the corner, like an actor "doing a stunt," he reappeared a few moments later with clean hands, wearing a gray jacket and cap. "Hurry, hurry!" he called. He was like a lad invited to go fishing or swimming.

"I've been all 'balled up' since you went away," he explained—"took a contract to produce a certain line of ornamental reliefs; it never pays to be mercenary. But there it is! I was greedy, I went out for money—now behold me in the grasp of a business agreement. Can't sleep, can't breathe country air—had to work all day Sunday."

"It'll pay some of our debts, though," explained Mrs. Moss, "and buy the children's summer suits."

"Summer suits! Why summer suits? I only had one complete suit a year when I was a child— and that was a buff."

All the way down the elevator he gazed admiringly at Bertha. "My, my! how fit you look. Julia, why don't you get a hat and cloak like that?"

"Why don't I? Do you know why?" Then as they came out in sight of the 'mobile she said, "Why don't you furnish me an auto-car like this?"

"I will," he said, as though the notion had just risen in his mind. "I'll secure one this week."

Mart, who had taken a seat with Lucius, was touched and warmed by their hearty greeting, and they rolled away up the street as merry as school-children—even the self-contained Lucius smiled at Joe's odd turns of speech. Bertha's heart swelled with the keen delight of giving pleasure to her friends. This was, indeed, the chief of all the wondrous powers of money—it enabled one to be hospitable, to possess a home wherein visitors were always welcome, to own a car in which dear friends could ride; for the moment her resolution to give it all up weakened.

Moss was delirious with joy as they went sweeping up the Lake Shore Drive. He took off his cap and stood up in the car in order to drink deep of the wind that came over the water, crisp and clean and crystalline.

On the park mead the boys were playing ball, and the combination of green grass and soft and feathery foliage was very beautiful. The water-fowl were out, the captive cranes crying, and the drives were full of carriages and cars. It was all very cheering, with death and winter far away.

Moss, sobering somewhat, began to set forth his plan for making Chicago a new and greater Venice by bringing the lake into all the city boulevards and spanning these waterways with stately bridges of a new type, "designed by Joe Moss, of course," he added; "'twould make Venice look like a faded print in a lovely old song-book."

His talk took hold of Bertha's imagination—not because she cared to see Chicago adorned, but because he was so singularly altruistic in his concernments. That a man should live to make the world more beautiful was a wondrous discovery for her. He was not specially troubled about the physical welfare or the morals of the average citizen, but the city's grossness, its willingness to perpetuate ugly forms, rasped him, angered him.

She was eager to tell him of her own change of view, but waited till their ride was over and they were seated in the studio and a moment's private conversation was possible. Tingling with the stimulus of his fragmentary exclamations, she impulsively began: "If I were a poor girl who wanted to earn a living in the world, what would you advise me to do?"

"Get married!" His answer was jocular, but, observing her displeasure, he added: "I'm sorry I said that in just that tone, but at the same time I really mean it. A woman can do other things, but marry she must if she is to fulfil her place in the world—and be happy."

She was balked and disappointed, he perceived, and he was forced to go further: "I certainly wouldn't advise any girl to study painting or sculpture in the hope of making a living by it. The only side of art that isn't hopelessly out of the running is the decorative—home decoration is a sure and worthy profession. People don't feel keen need of sculpture, but they do like pretty walls and nice furniture. I know several highly successful women decorators— but I wouldn't advise that work for any one as an easy way to make a living, for the decorative sense is either a gift at birth or acquired after hard study."

"Do they teach it over there?" She nodded towards the lake. "I liked it over there," she said, wistfully. "You see I didn't get much of a show at school. I began to stay out to help mother when I was fourteen. I missed a whole lot. I'd kind o' like to make it up now if I could."

Moss was eager to probe a little deeper. "Your life is thrillingly romantic to us—the kind of thing we read of. Congdon writes that you have a superb home. I should think you'd hate to leave it, even for a visit."

Her hands strained together as if in resistance to an impulse of pleading; then she answered: "Yes—but then, you see, it isn't really mine—it's the Captain's."

"Yours by marriage."

"That's what people say—but I don't know. Sometimes I think I have no right to any part of it. You have to earn what you own, don't you?"

What was this doubt at her heart? The unexplained emotion in her voice moved him profoundly. He cautiously approached. "Of course, we know Frank Congdon—he likes to 'string' us Easterners and we take his yarns with due discount. I suppose Captain Haney, like many other Western men, is ready to try his luck now and again, and in that sense really is a gambler."

She faced him squarely. "No, he has been the real thing. He kept a saloon—when I first knew him, but he gave it all up for me. I wouldn't promise to marry him till he did. Everybody out there knows his career, and most people think he got his money underhand, but he tells me he didn't, and I take his word. Every dollar he spends on me or on our home comes out of some mines he owns. I told him I wouldn't touch a dollar of the saloon money—and I won't. Some folks think I don't care, but I do. I don't like the saloon business, and he got out and he's livin' straight now, as straight as any man. It's pretty hard on him, too, though he won't admit it. He must get awful sick of sittin' round the way he does. I tell him he needn't cut out all his old cronies on my account. He says he ain't sufferin', but it's like shuttin' a bronco up in the corral and lettin' the herd go back into the hills."

"Perhaps he thinks you're better fun than any of his cronies."

She ignored the implied compliment and went on:

"All the same, it's drawin' mighty close lines on him. You can't take a man living a free-and-easy life the way he was and wing him all at once and tie him down to a chair without seein' some suffering. Don't you know it?"

"Does he complain?"

"Not a whimper. Sometimes I wish he would. No, he just waits—but I'm afraid he'll get lonesome some day and break loose and go back to the game."

In this way the sculptor had come very close to her secret, and she was trembling to deeper confidence, when he said, very gently: "Of course, it does seem a little strange to me that one so young and charming as you are should be married to a man of his type, but I suppose he was a handsome figure before his—accident."

Her eyes glowed. "He was one of the grandest-looking men! I never liked his trade—and I mistrusted him, at first; but when he cut himself out of the whole business—for me—I couldn't help likin' him; he was so big-hearted and free-handed. We needed his help, all right.

Mother was sick, and my brother's ranch was playing to hard luck. But don't think I married him for his money—I liked him then, and, besides—well, I *thought* I was doing the right thing—but now—well, I'm guessing." She ended abruptly, and in the tremor of that final word Moss read her secret. She had never loved her husband. Pity and a kind of loyalty to her word had carried her to his side, and now a sense of duty bound her there.

With sincere sympathy, he said: "We all do wrong at times that good may come out of it. You could not foresee the future—the best of us can *only guess* at the effect of any action. You did the best you knew at the moment. The question you have to face now has only slight relation to the past. No one can enter wholly into another's perplexity—I'm not even sure of a single one of my inferences—but if you are thinking of—separation, I would say, meet this crisis as bravely as you met the other. But I don't believe we should decide any such question selfishly. I am not of those who always seek the side on which lies personal happiness, because a happiness that is essentially selfish won't last. The Captain lives only for you—any one can see that. What he does for you springs from deep affection. What would happen to him—if you left him?"

He paused a moment and watched her subduing her tears; then added: "I won't say I was unprepared for what you've said, for the entire relationship, from our first meeting, seemed too abnormal to be altogether happy. Money will buy a great many desirable things, but it has its limits. At the same time, it is too much to expect of you—If your feeling for him has changed—"

His delicacy, his sympathy for her, was made apparent by the unusual hesitation of his speech, and she would have broken down completely had not Julia Moss called out: "Joe, turn on the lights—it's getting dark."

Conscious of Bertha's emotion, he did not immediately do as he was bidden. "I wish you'd talk this over with Julia," he ended gently; "she's a very wise little woman."

Bertha shook her head. "I didn't intend to talk it over with you. I don't know what possessed me. I had no business to say what I did."

He reassured her. "All you've told me and the part I've guessed is quite safe. I will not even permit Julia to share your confidence till you are willing to speak to her yourself."

As he slowly lighted the studio Bertha was surprised and a little troubled to find that two or three other visitors had slipped in through the dusk, and were grouped about the tea-table, and that the Captain was again the centre of an eager-eyed group. "They treat him as if he were an Eskimo," she thought bitterly, and rose to join the circle and protect him from their inquisition.

Haney was feeling extremely well, and talked with so much of his old time vigor and slash of epithet that his little audience was quite entranced. He enlarged upon the experiences of a year he had spent in Alaska. "Mining up there in them days made gambling slow business," he said. He had told Bertha that he had made an attempt to get out of "the trade," but she was content to have him put it on less self-righteous grounds. He contrived to make his hearers feel very keenly the pitiless, long-drawn ferocity of that sunless winter. He made it plain why men in that far land came together in vile dens to drink and gamble, and Moss glowed with the wonder and delight of those great boys who could rush away to the arctic edge of the world and die with laughing curses on their lips.

"What did you all do it for?" he asked, bluntly. "For money?"

"Partly—but more for the love of doing something hard. No man but a miser punishes himself for love of gold—it's for love of what the stuff will buy, that men fight the snows."

While Haney talked of these things Bertha's eyes were musingly turned on the face of the sculptor, and her mind was far from the scenes which Mart so vividly described. This side of his life no longer amused her—on the contrary she shrank from any disclosure of his savage career. She was now as unjust in her criticism as she had been fond in her admiration, and when with darkening brow she cut short his garrulous flow of narrative Julia perceived her displeasure.

Haney apologized, handsomely. "It's natural for the ould bedraggled eagle in the cage with a club on his wrist to dream of the circles he used to cut and the fish he set claw to. In them days I feared no man's weight, and no night or stream. 'Twas all joyous battle to me, and now, as I sit here on velvet with only to snap me fingers for anything I want, I look back at thim fierce old times with a sneaking kind o' wish to live 'em all over again. Bertie knows me weakness. I would talk forever did she lave me go on; but 'tis no blame to her—it was a cruel, bad, careless life."

"When I come West," said Moss, sincerely, "we'll go camping together, and every night by the fire we'll smoke and you can tell me all about your journeys. I assure you they are epic to me."

Dr. Brent, a little later, put in a private word to Bertie. "Now you're going back into the high country and you'll find it necessary to watch the Captain pretty closely. I suspect he'll find his heart thumping briskly when he reaches the Springs. He may stand that altitude all right, but don't let him go higher. He will be taking chances if he goes above six thousand feet. You'd better have Steel of Denver come down and examine him to see how he stands the first few days. I mention Steel because I know him—I've no doubt there are plenty of good men in the Springs."

"What'll I do if he's worse?"

"Bring him back here or go to sea level—only beware of high passes."

CHAPTER XXIV

THE HANEYS RETURN TO THE PEAKS

The forces that really move most men are the small, concrete, individual experiences of life. The death of a child is of more account to its parents than the fall of a republic. Napoleon did not forget Josephine in his Italian campaigns, and Grant, inflexible commander of a half-million men, never failed, even in the Wilderness, to remember the plain little woman whose fireside fortunes were so closely interwoven with his epoch-making wars.

As Ben Fordyce lost interest in the question of labor and capital and the political struggles of the state because they were of less account than his own combat with the powers of darkness, so Bertha had little thought of the abstract, the sociologic, in her uneasiness—the strife was individual, the problems personal—and at last, weary of question, of doubt, she yielded once more to the protecting power which lay in Haney's gold and permitted herself to enjoy its use, its command of men. There was something like intoxication in this sense of supremacy, this freedom from ceaseless calculation, and to rise above the doubt in which she had been plunged was like suddenly acquiring wings.

She accepted any chance to penetrate the city's life, determined to secure all that she could of its light and luxury, and in return intrusted Lucius with plans for luncheons and dinners, which he carried out with lavish hand.

Mart seconded all her resolutions with hearty voice. "There's nothing too good for the Haneys!" he repeatedly chuckled.

In the midst of other gayeties she had the McArdles over to mid-day dinner one Saturday, and afterwards took them all, a noisy gang, to the theatre—Patrick Haney as much of a boy as his grandsons, McArdle alone being unhappy as well as uneasy.

She went about the shops, buying with reckless hand treasures for the house in the Springs, and this gave her husband more satisfaction than any other extravagance, for each article seemed a gage of the permanency of his home. In support of her mood he urged her to even larger expenditures. "Buy, buy like a queen," he often commanded, as she mused upon some choice. "Take the best!"

There was instruction as well as a guilty delight in all this conjuring with a magic check-book, and Bertha grew in grace and dignity in her rôle as hostess. Her circle of acquaintances widened, but the Mosses, her first friends in the city, were not displaced in her affections. To them she continued to play the generous fairy in as many pleasant ways as they would permit. The theatre continued to be her delight, as well as her school of life, and a box-party followed nearly every dinner. She was like a child in the catholicity of her appetite, for she devoured Shakespearian bread, Ibsen roasts, and comic opera cream-puffs with almost equal gusto— and mentally thrived upon the mixture. To the outsider she seemed one of the most fortunate women in the world.

And yet every day made her less tolerant of the crippled old man at her side. She did not pout or sulk or answer him shortly, but she often forgot him—failed to answer him—not out of petulance or disgust, but because her mind was busy with other people. Gradually, without realizing it, she got into the habit of leaving him to amuse himself, as he best could, for she knew he did not specially care for the pursuits which gave her the keenest joy. In consequence of this unintentional neglect he very naturally fell more and more into the hands of the bar-room spongers who loitered about the hotel corridors. He dreaded loneliness, and it was to keep his companions about him that he became a spendthrift in liquors. Sternly and deliberately temperate during his long career as a gambler, he fell at last into drinking to excess, and on one unhappy afternoon returned to Bertha quite plainly drunk.

She was both startled and disgusted by this sign of weakness, and he was not so blinded by the mist of his potations but that he perceived the shrinking reluctance of her touch as she aided Lucius in lifting him into the bed. His inert, lumpish form was at the moment hideously repulsive to her, and physical contact with him a dreaded thing. What was left if he lost that self-control which had made him admirable? She had always been able to qualify his other shortcomings by saying, "Well, anyhow, he don't drink." She could boast of this no longer.

It was a most miserable night for her. At dinner she was forced to lie about him for the first time, and she did it so badly that Joe Moss divined her trouble and came generously to her aid with a long and amusing story about Whistler.

The play to which she took her guests did not help her to laughter, for it set forth with diabolic skill the life of a woman who loathed her husband, dreaded maternity, and hated herself—a baffling, marvellously intricate and searching play—meat for well people, not for those mentally ill at ease or morally unstable. Of a truth, Bertha saw but half of it and comprehended less, for she could not forget the leaden hands and flushed face of the man she called husband—and whom she had left in his bed to sleep away his hours of intoxication. She pitied him now—but in a new fashion. Her compassion was mixed with contempt, and that showed more clearly than any other feeling could the depth to which Marshall Haney had sunk.

When she came home at midnight she listened at his door, but did not enter, for Lucius—skilled in all such matters—reported the Captain to be "all right."

She went to her own room in a more darkly tragic mood than she had ever known before. Her punishment, her time for trouble, had begun. "I reckon I'm due to pay for my fun," she said to herself, "but not in the way I've been figuring on." Haney seemed at the moment a complete physical ruin, and the change which his helplessness wrought in her was most radical.

His deeply penitent mood next morning hurt and repelled her almost as much as his maudlin jocularity of the night before. She would have preferred a brazen levity to this humble confession. "'Twas me boast," he sadly asserted, "that no man ever caught me with me eyes full of sand and me tongue twisted—and now look at me! 'Tis what comes of having nothing to do but trade lies with a lot of flat-bottomed loafers in a gaudy bar-room. But don't worry, darlin', right here old Mart pulls up. You'll not see anny more of this. Forget it, dear-heart— won't you now?"

She promised, of course, but the chasm between them was widened, and a fear of his again yielding to temptation cut short her stay in the city, for Lucius warningly explained: "The Captain is settling into a corner of the bar-room with a gang of sponging blackguards around him, and every day makes it less easy for him to break away. I'd advise going home," he ended, quietly. "The Springs is a safer place for him now."

The hyenas were beginning to prowl around the disabled lion, and this the faithful servant knew even better than the wife.

"All right, home we go," she replied, and the thought of "home" was both sweet and perilous.

Haney met her decision with pathetic, instant joy. "I'm ready, I was only waitin'," he said. "After all, your own shack is better than a pearl palace in anny town, and it's gettin' hot besides."

Bertha parted from the Mosses with keen sorrow. Joe had come to be like an elder brother to her—a brother and a teacher, and, next to Ben Fordyce, was more often in her thought than any other human being. She had lost part of her awe of him, but her affection had deepened as she came to understand the essential manliness and simplicity of his character. He redeemed the artist-world from the shame men like Humiston had put upon it.

As she entered for the last time the studio in which she had spent so many happy hours and from whose atmosphere of work and high endeavor she had derived so much mental and moral development she was sad, and this sadness lent a beauty to her face that it had never before attained. She looked older, too; and contrasting her with the girl who had first looked in at his door, Moss could scarcely believe that less than half a year had affected this change in her. He was too keen an observer not to know that part of this was due to a refining taste in hats and gowns, but beneath all these superficial traits she had grown swiftly in the expression of security and power.

He greeted her as usual with a frank nod and his hands being free from clay advanced to shake hands. "Don't tell me you've come to say good-bye."

"That's what," she curtly said. "It's up to me to take the Captain home. He's getting into bad habits lying around this hotel."

His face clouded. "I've been afraid of that," he answered, gently. "Yes, you'd better go home. It's harder for a man to have a good, easy time than it is for a woman. But sit down, Julia will be in soon; you mustn't go without seeing her."

After some further talk on trains and other common-places she became abruptly personal. "I've been having a whole lot of fun buying things and planting dollars, but I'm beginning to see an end to that kind of business. After you've got your house filled up with furniture and jimcracks, what you going to do then?"

"Burn 'em."

"And begin all over again? You can't buy out the town. It's a real circus for a while, but I can see there's a limit to it. Once you find out you can just go down here to one of these jewelry-stores and order anything you want—you don't want anything. Here I am with a lot of money that ain't mine, having a gay whirl spending it, but I can see my finish right now. To go on in this line would take all the fun out of life. What am I to do?"

Moss took a seat and looked at her thoughtfully. "I don't know. I used to think if I had money I'd start out and 'do good to people,' but I'm not at all sure that charity isn't all a damned impertinence. A couple of years ago I would have said go in for 'Neighborhood Settlements,' free libraries, 'Noonday Rests,' 'Open-air Funds,' and all the rest of it, but now I ask, 'Why?' We've had our wave of altruism, and I'm inclined to think a wave of selfishness would do us all good—but you're too young to be bothered with these problems. Go home and be happy while you can. Enjoy your gold while it glitters. Work is my only fun—real, enduring fun— and I'm not a bit sure *that* will last. Whatever you do, be yourself. Don't try to be what you think I or some one else would like to have you. I like you because you are so straight-forwardly yourself; I shall be heart-broken if you take on the disease of the age and begin to prate of your duty."

She listened to him with only partial comprehension of his meaning, but she answered: "I was brought up to think duty was the whole works."

"Yes, and your teacher meant duty to God, duty to others. Well, there's duty to one's self. The war of money and duty is the biggest mix of our day. It's simpler to be poor; then all you've got to worry about is bread and shoes and shingles."

"That's just it. Sometimes I wish I was back in the Golden Eagle, where I—" she ended in mid-sentence.

He laughed. "You sound like a middle-aged financier who mourns tattooed with dollar-marks for the days when he used to husk corn at seventy cents a day." She saw the humor of this, but was aware that without a knowledge of Ben Fordyce Joe could not understand her problem, therefore she abandoned her search for light and leading. "Well, anyhow, right here I quit what you fellows call civilization. I hate to lose you and Julia and the rest of the folks, but it's me to the high hills. You'll never know how much you've helped me."

"I hope you'll never know how thoroughly we've *done* you. An evil-minded person would say we'd worked you for dinners and drives most shameful. However, if you have enjoyed our company as thoroughly as we've delighted in your champagne and birds, we'll cry quits. All my theories of art and life I advance *gratis*. I ought to do something handsome for you— you've listened so divinely."

Underneath his banter Moss was sincerely moved. It was hard to say good-bye to this curious, earnest, seeking mind, this unspoiled child in whose face the world was being reflected as in a magical mirror. He loved her with frank affection—a pure passion that was more intimate than fraternal love and more exalted, in a sense, than the selfish, devouring passion of the suitor. It would have been difficult for him to say what his relationship to her at the moment was. It was more than friendship, more than brotherly care, and yet it was definably less than that of the lover.

Julia came in and was quite as outspoken in her regret, and both refused to say good-bye at the moment. "We'll see you at the station," they said, and Bertha went away, feeling the pain of parting less keen by reason of this promise.

Afterwards, as the hour for departure came near, she hoped they would not come. It was less difficult to say "I'll see you again" than to utter the curt "good-bye" which means so much in Anglo-Saxon life.

They came, however, together with several others of her friends, but in the bustle and confusion of the depot not much of sentiment could be uttered, and, though she felt that she was going for a long stay, she was prodigal of promises to return soon.

Patrick Haney was there, but refused to go with them. "Sure I'm at the jumpin'-off place now, and to immigrate furder would be to put meself in the hands of the murtherin' redskins." His talk was the touch of comedy which the situation needed. "Av ye don't mind I'll stay wid Fan," he said, a little more seriously, to Haney, who replied:

"All right, 'tis as Fan says," and so they entered the train for the upward climb.

Haney himself had only joy of the return. He sat at one of the windows of the library car and studied the prairie swells with a faint, musing smile, till the darkness fell, and was up early next morning, eager and curious, to see how the increasing altitude would affect him. Only towards the end of the second day after eating his dinner did he begin to feel oppressed.

"I smell the altitude," he confessed—"me breath is shortenin' a bit, but 'tis good to see the peaks again."

In this long ride the girl-wife dwelt dangerously on the bright face of Ben Fordyce. It was the thought of seeing him again that came at last to steal away her regret at parting from her Eastern friends. The splendor of the Eastern world faded at last, and she, too, soared gladly towards the mountains. Every doubt was swallowed up in a pleasure which was at once pure and beyond her control.

Ben would be at the station, she was certain, for Lucius had wired to him the time of their arrival, and he had instantly replied. "I'll be there, and very glad to see you"—these words, few and simple, were addressed to Marshall Haney, but they thrilled her almost as if Ben had spoken them to her. Was he as glad to have her return as she was to meet him again?

"A fine lad," remarked Haney, as he pocketed the envelope. "I wonder does he marry soon? He'd better decide now. I reckon Alice is not long for this climate—poor girl!"

His remark, so simple in itself, pierced to the centre of Bertha's momentary self-deception. "I have no right to think of him. He belongs to Alice Heath!" But the feeling that she herself belonged to Marshall Haney was gone. That she owed him service was true, but since the night of his drunkenness she had definitely and finally abandoned all thought of being his wife, soul to soul, in the rite that sanctifies law. True, he had kept his word, he had not offended again, but the mischief was done. To return to the plane on which they had stood when she gave her promise was impossible.

The day and the hour were such as make the plain lover content with his world. The earth, a mighty robe of closely woven velvet, mottled softly in variant greens, swept away to the west, under a soaring convexity of saffron sky, towards a cloudy altar whereon small wisps of vapor were burning down to golden embers, while beneath lay the dark-blue Rampart range. It was a world for horsemen, for free rovers, and for swift and tireless desert-kine. The course of winds, it lay, a play-ground for tempests that formed along the great divide and swept down over the antlike homes of men, acknowledging no barrier, exultant of their strength of wing and the weight of their horizon-touching armament.

Bertha loved this land, but only because it was an approach to the hills. She would have shuddered at its desolate, limitless sweep, treeless, shelterless, had not the dim forms of the distant peaks she loved so well rose just beyond. She lost her doubt as they approached, welcoming them as the gates of home. She forgot all save the swelling tide of longing in her heart.

As the train drew slowly in she caught sight of Ben's intent face among the throng, and was moved to the point of beating upon the window. He seemed care-worn and older in this glimpse, but at sight of her his sunny smile came back radiantly to his lips and glinted like sunshine from his eyes. In tremulous voice she called: "*There he is!*"

Self-revelation lay in this ecstatic cry and in the glad haste which kept her on her feet; but Haney, unsuspicious, content, found no cause for jealousy in her innocent and unrestrained delight at getting home.

Progress down the aisle seemed intolerably slow, for the passengers ahead of her, stubbornly sluggish, barred her way, but at last she stood looking into her lover's face, her eager hand pressed between his palms.

"Welcome home!" he called, and drew her to him as if moved almost beyond his control with desire to clasp her to his bosom. In that instant they forgot all their doubts and scruples—overpowered by the sense of each other's nearness.

She was the first to recover her self-command, and, pushing him away with a quick, decisive gesture, turned to aid Mart, whom Lucius was bringing slowly down the step.

Her heart was still laboring painfully as she faced Congdon, but she contrived to return his greeting as he remarked with quizzical glance, "I hope you'll not find our little town dull, Mrs. Haney."

Dull! She wanted to scream out her joy. She felt like racing to the big black team to throw her arms about their necks. Dull! There was no other spot in all the world so exalting as this small town and its over-peering peaks.

"Where is Mrs. Congdon?" she succeeded in asking at last.

"She has visitors and couldn't come," he answered. "But where's that 'mobile we've heard so much about?"

"Coming by fast freight."

"Freight! From all I've heard of your doings in Chicago I expected it to come as excess baggage."

It was cool, delicious green dusk—not dark—with a small sickle of moon in the west, and as they drove up the broad avenue towards home the town, the universe, was strangely sweet and satisfying. It seemed as though she had been gone an age—so much had come to her—so thick was the crowd of new experiences standing between her going and her return—so swiftly had her mind expanded in these months of vivid city life. "I'll never go away again," she said to Ben. "This country suits me."

"I'm glad to hear you say that," he answered, softly. In the most natural way he had put Congdon with Haney in the rear seat and had taken the place beside Bertha, and this nearness filled her with pleasure and an unwonted confusion. How big he was! and how splendid his clear, youthful profile seemed as it gleamed silver-white in the light of the big street-lamps. Never had his magnetic young body acted upon her so powerfully, so dangerously. His firm arm touching her own was at once a delight and a dread. She was all woman at last, awake, palpitant with love's full-flooding tide—bewildered, dizzy with rapture. Speech was difficult and her thought had neither sequence nor design.

Fordyce was under restraint also, and the burden of the talk fell upon Congdon, who proceeded in his amusingly hit-or-miss way to detail the important or humorous happenings, of the town, and so they rolled along up the wide avenue to the big stone steps before the looming, lamp-lit palace which they called home.

Ben sprang out first, glad of another opportunity to take Bertha's hand, a clasp that put the throbbing pain back in her bosom—filling her with a kind of fear of him as well as of herself—and without waiting for the Captain she ran up the walk towards the wide doorway where Miss Franklin stood in smiling welcome.

Her greeting over, the young wife danced about the hall, crying: "Oh, isn't it big and fine! And aren't you glad it's our own!" She appeared overborne by a returning sense of security and ownership, and ran from room to room with all the ecstasy and abandon of a child—but she stopped suddenly in the middle of her own chamber as if a remorseless hand were clutching at her heart. "But it is *not* mine!—I must give it all up!"

Thrusting this intruding thought away, she hurried back to the library, where the men were seated at ease, sipping some iced liquor in gross content.

Haney was beaming. "It makes me over new to sniff this air again," he was saying. "'Tis a bad plan to let go your hold on mountain air. Me lungs have contracted a trifle, but they'll expand again. I'll be riding a horse in a month."

Ben was sympathetic, but had eyes only for Bertha, whose improvement in mind as in bearing astonished and delighted him. Her trip, coming just at the period when her observation was keenest and her memory most tenacious, had subtly, swiftly ripened her. Wrought upon by a thousand pictures, moved by strange words and faces, unconsciously changing to the color of each new conception, deriving sweetness and charm from every chance-heard strain of music and poetry, she had opened like a rose.

The middle-aged are prone to go about the world carrying their habits, their prejudices, and their ailments with them to return as they went forth; but youth like Bertha's adventures out into the world eager to be built upon, ready to be transformed from child to adult, as it would seem, in a day.

"She has achieved new distinction!" Ben exulted as he watched her moving about the room, so supple, so powerful, and so graceful, but, though he was careful not to utter one word of praise, he could not keep the glow of admiration from his eyes.

An hour later as he said good-night and went away with Congdon, his heart burned with secret, rebellious fire. "Was it not hateful that this glorious girl should be doomed to live out the sweetest, most alluring of her years with a gross and crippled old man?" To leave her under the same roof with Mart Haney seemed like exposing her to profanation and despair.

They were hardly out of the gate before Congdon broke forth in open praise of her. "When Mart dies, what a witching morsel for some man!"

Fordyce did not answer on the instant, and when he did his voice was constrained. "You don't think he's in immediate danger of it—do you?"

"Quite the contrary. He looks to be on the upgrade; but it's a safe bet she outlives him, and then think of her with a hundred thousand dollars a year to spend! Talk about honey-pots!—and flies!" After a moment's silence he added, musingly: "Funny how one's ideas change. A year ago I thought she was deeply indebted to him; now I feel that with all his money he can't possibly repay her for what she's giving up on his account. And yet his chink has made her what she is. Money is a weird power when applied to a woman. Tiled bath-rooms, silk stockings and bonnets work wonders with the sex. She's improved mightily on this trip."

After leaving Congdon, Ben went to his apartment and telephoned Alice to say that the Haneys had arrived and that he had left them under their own roof in good repair.

"How is the Captain's health?" she asked, with the morbid interest of the invalid gossip.

"He feels the altitude a little, but that is probably only temporary. They both seem very glad to get home."

"He's made a mistake. He can't live here—I am perfectly sure of it. How is she?"

"Very well—and beautifully dressed, which is the main thing," he added, with a slight return of his humor. "They asked after you very particularly."

Unable to sleep, he went out to walk the night, blind envy in his brain and a hot hunger in his heart, moved as he had never been moved before at thought of Haney's nearness to that glowing girl. Their union was monstrous, incredible.

He no longer attempted to deceive himself. He loved this young wife whose expanding personality had enthralled him from their first meeting. It was not alone that she was possessed of bodily charm—she called to him through the mysterious ways which lead the one man to the predestined woman. The affection he had borne towards Alice Heath was but the violet ray of friendship compared to the lambent, leaping, red flame of his passion for Bertha Haney. She represented to him the mysterious potency and romance of the West—typifying its amazing resiliency, its limitless capability of adaptation. In a way that seemed roundabout and strange, but which was, after all, very simple and very direct, she had lifted her family as well as herself out of poverty back into the comfort which was their right. Odd, masculine, unexpected of phrase, she had never been awkward or cheap. Congdon was right, she was capable of high things. She made mistakes, of course, but they were not those which a shallow personality would make—they sprang rather from the overflow of a vigorous and abounding imagination.

"All she needs is contact with people of the right sort. She is capable of the highest culture," he concluded.

That she was more vital to him than any other woman in the world he now knew, but he acknowledged nothing base in this confession. He was not seeking ways to possess her of his love—on the contrary, he was resolved to conduct himself so nobly that she would again trust and respect him. "My love is honorable," he said. "I will go forward as in the beginning—why should I not?—enjoying her companionship as any honest man may do."

The question of his relation to Alice was not so easily settled. She had come to irritate him now. Her changeable, swift-witted, moody, hysterical invalidism had begun to wear upon him intolerably. Everything she did was wrong. It was brutal even to admit this, but he could no longer conceal it either from himself or from her. It was deeply, sadly painful to recall the promise, the complete confidence and happiness with which they had both started towards the West. How sure of her recovery they had been, how gay and confident of purpose! Now she not only refused to listen to his demand for an early marriage, but hampered and annoyed him in a hundred ways. As he walked the silent night he was forced to acknowledge that she had been right in delaying their union. And yet how dependent upon him she was. Her life was so tragically inwound with his that to think of shaking away her hand seemed the act of a sordid egoist.

"And even were I free, nothing is solved."

The situation took on the insoluble and the tragic. In the fashion of well-bred, soundly nurtured American youth he had thought of such complications only as subjects for novelists. "There must be concealment, but not duplicity, in my attitude," he decided. He longed for the constant light of Bertha's face, the frequent touch of her hand. Her laughter was so endlessly charming, her step so firm, so light, so graceful. The grace of her bosom—the sweeping line of her side—

He stopped there. In that direction lay danger. "She trusts me, and I will repay her trust. She has chosen me to be her adviser, putting her wealth in my hands!—Well, why not? We will see whether an honorable man cannot carry forward even so difficult a relationship as this. I will visit her every day, I will enjoy her hospitality as freely as Congdon, and I will fulfil my promise to Alice—if she asks it of me."

But deep under the sombre resolution lay an unuttered belief in his future, in his happiness— for this is the prerogative of youth. The dim mountains, the sinking crescent moon, and the silence of the plain all seemed somehow to prophesy both happiness and peace.

CHAPTER XXV

BERTHA'S DECISION

It was good to wake in her old room and see the morning light breaking in golden waves against the peaks, to hear her dogs bay and to listen to the murmuring voice of the fountains on the lawn. It was deliciously luxurious to sit at breakfast on the vine-clad porch with the shining new coffee-boiler before her, while Miss Franklin expressed her admiration of the napery and china which the Mosses had helped her to select.

It was glorious to go romping with the dogs about the garden, and most intoxicating to mount her horse and ride away upon the mesa, mad with speed and ecstatic of the wind. No one could have kept pace with her that first day at home. She ran from one thing to the other. She unpacked and spread out all her treasures. She telegraphed her mother and 'phoned her friends. She gave direction to the servants and examined every thing from the horses' hoofs to the sewing-machine. She went over the house from top to bottom to see that it was in order.

She was crazy with desire of doing. Her mid-day meal was a mere touch-and-go lunch, but when at last she was seated in her carriage with Haney and Miss Franklin she fell back in her seat, saying, "I feel kind o' sleepy and tired."

"I should think you would!" exclaimed her teacher.

"Of all the galloping creatures you are the most wonderful. I hope you're not to keep this up."

Haney put in a quiet word. "She will *not*. Sure, she cannot. There'll be nothin' left for to-morrow."

Their ride was in the nature of a triumphal progress. Many people who had hesitated about bowing to them hitherto took this morning to unbend, and Mart observed, with a good deal of satisfaction: "The town seems powerful cordial. I think I'll launch me boom for the Senate."

At the bank-door, where the carriage waited while Bertha transacted some business within, he held a veritable reception, and the swarming tourists, looking upon the sleek and shining team and the gray mustached, dignified old man leaning from his seat to shake hands, wondered who the local magnate was, and those who chanced to look in at the window were still more interested in the handsome girl in whose honor the president of the bank left his mahogany den.

In truth, Bertha had won, almost without striving for it, the recognition of the town. Those who had never really established anything against her seized upon this return as the moment of capitulation. There was no mystery about her life. She was known now, and no one really knew anything evil of her—why should she be condemned?

In such wise the current of comment now set, and Mrs. Haney found herself approached by ladies who had hitherto passed her without so much as a nod. She took it all composedly, and in answer to their invitations bluntly answered: "The Captain ain't up to going out much, and I don't like to leave him alone. Come and see us."

She was composed with all save Fordyce, who now produced in her a kind of breathlessness which frightened her. She longed for, yet dreaded, his coming, and for several days avoided direct conversation with him. He respected this reserve in her, but was eager to get her comment on the East.

"How did you like New York," he asked one night as they were all in the garden awaiting dinner.

"It scared me," she answered. "Made me feel like a lady-bug in a clover-huller; but it never phased the Captain," she added, with a smile. "'There's nothin' too good for the Haneys,' says he, and we sure went the pace. We turned Lucius loose. We spent money wicked—enough to buy out a full-sized hotel."

Her quaint, shrewd comment on her extravagances amused Ben exceedingly, and by keeping to a line of questioning he drew from her nearly all her salient experiences—excepting, of course, her grapple with the degenerate artist.

"Lucius turned out the jewel they said he was?"

She responded with enthusiasm. "I should say he did! He knew everything we wanted to know and more too. We'd have wandered around like a couple of Utes if it hadn't been for him. *When in doubt ask Lucius*, was our motto."

She told stories of the elder Haney and the McArdles, and described the trials of the children in their new home till Ben laughingly said: "It's hard to run somebody else's life—I've found that out."

And Haney admitted with a chuckle that Mac was "a little bewildered, like a hen with a red rag on her tail—divided in his mind like. As for Dad, he still thinks me a burglar on an improved plan."

They also talked of Bertha's studies, for Miss Franklin began at once to give her daily instruction in certain arts which she considered necessary to women of Mrs. Haney's position, and always at the moment of meeting they spoke of Alice—that is to say, Haney with invariable politeness asked after her health, and quite as regularly Ben replied: "Not very well." Once he added: "I can hardly get her out any more. She seems more and more despondent."

This report profoundly troubled Bertha, and the sight of Alice's drawn and tragic face made her miserable. There was something in the sick woman's gaze which awed her, and she was careful not to be left alone with her. The thought of her suffering and its effect on Ben threw a dark shadow over the brightness of her world. She was filled, also, with a growing uneasiness by reason of Mart's change of attitude towards herself. In the excitement of his home-coming he seemed about to regain a large part of his former health and spirits. His eyes brightened, his smile became more frequent, the appealing lines of his brow smoothed out, and save for an occasional shortening of the breath his condition appeared to be improving.

This access of vitality was apparent to Bertha, and should have brought joy to her as to him; but it did not, for with returning vitality his attitude towards her became less of the invalid and more of the lover. He said nothing directly—at first—but she was able to interpret all too well the meaning of his jocular remarks and his wistful glances. Once he called her attention to the returning strength in his arm. "The ould man is not dead yet," he exulted, lifting his disabled arm and clinching his fist. "I feel younger than at any time since me accident," and as he spoke she perceived something of the lion in the light of his eyes.

One night as she was passing his chair he reached for her and caught her and drew her down upon his knee. "Sit ye down a wink. Ye're always on the move like a flibberty-bidget."

She struggled free of his embrace, her face clouded with alarm and anger. "Don't be a fool," she said, harshly.

He released her, saying, humbly: "Don't be angry, darlin', 'tis foolish of me, an ould crippled wolf, to be thinking of matin' with a fawn like y'rself. I don't blame ye. Go your ways."

She went to her room, with his voice—so humbly penitent and resigned—lingering in her ears, trembling with the weight of the burden which his amorous mood had laid upon her.

She resented his action the more because life at the moment was so full of joy. Each morning was filled with pleasant duties, and each afternoon they drove to the office to discuss the mines with Ben, and in the evening he called to sit for an hour or two on the porch, smoking, talking, till Mart grew sleepy and yawned. These meetings were deliciously, calmly delightful, for Mrs. Gilman or Miss Franklin was always present, and, though the talk was general, Ben talked for her ears at times, but always impersonally, and she honored him for his delicacy, his reserve, his respect for her position as a married woman, recognizing the care with which he avoided everything which might embarrass her.

And now, by force of Mart's humble suing, her half-forgotten scruples were revived. Her uneasiness began again. A decision was finally and definitely thrust upon her. Instantly she was beset by all her doubts and desires, and the sky darkened with clouds of trouble.

To make Mart happy was still her wish, but the way was not so easy of choice, nor so simple to follow as it had once seemed. The briers were thick before her feet. There was so much of personal gratification, so much of selfish pleasure, in remaining his companion, warmed and defended by all the comfort and dignity which his wealth had brought to her, that it seemed a kind of treachery to halt with her duty half done. To be his spouse, to become the mother of his children, this alone would entitle her to his bounty. "I can't do it!" she cried out—"I can't, I can't!" And yet not to do his will was to remain a pensioner and to be under indictment as an adventuress.

She had read somewhere these words from a great philosopher: "The woman who bears a child to any man should instantly be lawfully seized of one-half his goods, for by that sublime act she takes her life in her hand as truly as the soldier who charges upon an invading host. The anguish of maternity should sanctify every woman."

On the other side of her hedge lay enticing freedom. It seemed at times as though to be again in the little office of the Golden Eagle Hotel would be a more perfect happiness than this she now enjoyed—but that, too, was illusory. How could she repay the money she had used? The moment she left Marshall Haney she would not only be poor, she would be profoundly in his debt. Where could she find the money to repay him and to make her schooling possible?

Perplexity was in her darkened eyes. Happiness and sorrow, doubt and delight grew along each path—thickly interwoven—and decision became each day more difficult. It was hateful to lie under the charge of having married merely for a gambler's money, and yet to plunge her mother and herself back into poverty would seem to others the act of one insane. As she pondered the problem of her life she lost all of her girlish lightness of heart and lay in her luxurious bed a brooding, troubled woman.

She could have gone on indefinitely with the half-filial, half-fraternal relationship into which she and Mart had fallen, but the thought of that other most intimate, most elemental union which his touch had made more definite than ever before produced in her a shudder of repulsion, of positive loathing. She could no longer endure the clasp of his hand, and in spite of herself she was forced, by contrasting experience, to acknowledge the allurement which lay in Ben Fordyce's handsome face and strong and graceful body.

"I must go away—for a while at least. I'll go back to the ranch and think it over."

And yet even the ranch was partly Haney's! How could she escape from her indebtedness to him? To what could she turn to make a living? To leave this big house and her horses, her garden, her dresses and jewels, required heroic resolution, but what of the long days of toil and dulness to which she must return?

Worn with the ceaseless alternations of these thoughts, she fell into a dream that was half a waking vision. She thought she had just packed a bag with the gown she wore the night she came to Haney's rescue, when he came shuffling into her room and said: "Where are you goin', darlin'?"

She replied: "To the ranch—to think things over."

The tears came to his eyes, and he said: "'Tis the sun out of me sky when ye go, Bertie. Do not stay long."

She promised to be back soon, but rode away with settled intent never to return.

No one knew her on the train, for she had drawn her veil close and sat very still. It seemed that she went near the mine in some strange way, and at the switch Williams got on the train to stop her and persuade her to return. He was terribly agitated. "Didn't you know Mart is sick?" he said, in a tone of reproach. It seemed as if a broad river of years flowed between herself and the girl who used to see this queer little man enter her hotel door—but he was unchanged. "You can't do this thing!" he went on, his lips trembling with emotion.

"What thing?" she asked.

"Fordyce tells me you're going to throw poor old Mart overboard."

"That's my notion—I can't be his wife, and so I'm getting out," she answered.

"But, girl, you can't do that!" and he swore in his excitement. "Mart needs you—we all need you. It'll kill him."

"I can't help it!" she answered, with infinite weariness in throat and brain. "I pass it up, and go back to my brother."

"I don't see why."

"Because I've no right to Mart's money."

"You're crazy to think of such a thing. You a queen! Who's goin' to catch the money when you drop it?" he asked, and helplessly added: "I don't believe you. You're kiddin', you're tryin' us out."

"I'm doing nothing to earn this luxury."

"Doing nothing! My God, you've made Mart Haney over new. You've converted him—as they say, you've redeemed him. Let me tell you something, little sister, Mart worships you. It does him good just to *see* you. You don't expect the moon to fry bacon, do you? Stars don't run pumps! Mart is satisfied. Every time you speak to him or pass by him he gets happy all the way through—I know, for I feel just the same."

There was something in his eloquence that went to the heart of the dreaming girl. If any one in her world was to be trusted it was this ugly little man, who never presumed to ask even a smile for himself, and whose unswerving loyalty to Mart made her own flight a base and cruel act; and yet even as he pleaded his face faded and she fancied herself stepping from the train in Sibley, unnoticed by even the hackmen, who used to bring the humbler passengers of each train to the door of the Golden Eagle Hotel.

She walked up the sidewalk, surprised to find it changed to brick. The hotel was gone, and in its place stood a saloon marked, "Haney's Place." This hardened her heart again. "That settles it!" she said, bitterly. "He's gone back to his old business."

The road out to the ranch seemed very long and hot, but she had no money, not a cent left with which to hire a carriage, and she kept saying to herself: "If Mart knew this, he'd send Lucius and the machine. I reckon he'd be sorry to see me walking in this dust. It's a good thing I have my old brown dress on." She passed lovingly, regretfully over the splendid gowns which hung in her wardrobe. "What will become of them?" she asked. "Fan can't wear them." This called up a vision of Fan and her eldest daughter, sweeping about in her splendor, her opera-cloak only half encompassing the mother, while the girl swished over the floor in the gown she had worn at her last dinner in the East. She laughed and cried at the same time—it was painful to see them thus abused.

Then she seemed suddenly to enter the grove of twisted, hag-like cedars which stood upon the mesa back of the ranch-house. "By-and-by I will look like this," she dreamed, and laid her hand on one that was ragged and gnarled and gray with a thousand years of sun and wind, and even as she stood there, with the old crones moaning round her, Ben suddenly confronted her.

Her first impulse was for flight, so sad and bitter was his face. She began to pity him. His boyhood seemed to have slipped from him like a gay cloak, revealing the stern man beneath.

He met her gravely, self-containedly, yet with restrained passion, and his voice was sternly calm as he began: "I have come to ask you what you wish to do with Marshall Haney's inheritance? I will not be a party to your action. I helped him plan out his will, and he said he could trust you to do the right thing, and I have come to tell you that his will must be yours."

"What do you mean?" she asked.

"He is dead!" he replied.

Her heart turned to ice at the sound of his words, so clear, succinct, and piercing; then the cedars began to wail and wail, and sway in eldrich grief, but she who felt most remorse could not utter a sound to prove her own despair; and in the tumult her dream ended abruptly, and she woke to hear the night wind whistling weirdly through the screen of her open window.

She lay in silence, shuddering with the subsiding terror of her vision, till she came to a full realization of the fact that it was all but a night terror and that Mart was still alive and her decision not yet irrevocably made.

She shuddered again—not in grief, but in terror—as she relived the vivid hour of self-chosen poverty which her dream had brought her. Yes, the magic of wealth had spoiled her for

Sibley and the ranch. To go back there was impossible. "I will try the East," she said. "The Mosses will help me." And yet to return to Chicago—after having played the grand lady—would be bitterly hard. Suppose her friends should meet her with cold eyes and hesitating words? Suppose they, too, had loved her money and not herself? Suppose even Joe, who seemed as true as Williams, should prove to be a selfish sycophant. Ah yes, it would be a different city with the magic of Haney's money no longer hers to command.

In this hour of deepest misery and despair the sheen of his gold returned like sunlight after a storm; and yet, even as she permitted herself to imagine how sweetly the new day would dawn with her determination to remain the mistress of this great house, the old fear, the new disgust, returned to plague her. Her love for Ben Fordyce came also—and the knowledge that Alice was dying of a broken heart because of Ben's growing indifference—all these perplexities made the coming of sunlight a mockery.

She rose to the new day quite as undecided as before and more deeply saddened. One thing was plain—Ben should come no more to visit her—for Alice's sake he must keep the impersonal attitude of the legal adviser. In that way alone could even the semblance of peace be won.

CHAPTER XXVI

ALICE VISITS HANEY

Alice Heath was dying of something far subtler than "the White Death," to which Haney so often referred. Tortured by Ben's studied tenderness when at her side, she suffered doubly when he was away, knowing all too well that his keenest pleasure now lay in Bertha's companionship. Her doubt darkened into despair. In certain moments of exaltation she rose to such heights of impersonal passion as to acknowledge fully, generously, the claims of youth and health—admitting that she and Marshall Haney were the offenders and not the young lovers, whose desire for happiness was but an irresistible manifestation of the mystic force which binds the generations together.

"Why do we not quietly take ourselves off and make them happy?" she asked herself. "Of what selfish quality is our love? Here am I only a spiteful, hopeless invalid—I hate myself, I despise my body and everything I am. I loathe my wrinkled face, my shrivelled hands, my flat chest. I am fit only to be bride to death. I'm tired of the world—tired of everything—and yet I do not die. Why can't I die?"

These moods never soared high enough or sank quite low enough to permit the final severing stroke, and she ended each of them in a flood of tears, filled with ever-greater longing for the beautiful young lover whose heart had wandered away from her. It was hard not to welcome him when he came, but infinitely harder to send him away, for life held no other solace, the day no other aim.

In her saner moments she was aware of her own misdemeanor. She knew that her morbid questioning, her ceaseless grievings were wearing away her vital force, and that no doctor could ever again medicine her to sweet sleep, that no wind or cloud would bring coolness to her burning brain. "I am no longer worthy of any man's love," she admitted to her higher self.

She did not question Ben's honor—he was of those who keep faith. "He has no hope of ever being other than the distant lover of Bertha Haney, and he is ready to fulfil his word to me, but I will not permit him to bind himself to me. It would be a crime to lay upon him the burden of a wife old before her time, sterile and doomed to a slow decline." She revolted, too, at the thought of having a husband, whose heart was elsewhere, whose restless desire could not be held within the circuit of his wife's arms—and yet she could not give him up.

As her flesh lost its weight and her blood its warmth, her mind burned with even more mysterious brightness, sending out rays of such perilous sublimation that she was able to perceive, as no earthly inhabitant should do, the jealously guarded secrets of those surrounding her, and on the night of Bertha's struggle against her fate she divined in some supersensuous way the tumult in the young wife's mind.

She laughed at first with a cruel, bitter delight, but at last her nobler self conquered and she resolved to have private speech with Haney. She perceived a danger in the ever-deepening passion of the young lovers. She began to fear that their love might soon break over all barriers, and this she was still sane enough of thought and generous enough of soul to wish to prevent.

Her decision to act was hastened by a slurring paragraph in the morning paper wherein veiled allusion was made to "a developing scandal." She lay abed all the forenoon brooding over it, and when she rose it was to dress for her visit to Haney. Sick as she was and almost hysterical with her mood, she ordered a carriage and drove to the gambler's house, hoping to find him alone, determined upon an interview.

It chanced that he was sitting in his place upon the porch watching the gardener spraying a tree. He greeted his visitor most cordially, inviting her to a seat. "Bertie is down town, but she'll be back soon."

"I'm glad she is away, Captain Haney, for I have something to say to you alone."

"Have you, indeed? Very well, I've nothing to do but listen—'tis not for me to boss the gardener."

She looked about with uneasy eyes, finding it very difficult to begin her attack. "How much you've improved the place," she remarked, irrelevantly, her voice betraying the deepest agitation.

He looked at her white face in astonishment. "How are ye, the day, miss?"

"I'm better, thank you, but a little out of breath—I walked too fast, I think."

"Does the altitude make your heart jump, too?" he asked, solicitously.

"No, my trouble is all in my mind—I mean my lungs," she answered. Then, with a ghastly attempt at sprightliness, she added: "Now let's have a nice long talk about symptoms—it's so comforting. How are *you* feeling these days?"

Haney answered with unwonted dejection. "I'm not so well to-day, worse luck. This is me day for thinkin' the doctors are right. They all agree that me heart's overworked up here." His dejection was really due to Bertha's moody silence.

"I'm sorry to hear that. Do they think you may live safely at sea-level?"

"They say so. Me own feeling is that the climate is not to blame. 'Tis age. I'm like a hollow-hearted tree, ready to fall with the first puff of ill wind. I've never been a man since that devil blew me to pieces."

She put her right hand upon his arm. "Is it not a shame that you and I should stand in the way of two fine, wholesome, young people—shutting them off from happiness?"

He turned a glance upon her quite too penetrating to be borne. "You mane—what?—who?"

"I mean Bertha."

"Do I stand in the way of her happiness?"

She met the question squarely, speaking with tense, drawn lips. "Yes, just as I do in Ben's way. We're neither of us fit to be married, and they are."

His eyes wavered. "That's true. I'm no mate for her—and yet I think I've made her happy." He was silent a moment, then faltered: "Ye lay your hand on a sore spot—ye do, surely. 'Tis true I've tried to have the money make up for me other shortcomings." He ended almost humbly.

"Money can do much, but it can't buy happiness."

"That's true, too—but 'tis able to buy comfort, and that's next door to happiness in the long-run, I'm thinkin'. But I'm watchin' her, and I don't intend to stand in her way, miss. I've told her so, and when the conquering lad comes along I mane to get out of the road."

"Have you said that?" Her face reached towards his with sudden intensity, and a snakelike brilliancy glittered in her eyes. "You've gone as far as that?"

"I have."

"Then act, for the time has come to make your promise good. Bertha already loves a man as every girl should love who marries happily, and the gossips are even now busy with her name."

He was hard hit, and slowly said: "I don't believe it! Who is the man?—tell me!" He demanded this in a tone that was not to be denied.

She delivered her sentence quickly. "She loves Ben. Haven't you seen it? She has loved him from their first meeting. I have known it for a long time, almost from the first; now everybody knows it, and the society reporters are beginning their innuendoes. The next thing will be her picture in the sensational press, and a scandal. Don't you know this? It must not happen! We must make way for them—you and I. We cumber the path."

He sank back into his seat and studied her from beneath his overhanging eyebrows as intently, as alertly, as silently as he was wont to do when watching the faces of his opponents in a game of high hazard. There was something uncanny, almost elfish, in the woman's voice and eyes, and yet even before her words were fully uttered the truth stood revealed to him. His eyes lost their stern glare, his hands, which had clutched the arms of his chair, relaxed. "Are you sure?" he asked again, but more gently. "You've got to be sure," he ended, almost in menace.

"You may trust a jealous woman," she answered. "I don't blame them—observe that. We are the ones to blame—we who are crippled and in the way, and it is our duty to take ourselves off. What is the use of spoiling their lives just for a few years of selfish gratification of our own miserable selves?"

He felt about for comfort. "They are young; they can wait," he stammered, huskily.

"But they *won't* wait!" she replied. "Love like theirs can't wait. Don't you understand? They are in danger of forgetting themselves? Can't you see it? Ben talks of nothing else, dreams of nothing else but her, and she is fighting temptation every day, and shows it. It's all so plain to me that I can't bear to see them together. They have loved each other from the very first night they met—I felt it that day we first rode together. I've watched her grow into Ben's life till she absorbs his every thought. He's a good boy, and I want to keep him so. He respects your claim, and he is trying to be loyal to me, but he can't hold out. I am ready to sacrifice myself, but that would not save him. He loves your wife, and until you free her he is in danger of wronging her and himself and you. I've given up. There is nothing more on this earth for me! What do *you* expect to gain by holding to a wife's garment when she—the woman—is gone?"

The wildness in her eyes and voice profoundly affected Haney, who was without subtlety in affairs of the heart. The women he had known had been mainly coarse-fibred or of brutish directness of passion and purpose, and this woman's words and tone at once confused and appalled him. All she said of his unworthiness as a husband was true. He had gone to Sibley at first to win Bertha at less cost than making her his wife—but of that he had repented, and on his death-bed as he thought he had sought to endow her with his gold. Since then he had lived, but only as half a man. Up to this moment he had hoped to regain his health, but now every hope died within him.

Part of this he admitted at once, but he ended brokenly: "'Tis a hard task you set for me. She's the vein of me bosom. 'Tis easy talkin', but the doin' is like takin' y'r heart in your two hands and throwin' it away. I knew she liked the lad—I had no doubt the lad liked her—but I did not believe she'd go to him so. I can't believe it yet—but I will not stand in her way. As I told her, I did not expect to tie her to an old hulk; I thought I was dying when I married her, and I only had the ceremony then to make sure that me money should feed her and protect her from the storms of the world. I wanted to take her out of a hole where she was sore pressed, and I wanted to make her people comfortable. I've brought her to this house. Me money has always been to her hand. It rejoices me to see her spend it, and I've been hoping that these things— me money—would make up for me poor, old, crippled body. I've been a rough man. I lived as men who have no ties have always lived—till I met her, then I quit the game. I put aside everything that could make her ashamed. I'm no toad, miss—I know she has that in her soul that can take her out of my level. Were I twenty years younger and a well man I could folly her—but 'tis no use debating now. I'll talk with her this night—" He paused abruptly and turned upon her with piercing inquiry: "Have you discussed this with Ben?"

She was beginning to tremble in face of the storm which she foresaw looming before her. "No—I lacked the courage."

A faintly bitter smile stirred his upper lip. "Shall I tell him what you have said to me?"

"No, no!" she exclaimed, in sudden affright, "I will tell him."

"Be sure ye do. As for these editors, I have me own way of dealing with them. I will soon know whether you are right or wrong. Ye're a sick woman, and such, they say, have queer fancies. You admit you're jealous, and I've heard that jealous women are built of hell-fire and vitriol. Anyhow, you've not shaken me faith in me girl—but ye have in Ben, for I know the heart of man. We're all alike when it comes to the question of women."

"Please don't misunderstand me—it is to keep them both what they are, good and true, that I come to you—we must not tempt them to evil."

"I understand what you say, miss, and I think you're honest, but you may be mistaken. I saw her meet-up with fine young fellies in the East; I could see they admired her—but she turned them down easily. She's no weak-minded chippy, as I know on me own account—the more shame to me."

"Of course she turns others down, for the reason that Ben fills her heart." She began to weary of her self-imposed task.

He, too, was tired. "We'll see, we'll see," he repeated musingly, and gazed away towards the cloud-enshrouded peaks in sombre silence—the lines of his lips as sorrowful as those of an old lion dying in the desert, arrow-smitten and alone. He had forgotten the hand that pierced his heart.

Thus dismissed, she rose, her eyes burning like deep opals in the parchment setting of her skin.

"Life is so cruel!" she said. "I have wished a thousand times that love had never come to me. Love means only sorrow at the end. Ben has been my life, my only interest—and now—as he begins to forget—Oh, I can't bear it! It will kill me!" She sank back into her chair, and, burying her face, sobbed with such passion that her slight frame shook in the tempest of it.

Haney turned and looked at her in silence—profoundly stirred to pity by her sobs, no longer doubting the reality of her despair. When he spoke his voice was brokenly sweet and very tender.

"'Tis a bitter world, miss, and me heart bleeds for such as you. 'Tis well ye have a hope of paradise, for, if all you say is true, ye must go from this world cheated and hungry like meself. Ye have one comfort that I have not—'tis not your own doing. Ye've not misspent your life as I have done. What does it all show but that life is a game where each man, good or bad, takes his chance. The cards fall against you and against me without care of what we are. I can only say I take me chances as I take the rain and the sun."

Her paroxysm passed and she rose again, drawing her veil closely over her face. "Good-bye. We will never meet again."

"Don't say that," he said, struggling painfully to his feet. "Never is a long time, and good-bye a cruel, sad word to say. Let's call it 'so long' and better luck."

"You are not angry with me?" she turned to ask.

"Not at all, miss—I thank ye fer opening me eyes to me selfishness."

"Good-bye."

"So long! And may ye have better luck in the new deal, miss."

As she turned at the gate she saw him standing as she had left him, his brow white and sad and stern, his shoulders drooping as if his strength and love of life had suddenly been withdrawn.

While still in this mood she sent word to Ben that she wished to see him at once, and he responded without delay.

He was appalled by the change in her. Her interview with Haney had profoundly weakened her, chilled her. She was like some exquisite lamp whose golden flame had grown suddenly dim, and Fordyce was filled with instant, remorseful tenderness. His sense of duty sprang to arms, and without waiting for her to begin he said: "I hate to think of you as a pensioner in this house. You should be in your own home—our home—where I could take care of you. Come, let me take you out of this private hospital—that's what it is."

She struggled piteously to assure him that she would be back to par in a few days, but he was thoroughly alarmed and refused to listen to further delay.

"Your surroundings are bad, you need a change."

She read him to the soul, knew that this argument sprang not from love, but from pity and self-accusation; therefore, forcing a light tone, she answered: "I don't feel able to take command of a cook and second girl just yet, Bennie dear; besides, you're all wrong about this being a bad atmosphere for me. I'm horribly comfortable here, my own sister couldn't be kinder than Julia is. No, no, wait a few months longer till you get settled a little more securely in business; I may pick up a volt or two more of electricity by that time." Then as she saw his face darken and a tremor run over his flesh, she lost her self-control and broke forth with sudden, bitter intensity: "Why don't you throw me over and marry some nice girl with a healthy body and sane mind? Why cheat yourself and me?"

He recoiled before her question, too amazed to do more than exclaim against her going on.

She was not to be checked. "Let us be honest with ourselves. You know perfectly well I'm never going to get better—I do, if you don't. I may linger on in this way for years, but I will never be anything but a querulous invalid. Now that's the bitter truth. You mustn't marry me—I won't let you!" Then her mood changed. "And yet it's so hard to go on alone—even for a little way."

Her eyes closed on her hot tears, her head drooped, and Ben, putting his arm about her neck and pressing her quivering face against his breast, reproached her very tenderly: "I won't let you say such things, dearest—you must not! You're not yourself to-day."

"Oh yes, I am! My mind is very clear, too horribly clear. Ben dear, I mean all I say—you shall not link yourself to me. I have no delusions now. I'll never be well again—and you must know it."

"Oh yes, you will! Don't give up! You're only tired to-day. You're really much better than you were last week."

"No, I'm not! Let us not deceive ourselves any longer. The change of climate has not done me good. We waited too long. It has all been a mistake. Let me go back to Chester—I'm afraid to die out here. I can't bear the thought of being buried in this soil. It's so bleak and lonely and alien. I want to go back to the sweet, kindly hills—perhaps I can reconcile myself to death there—to sink into the earth on this plain is too dreadful."

He struggled against the weight of her sorrowful pleadings. "This is only a mood, dearest; you are over-tired and things look black to you—I have such days—everybody has these hours of depression, but we must fight them. It would be so much better for us both if I were your husband, then I could be with you and watch over you every hour. I could help you fight these dismal moods. It would be my hourly care. Come, let's go out and seriously set to work to find a cottage."

She was silenced for the moment, but when he had finished his counter-plea she looked up at him with deep-set glance and quietly said: "Ben, it's all wrong. It was wrong from the very beginning. You are lashing yourself into uttering these beautiful words, and you do not realize what you are saying. I am too old for you—Now listen—it's true! I'm twenty years older in spirit. I haven't been really well for ten years. You talk of fighting this. Haven't I fought? I've danced when I should have been in bed. I've had a premonition of early decay for years—that's why I've been so reckless of my strength. I couldn't bear to let my youth pass dully—and now it's gone! Wait!—I've deceived you in other ways. I've been full of black thoughts, I've been jealous and selfish all along. You deserve the loveliest girl in the world, and it is a cruel shame for me to stand in the way of your happiness just to have you light my darkness for a few hours. I know what you want to say—you think you can be happy with me. Ben, it's only your foolish sense of honor that keeps you loyal to me—I don't want that— I won't have it! Take back your pledge." She pushed away from him and twisted a ring from her finger. "Take this, dear boy, you are absolutely free. Go and be happy."

He drew back from her hand in pain and bewilderment. "Alice, you are crazy to say such things to me." He studied her with suffering in his eyes. "You are delirious. I am going to send the doctor to you at once."

"No, I'm not delirious. I know only too well what I'm saying—I have made my decision. I will never wear this ring again." She turned his words against himself. "You must not marry a crazy woman."

"I didn't mean that—you know what I meant. All you say is morbid and unreasonable, and I will not listen to it. You are clouded by some sick fancy to-day, and I will go away and send a physician to cure you of your madness."

She thrust the ring into his hand and rose, her face tense, her eyes wonderfully big and luminous. She seemed at the moment to renew her health and to recover the imperious grace of her radiant youth as she exaltedly said: "Now I am free! You must ask me all over again—and when you do, I will say *no*."

He sat looking up at her, too bewildered, too much alarmed to find words for reply. He really thought that she had gone suddenly mad—and yet all that she said was frightfully reasonable. In his heart he knew that she was uttering the truth. Their marriage was now impossible—a bridal veil over that face was horrifying to think upon.

She went on: "Now run away—I'm going to cry in a moment and I don't want you to see me do it. Please go!"

He rose stiffly, and when he spoke his voice was quivering with anxiety. "I am going to send Julia to you instantly."

"No, you're not. I won't see her if you do. She can't help me—nobody can, but you—and I won't let you even see me any more. I'm going home to Chester to-morrow; so kiss me good-bye—and go."

He kissed her and went blindly out, their engagement ring tightly clinched in his hand. It seemed as if a wide, cold, gray cloud had for the first time entirely covered his sunny, youthful world.

CHAPTER XXVII

MARSHALL HANEY'S SENTENCE

After Alice Heath's carriage had driven away, Haney returned to his chair, and with eyes fixed upon the distant peaks gave himself up to a review of all that the sick woman had said, and entered also upon a forecast of the game.

He was not entirely unprepared for her revelation. He was, indeed, too wise not to know that Bertha must sometime surely find in another and younger man her heart's hunger, but his wish had set that dark day far away in the future. Moreover, he had relied on her promise to confide in him, and it hurt him to think that she had not fulfilled her pledge; yet even in this he sought excuses for her.

"She may love him without knowing it. Anyhow, he's a fine young lad, far better for her than an old shoulder-shot cayuse like meself." His sense of unworthiness became the solvent of other and sweeter emotions. His wealth no longer seemed capable of bridging the deep chasm widening between them.

This day had shown a black sky to him, even before Alice Heath's disturbing call, for Bertha had been darkly brooding at breakfast, and silent at lunch, and immediately after rising from the table had gone away alone, without a word of explanation to any member of her household. She had not even taken her dogs with her, and her face was set and almost sullen as she passed out of the door and down the walk. All this was so unlike her that Mart was greatly troubled. It gave weight and significance to every word of Alice Heath's warning.

Bertha was gone till nearly six o'clock, and her mood seemed no whit lightened as she entered the gate and came slowly up the walk. To Mart's humbly spoken query, "What troubles ye, darlin'?" she made no reply, but went at once to her room.

The old gambler seemed pitiably helpless and forlorn as he sat there in his accustomed chair waiting her return. The bees and birds were busy among the vines, and all the well-oiled machinery of his splendid home was going forward to the end that his sweet girl-wife should be served. If she were unhappy, of what value were these soft rugs, these savory dishes, this shining silver? There was, in truth, something mocking and terrifying in the swift, well-trained action of the servants, who went about their tasks unmoved and apparently unacquainted with any change in the mind of their young mistress.

In the kitchen the cook was carefully compounding the soup while watching the roast. Lucius, deft and absorbed, was preparing the table, arranging the coffee service and deciding upon the china. On the seat under the pear-trees Miss Franklin was chatting with Mrs. Gilman, and in the barn the coachman could be heard giving the horses their evening taste of green grass—"and yet how empty, aimless, and foolish it all is if Bertha is unhappy," thought the master.

He grew alarmed for fear she would not come down; but at last he heard her light step on the stairs, and when she came in view his dim eyes were startled by the transformation in her. She had put on the plainest of her gowns, and she wore no jewels. By other ways which he felt but could not analyze she expressed some portentous shift of mood. He could not define why, but her step scared him, so measured and resolute it seemed.

She called to her mother and Miss Franklin and then asked, "Has dinner been announced?"

Her tone was quiet and natural, and Mart was relieved. He answered with attempt at jocularity, "Lucius is this minute winkin' at me over the soup-tureen."

As they took seats at the table Mrs. Gilman exclaimed, "Why, dearie, where did you dig up that old waist?"

"Will it do to visit Sibley in?"

"No indeed! I should say not. When you go back there I want you to wear the best you've got. They'll consider it an insult if you don't."

A faint smile lighted Bertha's pale face. "I don't think they'll take it so hard as all that."

"Are you goin' to Sibley?" asked Mart, an anxious tone in his voice.

"I thought of it. Mother is going over to-night, and I rather guess I'll run over with her. I've never been back, you see, since that night."

There was something ominous in her restraint, in her abstraction of glance, and especially in her lack of appetite. She took little account of her guests and seemed profoundly engaged upon some inward calculation. The beautifully spread table, which would have thrilled her a few short weeks ago, was powerless to even hold her gaze, and it was Lucius deft and watchful who brought the meal to a successful conclusion—for the mother was awed and helpless in the presence of the queenly daughter whom wealth had translated into something almost too high and shining for her to lay hand upon.

Miss Franklin did her best, but she was not a person of light and dancing intellectual feet, and she had never understood Haney, anyhow. Altogether it was a dismal and difficult half-hour.

When the coffee came on Bertha rose abruptly, saying, "Come out into the garden, Mart, I've got something to say to you."

He obeyed with a sense of being called to account, and as they walked slowly across the grass, which the light of a vivid orange sunset had made transcendently green, he glanced to the west with foreboding that this was the last time he should look upon the kingly peak at sunset time. A flaming helmet of cloud shone upon the chief, and all the lesser heights were a deep, purple bank out of which each serrate summit rose without perspective, sharply set against the other like a monstrous silhouette of cardboard.

It should have been indeed a very sweet and odorous and peaceful hour. The murmur of the water from the fountain had the lulling sound of a hive of bees as they settle to rest, and to the suffering man it seemed impossible that this, his cherished world, could change to the black chaos which the loss of his adorable wife would bring upon it.

The settee was of wire, and curved so that when they had taken seats they faced each other, and the sight of her, so slender, so graceful, so womanly, filled him with a fury of hate against the assassin who had torn him to pieces, making him old before his time, a cripple, impotent, inert, and scarred.

Bertha did not wait for him to begin, and her first words smote like bullets. "Mart, I'm going back to Sibley."

He looked at her with startled eyes—his brow wrinkling into sorrowful lines. "For how long?"

"I don't know—it may be a good while. I'm going away to think things over." Then she added, firmly, "I may not come back at all, Mart."

"For God's sake, don't say that, girlie! You don't mean that!" His voice was husky with the agony that filled his throat. "I can't live without ye now. Don't go—that way."

"I've *got* to go, Mart. My mind ain't made up to this proposition. I don't know about living with you any more."

"Why not? What's the matter, darlin'? Can't ye put up with me a little longer? I know I'm only a piece of a man—but tell me the truth. Can't you stay with me—as we are?"

She met him with the truth, but not the whole truth. "Everybody thinks I married you for your money, Mart—it ain't true—but the evidence is all against me. The only way to prove it a lie is to just naturally pull out and go back to work. I hate to leave, so long as you—feel about me as you do—but, Mart, I'm 'bleeged' to do it. My mind is so stirred up—I don't enjoy anything any more. I used to like everything in the house—all my nice things—the dresses and trinkets you gave me. It was fun to run the kitchen—now it all goes against the grain some way. Fact is, none of it seems mine."

His eyes were wet with tears as he said: "It's all my fault. It's all because of what I said last night—"

She stopped him. "No, it ain't that—it ain't your fault, it's mine. Something's gone wrong with *me*. I love this home, and my dogs and horses and all—and yet I can't enjoy 'em any more. They don't belong to me—now that's the fact, Mart."

"I'll make 'em yours, darlin', I'll deed 'em all over to you."

"No, no, that won't do it. My mind has got to change. It's all in my mind. Don't you see? I've got to get away from the whole outfit and think it all out. If I can come back I will, but you mustn't bank on my return, Mart. You mustn't be surprised if I settle on the other side of the range."

"I know," he said, sadly. "I know your reason and I don't blame you. 'Tis not for an old derelict like me to hold you—but you must let me give you some of me money—'tis of no value to me now. If ye do not let me share it with you me heart will break entirely."

"I haven't a right to a cent of it, Mart—I owe you more than I can ever pay. No, I can't afford to take another cent."

In the pause which followed his face took on a look of new resolution. "Bertie, I've had something happen to me to-day. I've learned something I should have known long since."

Her look of surprise deepened into dismay as he went on: "I know what's the matter with you, girlie. 'Tis after seeing Ben your face always shines. You love him, Bertie—and I don't blame you—"

A carriage driving up to the gate brought diversion, and she sprang up, her face flushed, her eyes big and scared. "There comes Dr. Steele! I'd plumb forgot about his call."

"So had I," he answered, as he rose to meet his visitor.

Dr. Steele, a gray-haired, vigorous man, entered the gate and came hurriedly up the path, something fateful in his stride. He greeted them both casually, smilelessly. "I've got to get that next train," he announced, mechanically looking at his watch, "and that leaves me just twenty minutes in which to thump you."

Bertha was in awe of this blunt, tactless man of science, and as they moved towards the house listened in chilled silence while he continued: "Brent writes me that you were doing pretty well down by the lake. Why didn't you stay? He says he advised you not to come back."

"This is me home," answered Haney, simply.

Lucius took Bertha's place at Mart's shoulder and the three men went into the library, leaving her to wait outside in anxious solitude. There was something in the doctor's manner which awed her, filled her with new conceptions, new duties.

Steele was one of these cold-blooded practitioners who do not believe in the old-fashioned manner. "Cheery suggestion" was nonsense to him. His examination was to Bertha, as to Haney, a dreaded ordeal. However, Brent had advised it, and they had agreed to submit to it, and now here he was, and upon his judgment she must rest.

For half an hour she waited in the hall, almost without moving, so far-reaching did this verdict promise to be. Her anxiety deepened into fear as Steele came out of the room and walked rapidly towards her. "He's a very sick man," he burst forth, irritably. "Get him away from here as quickly as you can—but don't excite him. Don't let him exert himself at all till you reach a lower altitude. Keep him quiet and peaceful, and don't let him clog himself up with starchy food—and above all, keep liquors away from him. He shouldn't have come back here at all. Brent warned him that he couldn't live up here. Slide him down to sea-level—if he'll go—and take care of him. His heart will run along all right if he don't overtax it. He'll last for years at sea-level."

"He hates to leave—he says he won't leave," she explained.

The man of science shrugged his shoulders. "All right! He can take his choice of roads"—he used an expressive gesture—"up or down. One leads to the New Jerusalem and is short—as he'll find out if he stays here. Good-night! I must get that train."

"Wait a minute!" she called after him. "Is there anything I can do? Did you leave any medicine?"

He turned and came back. "Yes, a temporary stimulant, but medicine is of little use. If you can get away to-morrow, you do it."

She stood a few minutes at the library door listening, waiting, and at last hearing no sound, opened the door decisively and went in.

Haney, ghastly pale, in limp dejection, almost in collapse, was seated in an easy-chair, with Lucius holding a glass to his lips. He was stripped to his undershirt and looked like a defeated, gray old gladiator, fallen helpless in the arena, deserted by all the world save his one faithful servant—and Bertha's heart was wrenched with a deep pang of pity and remorse as she gazed at him. The doctor's warning became a command. To desert him in returning health was bad enough, to desert him now was impossible.

Running to him, all her repugnance gone, all her tenderness awake, she put her arm about his shoulders. "Oh, Mart, did he hurt you? Are you worse?"

He raised dim eyes to her, eyes that seemed already filmed with death's opaque curtains, but bravely, slowly smiled. "I'm down but not out, darlin'. That brute of a doctor jolted me hard; I nearly took the count—but I'm—still in the ring. Harness me up, Lucius. I'll show that sawbones the power of mind over matter—the ould croaker!"

He recovered rapidly and was soon able to stagger to his feet. Then, with a return of his wonted humor, he stretched out his big right arm. "I'm not to be put out of business by wan punch from an old puddin' like Steele. I am not the 'stiff' he thinks. He had me agin the ropes, 'tis true, but I'll surprise him yet."

"What did he say?" she persisted in demanding.

He shook his head. "That's bechune the two of us," he nodded warningly at Lucius. "For one thing, he says me heart can't stand the high country. 'It's you to the deep valley,' says he."

Her decision was ready. "All right, then *we go*!"

He faced her quickly. "Did ye say WE, Bertie? Did ye say it, sweetheart?"

"I did, Mart—I've changed my mind once more. I'm goin' to stick by you—till you're settled somewhere. I won't leave till you're better."

The tears blinded his eyes again, and his lips twitched. "You're God's own angel, Bertie, but I don't deserve it. No, stay you here—I'm not worth your sacrifice. No, no, I can't have it! Stay here with Ben and look after the mines."

Her face settled in lines that were not girlish as she repeated: "It's up to me to go, and I'm going, Mart! I didn't realize how bad it was for you here—I didn't, really!"

"It's all wrong, I'm afraid—all wrong," he answered, "but the Lord knows I need you worse than ever."

"Shut off on all that!" she commanded. "Lucius, help me take him outside where the air is better."

Mart put the man away. "One is enough," he said, brusquely; and so, leaning on his strong, young wife, he went slowly out into the dusk where the mother and Miss Franklin were sitting, quite unconscious of the deep significance of the doctor's visit. "Not a word to them," warned Haney—"at any rate, not to-night."

They were now both facing the pain of instantly abandoning all these beautiful and ministering material conditions which money had called round them. It seemed so foolish, so incredibly silly—this mandate of the physician. Could any place on the earth be more healthful, more helpful to human life than this wide-porched, cool-halled house, this garden, this air? What difference could a few thousand feet make on the heart's action?

The thought of putting away all hope of seeing Ben Fordyce came at last to overtop all Bertha's other regrets as the lordly peak overrode the clouds—and yet she was determined to go. Very quietly she told her mother that she had decided to put off her visit to Sibley, and at 10:30 she drove down to the station and sent her away composedly. At the moment she was glad to get her out of the town, so that she should not share in the grief of next day's departure. To Miss Franklin she then confided the doctor's warning, and together they began to pack.

Haney, with lowering brow and bleeding heart, went to his bed denouncing himself. "I have no right to her. 'Tis the time for me to step out. If the doctor knows his business, 'tis only a matter of a few weeks, anyhow, when my seat in the game will be empty. Why not stay here in me own home and so end it all comfortably?"

This was so simple—and yet he spent most of the night fighting the desire to live out those years the doctor had promised him. It was so sweet to sit opposite that dear girl-face of a morning, to feel her hand on his hair—now and again. "She's only a child—she can wait ten years and still be young." But then came the thought: "'Tis harder for her to wait than it is for me to go. 'Tis mere selfishness. What can I do in the world? I have no interest in the game outside of her. No, Mart, the consumptive is right, 'tis up to you to slip away, genteel and quiet, so that your widow will not be troubled by anny gossip."

To use the pistol was easy, the handle fitted his hand, but to die so that no shock or shame would come to her, that was his problem. "I will not leave her the widow of a suicide," he resolved. "I must go so sly, so casual-like, that no one will be able to point the finger at her or Ben."

"Can I visit the mine once more?" he had asked Steele. "No," the doctor had replied. "To go a thousand feet higher than this would be fatal."

As he mused on this he began to feel the wonder of the body in which he dwelt. That a machine so bulky and so gross could be so delicate that a change in the pressure of the atmosphere might be fatal astonished him. "I'll soon know," he said, "for I cross the range to-morrow."

The dark shadow of the unseen world, once so dim and far, now rose formidable as a mountain on the horizon of his thought. It was so difficult to leave the house in which he had found peace and a strange kind of happiness the happiness of a soldier home on parole, convalescent and content under the apple-trees—it was very hard—and the tenderness, the care, to which his little wife had returned and which filled his heart with sweetness, added to his irresolution.

He fell into deep sleep at last, still in debate with himself.

He woke quietly next morning, like a child, and as his eyes took in the big room in which he had slept for a year, surrounded by such luxury as he had never dreamed of having even for a day, life seemed very easy of continuance, and Steele a mistaken egotist, a foul destroyer of men's peace; but as he rose to dress and saw himself in the glass, the figure he presented decided his hand. Was this Mart Haney—this unshaven, haggard, and wrinkled old man?

Leaning close to the mirror, he studied his face as if it were a mask. Deep creases ran down on either side of the nose, giving to his gaze the morose expression of an aged, slavering mastiff. His nerveless cheeks depended. His neck was stringy. Puffy sacs lay under the eyes, and the ashen pallor of his skin told how the heart was laboring to maintain life's red current in its round.

As he looked his decision was taken. "Mart, the game has run mostly in your favor for twenty-five years—but 'tis agin ye now. The quiet old gentleman with the bony grin holds the winning fist. Lay down your cards and quit the board this day, like a man. Why drag on like this for a year or two more, a burden to yourself and a curse to her."

And yet, though crippled and gray, death was somehow more dreadful to him at this moment than when in his remorseless and powerful young manhood he had looked again and again into the murderous eyes of those who were eager to shed his blood. He shivered at the thought of the dark river, as those whose limbs having grown pale and thin dread the cold wind of the night.

"I wonder is the mother over there waitin' fer me?" he half whispered. "If ye are, your soul will be floating far above me in the light, while I—burdened by me sins—must wallow below in purgatory. But I go, and the divil take his toll."

There was not much preparation to be made. His will was written, fully attested, and filed in a safe place. His small personal belongings he was willing to leave in Bertha's hands. It was hardest of all to vanish without a word of good-bye to any soul, but this was essential to his plan. "No one must suspect design in me departure," he muttered. "I must drop out—*by accident*. I must cut loose during the day, too—no night trips for me—in a way that will look natural. If Steele knows his business, Mart Haney will go out of the game on the summit, if not, 'tis easy for a cripple to stagger and fall from a rock. Thank God, I leave her as I found her—small credit to me in that."

Lucius, coming in soon after, found his master unexpectedly cheerful and vigorous.

In answer to his query, the gambler said: "I take me medicine, Lucius, like a Cheyenne. 'Tis all in the game. Some man must lose in order that another may win. The wheel rolls and the board is charged in favor of the bank. Damn the man that squeals when the cards fall fair."

CHAPTER XXVIII

VIRTUE TRIUMPHS

Mart maintained his deceptive cheer at the breakfast-table, and the haggard look of the earlier hour passed away as he resolutely attacked his chop. He spoke of his exile in a tone of resignation—mixed with humor. "Sure, the old dad will have the laugh on us. He told us this was the jumpin'-off place."

"What will we do about the house?" asked Bertha. "Will we sell or rent?"

"Nayther. Lave it as it is," replied he quickly. "So long as I live I want to feel 'tis here ready for ye whinever ye wish to use it. 'Tis not mine. Without you I never would have had it, and I want no other mistress in it. Sure, every chair, every picture on the walls is there because of ye. 'Tis all you, and no one else shall mar it while I live."

This was the note which was most piercing in her ears, and she hastened to stop it by remarking the expense of maintaining the place—its possible decay and the like; but to all this he doggedly replied: "I care not. I'd rather burn it and all there is in it than turn it over to some other woman. Go you to Ben and tell him my will concerning it."

This gave a new turn to her thought. "I don't want to do that. Why don't you go and tell him yourself?"

"Didn't the doctor say I must save meself worry? I hate to ask ye to shoulder the heavy end of this proposition." His face lost its forced smile. "I'm a sick man, darlin'; I know it now, and I must save meself all I can. Ye may send Lucius down and bring him up, or we'll drive down and see him; maybe the ride would do me good, but I can't climb them stairs ag'in."

The temptation to see Ben once more, alone in the bright office, proved too great for Bertha's resolution, and she answered: "All right, I'll go, but only to bring him down to you. You must give the orders about the house."

In spite of his iron determination to be of good cheer in her presence, Mart's lips quivered with pain of parting as he looked round the splendid dining-room, into which the sunlight was pouring. Suddenly he broke forth: "Ye *must* stay here, darlin'—never mind me. 'Tis a sin and a shame to ask ye to lave all this to go with a poor old—"

"Stop that!" she called, sharply. "I won't listen to any such talk," and he said no more.

They decided to go down about ten o'clock, when the daily tide of his life rode highest. This hour suited his own plan, for a train left for the mountains not long after, and he had resolved to make his escape while Bertha was with Ben in the office. "There will be no need of any change in the house," he thought, "but 'twill do no hurt for them to talk it all over."

For an hour or two he hobbled about the yard and garden, taking a final look at the horses and dogs, and his face was very lax and gray and his voice broken as he talked with his men, who had learned of the doctor's orders, and were awkwardly silent with sympathy. He soon grew tired and came back to the porch to rest and wait for the hour of his departure. Settling into his accustomed chair, which faced directly upon the mountains over which the sun, wearing to the south, was beginning to hang its vivid shadows, he sat like a man of bronze. The clouds which each day clothed the scarred and naked peaks with a mantle of ermine and purple, were already assembling. The range assumed a new and overpowering grandeur in his eyes, for it typified the Big Divide, which lay between him and the country of the soundless, dawnless night.

Up that deep fold which lay between the chieftain and his consort to the north ran the western way—a trail with no returning footprints; and the thought made his heart beat painfully, while a sense of the wonder and the terror of death came to him. He was going away as the wounded grizzly crawls to the thicket to die, unseen of his kind, even of his mate.

To never return! To mount and mount, each league separating him forever from the mansion he had come to enjoy, the wife he loved better than his own life. "I cannot believe it," he whispered, "and yet I must make it so."

Then he began to wonder, grimly, just when his heart would fail, just where it would burst like a rotten cinch. "Will it be on the train? Suppose I last to the coal-switch, then I must climb to the mine. Suppose I live to reach the mine, then what? Oh, well, 'tis easy to slip from the cliff."

Meanwhile, out under the trees, the gardener was spading turf, the lawn-mower was purring briskly and as though no sentence of death had been passed upon the master of the place. In this Haney saw the world's action typified. The individual is of little value—the race alone counts.

He shuffled down to meet the carriage at the gate, and Lucius helped him in before Bertha could reach him, and they drove off down the street so exactly in their usual way that Bertha was moved to say: "I don't believe it! I can't realize we're quitting this town to-morrow."

"No more can I, but I reckon it's good-bye all the same—for me, anyhow. I despise meself for asking ye to go, darlin'—I *don't* ask it. Stay you! I'm not demanding anything at all. 'Tis fitter for me to go alone. Stay on, darlin'—'twill comfort me to lave ye safe and happy here."

She shook her head with quite as much determination as he. "No, Mart, my mind is made up—I know my job, and I'm going to muckle to it like a little lady, so don't fuss."

The air was beautifully clear and bracing, and a minute later Haney remarked, sadly: "I reckon the doctor knows his trade, but 'tis bitter nonsense to me when a man says the murky wind of the low country is better for a sick man than this."

She was very tender at heart as she replied: "I'm afraid he's right, Mart. I could see you weren't so well here; but I was selfish—I tried to argue different. You'll be better down below, that's dead certain."

"Well, the bets are all laid and the wheel spinning. I'm ready to take me exile—but I hate to drag ye down with me."

"Don't worry about me," she answered, with intent to reassure him. "To be honest, I kind o' like the East."

At the door of Ben's office building she got out, leaving him in the carriage. As she looked back at him from the doorway something which seemed like anguish in his face moved her, and she returned to the wheel to say, "Never mind, Mart, we'll buy a new home down there."

He was struggling as if with the pangs of death, but he said, "'Tis childish, I know, but I hate to say good-bye to it all."

She patted his hand as if soothing a child, and, turning, mounted the stairway. How weak and old he seemed at the moment!

Fordyce was at work. She could hear his typewriter click laboriously he was his own typist as yet, and she stood for a moment in the hall with hand pressed hard upon her bosom, the full significance of this last visit overwhelming her. Here was the end of her own happiness—the beginning of long-drawn misery and heart-hunger. Her blood beat tumultuously in her throat, and each throb was a physical, smothering pain.

At last she grew calmer and knocked. Ben opened the door, and his face shone with joy. "You're late!" he reproachfully exclaimed; then, as he peered into the hall, he asked, "Where's the Captain?"

She was very white as she answered: "He can't come up this morning. He ain't able."

"Is he worse?" His face expressed swift concern.

"Yes—Dr. Steele came last night and examined him—"

"What did he say?"

"He told us to 'get out' of here—quick."

He drew her in and shut the door. "Tell me all about it. What is the matter?"

"It's his heart. He can't stand it here. We've got to get away—down the slope—to-morrow."

"Not to stay?"

"That's what Steele says. Mart's in bad shape."

He searched her face with earnest gaze. "I can't understand that. He seemed so happy and so much better, too."

"He's been a good deal worse than he let on, or else he fooled himself. The doctor found his heart jumping cogs right along."

"And he positively ordered you to go below?"

"Yes—he scared me. He said Mart might die any minute—if he stayed."

In the silence that followed his face became almost as white as her own, for he understood and shared her temptation. At last he said, slowly, "And you are going with him?"

"Yes, I must. Don't you see I must?"

He understood, too. Haney had refused to go without her, and to stay would be to shorten his life.

"How did the Captain take it?" he asked with effort.

"Mighty hard at first, but he's fairly cheerful to-day. He wants to leave me here—but I'm going with him. It's my business to be where he is," she added. "He sure needs me now."

"What are you going to do with the house?"

"Leave it just as it is. He won't sell it or rent it. He wants you to look after all his business just the same—"

"I can't do that."

"Why not?"

"Because I don't intend to stay here." As he spoke his excitement mounted. "My little world was all askew before you came. You've put the finishing-touch to it. I'm ready to make my own will at this moment."

"You mustn't talk that way," she admonished. "I don't like to see you lose your grip." Her words were commonplace, but her hesitating, tremulous voice betrayed her and exalted him. "I'm—we are depending on you."

His face, his eyes, filled her with light. She forgot all the rest of the world for the moment, and he, looking upon her with a knowledge that she loved him and was about to leave him, spoke fatefully—as if the words came forth in spite of his will. "You don't seem to realize how deeply I'm going to miss you. You cannot know how much your presence means to me here in this small town. I will not stay on without the hope of seeing you. If you go, I will not remain here another day."

She fought against the feeling of pride, of joy, which these words gave her. "You mustn't say that—you've got to stay with Alice."

"Alice!" his voice rose. "Alice has given me back my ring and is going home. When you are gone, what is left in this town for me?" He rose and walked up and down, a choking sob in his throat. "My God! It's horrible to feel our good days ending in a crash like this. What does it all mean? I refuse to admit that our shining little world is only a house of cards. Are we never to see each other again? I refuse to say good-bye. I won't have it so!" He faced her again with curt inquiry. "Where are you going to live?"

"I don't know—maybe in Chicago—maybe in New York."

"No matter where it is, I will come to you. I cannot lose you out of my life—I will not!"

"No, you mustn't do that. It ain't square to Mart—I can't see you any more—now."

He seized upon the significance of that little final word. "What do you mean by *now*? Do you mean because Mart is worse? Or do you mean that I have forfeited your good-will by my own action?" He came closer to her and his voice was low and insistent as he continued: "Or do you mean—something very sweet and comforting to me? Do you love me, Bertie? Do you? Is that your meaning?"

She struggled against him as she answered: "I don't know—Yes, I do know—it ain't right for me—for you to say these things to me while I am Mart Haney's wife."

He caught at her hands and looked upon her with face grown older and graver as he bitterly wailed: "Why couldn't we have met before you went to him? You must not go with him now, for you are mine at heart, you belong to me."

She rose with instinctive desire to flee, but he held her hands in both of his and hurried on: "You do love me! I am sure of it! Why try to conceal it? You would marry me if you were free?" His eyes pierced her as he proceeded, transformed by the power of his own plea. "We belong to each other—don't you know we do? I am sorry for Alice, but I do not love her—I never loved her as I love you. She understands this. That is why she has returned my ring—there is nothing further for me to say to her. As for Marshall Haney I pity him, as you do, but he has no right to claim you."

"He don't claim me. He wants me to stay here."

"Then why don't you?"

"Because he needs me."

"So do I need you."

"But not the way—I mean he is sick and helpless."

He drew her closer. "You must not go. I will not let you go. You're a part of my life now." His words ceased, but his eyes called with burning intensity.

She struggled, not against him, but in opposition to something within herself which seemed about to overwhelm her will. It was so easy to listen, to yield—and so hard to free her hands and turn away, but the thought of Haney waiting, and a knowledge of his confident trust in her, brought back her sterner self.

"No!" she cried out sharply, imperiously. "I won't have it! You mustn't touch me again, not while he lives! You mustn't even see me again!"

He understood and respected her resolution, but could not release her at the moment. "Won't you kiss me good-bye?"

She drew her hands away. "No, it's all wrong, and you know it! I'll despise you if you touch me again! Good-bye!"

Thereupon his clean, bright, honorable soul responded to her reproof, rose to dominion over the flesh, and he said: "Forgive me. I didn't mean to tempt you to anything wrong. Good-bye!" and so they parted in such anguish as only lovers know when farewells seem final, and their empty hearts, calling for a word of promise, are denied.

CHAPTER XXIX

MARSHALL HANEY'S LAST TRAIL

Marshall Haney was a brave man, and his resolution was fully taken, but that final touch of Bertha's hand upon his arm very nearly unnerved him. His courage abruptly fell away, and, leaning back against the cushions of his carriage, with closed eyelids from which the hot tears dripped, he gave himself up to the temptation of a renewal of his life. It was harder to go, infinitely harder, because of that impulsive, sweet caress. Her face was so beautiful, too, with that upward, tender, pitying look upon it!

While still he sat weak and hesitant, a roughly dressed man of large and decisive movement stopped and greeted him. "Hello, Mart, how are you this fine day?"

Haney put his tragic mask away with a stroke of his hand, and hastily replied: "Comin' along, Dan, comin' along. How are things up on the peak?"

"Still pretty mixed," replied the miner, lightly; then, with a further look around, he stepped a little nearer the wheel. "Hell's about to break loose again, Mart."

"What's the latest?"

"I can't go into details, and I mustn't be seen talking with you, but Williams is in for trouble. Tell him to reverse engine for a few weeks. Good-day," and he walked off, leaving the impression of having been sent to convey a friendly warning.

Haney seized upon this message. His resolution returned. His voice took on edge and decision. "Oscar," he called quickly, "drive me down to the station, I want to get that ten-thirty-seven train."

As the driver chirruped to his horses and swung out into the street, Marshall Haney, with full understanding that this was to be his eternal farewell, turned and looked up, hoping to catch a last glimpse of his wife's sweet face at the window. A sign, a smile, a beckoning, and his purpose might still have faltered, but the recall did not take place, and facing the west he became again the man of will. When the carriage drew up to the platform he gave orders to his coachman as quietly as though this were his usual morning ride. "Now, Oscar, you heard what that friend of mine said?"

"Yes, sir."

"Well, forget it."

"Very well, sir."

"But tell Mrs. Haney I've gone up to the mine. You can say to her that Williams sent for me. You can tell her, but to no one else, what you heard Dan say. You understand?"

"Yes, sir."

"All right, that stands. Now you go home and wait till about twelve-thirty. Then go down for Mrs. Haney."

The coachman, a stolid, reliable man, well trained to his duties, did not offer to assist his master, but sat in most approved alertness upon his box while Haney painfully descended to the walk.

The train was about to move, and the conductor had already signalled the engineer to "go ahead," but at sight of the gambler, whom he knew, stopped the train and helped Haney aboard. "A minute more and you would have been left. Going up to the mine, I reckon?"

They were still on the platform as Mart answered, "Yes, I'm due to take a hand in the game up there." He said this with intent to cover his trail.

He was all but breathless as he dropped into a seat near the door. The sense of leaden weakness with which he had come to struggle daily had deepened at the moment into a smothering pain which threatened to blind him.

"I must be quiet," he thought—"I will not die in the car." There seemed something disgraceful, something ignominious in such a death.

Gradually his fear of this misfortune grew less. "What does it matter where death comes or when it comes? The quicker the better for all concerned."

Nevertheless, he opened the little phial of medicine which Steele had given him and swallowed two of the pellets. That they were a powerful stimulant of the heart he knew, but that an overdose would kill he only suspected from Steele's word of caution.

They were, indeed, magical in their effect. His brain cleared, his pulse grew stronger, and the feeling of benumbing weakness which dismayed him passed away.

The conductor, on his round, found him sitting silently at the window, very pale and very stern, his eyes fixed upon the brawling stream along whose winding course the railway climbed. While noting the number of Mart's pass the official leaned over and spoke in a low voice, but Haney heard what he said as through a mist. He was no longer moved by the sound of the bugle. A labor war was temporary, like a storm in the pines. It might arrest the mining for a few weeks or a month, but through it all, no matter what happened, deep down in the earth lay Bertha's wealth, secure of any marauder. So much he was able to reason out.

One or two of the passengers who knew him drew near, civilly inquiring as to his health, and to each one he explained that he was on the gain and that he was going up to the camp to study conditions for himself. They were all greatly excited by the news of battle, but they did not succeed in conveying their emotion to Haney. With impassive countenance he listened, and at the end remarked: "'Tis all of a stripe to me, boys. I'm like the soldier on the battle-field with both legs shot off. I hear the shouting and the tumult, but I'm out of the running."

Without understanding his mood, they withdrew, leaving him alone. His mind went back to Bertha. "What will she do when she finds me gone? She will not be scared at first. She will wire to stop me; but no matter—before she can reach me, I'll be high in the hills."

He could not prevent his mind from dwelling on her. He tried to fix his thoughts upon his life as a boyish adventurer, but could not keep to those earlier periods of his career. All of his days before meeting her seemed base or trivial or purposeless. She filled his memory to the exclusion of all other loves and desires. She was at once his wife and his child. He possessed a thousand bright pictures of her swift and graceful body, her sunny smile, her sweet, grave eyes. He recalled the first time he saw her on the street in Sibley, and groaned to think how basely he had planned against her. "She never knew that, thank God!" he said, fervently.

Then came that unforgetable drive to the ranch, when she put her hand in his—and on this hour he dwelt long, searching his mind deeply in order that no grain of its golden store of incident should escape him. His throat again began to ache with a full sense of the loss he was inflicting upon himself. "'Tis a lonely trail I'm takin' for your sake, darlin'," he whispered, "but 'tis all for the best."

Slowly the train creaked and circled up the heights, following the sharp turnings of the stream, passing small towns which were in effect summer camps of pleasure-seekers, on and upward into the moist heights where the grass was yet green and the slopes gay with flowers. A mood of exaltation came upon the doomed man as he rose. This was the place to die—up here where the affairs of men sank into insignificance like the sound of the mills and the rumble of trains. Here the centuries circled like swallows and the personal was lost in the ocean of silence.

At one of these towns which stood almost at the summit of the pass the conductor brought a telegram, and Mart seized it with eager, trembling hands. It was as he expected a warning from Bertha. She implored him to let the mine go and to return by the next train.

He was too nerveless of fingers to put the sheet back within its envelope, and so thrust it, a crumpled mass, into his pocket. It was as if her hand was at his shoulder, her voice in his ear, but he did not falter. To go back now would be but a renewal of his torture. There could not come a better time to go—to go and leave no suspicion of his purpose behind him.

Just over the summit, at a bare little station, the train was held for orders, and Haney, who was again suffocating and almost blind, took another dose of the mysterious drug, and with its effect returned to a dim perception of his surroundings. He was able vaguely to recall that a trail which began just back of the depot mounted the hill towards his largest mine. A desire to see Williams, his faithful partner, his most loyal friend, came over him, and, rising to his feet, he painfully crept down the aisle to the rear of the car and dropped off unnoticed, just as the conductor's warning cry started a rush for the train.

As the last coach disappeared round the turn the essential bleak loneliness of the place returned. The station seemed deserted by every human being, even the operator was lost to sight, and the gambler, utterly solitary, with clouded brain and laboring breath, turned towards the height, his left leg dragging like a shackle.

For the first half-mile the way was easy, and by moving slowly he suffered less pain than he had expected. Around him the frost-smitten aspens were shivering in the wind, their sparse leaves dangling like coins of red-and-yellow gold, and all the billowing land below, to the west, was iridescent with green and flame-color and crimson. A voiceless regret, a dim, wide-reaching, wistful sadness came over him, but did not shake his resolution. He had but to look down at his crippled body to know that the beauty of the world was no longer his to enjoy. His days were now but days of pain.

He had always loved the heights. From the time he had first sighted this range he had never failed to experience a peculiar exaltation as he mounted above the ranch and the mine. Gambler and night-owl though he had been, he had often spent his afternoons on horseback riding high above the camps, and now some small part of his love of the upper air came back to lead him towards his grave. With face turned to the solitudes of the snows, with ever-faltering steps, he commenced his challenging march towards death.

At the first sharp up-raise in the way his heart began to pound and he swayed blindly to and fro, unable to proceed. For an instant he looked down in dismay at the rocky, waiting earth, a most inhospitable grave. A few minutes' rest against a tree, and his brain cleared. "Higher—I must go higher," he said to himself; "they'll find me here."

As he rose he could see the town spread wide on the hill-tops beneath him—the cabins mere cubes, the mill a child's toy. He could discern men like ants moving to and fro as if in some special excitement—but he did not concern himself with the cause. His one thought was to mount—to blend with the firs and the rocks. He drew the phial from his pocket and held it in his hand in readiness, with a dull fear that the chemical would prove too small, too weak, to end his pain.

It was utterly silent and appallingly lonely on this side of the great peak. Hunters were few and prospectors were seldom seen. These upward-looping trails led to no mine—only to abandoned prospect holes—for no mineral had ever been found on the western slope. The copses held no life other than a few minute squirrels, and no sound broke the silence save the insolent cry of an occasional jay or camp-bird. To die here was surely to die alone and to lie alone, as the fallen cedar lies, wrought upon by the wind and the snows and the rain.

Nevertheless, his suicidal idea persisted. It had become the one final, overpowering, directing resolution. There is no passion more persistent than that which leads to self-destruction. In the midst of the blinding swirl of his thought he maintained his purpose to put himself above the world of human effort and to become a brother of the clod, to mix forever with the mould.

Slowly he dragged himself upward, foot by foot, seeking the friendly shelter and obscurity of a grove of firs just above him. Twice he sank to his knees, a numbing pain at the base of his brain, his breath roaring, his lips dry, but each time he rose and struggled on, eager to reach the green and grateful shelter of the forest, filled with desire to thrust himself into its solitude; and when at last he felt the chill of the shadow and realized that he was surely hidden from all the world, he turned, poised for an instant on a mound where the trail doubled sharply, gave one long, slow glance around, then hurled himself down the rocky slope. Even as he leaped his heart seemed to burst and he fell like a clod and lay without further motion. It was as if he had been smitten in flight by a rifle-ball.

Around him the small animals of the wood frolicked, and the jay called inquiringly, but he neither saw nor heard. He was himself but a gasping creature, with reason entirely engaged in the blind struggle which the physical organism was instinctively making to continue in its wonted ways. All the world and all his desires, save a longing for his fair young wife, were lost out of his mind, and he thought of Bertha only in a dim and formless way—feeling his need of her and dumbly wondering why she did not come. In final, desperate agony, he lifted the phial of strychnine to his lips, hoping that it might put an end to his suffering; but before this act was completed a sweet, devouring flood of forgetfulness swept over him, his hand dropped, and the unopened bottle rolled away out of his reach. Then the golden sunlight darkened out of his sky, and he died—as the desert lion dies—alone.

When they found him two days later he lay with his head pillowed upon his left arm, his right hand outspread upon the pine leaves—palm upward as if to show its emptiness. A bird—the roguish gray magpie—had stolen away the phial as if in consideration of the dead man's wish, and no sign of his last despairing act was visible to those who looked into his face. His going was well planned. Self-murder was never written opposite the name of Marshall Haney.

THE END